BLUEPRINT

Kizzie French

POMEGRANATE · PRESS ·

Published by Pomegranate Press,
Dolphin House, 51 St Nicholas Lane, Lewes, Sussex BN7 2JZ
pomegranatepress@aol.com
www.pomegranate-press.co.uk

ISBN 978-0-954-89754-3

Cover images courtesy of http:photoeverywhere.co.uk

Printed and bound by CPI Antony Rowe, Eastbourne

1

As Calla Marchant swung her bright red Porsche through the impressive gateway (Portland stone pillars, decorative ironwork with the aristocratic crest inlaid) she was muttering 'Damn the roads, blast the weather and screw the Duke of Mercia!'

The tyres spat up gravel. Never mind the damp conditions and the fog, she handled the car with the practised ease of a woman used to travelling at speed and knowing that she was capable of coping with any of life's sudden emergencies.

'The blasted man has properties galore in London,' she continued arguing to her unseen audience, 'so why does he have to drag everyone more than a hundred miles down to this barbaric wilderness?'

At this moment one of life's sudden emergencies occurred. Her front wheels struck what the British call 'a sleeping policeman' – a hump in the roadway designed to persuade motorists that they ought to slow down – and she felt herself taking flight. The Porsche sailed through the air like one of the Duke's pheasants and slammed onto the tarmac with a shudder.

'Bloody hell!' she protested, flicking off the ignition and springing out to inspect the damage. 'That's what I call an unfriendly welcome.'

If Calla Marchant angry was an awesome sight, Calla Marchant furious partook of the supernatural. Yet the intensity of her emotion, by some trick of the flesh and the psyche, only made her natural beauty the more distinctive. Many a red-blooded male had been known to stir her wrath precisely in order to exult in the female of the species in sharp focus.

Now she crouched in front of the engine to inspect the tyres, and the glare of the lights emphasised the generosity of her full mouth, the high line of her cheekbones, the raven lustre of her hair. Most startling of all, however, it picked out the magical tincture of her eyes, that violet glint which was so improbable that a man had every excuse for looking rather longer into them than would otherwise have been acceptable.

'May I assist you, Madam?'

A uniformed flunkey stood at a respectful distance. Probably, she thought, it was at exactly the right distance as specified in some book of English country house etiquette. Just as the size of his bowtie and the cut of his jacket and the width of his trouser leg would all be precisely, stupidly correct. And the parting in his greying hair, too. She was in no mood to be accommodating.

'Is there some problem, Madam? I noticed from the house that you appeared to have come to a stop.'

'Which isn't surprising since you've taken to laying tank-traps across your grounds. But I don't think there's any damage. Are there any more of these things in the way?'

'Only two, Madam, each thirty yards apart. Then Madam will come to the car park. Would Madam like some assistance in parking her car?'

'No Madam would not!' Calla exploded. 'Madam would like a stiff drink.'

'Of course, Madam. And how shall I announce Madam?'

Out of the corner of your mouth, she wanted to scream. Or perhaps with real roistering gusto, like a newspaper seller. Or how about singing it? But instead she ignored him and slid onto the seat of the car, slamming the door with an awesome finality.

'Oh dear, Calla, you've landed yourself in a spot of bother here,' she told herself, the cold February air clearing her brain. 'You've gate-crashed a few parties in your time, but never at a ducal palace.

'And anyway, don't you think that at twenty-nine you're a little bit old for this kind of thing?'

As she negotiated the remaining two sleeping policemen, she could see the servant standing under the lamp on the wide front steps. There was something in his head-up, legs-apart stance which she recognised, a bulldog determination not to yield. And it inspired in her, as it always did, an even greater determination to outwit the dull, the conforming, the conservative. She hadn't taken her world by storm by playing the delicate wallflower.

'Not too old to put one over old Jeeves,' she said aloud as she pulled into the car park at the side of the house and reversed smoothly between a jet-black Ferrari Testa Rossa and a gold Mercedes convertible with smoked-glass windows.

In her headlamps landscaped gardens rolled away, punctuated by mighty beech trees and great drifts of rhododendron bushes. In the distance was the hazy suggestion of a lake and beyond that a columned building like a small Greek temple.

Late eighteenth century neo-Classicism, she registered almost unconsciously. In the Palladian manner. A 'feature' giving perspective at the end of an avenue. Possibly a mausoleum, probably a folly.

'And in the circumstances, Calla Marchant,' she chided herself, 'who are you to talk about follies?'

She reached into her Mulberry bag for her illuminated compact mirror. A quick slick of scarlet would do the trick nicely. Steady on the scent, though: 'You don't want to shock the man. He's old money and high breeding. We mustn't frighten the horses round here.'

She swung long sheer-clad legs out of the car, slamming the door nonchalantly behind her. It wasn't the sort of neighbourhood where you needed to lock up.

In front of her stretched one wing of the extensive house.

'Now, if I had the mortgage on this stately pile, where would I hold this particular thrash?' she mused, sizing up the options. 'Yes, I think my guests might just enjoy an evening drink with a misty view over the grounds.'

She walked smartly up a flight of steps at the end of a long terrace at the back of the house. Lit up to one side was a noisily splashing fountain, supported by a naked Colossus. It was damn chilly for that kind of thing, she thought, although she couldn't stop herself running an appreciative eye over the spectacularly endowed stone form.

A long room in the centre of the house was richly aglow with light from huge crystal chandeliers. She could see clearly inside, and a shadow of anger passed over her set face. There, shoulder to bruising shoulder, elbow to sharp elbow, were the rivals she normally dealt with at a safe professional distance. At a rough count there were two dozen people in that room, and she knew more than half of them. It didn't escape her notice that all of those inside were men. To hell with etiquette, this was one party it would be a real pleasure to crash.

'Who'd have thought I'd see so many dear friends and colleagues under such a stately roof – and being so unnaturally polite to one another?' she murmured sardonically. 'And won't they be surprised to clap eyes on me!'

But someone inside the book-lined room had already seen Calla, and recognised her in spite of the outer gloom. After all, she wasn't the sort you forgot. Not if you were a man, at any rate. And Grant Locke was not only a man, but a man with an eye for a woman's style.

Where he came from, there hadn't been many women like Calla and he'd learnt their ways bit by bit, noticing the walk, the clothes, the way such women held their confident heads. He knew how to tell the real from the paste, and this was the 24-carat inimitable genuine article.

Oh yes, he recognised Calla Marchant. The black and white Chanel jacket cropped to the waist, the black narrow skirt above the knee, the shapely ankles set off by shoes which were almost certainly Jimmy Choos.

Things were about to get interesting, he thought. Especially as Calla's name hadn't been on the guest list. He'd suspected at the time that the omission wouldn't stop her. That wouldn't be Calla's style at all.

It wasn't. Calla, her investigation over, stalked back along the terrace and strode up to the main entrance, where the flunkey stood squarely and immoveably in her way. The gravel was probably doing unspeakable things to her leather-covered high heels and she was in no mood to mess around.

'Here's my card,' she said in impatient tones. 'I've no idea what all this is about, but my secretary took an urgent phone call from the Duke's personal assistant. It seems his Grace just can't do without me.'

He read her card. 'Calla Marchant, Architect.' An address in Mayfair. A telephone number. Nothing more, but, like the woman herself, the card had style. It had an undeniable authority. It was an opener of doors, and she could tell that it already had a foot in this one.

'In the library,' snapped Calla. 'That was the message, and if it's wrong I've a long journey back to Mayfair.'

The manservant met Calla's unwavering glance and, despite his years of training in the art of refusal, succumbed. He led her through an atrium to a pair of heavy oak doors and swung them open.

Just as a firework bursts in an ebony sky and the onlookers stand transfixed, sharing its stark beauty, so the gathering now stared as one, gazing with a communal appreciation that was close to awe upon the striking young woman who had thrust herself into their midst. And she, for her part, outfaced them with a characteristic brazenness which made the formal announcement quite unnecessary.

'Miss Calla Marchant.'

2

'I'll have a Bloody Mary.'

How did she know it would work? What made her so sure that, within seconds, a glass would find its way into her hand and that she would be inside the large room, safely swallowed up by the jabbering crowd?

Simply from experience. Calla had once been as nervous and shy as 99 per cent of the human race, but she had long since stumbled on the secret of social ease. Make it seem natural. Don't give a damn. Let the others worry.

The first time it had been an accident. As a teenager she had once taken a minor acting role in the school play and, mixing up her dates, had turned up for the first performance thinking it was the full dress rehearsal.

She arrived, with seeming insouciance, just two minutes before she was due to go on. She didn't have time for make-up and her costume was thrown on in great haste, with everyone backstage whispering and urging and pointing. Not surprisingly, she still didn't know that it was for real when she was pushed through the curtains and stumbled onto the stage.

The glare of the lights hid the audience from her until it was far too late – until she had stumbled, fallen, risen with a smile on her lips and, thinking she was only among friends, had improvised a witty little sketch which neatly returned her to the main action.

It was the roar of approval which woke her to the true situation, but by then she was into her stride. Not even thinking to be terrified, she soaked up the applause and stole the show with a performance her friends and teachers had never imagined her capable of.

A lucky break was how she thought about it afterwards. Despite her looks and her intelligence, Calla was never a conceited girl. She'd simply had the good fortune to learn a lesson sufficiently early in life to make all the difference when it mattered, and she ever afterwards milked that lesson for all it was worth.

That was why she now found herself among a gathering of some of the best architects in the land for a meeting which she suspected might change a few of their lives, for good or ill.

'A bravura performance, dear girl,' came a sibilant voice close to her ear. 'If not playing quite by the rules, eh?'

'What do you know about rules, Meredith?'

All her anger returned in an instant. Langton Meredith, a partner with Broughton, Hughes, Lorimer, had always managed to touch a raw nerve with Calla. It was the insolence of the man, his belief that small firms counted for nothing, especially if run by a mere woman.

He stepped close to her now, a handsome man in his late thirties, impeccably dressed. With his wellgroomed dark hair, his haughty Roman nose and his firm jaw, he looked every bit the typical English gentleman. But an unlikely wisp of white hair at one temple and that hissing quality in his speech added a rather sinister, deviant touch, and Calla shivered at his proximity.

'I do know about invitation cards,' he replied with a smile, 'and what's regarded as good form. Perhaps you imagined that the Duke had simply forgotten?'

'Let's just agree, Meredith, that you have much better breeding than me.'

'Than *I*, dear girl,' he sang. 'Than *I*. But I never had the benefit of attending a convent school.'

'Damn you, what do you know about that?'

Of course it didn't matter at all, but it rankled that he should know anything about her past. He was the kind of man who sullied everything he touched, even if it did happen years ago.

He laughed: 'More than would be decent to mention in this company, I'm sure.'

She turned her back on him and pointedly moved away. There was nothing to be ashamed of in those early days. Those were the precious days before she knew what shame was, she thought. Perhaps that was why his stupid remark annoyed her so much.

What, she wondered, would Mother Angelica make of her now? Would she be proud of her star pupil, or would she lament the fact that she had fallen among the worldly?   Certainly there were none more greedy, more cunning, more rapacious than some of those who were buzzing about the Duke's brimming honey-pot.

Calla remembered those far-off childhood days with deep affection. She could easily bring back to mind so many memories – the reverend sisters in their faded habits, shuffling into the tiny chapel; the simple, but wholesome meals, at the large, scrubbed refectory tables, with water poured into their glasses from tall earthenware pitchers; the dusty schoolroom, where they were first taught simple English and mathematics, but later progressed with the help of enthusiastic teachers to the intricacies of calculus, the complexities of Latin, to history, geography and the sciences.

There was a time, she recalled with a pang, when she had seriously considered taking the vows. Most girls in that position go through such a phase, but with Calla it was more than a passing fancy. She was a serious-minded girl, and she loved the quiet of the life.

One morning Mother Angelica had called for her, and asked her if she would consider becoming a novice 'if you feel that the Lord has called you'. And she had considered it, and had been minded to answer the call. If the other thing haddn't happened . . .

So what, she demanded of herself, was such a veritable paragon of virtue doing in this bear-pit? Had she changed so very much? Had she sold her soul? Perhaps the very fact that she was here meant that she was about to make a trade with the devil.

'Calla-lily!'

'Bunny!'

All these sombre thoughts were dashed out of her mind by the sight of a large, round man of about fifty-five, whose balding dome shone between bushes of grey hair and whose ample belly argued with crumpled trousers that were poorly supported by a pair of bright yellow braces.

Bunny Simkins was an architect of the old school, and the man who had taught the apprentice Calla Marchant all she knew. Or rather, all she knew *then*. She threw herself at him, spilling a little of her drink over her fingers. She licked them dry.

'And how's my innocent beginner?' he asked, just as if he'd been reading her mind. 'You're looking magnificent, Calla. I searched the guest list and ordered a hemlock when I saw that you weren't on it.'

'Ssssh!' she warned him with a twinkle in her eyes. 'Don't let everyone know. Langton Meredith has already been doing his worst to condemn me in the world's eyes.'

'As if anyone would believe anyone who spoke a word against you.'

They had the easy camaraderie and fondness of a man and a woman too far separated by age and type for the difficulties of romance to intervene. They simply loved one another's company on those few occasions these days when they were thrown together. She warmed to his openness and generosity.

'But tell me,' he said quietly, 'what this is all about. I'm rather out of touch. Got the invitation, said "Righty, righty" and toddled along. What's happening?'

'Don't know,' Calla replied. 'But with this lot invited, it's got to be something pretty big. It's more a case of who's *not* here.'

'No Richard Rogers,' Simkins said. 'No Frank Gehry.'

'And no Pei. But they wouldn't fit into the Duke's scheme of things, would they? Not his type at all.'

Now for the first time she saw the Duke of Mercia. Harry Willoughby was 40 years old, upright, somewhat starchy and obviously conscious of his position in the world. His position, that is, of a man with a wealth second only to that of his sovereign and so much property that it was said he could walk for a whole week and still be on his own land.

'Do you know our host?' asked Bunny, following the direction of Calla's gaze. 'Rather a young fogey, I should say. Not quite as at ease with his fellow man as you might expect. Not *this* type of fellow man, at least, eh?'

His former pupil nodded. The man she saw was courteously attentive to his guests, with the air of one who need not listen to others but was too well-mannered not to. His rather old-fashioned clothes had the easy look which belonged only to well-worn garments of generous cut and best quality cloth – the hallmark of the gentleman. Not for the Duke the sharp suiting of some of his guests. He didn't have to prove anything to anyone. This was a man at home in his clothes, in the house of his ancestors and in his wealth, Calla thought.

But there was no arrogance, nothing ugly in his bearing, none of the greed and eagerness in some of the faces around her. For a moment she wondered uncomfortably how her abrupt arrival must have struck such a man. There hadn't been many closed doors in *his* life, she thought.

But Calla could see more than just an assured aristocrat putting on his public face. Replacing his glass on a waiting servant's tray, the Duke began illustrating his conversation with gestures, restrained, but emphatic.

'He cares about whatever it is he's saying,' thought Calla. The hands were soft and square-fingered, not the slim and nimble hands of a musician or a draftsman, but of a visionary with the determination to make his dream come true.

As he stopped talking in order to listen, he toyed with his cufflink, not enough to distract Meredith, with whom he was standing, but just enough to put up a slight barrier between them. He had, after all, the reserve of his class and for all his apparent interest would not be a man easy to get close to.

But how little he needed to exert himself to seem different from, better than most of the others in this room! There was no obvious statement of his wealth, nothing showy, no flash Rolex wristwatch – just a black-stoned ring on his little finger, something else to pretend to adjust and so keep that precious distance from others. He would be a remarkable man to work with, thought Calla, a fascinating combination of nonchalance and power.

The Duke wasn't especially aware of being watched though, had someone asked him, he would have said he supposed it quite possible. He was used to moving among people whose duty or whose interest lay in watching him. Because of that, he had inevitably developed a range of social masks which his features readily assumed whenever he was not alone. It would scrcely do if people knew what one was thinking.

This Meredith to whom he was speaking now for instance. Skilled chap in his field, no doubt, with a dashed clever reputation, but here in the Duke's library, he seemed a little...well, overgroomed. Spoke agreeably though, no doubt of that. Could be just the man for the job.

If it *had* to be a man, thought the Duke, as he looked over Meredith's well brushed shoulder towards Calla. What an entrance that had been. Could have had her thrown out, but it would have embarrassed her and got the party off to a bad start. Besides, one liked to avoid scenes at all times.

She had remarkable eyes, though. Never seen anything that colour. As if she'd chosen the shade from a rainbow. In her City rich clothes, she stood out against the worn leather bookspines around the room. She even stood out against the rich old Persian carpet presently being indented by her high heels. He supposed the old place had never seen anything like her. But just who was Calla Marchant, architect? He must find out.

Harry Willoughby wasn't the only one looking, though Grant Locke had no need to wonder who Calla was. He had reason to know her well enough, more reason than even she knew. Locke was leaning against a nineteenth century French table, unabashed at being alone and boldly watching everyone else. He would quite like a word with young Calla though. She had the sort of guts Locke admired and if she was offhand with him, well, his skin was thicker than most and he could stand it.

Most men would have subtly caught Calla's eye and moved over to join her. Not Locke. He only played social games when there was money to be had out of them. This was just for the hell of it, so he fixed her with a stare across the room, blatantly gazing at her long legs. Then his eyes travelled up her almost perfect figure until, as he knew they would, they met hers. There was no blush on those fine features of hers, no anger, just icy inquiry. Locke nodded at her and laughed. She was good value for money, he thought. The world of architecture was all the more colourful for this high-flying bird of paradise. But Calla was such a magnificently determined creature and such a gifted architect that he wondered whether it would always be a pleasure to meet this particular rival.

Just now, however, the drinks were coming towards Calla, and Locke reasoned that she must need rescuing from that bore Bunny Simkins. He detached himself from the highly polished heirloom and crossed the floor towards her.

'Not quite our usual habitat,' he remarked. Locke had no patience with 'How are you?' inquiries. No one ever stopped to listen to the reply, so it was just a waste of breath.

'I suppose it is a shade respectable for you, Grant,' riposted Calla coolly. 'If you'd asked, I'm sure the Duke would have had sawdust put down to make you feel at home. How's everything?'

'Not being in the position of the Almighty, I don't know,' replied Grant. His vowels still gave away his northern origins, but he was the last person to put on a cultured voice. You took Grant Locke as you found him, or not at all, as he often said. Meredith, a sycophantic snob, preferred the not-at-all option, but most people in architecture admired Locke for his robust attitude towards taboos. He usually thought the unthinkable and frequently said it, even in the most inappropriate circumstances.

Like the Duke, he too looked entirely at ease in his evening clothes, but that was because he hadn't bothered to change. His corduroy jacket bagged at the elbows and the pockets. His tie was loosened and he wore an old tan leather belt. At forty, Grant Locke was still young enough to enjoy tilting at the Establishment. Even in the Establishment's own library.

Now his sharp eyes saw the Duke make a sign to the butler, who promptly led the waiters from the room. 'For what we are about to receive,' Locke murmured to Calla. 'His Grace is about to speak. Is he going to have the gatecrashers shot, do you think?'

The babble of chattering voices subsided like a sail when the wind has gone out of it. Such was the power of this one man, who strolled comfortably to a small Louis XV lectern and brushed a hand confidently across a waiting file of papers.

'No sign of the Duchess,' Calla whispered, having expected her presence even if this was something other than a strictly social event.

Grant Locke raised his eyebrows at this remark: 'Such innocence, dear girl. The good lady is certainly at home – I saw the car arrive. But upstairs tends to be her province.'

The fact that several heads turned in his direction, with reproving scowls for his temerity in continuing to talk, worried Locke not at all.

'And off her feet,' he added, defiantly.

The Duke looked carefully around the room for a full minute before he began to speak. Calla noticed that his air of polite distraction had entirely disappeared. Something vital within the man had risen to the surface, affecting the way he stood, the expression on his face, even the colour of his skin. He seemed to be buoyed up by some hidden inner excitement. Like, she thought – yes, just like a small boy who has a special secret which he can hardly contain within himself. The Duke looked similarly fit to burst!

'Thank you for coming, gentlemen,' he began, immediately checking himself. His glance in Calla's direction was, she registered with great relief, full of amusement: 'And lady.' He allowed the correction to hang in the air, so that a good-humoured ripple ran around the room. This was a man who knew how to handle a gathering, to manipulate it.

'I have had the pleasure of conversation with several of you already this evening, and I trust that there will be time for me to talk to everyone before you go. Many of you are already known to one another, and you will have realised that we have gathered here the cream of the post-war architectural generation.

'Indeed, I would go so far as to say that, with one or two controversial exceptions, every partnership of quality within the profession is here represented.'

'Norman Foster eat your heart out,' muttered Locke.

'There would be little point,' the Duke continued, 'in hiding from you my own rather strong views about the kind of buildings the British people have had to put up with over the last few decades. I'm quite sure that some of you in this room have had a few unkind things to say about this rather nutty character who meddles with things he knows nothing about. I do seem to have the knack of stirring up the proverbial hornet's nest whenever I open my mouth to speak on the subject.'

'Warts,' threw in Locke with a suppressed chuckle.

'I recall, for instance, no end of a kerfuffle when I referred to that proposed extension to the Tate Gallery as a hideous warty excrescence. The fact that the extension has not, after all, been built is attributed to the intervention of a sort of architectural Luddite, fanatically opposed to so-called progress and yearning for a nostalgic England full of milkmaids and handsome young swains.'

'Ee by gum,' commented Locke in an exaggerated northern accent, causing heads to turn again. 'Could we possibly 'ave it in English, please, sir?'

'I have to suggest, however, that perhaps it is rather the case of good sense and good taste coming to prevail. There has, I believe, been a shift in the public's perception of what makes a good building, and if I, in my small way, have done something to bring that about, I am very proud of my contribution.

'I beg your pardon, Mr Locke?'

Grant Locke had made one remark too many, for the Duke had obviously seen the movement of his lips. Calla sensed a new mood in the room. Locke's fellow architects scented blood. All eyes were upon him, and they were eyes narrowed with expectation of an entertainingly vicious scene. Yes, thought Calla, they couldn't help having a sneaking regard for his individualism, but despite this – or perhaps because of it – they relished the idea of his being torn apart in front of their eyes.

'Perhaps you would like to tell me, Mr Locke, that pride is a sin? I am aware of what the Good Book has to say about the matter.'

'I don't imagine, your Grace,' Grant Locke replied in tones of easy familiarity, 'that many people in this room are in a position to give a lecture on the deadly sins. I'm certainly not. But since you ask my view, I must say I'm surprised that you've included in this little soiree of yours people who wouldn't know how to tile a backyard lavatory.'

'What's wrong with modern architecture comes down to just one word – incompetence.'

The Duke toyed with a cufflink, a thin smile playing on his lips. If he was angry, his breeding didn't let him show it. But Calla thought he seemed rattled. He wasn't accustomed to such a direct criticism, and just for a moment he seemed to have lost control of the situation.

'That's preposterous!'

A small, swarthy man stepped forward, waving his arms towards Locke's face as if he intended a physical attack. Darl Pannick's rugged central European features were distorted in an expression of loathing. It was the face of a man who had been through the furnace of life and survived with knowledge he would rather not have. It wasn't, Calla thought, a face that it would be pleasant to have turned against you.

'You think,' Pannick shouted, the trace of an accent in his speech,'to come here, to accept the Duke's hospitality and then to . . . to spit in his face like this? You think you're so high and mighty you can accuse others of incompetence? Tell us what you have built!'

'I've won awards,' said Locke quietly, in a mocking voice.

'Ha! Awards! What do they matter? It's buildings I'm talking about.'

Calla remembered what she had heard about Darl Pannick, how as a child he had been ferried between the Middle East and Middle Europe by a mother who had survived the ghastliest horrors of the last war, her husband having been tortured and killed in front of her eyes, only to run up against new conflicts and new cruelties at every turn. They had at last arrived in England, penniless, homeless, hopeless. But young Darl had guts and determination as well as a quick wit. He had the immigrant's hunger. He learnt quickly and he took two steps forward while his schoolfriends and then his workmates took one.

He had the urge to build. It was a primitive drive with the young Pannick. He had seen so much destruction, so much desolation. He told his mother he would build her a palace. He learned the art, studying frantically at night school, but he still learned it too late for his mother. She died, worn out, a month before he completed his studies.

'But I'll do it, momma,' Pannick said to her ghost. 'You'll see that I still do it.' And he threw himself into the designing of buildings with an even greater zeal. It was a crusade, not a job of work. His buildings, however strange and innovative, were inspired by memories of flesh and blood. They weren't empty aesthetic exercises.

'So don't talk about incompetence,' he railed, 'when you have never built anything but little brick terraces!'

As soon as he paused for breath, he realised that he had behaved inexusably. Grant Locke only shrugged, but Pannick gave the Duke a pathetically imploring look, wrung his hands and began to stammer an apology.

'Gentlemen,' assured the Duke, both hands extended in a conciliatory gesture. 'I am the last person to need telling that architecture arouses great passions. I didn't bring you here, however, so that you might fight to the death over great principles. There will be a time for that, perhaps.'

Calla could not begin to guess why, but this last throw-away remark sent a chill through her body. Perhaps she simply knew all too well the passions which raged in a profession which seemed, to the naive outsider, so controlled and so civilised.

'Tomorrow morning,' the Duke continued, in businesslike tones which indicated that he was in charge once again, 'there is to be a press conference at which certain plans will be unveiled. I have invited you here for two reasons. First, out of courtesy. I felt that you should be the first to know. Secondly, because I may well use the services of one among your number, and this is, for me, an excellent opportunity to gauge your views in an informal manner.'

He raised a hand high in the air and soundlessly clicked his fingers. At once two servants hurried forward with a scroll of paper which they unrolled on a long table, holding down the ends with large onyx weights. Powerpoint obviously hadn't penetrated the ducal awareness.

'Plans,' he explained, 'for a new town. Or, properly speaking, for the extension of our existing county town. At present the population of Charlesbury is some 15,000. Within a few years my projection is for a population of 30,000 with the development of two thousand acres of the Duchy's land.'

He paused in order to enjoy the reaction of his audience. Calla felt her pulse quicken. Because of his influence, working for the Duke on any project was a feather in the cap. This, however, was something on the grand scale. The architect who won this project was made for life – financially, professionally, socially. She glanced round the room and saw each man an island of concentration, of wildfire dreams. She knew the gloves were off and that the fight would be dirty.

'You won't be surprised to learn,' said the Duke, speaking more easily now, 'that I have special plans for my new town. In fact it won't be a town, but a series of villages. And it is my intention that this development will be on the human scale, and will put into practice the principles which I have been so tirelessly – and, I dare say, tiresomely – promoting over the past few years.

'The design will be open to competition. I am inviting outline architectural schemes by the first day of September. I shall then draw up a short list of the designs which best meet my requirements and I shall invite the practices concerned to develop detailed blueprints.

'If you will step closer, you may inspect the plans and ask any questions at your leisure.'

Such was the tension that the architects seemed poised to swoop upon the Duke with one united rush, but before one of them could make a move there came a furious scrabbling sound at the library doors, as if someone on the other side was uncertain whether to push or to pull.

The doors flew open and a tall, wild-eyed young man, his dark hair falling into eyes that were preternaturally bright, half fell, half ran into the room. He swayed on the carpet with an almost idiotic calmness. The carelessly floppy hair, the heavy dark eyebrows raised questioningly at the startled onlookers, the girlish pout of the lips, were the sort of looks which might be at home on a cricket pitch or leaning on a snooker cue or propping up the railings of a cruise liner. They said money and they said magnetism.

But there was more than complacent good looks to this man. Something sadder, something infinitely deeper was etched on that face, so pale in stark contrast to his dark hair. There was a weakness, a waywardness, which was both winning and a warning. It said beware. It said that this man,who must be in his thirties yet carried something boyish in his every feature, was dangerous to women.

He tottered forward, held both hands together in front of his body as if aiming a pistol, and began to wheel slowly round, staring with a fixed and manic gaze at each person in turn. They fell back as if they were genuinely in danger, shocked and scared by the weird interloper.

'Brunson!' the Duke called to his butler, regaining his composure before anyone else. 'Fetch the police!'

But at this moment Calla sprang forward. Seizing the man by the arm, she dragged him away, forcing him it seemed by sheer strength of will. 'Damn, damn, damn!' she was muttering to herself as, tears in her eyes, her bosom heaving with a barely suppressed passion, she pushed him out of the room and slammed the heavy doors behind her.

3

Jason Andover had been the love of her life, that was her problem. He'd been her joy and her anguish, her support and her handicap, her friend and her enemy. Her life was so inextricably linked with his that there was never a good moment or a bad that was without an echo of him. She loved him and she hated him and there was no way that she could imagine that she could be without him.

It had begun on the night of her seventeenth birthday, at the very worst time of her life. She remembered the clear skies of that September evening, the air still warm, the stars shining brightly, the moon full. But it was typical of her relationship with Jason that she was never allowed a memory that was free from pain. She had only met him because she had been running away.

Calla had an older sister, Nerissa, who was ten years her senior. They were too much apart in years for rivalry. The young Calla worshipped her sister with a fierce loyalty, trailing her through her sparkling life at an awed distance. Nerissa was beautiful and carefree. Whereas Calla applied herself to study, thought hard about her friendships, was generally a serious young woman, Nerissa allowed people and events to wash about her. She seemed to succeed with no effort at all.

She had made no great effort at school yet garnered a useful crop of examination results. She declared that she had no great professional ambitions, but she stumbled into photography and within a couple of years was in demand by top magazines who admired her distinctive style, her ability to read things in any situation which nobody else had noticed.

During Calla's years in the convent school she read reports of her big sister's doings with pride, and showed cuttings of her work to her friends. Journalists were writing feature articles about her now. She was becoming a celebrity. And Nerissa, for her part, although she was busy, kept in touch with Calla and sometimes sent her money. These gifts were erratic, in keeping with her spontaneous, unpredictable nature, just as her letters were erratic, both in their frequency and in their content. Sometimes there would be nothing more than a single page, with a pen and ink drawing and a rudimentary caption above that sprawling signature and a row of kisses. On other occasions there would be pages of news, hilarious accounts of life in magazine-land, of fashion shoots and exciting expeditions to far-off climes.

'Think big and think wild, little sis,' used to be her watchword, perhaps because she sensed that Calla was a little too serious to be true.

'They won't bite,' she used to add.

It was, Calla came to think later, a charmed life she herself was leading – and charmed lives can't last. Her elderly parents had plenty of money, although how much she couldn't guess (Daddy was in insurance). Her sister was famous and she was happy at school.

The dreadful realisation that the spell had been broken came to her by degrees. At first she hardly noticed that her parents made no mention of Nerissa in their letters. A gap in Nerissa's own correspondence was not unusual, though it did begin to lengthen. Then, as she made plans to return home for the long vacation, the sense of a family crisis began to loom. She spoke to her mother on the telephone and heard an embarrassed edge to her voice when Nerissa was mentioned. Perhaps her older sister would be visiting, perhaps she wouldn't.

'But why ever not?'

'It may be better that she doesn't, Calla, that's all.'

Why should her beloved sister not be at home for weeks at a time? Of course, she had her own flat in London now, she'd been independent for two or three years. She had her own friends and she was travelling the world. But Calla couldn't imagine that her sister wouldn't come dancing through the front door and throw her arms around her, all the while telling her of the latest escapade in a life full of the most spendid gaiety.

It was worse than she could have imagined. Nerissa was already home when Calla arrived in a taxi from the station, clutching her school bag and a light suitcase. The cabbie was waiting for his money, but she couldn't approach any of the adults in the house because of the terrible row which was going on.

'This is a respectable home,' her father was shouting like some rabid fundamentalist preacher. 'It's been unsullied by filth and lewdness.'

'I'm 23 years old, for Christ's sake,' Nerissa bawled back. 'What rights do you have over my body?'

'The right to know when a woman's made a bitch of herself,' her father went on, and all the while her mother, red eyed, was imploring both of them not to shout, not to make it worse, not to say things they didn't really mean.

'I mean every word,' her father yelled. 'She's been whoring around and she's not welcome in a home of mine.'

Calla, white with shock, fumbled in a kitchen drawer for loose change and fled down the drive, where, hardly knowing what she was doing, she pushed a fistful of coins into the cabman's waiting hand. Then she returned very slowly, as if she could in some way make it all not happen, so that when she entered the house again none of this would have happened and her beloved sister would be laughing out loud and telling colourful stories of her world far away.

But the charm had ceased to work. Even as she reached the door Nerissa came flying out of it, her eyes wild, her cheeks flushed. Their father's shouting could be heard inside the house. It seemed for a moment as if Nerissa's headlong flight would take her down the drive and away without so much as a word, but then she turned and, her eyes brimming with tears, smothered Calla in a warm embrace.

The two clung together, silently, their cheeks touching so that each could feel the other's tears. Then their father's voice came nearer and Nerissa disengaged herself, backing away from her younger sister with a look of unbearable tenderness on her face.

'Think big, little sis,' she said, her voice cracking. 'And think wild.'

'I will,' Calla whispered, watching her disappear. 'I will.'

This was in 1990, when young people were much more free than ever before to live their own lives, but her parents were elderly and conservative and it was some time before they could bring themselves to tell her what had happened. When they did tell her she couldn't understand, in her young innocence, why they were so angry. She couldn't understand, that is, why they were heartbroken, that they felt their plans for their elder daughter had been needlessly wrecked.

Nerissa, quite simply, was pregnant and she intended to keep the child. This they found appalling. They hadn't read the right agony aunts and they didn't mix with people who were the slightest bit liberal. She wasn't married and had no immediate plans to marry. And when they asked about the father, she was offhand about him, as if he hardly came into the equation. Perhaps this was bravado, but it made her appear cheap in their eyes. They thought it was dirty, and that the dirt rubbed off on them. They told her she wasn't welcome in their home and she took them at their word. She said, in turn, that she would never return, and she kept her word.

Who was the father? They didn't know. Nerissa reasoned that if they were so vicious towards their own daughter, they were likely to behave intolerably towards the father of her child. So she kept the name secret. They never knew.

Calla was devastated. She loved her parents, but she worshipped her sister. It wasn't a question of taking sides: she simply pined for Nerissa. There was an early letter from her, which was in effect a farewell note. She didn't want to involve Calla in the feud with their parents. It was best, she wrote, that she keep away 'even from my little sis', at least for a period. She urged Calla to carry on with her studies and, needlessly, to remember her Nerissa.

This was the end of Calla's childhood, and she was only thirteen years old. She hadn't known how much she depended upon her older sister until she disappeared. Then she began to examine her own life and to consider how poorly it compared with Nerissa's. She would rather be like Nerissa than anything in the world. If that meant being wild, that's what she would do. She didn't have to be a blue-stocking.

It would doubtless have been better had she known that their father, despite his hurt and the feeling of disgust he couldn't control, had sold a large tranche of blue chip shares and, on the birth of the baby, had sent the cash to Nerissa as a love offering. He could not bring himself even to tell his wife what he had done, because in truth he despised himself for his weakness. And he maintained the silence against his elder daughter for the rest of his life.

If Calla had known this it might have softened her resolve to follow her sister's path. She might have accommodated herself to her parents' wishes. As it was, she determined to strike out for herself, even if it meant another storm in the family. Nerissa had made storms respectable.

She bided her time, spending the best part of four years in a mood of rebellion artfully concealed. Of course she had her famous rages from time to time, but they were expected. That was Calla. She still managed to study, even though her heart wasn't in it. Nobody suspected. Then, a week before her seventeenth birthday, she climbed over the convent wall at dusk and made her way to London.

Mercifully, there was someone she knew. Mardi, a jolly, gauche brunette, had just left the convent school at the age of eighteen and was training to be a nurse. She was living in a bedsit in Southwark and was happy for Calla to sleep on her floor. There were other student nurses in the same house, and Calla felt that she was among friends.

The nurses often slept through part of the day and worked at night, and Calla would spend the evening hours wandering about the city, getting to know the different areas. She soon learned that the south of the Thames is another world from the north, and that London is a collection of villages which retain their identity despite the anonymous work of the planners. She came to admire this diversity and to understand how the different buildings created a local character.

On her seventeenth birthday Mardi organised a lunchtime party for Calla, which spread late into the afternoon. Eventually the nurses put on their uniforms and trooped off to the training hospital and their bedpans and syringes, leaving Calla in a mellow mood, rather wistful about the circumstances of the celebrations and still a little tipsy from the cheap wine they had drunk. She walked to the river, crossed Blackfriars bridge and strolled along the Embankment.

There's no time for feeling lonely like the hour when lovers are strolling hand in hand, and there's no place for it like a big city where the lights seem to be calling everyone to have a good time. Calla suddenly felt that desolation as she came upon the obelisk Londoners call Cleopatra's Needle, and she sat down at the foot of it and felt ready to cry.

She seemed a long way from home. But where was home? Certainly not with the father and mother who had turned their backs on her beloved sister. Certainly not in the stifling safety of the convent. Mardi's flat, the crowd of nurses, her makeshift bed on the floor. Could any of those be home?

A drunk lurched by, waving a friendly bottle at her. Calla shuddered and tried to shrink back into the shadows. She had seen down-and-outs sleeping on benches and under the capital's many bridges, covered in newspaper, their hair and breath foul with dirt and drink. She feared them. She feared being sucked into that dreadful netherworld of the hopeless and forgotten.

In the lamplight some way off she saw a merry group of young people in evening dress drifting towards her. Laughing and shouting, they were pivotting around a central member of their group, a young man who was in high good spirits and who, with extravagant gestures, was giving a brilliant impersonation of an orchestra conductor. He was walking backwards as he led his orchestra of friends, each imitating an instrument as they moved closer, laughing their tune along.

Calla was so fascinated that she didn't realise the young man was on collision course for her perch at the foot of the column. His friends were either too drunk to notice or perhaps thought it would add to their merriment if the conductor took a tumble.

It happened in a split second. Arms upraised, about to direct the crashing end of an unrecognisable symphony, he fell backwards into her lap as the orchestra broke up in riotous disarray. Such is the ludicrously insignificant way great events often begin. The young man scrambled to a sitting position and faced her, pushing an unruly lock of hair out of his playful blue eyes.

'Sorry! I didn't realise we had a soloist,' he said to her, with a disarming grin. 'What do you play?'

Youthful banter hadn't been part of the curriculum at St Jude's – the patron saint of lost causes, the girls often reminded themselves – and there had been no lessons in coping with larky young men.

She answered truthfully: 'The flute actually,' adding ridiculously, 'but I'm frightfully out of practice.'

Her straightforward, guileless answer seemed to have a sobering effect on her companion, who straightened his bow-tie and examined her closely.

'Are you all right?' he asked.

Calla looked back at him. There was something direct about him. For all his careless air, there was a genuine concern which forced the truth out of her. Idiotically, she repeated: 'I'm out of practice. And I'm lost.'

He continued to stare at her, wondering what this unworldly girl was doing on the Embankment late at night and alone. Several minutes passed in trance-like silence. They were both aware that there was movement around them, that the rest of the group had called taxis and were climbing into them. Each somehow knew that the other was aware of all this and that it didn't matter at all. Rough hands shook his shoulders: 'Come on, Jason! Bring your flautist, if you like!'

But Jason, coming suddenly to life, shook his head and waved the party off with his imaginary baton: 'Much too early for the conductor to go home,' he said with a lopsided smile. 'Especially when he has a new score to study.'

He put an arm round her and, seeing the tears begin to form, pressed a soft handkerchief to her eyes.

'Now tell me,' he said, once they were alone.

She told him, as they walked along. Everything came out, from her days at the convent to Nerissa's fate and her own flight from home. Jason Andover wrapped his jacket around her shoulders and led her away from the river and into his life.

Years later and years wiser, Calla was to wonder why she had trusted herself to a foppish stranger on his drunken way home from one of the Promenade concerts at the Albert Hall. But it seemed quite natural at the time. She had never felt so understood, so unjudged. And she had never met a man quite like Jason, so assured, so dashing.

In his house they talked. Even then, there were signs of those distinctive ingredients of character, the strength allied to an almost wilful weakness, which were to make her both glory in him and to wish that they had never met.

Through hints and little anecdotes he sketched his life in the art world. He admired paintings and wrote about them in glossy magazines. He loved music, and played the piano. There were shelves of books in the flat, and he spoke about this and that novelist who were popular at the time. Some of them he seemed to have met, in circumstances which weren't clear to her.

Despite this impressive CV, however, it was evident that Jason Andover only played at the things he enjoyed. He was a dilettante. He was twenty-one years old and he didn't need to work. The money in his life rang and echoed around the flat. Framed pictures of public school cricket elevens were irreverently hung in the loo. Stiff white invitation cards were stuck any old how behind the clock. The unwashed plates in the kitchen were the kind most people hid safely away in glass cabinets. Jason belonged to a world of privilege.

Sons of that world tend to be spoilt and Calla when she was older often thought of the Jason of that night, leaning back on a battered chaise longue smoking the pot which was even then a habit with him. But she was just seventeen, and the air of romance clung to him even more thickly than the marijuana clouds. He was devil-may-care about everything, knowledgeable about things she had never heard of, and (most winning of all) he was kind and gentle, as if he understood everything that she thought and felt.

Damn it, he even knew how unsure she felt about being with him in the foreign territory of his flat. More, he was so generous that he was prepared to deny his own masculine desires in order that she shouldn't be hurt. She knew that he wouldn't pester her and force her as most men certainly would. So why did her heart beat so violently when he brought in a pillow and blankets and threw them on the living room floor?

'My bed,' he said, with a smile. 'The master bedroom is yours.'

She said nothing, only watching him fussing with the blankets. Then she rose and entered the bedroom. Her sister's words were running through her brain. 'Think big and thing wild,' was what Nerissa used to say. And she had replied, outside their parents' house, 'I will, I will'. And so she would, she thought. She was no longer a schoolgirl. She was in charge of her own destiny. She would – if only she knew how!

But she didn't need to think. Strange how innocence knows, as if by instinct, how to seduce. She entered the bedroom and sat on the bed, but she left the door open. What man could resist an open bedroom door?

'Comfortable?' he asked, putting his head in. 'I know how virtuous you convent girls are.' He smiled. 'You're almost a nun, after all.'

She remained silent and he didn't go away. He stood watching the leggy girl sitting on the bed, gazing down at her feet making shadows on the carpet. And of course he came in, sitting next to her as cautiously as if she were a fawn he mustn't startle. He put a finger under her chin, bringing her face round to his. He was startled by the largeness of her pupils. The thin ring of her irises was deep violet.

There was no alarm on her part. She looked back at him without fear and he drew her head towards him, kissing lips which were quite still, but warm and soft. Calla had only ever felt the bristly brush of male relatives against her cheeks before. She'd never known this firm claim of mouth on mouth.

Jason drew back to look at her face. Those wide eyes looked straight back at him still. He would make her close them. Cupping her face in his hands, he planted tiny kisses all along her mouth. Then, beginning in one corner, he pushed the tip of his tongue gently between her lips, going only the slightest way in each time until he reached the other corner.

She gasped slightly, her mouth parting, allowing his tongue inside, exploring, moving against hers, drawing out again to caress inside her lips and finally pull away with a little sucking kiss. Her eyes were closed now, as he rested his hands on her shoulders and ran his tongue down her arched white neck, from her chin to the soft cup of warm flesh between her collar bones.

His hands moved down to her breast. He heard a catch in her breath. Her arms came up around him and she sought his mouth with hers, respondingly uncertainly to his gentleness with kisses which grew in passion as his hands explored the secret of her. His fingers were under her blouse now, feeling for the nipple, which Calla knew was as hard as if she had been under the cold shower after school swimming.

Oh, but she had never felt quite like this before. As Jason's hand moved down inside her skirt, rubbing the tautness of her stomach, she felt a leap of desire within her. Her thighs loosened in a delicious yielding, and a moan escaped her lips. Suddenly his hands were under her elbows and she felt herself lifted off the bed. They were on their feet, he holding her tight against him. She could feel his hardness against her belly. It both excited and frightened her, and there was another emotion there too. It was a gratification that she, Calla, had caused his arousal, that she was desired.

This craving for flesh on flesh she had never imagined in its heat and ferocity. She wanted to tear her clothes off, but felt it a kind of immodesty and held back. Once again he understood. With patience he undid each of her buttons, kissing each newly revealed area of flesh, gently unfastening her bra and licking, licking, with slowly circling tongue, each dark pink nipple.

She could bear it no longer, but felt blindly for his trouser belt, tugging violently at it until it loosened, then pulling at the zip and forcing the material down over his thighs. She wanted his body as she had never wanted anything in her life. His hands reached out to slide her pants below her knees, she all the time pressing her breasts against his chest, rubbing flesh against flesh, aroused beyond endurance. What could ever stop this wanting, this needing?

They stood apart for a brief moment, watching, savouring. He saw the perfect tautness of her young woman's belly, the soft-muscled contours of her thighs with the tousle of pitch black hair between. She saw with an ache the sinews of his upper arms, the thread of hairs on his chest, the proudly rearing cock with its empurpled, engorged vein.

They clasped, pressed close, and Calla felt that proud member hard against her womanhood and pushing, pushing. She spread her legs, opening to it, offering herself to him, and she felt a little spasm of pain which became a lambent flame of pleasure as it slid along her moist canal, nosed firmly to its very end. How indescribably good it felt to be full of him, rocking to his gentle motion, the tender motion of love which began to flood her being with a euphoric drenching sensation until she felt she must fall to the ground.

He turned her then, his sinewy strength grasping her thighs and lifting her, swinging her towards the bed. Without leaving her, he lowered her onto it. She felt him upon her, moving, moving, and that feeling came in waves, pulsating through every nerve in her grateful, rejoicing body.

Afterwards, as they lay comfortable in an indolent closeness, she remembered what day it was.

'It's my birthday,' she said.

Jason smiled, a finger lazily exploring the matted moistness of her pubic hair: 'Many happy returns,' he wished her.

● ● ●

It was inevitable that her father should find her.

Those first few months of her life with Jason had been the stuff of dreams, pleasure without the slightest responsibility. They had toured the parks and galleries of London, the restaurants and the night spots, where he introduced her to as motley a crowd of zany individualists as she could ever hope to imagine. Everyone seemed to agree that Jason Andover was the most amusing, captivating companion, and Calla warmed herself in the reflected glow.

When he was busy on one of his forays into the art world, helping to organise an exhibition of sculpture, perhaps, or flying to a symposium of European ceramics, she would resume her habit of exploring the intricacies of the city. Where the knack had come from she couldn't guess (was it some ancient family gene resurfacing?) but she quickly learned to place a style, to date a building, to tell from a swift tour of an area how it had developed.

Jason was always encouraging about the things she enjoyed doing, and when he realised that her love of buildings and their geography was more than a passing whim he bought her books on the subject, and asked intelligent questions which fired her enthusiasm even more. Returning from one of his trips, he would make her explain what she had learned. They would wander the streets together, hand in hand, as she explained the features of the cityscape, which seemed to become more and more their own.

One morning, minutes after Jason had left the house, there was a knock on the door and her father stood outside, his face grim, his fingers bunched into two tight fists.

'My baby,' he said.

'No,' she replied. 'I'm Calla. Don't think of me as a little girl. I don't want that.'

She had felt strong when she said this, but when the tears welled up in his eyes she lost her resolve. The moment had been long expected, and she had rehearsed the scene in which she ordered him out of her life. Now she reached forward, took him by the arm and gently pulled him inside.

'I don't want that,' she repeated, though in truth she didn't know just what it was that she wanted at this moment. She only knew that she would not long be able to bear the pain in his eyes.

He sat down at last, heavily, and stared at her as if she belonged to another world. As she did, of course. He knew nothing of her life now. She had always thought of him as strong and masterful, but here he seemed diminished, so that she felt protective towards him.

'Your mother . . .' he began, but the words choked in his throat.

'Forget that speech, Daddy,' she said flatly, forcing herself. 'We don't need it. We've seen the film. Tear-jerking isn't going to work.'

'Why?' he asked. 'Why did you do it?'

She shrugged her shoulders. What about her rehearsed speech? Now the opportunity had come she had forgotten it.

'Nerissa,' she said.

'She made you do it – is that it? Has she been filling your head with these things?'

Calla shook her head: 'I've lost Nerissa.' She had meant to say that she hadn't seen her sister, but the bitter truth of the situation came out. It hit her with the greater force because it was something she daily put out of her mind.

'You've been looking for Nerissa? In London? That's why you came here?'

'No.'

'Because if that's it, you've been wasting your time. She went to America. She's been there ever since . . .'

He didn't need to finish his sentence. How pitiful he seemed, she thought. It was cruel to hurt him. He had suffered so much these last years that there were lines in his face she had never been aware of, and his skin had the pallor of an illness.

'I can have you brought back,' he suddenly shouted, as if it was a threat he had been tussling with all along. 'You're under-age. The authorities would say you were in danger, living in a place like this.'

For the first time he allowed himself to look at his surroundings. They were untidy, though clearly not sordid. He could tell that she was not without money. But he didn't need to look, she was sure. He must have been spying on her for some time.

'I'm seventeen,' she said. 'Half way to eighteen. It's too late, Daddy. No one's going to make me go anywhere. I've chosen the life I want to live. You'd better just accept it.'

'I don't have to accept it!'

'That's your problem, then. Do what you like.'

She turned from him, crossed the room and opened the front door. The gesture was unmistakable in its intention. His time was up He had made his effort and failed. There was nothing more to be said.

'No, wait,' he said. He made a pacifying motion with his hands, as if to say 'Let's start again; let's pretend none of this has happened and that I've said nothing yet.' Plan B, thought Calla, all at once feeling incredibly tired. She swung the door closed and sat down again.

'Let's have it,' she said.

The realisation came to her at that moment that she had, in fact, won. She knew that she would have been able to watch him walk through the door and away. It would have hurt, yes – but she could have done it. Therefore she was free. She could afford to be magnanimous. She would listen.

'Calla,' he said, 'we miss you, your mother and I. We never wanted any of this. We wanted you to be happy. That's what we still want.'

'You threatened me.'

'I'm sorry. I was wrong. I thought that if I held out a threat I could make an offer to set against it. That sounds like blackmail, but I didn't want it to be like that. There's something I wanted to suggest to you.

'Forget the authorities, I was going to say. I won't tell the authorities if you'll agree to two things. I'm sorry that it sounds like blackmail.'

Threats. The authorities wouldn't be interested, she knew.

'So what were the two things.'

'One,' he said swiftly, 'that you'll see your mother from time to time. She doesn't expect much. You don't have to stay over. Just a quick visit. She wants to look at you and to know you're all right.'

'And number two?'

'That you'll take up your studies again.'

He saw the surprise on her face. It was the last thing she'd expected. What she had expected was something about Jason and her not seeing him again. Now he'd wrong-footed her.

'I'll pay,' he urged her. 'You're not far behind. Plenty of girls miss a year. You could get yourself qualified. Choose anything you like.' He saw her indecision and pressed home the advantage. 'What would you choose if you had the field to pick from? Anything.'

'Architecture,' she said.

• • •

What she had hidden from herself was a growing listlessness, a sense that she lacked direction. The happiness of her early days with Jason had seemed without flaw, but now she realised that there had been moments, albeit fleeting ones, when she had wished for something more. There was a want in Calla, a want to achieve, to win.

Once she had fallen in with her father's plan her life became completely fulfilled. If she saw less of Jason during the daytime, the joy of returning to him in the evening became so much the keener. Their love became more passionate than ever before, their love-making more tender and more thrilling.

He knew she would make a fine architect. He understood when she felt too tired for her work, but he would never allow the excuses which would have hampered her success. And after she had passed the first few necessary examinations, he used his incredible range of contacts to find the very best practice for her to join for her apprenticeship.

Bunny Simkins was a gentleman architect in a world where the smart and the glossy prevailed. And he was traditional in the best sense of the word. He used the latest technology, but he also knew the weaknesses of computer-aided design. Trained in a world of drawing boards, scales, set-squares, pens of different gauges and razor blades for erasing mistakes on tracing paper, he instructed Calla in the vital coordination between hand and eye. Sketching by hand, he told her, was the quickest way of discovering whether a space or a vista could work.

He owed his success to two things. First, he was so genuinely good-natured that few could find it themselves to dislike him – and,liking him, they were unable to carry out the deft stab in the back the profession expected. Secondly, he was bloody good.

'You can try to be a friend to your client,' he told Calla as she worked at the drawing board during her first week with the firm, 'and give him exactly what he wants. In which case it will probably be something awful. Most clients don't really know what they want at all, so they'll give you a crazy brief.

'Or you can put the building first and hope the client doesn't notice what you're up to. That's the way to earn the respect of the quality journals, but it'll soon put you out of business. The chances are that the client won't have a clue that you've just designed him the most subtle and innovative mansion in the western hemisphere. He hates living there.'

'Which means this job is mission impossible,' she laughed, holding the rule steady to trace the outline of a hospital liftshaft. 'Perhaps I should try something which offers more chance of success.'

'Believe me, Calla,' he replied, 'I wouldn't have taken you on unless I knew you were going to succeed. It's a tough world out there, and it's tougher still for a woman.

'No, it's an art, not a science, that's my point. Of course you need the scientific base – the physics, the mathematics – but it's sheer human skills that will take you to the top.'

Sometimes she wondered about her drive to reach that pinnacle. Why did it seem so necessary? Surely there were plenty of architects, just as there were plenty of dancers and teachers and journalists, who were content just to do a job well. Wasn't she happy with the rest of her life?

She thought she was. Jason was no less loving to her than before, and he took pleasure in her obvious progress. Sometimes they would visit a building site and, shy of being seen, would watch the beginning of a project she was involved in. They felt as close as ever in those moments.

Immersed in her work, though, she had ceased to observe his moods as keenly as once she did. She carelessly imagined that he was as happy and fulfilled as she was. His increased use of marijuana she barely registered, and when it did cross her mind she put it down to a temporary phase. It took the comment of an outsider to jolt her into frightful reality.

'He can afford that junk,' said her friend Mardi, only an occasional visitor now, 'but it's doing him no good.'

'If you've got to smoke,' Calla replied, 'it's better than cigarettes.'

'It's not smoking I'm talking about.'

'What are you saying, Mardi. What are you trying to tell me?'

'The coke, dunderhead. Don't tell me this is news.'

She suddenly felt ill. It wasn't only the bombshell that Jason was sniffing cocaine. That was dreadful, frightening, it opened a void of despair inside her. Even worse, however, was the realisation that she hadn't cared enough to notice. She had drifted a little away from him and, moreover, he hadn't cried out to her for help. Perhaps the distance between them had somehow grown too great. For the first time she felt that their relationship might be fragile, mortal.

'Concentration,' Jason said when she challenged him about the habit. 'That's all it's for. It's a simple tool, and I use it only when I need it.'

'And how often do you need it?'

'As often as I use it,' he giggled. 'Does that sound like something out of Alice in Wonderland?'

'You're beginning to seem like someone in Alice in Wonderland, Jason,' she heard herself saying. 'You're not in the real world any more.'

For that was increasingly how she felt about him. The more she advanced in her training, the more responsibility she took for designing buildings and agonising over their every significant detail, the less there seemed to be of value in Jason's life. He worked hardly ever now. When he attended exhibitions they seemed to have little impression on him. Even his frivolous pleasures seemed to be endured rather than enjoyed.

She was aware that they clung to one another almost from desperation. The love was still there, and sometimes it spouted like the steaming upthrust of a geyser, leaving them soaked and spent. But it seemed to Calla that they communicated now only through such moments of high passion, never in the casual comradeship of the day-to-day.

As the end of her apprenticeship drew close she found herself taking stock of her life afresh. The success she craved was possible now. She felt that she was a good architect. Of course she was: Bunny Simkins, now a friend as much as an employer, had said she was the most promising pupil he'd ever had. Soon she would be taking new strides, making a name for herself. She shouldn't allow herself to be shackled. But even as she entertained such thoughts, she felt guilty about them. You, Calla Marchant, she thought, are just a selfish bitch.

They were at a table for two at The Ivy late one evening when Jason reached forward and grasped her wrist. He had a feverish look in his eyes.

'That's hurting me,' she said. Had he been snorting that stuff? Was he trying to hurt?

'Sorry, but I've had this wonderful idea.' He waited for a reply. 'Can you guess what it is?'

'Of course not.'

'Try. Go on, try!'

'We should go on to Boujis for the disco.'

'No, something much more serious.'

'We should go home and read Proust.'

'I'm talking you,' he said, smiling. 'You and me, but principally you.'

'I should rise from this table, leave the restaurant and take a walk in the cool night air to rid my head of my insufferable inquisitor.'

He seemed to have missed the note of disdain in her jokey responses. Leaning forward, he took both her hands in his.

'You,' he said, 'will soon be an independent architect. You will be looking for new opportunities. You aim to be the best architect this country has ever seen.'

'Not so loud,' she counselled, 'this may sound a shade presumptuous to the clientele.'

'And you're ready to start now,' he added. 'Isn't that so?'

'If you like,' she said.

'No, tell me. Aren't you ready?'

'I'm ready.'

'Then you're in business. What shall we call it? The   Calla Marchant Partnership? Marchant Architectural Consultancy?'

'What *are* you talking about, Jason?'

'I'm talking money, my love. I do have a bit, you know. I'm talking of an investment in six figures to put the woman I love into her own business. I'm talking about Calla Marchant's future.'

He lifted her fingertips to his lips and kissed them, one by one. Calla felt the salt tears flooding into her mouth.

● ● ●

It wasn't until years after they met that she learned he had a younger brother. Jason was strangely reluctant to talk about his family or his childhood. Obviously there was money about, and she picked up the occasional hint about his businessman father, now dead, and his artistic mother. But they *were* only hints, as if there was something in the past which haunted him and must never be mentioned. The brother had come as a surprise.

Now, years later, the surprise was in the form of a crisp white envelope, hand-delivered to Calla's small new offices in Pimlico, one of the few commercial premises in that area of whitewashed Georgian terraces, discreet London homes of Government ministers and the well-to-do of the newspaper world – useful contacts for a young woman about to take the place by storm, she smiled to herself.

But some storm it would have to be, she thought, taking up a silver-bladed knife and deftly slitting the envelope. This wasn't much of a place, with its shabby decorations and its narrow staircases. But it was a start, a step towards the world she had dreamed of for years as she studied and wandered around the pomposity, the grandeur and the young daring of London's richly patterned architectural landscape.

She would do great things, starting with these offices, thought Calla, as she stood at the high window, looking down on the street beneath. Jason was so keen for her to win, so proud of the unexpected treasure he had found on the Embankment all those years ago. It was his money, she was keenly aware, which had bought this for her. And he was taking on all the costs of setting the business up properly.

'Look upon it as my investment, angel,' he had said to her one day as they gazed at the unsung Victorian splendour of St Pancras Station on one of their long Sunday strolls round a sleepy London whose walls, towers and courtyards were naked to the inspection of the few souls who cared to be up and about that quiet day.

'You never thought of me as a businessman, did you?' he had smiled. 'Why, my brother would be proud of me.'

Calla, for whom her sister had been everything she wanted and yearned to be, had hardly understood Jason's offhandedness and demanded full details of this mystery figure. After all, he must have shared her lover's toys, tantrums and boyhood triumphs. She rather wished to meet him, even if he sounded distinctly less than sympathetic.

Patrick Andover, two years the junior, couldn't have been more different from his brother, apparently. While Jason had grown into a sensuous adolescent, relishing everything which was beautiful, enjoying his own carefree life, and learning about the world of art and music, Patrick had been a driven youth. He'd been driven, that is, to succeed, to achieve and to make money. And he'd succeeded.

Jason, shrugging, had told Calla with a laugh: 'If a boy gets called Pat by the rest of the school, no wonder he grows up hard. Anyhow, he wanted precious little to do with his wastrel brother.

'And I can't say I missed him as a soulmate. Take Patrick to a concert and he'll be working out the advertising revenue you could make if the entire orchestra wore sponsors' tee-shirts.'

While both young men had a more than comfortable private income, they'd gone very different ways. Patrick had never considered any other career but the City, where long days are filled with dealing, buying and selling in a dizzying variety of currencies all over the globe. Lives so far asunder hardly ever impinged on each other. Jason found it amusing that the first time in years he should hear from his brother had been over a large holding of family shares.

'Patrick had plans for the old company, which involved getting his hands on big brother's bits of paper. But I'm rather attached to those scraps of paper, wherever they are at the moment,' Jason had told Calla. He'd given Patrick a similarly irritating answer and held firm, annoying his brother by his refusal to take the idea seriously or even get angry about it.

'I don't go round to *his* house and advise him on the no doubt dreadful paintings he's got on his walls, do I? I leave him in his swinish ignorance, where he's happy. And he should leave me with my bits of paper,' Jason had remarked to Calla one evening, before saying in the same breath: 'Care to go to Wheeler's and test the aphrodisiac quality of their oysters? You'll have to keep your hands off the waiters during pudding though. I want my desserts when we come back.'

He'd never mentioned Patrick since, and now here she was with his letter in her hand, a brief message saying that he needed to see her urgently. Not 'might he?' but that he needed to. Would she ring his secretary to confirm that she was coming over right away?

Andover's offices were in the heart of the City, an area Calla and Jason had often wandered through, remarking on the architectural variety to be found in those temples of money. From the staid to the garish, they housed the moneymen whose frenetic actions and lightning decisions reverberated throughout the world, affecting many millions of ordinary men and women who had never even seen these high walls of Portland stone and granite.

The black cab swept past the domed splendour of St Paul's and into the City itself. Glass and concrete towers of the sixties burst through their more dignified pale stone seniors, like the cheeky, thrusting young brokers who had invaded the musty world of the stock exchange, sweeping aside the paper and the handshakes with their computer screens, their mobiles and their loud, brash voices. And now there was a new generation of exciting buildings to ensure that this great capital kept on reaching out for the future – the crazily shaped Gherkin, the dazzling Lloyds Building, the hard-edged Tower 42, City Hall on the south side of the river.

They stopped outside a huge tower of reflecting glass which showed the sky and the bustling world about it without revealing to the passing observer a trace of what went on inside. Calla pushed through swing doors, automatically taking note of the style of the place, guessing at the architect and the designer as she walked to the reception desk.

Andover's office was on the 19th floor, so high up it could hardly be seen from outside. Remarkable, thought Calla, how bold money could be, how it could say: 'I'm here. You might not like the look of me, but don't I make you look small?'

A secretary looked up as Calla stepped out of the express lift and stood before her on the deep pile carpet. There were the inevitable big office plants, perfectly green, unflowering, unlovely plants. And there was a door labelled *Patrick Andover* behind the secretary's desk. For a second Calla tried to imagine Jason in these surroundings, but it was impossible. He'd laugh at the pale, boringly tasteless art on the walls, she thought. He'd mock those unreal plants.

She was led through the door by the secretary. 'Miss Marchant,' said the girl. 'Miss Marchant,' repeated Patrick Andover, as he swung round from his computer screen to look at her.

Only he didn't look: he stared. Patrick Andover stared at her as if he wielded absolute power over her. Nobody had ever looked at her like that before. As a ferret must look at a cornered rabbit, was the thought that crossed her mind. It fascinated her, and she had to struggle not to be mesmerised.

She was instantly aware of a dynamism about him. There was an echo of Jason in his features, but he was somehow sharper round the edges. His eyes were a piercing blue, but there was no humour in them as there was in his brother's. Where Jason's face was ever-changing, reacting with amusement to the world around him, Patrick's was more definitely drawn. There was a firmer jaw, those full lips were thinner, that wayward hair was somehow just in the right place. There were no signs of wear about this brother, none of Jason's air of having lived a long while in London's bohemia.

This was a man who knew what he wanted, Calla thought, a man who looked neither to his right nor to his left and was accustomed to having his way. Although he was the younger brother, anyone would immediately have said he had least of the child about him. In fact you couldn't believe that Patrick Andover had ever had a childhood. Calla, a woman of drive herself, in these few seconds recognised his energy and experienced an unpleasant magnet-like pull, force to force. But she could not like him.

Andover didn't ask her to sit down. He had none of his brother's instinctive courtesy. Courtesy, like the commodities of the stock market, was something to be put to profitable use. It had its price. He would make her wait a little. Andover was a manipulator.

He stood up, and Calla saw the expensive City suit which declared membership of the world of moneymaking. It protected its wearer from individuality and emotion as much as armour had protected knights of old from enemy arrows. He was a fraction taller than Jason, she idly thought, as she waited for him to speak.

But he was in no hurry. He wanted to look at this woman who had walked into his dilletante brother's life. He came closer, because he wanted her to savour his looking, and in spite of his control, his face registered slight surprise. A head-in-the clouds artist, all campus clothes outside and colourful impracticalities inside, wouldn't have surprised him. Nor would a dim but pretty young Sloane, bored with her job at Sotheby's or Christie's and thinking it would be fun to dabble with buildings.

This Calla was very different from the inexperienced young girl who had first come to London. There was the same wilfulness and the same ability to look the world squarely in the face, but she was no longer one of those arty young girls who dream of being different while they dress in identical layers of tired clothes and sit on cushions in their tatty top floor flats.

The woman standing before him had assurance. She knew she had worth, he could see that in her clothes – sexy without pleading for attention, a no-nonsense black dress cut right to her figure, an acid green jacket tossed over her shoulder. She had the rare figure which could wear an LBD perfectly, able to move confidently, knowing the precise outline was unspoilt, moulded perfectly to her curves. How had Jason found her? More amazingly, how had he kept her?

Patrick Andover, however, wasn't the sort to be won over by a lovely face, even by such rare beauty as Calla's, not even by the dark eyebrow which was now arching in enquiry. Calla was not a lost young girl, he could see that now, but he had the whip-hand and he meant to use it.

'I won't detain you long, Miss Marchant,' he said in a voice accustomed to coming straight to the point. 'I want to talk about money.'

'Whose money?'

'My poor brother has, I understand, advanced you cash for your little architecture project. That money came from my family and I don't like that. Jason has as much business sense as one of his paintbrushes. He gets carried away. He's a soft touch.'

Calla felt the colour rising in her cheeks. She was about to spring to Jason's defence, but something in those blue eyes, so like his and yet so unlike, held her still.

'You, Miss Marchant, are a bad risk. A young woman with no track record, who likes to draw pictures of buildings, who has no idea of the stuff which really puts them up and holds them together. You, like my brother, know nothing about money except how to spend it.'

There was contempt in his voice as he said the words 'my brother'.

'I must protect my family, Miss Marchant. There's a paper here which I want you to sign. It doesn't stop you from going ahead with your scheme, but it does protect my brother from being dragged down with you. You may sit down in this chair.'

Calla took the paper and did not sit down. Nor did she read it.

'What the hell do you know about my affairs?' she demanded, making no attempt to keep the loathing out of her voice, but wishing she could control its angry shaking. 'What do you know about my skill as an architect?'

'I *do* know, and that is enough for you, Miss Marchant. If you care for my brother, you'll want to protect him. That piece of paper merely gives him the right to withdraw his money from the business when he sees fit. After a reasonable period from the date of notification, obviously.

'It also secures his position as your major creditor, in the event that your enterprise should go to the wall. Moreover, in the unlikely event of your success, it commits you to repaying his investment with interest. That's all.'

His voice was even and hard: 'Will you please sit down and sign it.'

'Has it occurred to you,' she answered, her eyes full of fire, 'that there's not the slightest reason why I should. What good will it do me?'

'None at all. It's what will happen if you don't.'

Now she sat down: 'Do I hear blackmail in this?'

'It's not a word any of us likes, Miss Marchant. But look squarely at the facts for a moment. My brother hardly knows what he's doing. A wasted life – in which you've probably played a large part – has left him entirely unsuited to conduct financial dealings.'

'That's a lie!' she blurted. 'Jason knows exactly what he's doing. He's not a child.'

'There, I'm afraid, we have to differ. But let's not play with words. He's a wreck. His judgement's gone. As the senior responsible member of the family I have to make sure that he doesn't squander money which has been hard-earned over many generations and which is destined for the junior members of my family when they're old enough to enjoy it. I'm sorry if that sounds awfully Victorian to you.

'If you refuse to sign that paper I can promise you that I shall take steps to have brother Jason dealt with by the authorities. He's a known drug-user and I can think of several doctor friends of mine who would vouch for the fact that he's not responsible for his own actions.'

'You creep!' she yelled, half rising from the chair.

'That wouldn't directly affect the money he's thrown at your little bagatelle, Miss Marchant, but I don't suppose that an action by us to retrieve the cash on grounds of his diminished responsibility would do your reputation much good.'

All Calla wanted to do was to get out of the building, to be away from Patrick Andover and his warped values. She wanted never to see the man again. She wanted that more than she wanted to read the details of the document which sat on the desk in front of her.

In any case, she reasoned to herself, she'd always wanted to be her own woman. She wouldn't want to cling on to Jason's money for a second longer than he wanted her to have it. Therefore she really had nothing to lose that she wasn't fully prepared to lose.

She signed her name with a heavy flourish, glowered into those relentless blue eyes, hurled the pen across the desktop and stamped out of the room.

• • •

'Thing big and think wild.' Calla repeated the urgent motto to herself over and over during the first years of running Calla Marchant Practice. Aim for the stars. Don't settle for second best. Don't let the bastards do you down. Never mind that they were hackneyed phrases, she'd use anything which would keep her spirits high through whatever adversity.

She was soon running a staff of a dozen, with several more freelance pofessionals on stand-by and eager to work for someone who carried that authentic aura of drive and success about her. For Calla soon found that she didn't need to pretend, to whistle in the dark. She was right out there in the dazzling light, picking up contracts which more experienced architects would have given a year of their lives for.

'It's got to be luck, Bunny,' she said to her old mentor on one occasion, 'and luck can change.'

But he was wiser: 'You make your luck,' he told her. 'If I'd got a piece of real estate I needed developing I'd pick you out from the crowd for several reasons put together.'

'One of them being favouritism?' she grinned.

'*Two* of them being favouritism. But how about flair and acuity and sensitivity for a few more?   And that's ignoring a factor which an old man like me should be ashamed of mentioning.'

She never consciously used her feminine charms, but the inescapable fact was that power and success had given a sheen to the sexual attraction which nature had seen to bless Calla Marchant with. That violet in the eyes glinted the sharper for her perpetual excitement. The cloth clung to those pert breasts the firmer for her brimming vitality. That little kick in the walk was a product of the configuration of her hips allied to an irrepressibly buoyant spirit. Men lusted after her, and even when they subordinated their animal appetites to the dictates of business they knew they'd damn sure rather work alongside an architect who made them feel good in places which blueprints didn't usually reach.

But CMP, as the company was widely known, was securely founded on a base of experience. Calla had read widely even in the days before she began her training, and now she travelled as much as her business would allow, eager for a first-hand knowledge of the world's finest buildings. While older architects were stuck in a timewarp between tired tradition and the once-heady freedoms of post-modernism, she had moved into another dimension – knowing that she could draw on any ideas that came to hand and rearrange them into something new. CMP had the freshness of youth.

She visited the Grande Arche and the Tour EDF at La Defense in Paris. At Rogers' Centre Pompidou in Les Halles she stood among the crowds swarming all over the escalators. It wasn't only the structure she observed (the bold exposure of pipes and service ducts which were flaunted on the outside rather than primly hidden away) but the crowds themselves and how they used the building.

For architecture, as Bunny had stressed, was an art form. People related to it. She marvelled at Foster's dramatic Hongkong and Shanghai Bank in Tokyo, with its exterior resemblance to a giant rocket launcher, its cavernous interior with suspended floors. She toured the opera house in Sydney, with its echoes of the sails in the harbour, and the crystal skyscraper of the Bank of the South West in Houston, Texas, like a huge Wurlitzer organ. She learned so fast that sometimes it seemed as if her brain burned.

What Calla was unable to hide from herself, however, was that, even as she thrived on the challenges of her profession, so Jason retreated into that other world for which she lacked the key. His silences grew longer and longer, induced by heaven knew what potion he was sniffing or injecting. She tried to get through to him, but they communicated through a haze. They lived together but far apart.

'It's no good, Jason,' she would say, finding him flopped in a trance on the floor when she returned from a high-level meeting with clients. 'This isn't working. We're not giving each other anything.'

He would reach out for her hand and hold it close to his chest, like a ham actor in Shakespeare. Only, God help them both, he meant it. She knew that.

'We should try going it alone,' she would say weakly, knowing that he would only protest his love. He'd even wept with his head on her lap.

Yes, she accepted that she still loved him, but the word had ceased to have meaning. She felt she was merely walking in the shadow of the passion they'd once known. Why *didn't* she break away? She was twenty-nine, a successful businesswoman with the world before her. There were men who would flock to her at the slightest hint of an offer. So why?

This was something she hated to admit to herself, but she knew there was an impure mixture of motives. There was that memory of love. There was pity, which she felt degraded him.

And there was something else which she really couldn't bring herself to think about.

All right, for Christ's sake, there was the question of the money. She was some way off being able to exist without that investment. That was what she didn't like to admit to herself. That was the horrible, sordid reality, and she loathed herself for it.

That was why, as she slammed the door behind her, and dragged the limp Jason through the Duke's grounds to her car, her tears were sad and angry and bitter at the same time. And that was why she looked at Jason's gaunt face with fond pity and at the same time berated him over and over again: 'You bastard, you stupid, clumsy bastard – you've just ruined the biggest chance I ever had!'

4

Rona Kurtz was in a fluster. She looked at the clock and it told her she had five minutes to make the coffee, to spread the Langues de Chat biscuits on a plate and load the tray. Then, with any luck, she might get through the boardroom door without dropping the lot, though she rather doubted it.

This hadn't been a good week, especially for a first week. They'd told her Broughton, Hughes, Lorimer was a good firm to work for. It had class, they said. One of the best architectural partnerships you could find. That didn't mean much to Rona, who was an ordinary working class girl without pretensions, but it made her feel better all the same.

Things went wrong from the start. Mr Meredith, who was her particular boss, was very particular indeed. She wouldn't have called herself the best secretary in town, but she'd worked for some very decent people without any trouble. It was different here. This Mr clever Langton Meredith seemed to think she should be some kind of wonder woman for the money he paid. He asked her to do a dozen different things in the time she'd usually manage three, and he was pretty nasty about anything she did wrong.

All right, she thought, she had made a few lulus this first week. On the first day she'd mailed all the demands for outstanding payments to a separate list of people who were apparently only potential clients of the firm. She'd had to deal with phone calls for the rest of the day. Rona knew how the mix-up had occurred, so she found it quite possible to be forgiving of herself, but Mr Meredith got very angry.

Then there was the mistake about the quantities of certain materials. Actually there were several mistakes, but they were very small. Mr Meredith said a missing zero here and there might be small as far as she was concerned, but it made the difference between a proper set of foundations and a spare mountain of sand which wouldn't look out of place in the Sahara. She thought he meant that as a joke, but when she laughed he got even more cross and told her she was a very stupid young woman, which wasn't the kind of thing you expected to put up with in a place of employment.

Perhaps the worst mistake was this morning, when she'd managed to spill Mr Meredith's early cup of coffee down his shirt. It must have been rather warm, she admitted, if not quite hot. But most of it had missed, and the stain didn't look very bad, really. Anyway, she seemed to be forgiven, because Mr Meredith had asked her to take in the coffee and biscuits for the board meeting, and that was normally Sally's job, and Sally was Mr Lorimer's personal assistant.

She checked the clock again as she placed the coffee pot on the tray. It was heavy, so she put it in the middle, knowing the sort of thing that could happen with coffee pots. Then she lifted the tray, walked gingerly down the corridor, kicked her foot against the door by way of a knock and pushed inside. She was extremely careful. She only registered that Mr Meredith was at one end of the table, that Mr Lorimer at the other and that Mr Broughton was one of about half a dozen other people in the room. They were all men. There wasn't a Mr Hughes, because he'd died several years ago, so she'd been told.

Rona had deposited the tray and was turning away when Langton Meredith called out to her: 'Miss Kurtz, a moment please.'

'Sir?'

'Would you do me a favour? You see that chair by the wall – would you be good enough to climb onto it?'

'I beg your pardon, Mr Meredith?'

'Onto the chair,' he repeated, and in such an authoritative voice that there was little else she could do. It wasn't a high chair, but she was short and rather dumpy and had to stretch a little. She was facing the wall. They would all see that her lovely red hair needed trimming. She was going to the hairdresser this lunchtime.

'Thank you. Now will you please tell everyone your name. No – don't turn round.'

'I'm Rona Kurtz.'

'And what's your job, Miss Kurtz?'

'I'm your secretary, aren't I?'

'Let's not be truculent, Miss Kurtz,' said Meredith, beginning to enjoy himself. 'It was a simple question. And what are secretaries supposed to do?'

'I don't know,' she faltered, realising too late that she was, in effect, trapped. 'Typing, and things like that.'

'Very good, Miss Kurtz.'

There was a feeling of unease in the boardroom. A couple of the men chuckled lightly, but the others had strained looks on their faces. Jake Broughton, son of the founder and a man of about thirty-five, rose in his chair and sat down again. You shit, Meredith, he was thinking. You great slimy odiferous shit.

'Now tell us, Miss Kurtz, what a particular secretary – shall we say a Miss Kurtz? – managed to do this week with the blueprint for the new district hospital. What did she do with it?'

The voice sank to a whisper: 'Put it in the incinerator, Mr Meredith.'

'Didn't quite hear, Miss Kurtz. Louder, please.'

'That'll do,' said Broughton.

'Put it in the incinerator.'

'And what did this same Miss Kurtz say to our most valuable client, Rowland Matthewson?'

'Meredith, I said that'll do,' Broughton repeated.' For God's sake.'

'I thought he was the postman,' replied Rona Kurtz. 'I didn't know. The postman was late. It was an accident.'

'And you said?'

'I said he'd better get his act together because time-keeping was important where I came from.'

'Well, I'll tell you something, Miss Kurtz. You can turn round now, because Mr Broughton has kindly come to your aid. Where you came from, Miss Kurtz, isn't important. It's where you're going that counts. And do you know what? You're going out of here and you're never coming back. In short, Miss Kurtz, I have great pleasure in telling you that you're fired.'

The red-faced girl took the helping hand of Jake Broughton and, despite a heroic attempt at self-possession, burst uncontrollably into tears. She was helped from the room and could be heard for more than a minute, her sobbing gradually retreating down the corridor and away.

'I believe,' said Brent Lorimer, who was in the chair, 'that we should begin our meeting.'

Broughton, returning to the boardroom, glared venomously at Meredith, who laughed harshly: 'I'd say the meeting's already begun, Brent. Most entertaining. Pass the biscuits, would you?'

Lorimer frowned and fussed with his papers. He was getting too old for this job, he thought. He'd been the senior partner for six years now, nearly seven, and the strain was beginning to tell. The practice had grown so rapidly recently that it was impossible to keep abreast of everything. Once upon a time he'd regarded the plethora of new planning laws, the regular development of new materials, as challenges it was stimulating to do battle with. In those days he had a reputation for meticulousness. He wasn't the number one creative man, but he kept the firm on the rails. He was dependable.

The trouble had started, he supposed, with the arrival of Langton Meredith. It wasn't that the man was incapable: just the reverse, in fact. He'd come to them with the reputation of being dynamic and unconventional, and he had an incredible contacts book that assured his new firm of juicy contracts overnight. The problem was that Lorimer couldn't control the man, and neither could anyone else. Look how he'd just sabotaged the opening of the meeting – that nonsense with the girl.

Theoretically Meredith was the equal of the other partners, and a shade less equal than Lorimer. The reality was that he dominated the firm through the force of his personality. He was a hard man, Lorimer thought, quite ruthless. He was intent on a rapid expansion of their business, his view being that small practices were about to go to the wall in the tough economic circumstances of the time. The danger as Lorimer saw it was that they'd overstretch themselves, run into cash-flow problems and find there were jobs they couldn't complete. That way lay ruin. He'd seen it happen too often.

'You're all aware of this scheme of the Duke of Mercia at Charlesbury,' Meredith now addressed the meeting. 'I visited the Duke on our behalf last week and had a useful conversation with him.'

Typical, Lorimer thought ruefully. I'm supposed to be running this damn meeting and he's already taken it over.

'Perhaps you'd be good enough, Langton,' he said quickly, saving face as best he could, 'to brief us on your deliberations.'

'Of course, Brent. Isn't that the point of today's meeting?'

Damn, damn, damn him, why did he have to be so supercilious? Lorimer gazed around the room. Surely they were all thinking the same. It wasn't possible that anyone could actually like Langton Meredith. It was quite easy to admire his drive and acumen, yes, but just wait until he made a mistake. Then the knives would be out.

'The question is,' Jake Broughton broke in, 'do we want to get involved in this scheme. Is it our kind of work?'

'I wasn't aware,' Meredith replied icily, 'that we had a kind of work. Aren't we prepared to tackle anything that will make us a decent profit? I certainly understood that this is why I was invited to join this partner-ship. Its reputation beforehand was that of a tired, stick-in-the-mud organisation. I hope we've been changing in recent years.'

'It's possible to change too fast,' cautioned Lorimer. 'Isn't it?'

'Listen, Brent,' Meredith said impatiently, 'we're talking here about the biggest communal development in Britain. Ever. We're talking about a project with an overall price tag of more than a hundred million pounds. Whatever percentage of that you allow for the design of the place, we're talking megabucks. The architect who lands this contract is going to clean up, believe me.

'But that's not all – so you can keep quiet for a bit longer, Jake. You'll get your turn. We're also talking reputation here. I don't like it any more than any of you, but the Duke has captured the public imagination. If he likes a building you can be pretty sure Jack and Jill out there will go along with it. If he hates it, kaput. That may be because he's touching a genuine nerve, or it may be that the guy has charisma. That's irrelevant. The point is that whoever designs this scheme for the Duke of Mercia is going to be seen as the number one architectural genius of the modern age. Bar none. There'll be offers enough to keep him in work until the second coming.'

He leant back and opened his hands widely, inviting comments. That, thought Lorimer helplessly, should be my job.

'If I'm allowed to speak now,' began Jake Broughton, with a curl to his lips. He, too, was accusing himself of a spineless subservience to Meredith. Broughton's problem was that he'd never overcome his position as the founder's son. Before his father died he had kept a low profile, not wishing to be seen gaining any improper favours. After his death he found that the same restraint seemed to operate. He told himself that he shouldn't give the impression he was anyone special, that he thought he was running the place. Consequently he hamstrung himself all along.

'Go ahead, Jake,' said Meredith, as if he were granting a favour.

'I'm going to repeat my point about this not being our kind of work. We all know the type of scheme the Duke favours. It's a throwback to some idealisation of a once-upon-a-time Merrie England. That's not the style of commission we're used to, so there are two questions we need to ask ourselves – one, do we want it and two, are we up to it?'

'Personally,' broke in Stew McClear, a thin, bespectacled Scot who was the youngest of the partners, 'I'd not be happy playing that kind of game. And if I wasn't happy it would mean I wouldn't do it very well.'

'All that tells us,' Meredith threw at him, 'is that you're not the man for the job. I agree that anybody who lacks the balls for it shouldn't be considered. That includes anyone who has grand principles about the precious work architects ought to do. Forgive me if I'm wrong in thinking we're running a business, not a moral crusade.'

'Let's not make this personal,' Lorimer murmured.

'Look what happened to the Ambrose Partnership after the Duke ridiculed their Tate Gallery plans,' Meredith continued without a break. 'They got a lousy press and nobody wanted to touch them again. They folded. Johnny Ambrose is wandering about town like a blind man who's lost his white stick.

'We're sound architects, we know that. But it's the image we've got to work at right now. Forget the Bauhaus, Le Corbusier and Mies van der Rohe. Swallow your pride. We've got to get this contract and milk it for all its worth. If we have to act dirty, so be it.'

'When you say act dirty . . . ' Lorimer interrupted.

'I mean hitting below the belt, Brent, that's what I mean. There are going to be plenty of people pitching for the Duke's business, and I aim to be the one to win it – with your consent, of course. That may mean more than showing how brilliant we are. It may mean spiking the guns of our rivals.'

'Who are?' Broughton asked.

'Couldn't we all name several, Jake? Most of them were at the Duke's country house last week. But if you were to press me on who'll make the short list in six months time I'd say ourselves – if we don't shoot ourselves in the foot – Pannick, Simkins and Locke, plus any two of another dozen.'

'Can't agree about Pannick,' said McClear. 'He's very much in direct line from the Bauhaus. He's passionate and pretty unbending. Look at his National Biscuits building. It's everything the Duke hates.'

'And Simkins has done nothing original for twenty years,' Broughton offered. 'Though I suppose,' he conceded, 'that may be in his favour. But he's tired. He hasn't got what you like to call balls, Langton.'

Meredith shook his head in apparent disbelief: 'Hasn't anyone else in this room ever felt the pricking in his palms when big money was up for grabs? Am I really an old roue among virgins? This little party at Charlesbury is going to waken the dead, Jake. There's going to be blood spilt on the carpet.'

'I'd like to clarify something you said, Langton,' Lorimer spoke falteringly. 'About playing dirty and spiking guns. What exactly did you have in mind?'

Jake Broughton's mind returned to the cruel episode before the meeting had got under way. He'd seen the look on Meredith's face as he humiliated that poor secretary, and in it there was an exultation which was indecent, vile, almost as if he was indulging in some kind of sexual perversion. A cynic would say it was better to have such a man on your side rather than against you, but Broughton felt contaminated.

'Nothing *exactly*,' Meredith replied, 'but anything in general. If we can unearth anything about our competitors which will diminish them in the Duke's eyes so much the better – poor buildings, doubtful associates, personal scandals, that sort of thing. I've already briefed one or two people to do some judicious digging.

'On what you may perhaps regard as a more positive note, I believe we should foster profitably warm relations with those close to the Duke.'

'Tea and cucumber sandwiches with the Duchess,' quipped McClear dismissively.

'Exactly so,' Meredith said. 'The Duchess may indeed prove to be the key.'

5

What were those little blue crosses doing on the plan of Willoughby Hall, Martin Kingsley's journalistic training made him wonder. He had time to wonder while he waited for the bell to sound in some distant part of the house. It was a vast mansion, with dozens of rooms, and the marks were liberally scattered among them. There was one in the conservatory, for instance, but not in the pantry. Why was that?

Kingsley had been sent on some bum assignments in his time, but never anything quite like this one. As a reporter for the *National Herald* he'd done most things, from paying ex-choirboys to reveal the precise sexual inclinations of the vicar to getting horsewhipped by a master of foxhounds for asking difficult questions during the hunt.

If this job seemed pretty tame compared with those, why did his stomach wobble with nerves? Because he'd never been invited to take tea with a Duchess before. He was used to sticking his foot in doors, not to finding them swung back wide on their hinges by a butler. He was used to talking his way into places rather than being told that her ladyship was expecting him.

And he was used to dealing with people who were hoodwinked by his open face, his smart clothes and his flashy minidisk. Here at a grand country house he had the unusual feeling of being rather out of his league as he parked his nippy black Golf GTI in front of the broad steps.

'What am I doing here?' he asked himself. 'Why didn't they send the society page staff? What do they know that I don't?'

It was a damn sight too rural for his liking – the drive up to the house wound its way through fields of sheep, and there was a smell of fresh air and stables which his city lungs didn't relish. Kingsley liked traffic and bustle. He needed the adrenalin of the city, the kick to his system which working to a deadline gave him. His was a world of tubes and taxis, snatched lunches and snatched quotes, a high pressure do-it-now world where there was no time to think fine thoughts or dream impossible dreams.

It was someone's impossible dream which had brought him here, he thought, so far away from his natural habitat. Who was this guy Willoughby to start building towns, for God's sake? As far as newspapers were concerned, dukes and the like were gossip column fodder, good value for their eccentricities, their marital difficulties or their drug habits. Crackpot long-term schemes for turning a vision into bricks and mortar excited Kingsley about as much as covering the Women's Institute tent at an agricultural show.

'Your big chance,' Hacker had said with his news editor's dry humour. 'This is where you make a name for yourself.'

'As a stupid pratt,' he'd wanted to reply.

'It's the story of the decade. It'll run and run.'

'Like shit out of a cow's arse,' he'd thought of saying.

For this, he'd been taken off the hell of a story about a man with two wives, one who slept in a caravan at the bottom of the garden while he made merry with the other in the house. Kingsley liked that kind of yarn. He had a dirty mind.

'Best of all,' went on Hacker, 'it's a long-term assignment. Stay with this story, Marty baby. Live it, breathe it, sleep it.'

'Stuff it,' is what he should have replied.

His brief for the first story was simple: 'Write about Willoughby Hall, Marty.' (Nobody ever called him Marty – the editor thought himself bloody Rupert Murdoch for God's sake). 'The Duke likes to tell everyone else how to live, so let's find out how *he* lives.'

'Let's have a tale from inside the Hall, let's hear about his taste in everything from paintings to kitchen maids. And this time, Marty, stick right to the facts.'

'And forget all I've been taught,' he thought.

'Colour, yes, but the facts. Willoughby's co-operating with us all the way ' he wants the publicity. But remember, this one's got the money to sue if we get it wrong. You're not dealing with Joe Public here. It matters what we say.'

'And try not to shock the Duchess, you foul-mouthed young bugger.'

They bought you body and soul in Fleet Street. And with the sort of money they paid you, they didn't expect you to raise objections. There were always more hungry newshounds panting to take your place if your appetite dulled. So Kingsley hadn't groused too much as he scanned the map for this godforsaken spot, further away from the comforting security of the M25 than he cared for and in a county which to his eyes looked very boringly green indeed.

'I suppose her ladyship will serve cucumber sandwiches,' he thought, wondering how on earth he could pretend to match her austere regality. But he waited steadfastly for a response to his ringing. In spite of his youth, or maybe because of it, he already had a reputation in Fleet Street for being cheeky, charming and about as likely to let go of a story as a terrier to release its teeth from the backside of a rat. In short, he was irrepressible.

He was also jauntily good-looking, something which didn't escape a pair of pale green eyes watching lazily from a window on the landing of the grand staircase of Willoughby Hall. There was a spring in his step, an alertness in his face, which suggested a young man ready for just about anything.

And that was a quality which appealed to Fern Willoughby, who now gracefully detached herself from the windowsill where she was leaning, one leather-booted calf behind the other. She'd been wondering what he might be like, the young reporter whom she'd agreed to take in hand on her husband's behalf.

'It'll keep you out of mischief while I'm away,' the Duke had said to her, with a quick and uncertain glance.

And she had smiled her calm catlike smile back at him: 'I'll look after your journo, Harry,' she'd murmured. 'As long as he comes after my morning ride. I'll make sure he knows all about the ancestral portraits in the long gallery. I'll tell him dutifully about the first Duke, who was oh-so-fond of the local village boys. I'll tell all about your darling grand-ma who had that fascinating collection of horse-whips. I'll miss nothing out. Nothing at all.'

'I know you'll be more discreet than that, Fern,' he smiled, desperately. 'The editor of the *Herald* lunched with me last week at the Athenaeum. I have what they call "copy approval". In other words, it only goes into print if I sanction it.

'Journalists,' he added, 'can be rather exhausting company, I'm afraid, my dear.'

'So I've heard, Harry.'

'You must try to be as accommodating as possible and not get angry.'

'I promise,' she said, 'to turn the other cheek.'

Now, with an agility her apparent languour belied, the Duchess was at the foot of the grand staircase and standing to one side as the butler opened the door.

Quite what Martin Kingsley had expected of a duchess he didn't know – perhaps a hearty back-slapping horsewoman or a fragile aristocrat with porcelain features. Fern Willoughby was neither. She was pale and languid to be sure, but there was both a waywardness and an authority about her which was emphasised by her riding gear.

Kingsley took in, with the exactness of his trade, the fair curling hair, the ever-escaping green eyes and the lissome figure. He was used to summing up a person at a glance. Her hacking jacket was tailored to her slender waist, but it was unbuttoned over a loose shirt, and the shirt was open at a very white neck indeed. Jodphurs clung to long thighs – the only part of her body which suggested muscularity '– and were tucked into knee-high leather boots. He flushed slightly to see the amusement on her face. She had patiently waited for him to finish exploring her, and Kingsley felt discomfited, wrong-footed.

'I'm Fern Willoughby,' she drawled as she moved towards him. 'You can go, Brunson, I'll look after Mr Kingsley. And will you ask Jessica for coffee in the library?'

The butler nodded and melted away. Kingsley swallowed hard as he shook her cool hand, which seemed to rest in his a second longer than he expected.

'A chilly spot, this,' she said. 'Just right to keep the moose heads from going off, I suppose. My husband's from a great hunting family you know, though he has grave doubts about it these days – he's becoming quite a green duke.'

Kingsley was beginning to feel more like his old self. Coffee was on the way and the company was pretty enough, if rather insipid. He'd done his homework in the *Herald*'s library before setting off on the job and had a vague idea of the Duke's ancestry, how the title had been created and how the dynasty of landowners had amassed its fortune. There was rather less about the Duchess, who rarely appeared on his public engagements. The couple were childless though, being somewhat younger than her husband, she presumably still had time for that.

'Let's go through to coffee,' she said. 'Forgive my jods. I practically live in them and it's such a fag peeling everything off in the middle of the day for no good reason. Don't you think?'

He nodded and followed her up the few steps to the library. From below he couldn't help but notice her full high buttocks skimmed by the short riding jacket. Willoughby was a lucky bastard, he thought. Whatever else he'd expected from this story, it wasn't a hard-on. His mind was just racing on to what that rump must look like flinging itself on a saddle when her drawling voice brought him back down to earth.

'I asked if you'd prefer milk or cream, you know. I shall call you Martin, so, if I may be so bold, sit down and tell me what you'd like, Martin.'

That tone of amusement never left her, thought Kingsley as he cleared his throat and asked for milk. She leant forward over the tray, the neck of her shirt falling open before him revealing a fine spray of freckles and the whitest breasts, their roundness just restrained by a black lace bra. He swallowed again and thanked God silently that he was sitting down.

As she straightened up, her face was a picture of unconsciousness. She dropped lightly into a chair and threw one leg over the other, slipping her hand between them, high up, near her crotch.

'It's a huge house,' he blurted, sipping dangerously hot coffee. 'I was looking at the plan outside.'

'Vaaaast,' she breathed, in a low whisper.

'Those little crosses – what are they for?'

'Oh Martin, there's always something to do in each room. One likes to keep a record.'

He turned his tape recorder on and she began, in her careless voice, to tell the story of the house, interspersing it with anecdotes. This creature, who seemed easy almost but not quite to the point of listlessness, what made her tick? What was her passion?

'Which brings us to the Victorian era, when the fourth Duke established this library,' she was saying, lifting one arm behind her head, making her shirt, Martin restlessly noticed, ride up against her breast at that side. 'The fourth Duke had a rather esoteric taste in books. Care to see?'

She wandered across to a glass-fronted case and took down three or four leather-bound volumes, not thick, but large, and came back with them to sit by Martin on the settee. He felt, rather than saw, that tightly dressed backside come down next to him. Was he imagining it or, as she laid the book in his lap, did the back of her hand linger just long enough to assess his hardness? If so, it was gone now, turning over the pages with long pale fingers, as one fantastically erotic painting succeeded the next, showing act after act of decadent sex.

'The fourth Duke travelled widely in Africa,' said the Duchess, her voice remarkably even, 'which was where he had this volume painted.' In the second book, black women with brightly coloured wraps in disarray knelt or lay in a variety of positions, thrusting exaggerated buttocks, everything between them a pinky purple, towards the painter.

'His own favourite, and mine, is at the back of the book. The man in the picture has the face of the fourth Duke.'

She turned to a scene where a black woman lay back on a bed, her feet spread wide on the floor, her fingers dabbling in her own deep and wiry pubic hair, while a white man with the largest erect prick Kingsley had ever seen stood over her.

'Either the artist flattered or the fourth Duchess was a lucky woman,' said Fern Willoughby, her voice deepening.

Kingsley felt so tight he could hardly breathe. Was this an outrageous come-on or was he imagining the whole thing? He could hardly assume anything with a Duchess, for Christ's sake. He looked at her pale face. The green eyes were elsewhere, the face as bland as usual, but there was a deep flush on that white throat. She wanted it. Jesus, she wanted it.

But what should he do? He wasn't usually backward at coming forward. As a good-looking young man with a brash self-confidence, he didn't get many refusals from the girls. Sometimes they stayed a while, hoping for something longer-term. Others were simply after a good time, like him.

And they got it. Kinglsey was an enthusiastic lover, never likely to give up with the job half done. He'd always make sure she got there too, but he wasn't old enough or experienced enough to be sophisticated. He went about this in an animal and instinctive way, untroubled by imagination.The Duchess could see all that and she had quite enough imagination for both.

'Let me show you some more of the house,' she said. 'Come upstairs.'

It sounded like an order. He obeyed, walking up the wide steps behind her as she casually removed her riding jacket, revealing her waist, its narrowness emphasised by those horsewoman's hips which sprang out below. He watched her thighs brush against each other.

'This was the fourth Duke's dressing room,' said the Duchess, closing the door firmly behind them. 'It's not used much these days unless we have a full house. Women weren't allowed in it, not even the Duchess. It's a very masculine room.' She was breathing rather fast, Kinglsey noticed.

It was a small room, in a corner of the house, with two narrow windows looking in different directions over the grounds. There was a small tiled fireplace, a leather armchair, a heavily tooled chest and a worn carpet on the floor. She turned towards Martin: 'Christ, I'm hot. Take my shirt off.' Her languid tones had gone. There was real urgency in her voice.

He obeyed, hurriedly and with clumsy hands. God, her flesh was burning! She didn't complain, but sat in her jodphurs on the chest, her arms spread out on both sides, her head flung back, showing taut muscles in her neck.'

'Off,' she commanded, running her eyes over his clothes. 'But slowly.'

Fern Willoughby was gazing at him. She liked what she saw. The flush had spread to her chest.

'Oh shit, Duchess,' he choked, pulling her to her feet and tearing at her clothes. She was helping him, feverishly, kicking off her boots and wriggling out of her jodphurs. He slipped a hand under silk knickers. 'Shit, you're damn sodding soaking wet.'

Down they came, revealing astonishingly fair soft hair. She moaned and dropped to her knees, licking him all down his chest to his belly and the tip of his penis. He could take no more and tried to lay her on the floor, but she wasn't having that. She took his penis in her hand and firmly squeezed the end, pushing him back from the brink of orgasm.

'Wait,' she said, her voice husky with lust. 'Something the fourth Duke would approve of.'

She clambered onto the leather armchair, squatting on its edge with her back to Kingsley.

'Now,' she said. 'Now.'

Those magnificent haunches were open for him. He ran his fingers just once from cleft to clitoris and, standing, entered her from behind. She came loudly on his third thrust.

• • •

Fern Willoughby had fallen back into her old ways (and falling back was just one of her ways) after only two years of marriage to the Duke. Not that they'd been bad years, in spite of some disappointments. No, that wasn't it. It was quite simply that she couldn't help herself. She had to have men. And often.

She was amazed by friends who found their husbands enough, even too much. It was an accepted fact that women had more sexual capacity than men, that, far from being exhausted and incapaciatated by the act, a woman could keep going on and on to multiple pleasures. So what did they do with those sudden pangs, these chaste friends of hers? How did they cope with those moments that she found so heady, when flirtatious possibility turns to all-consuming lust?

Perhaps they didn't have those moments. Perhaps she, Fern, was odd, even a nymphomaniac. But if so, there it was, something to be lived with. Lived with and enjoyed too, damn it, like any other passion, like her other passion – riding. Now, in her thirty first year, these were her twin obsessions, and in her rare reading moments she turned happily from erotica to *The Field*.

She saw no shame in her sexuality now. it was a physical need to be slaked like any other. And if plain water got boring, well, there were sexual cocktails too. But her attitude to sex had not always been like that. In fact, her rather exotic sexual taste was due as much to early repression as to a need to titillate a jaded palate.

Orphaned while on the very brink of womanhood, she'd been brought up by a spinster aunt in a rambling old former rectory deep in Cornwall. At her stuffy boarding school, weekend leave was granted only twice a term and was limited to home visits. On those weekends, and during the holidays, young Fern Sherwood rode like a demon. On the Cornish heath she rode out the misery of her parents' deaths, and as adolescence came she rode out her teenage longings straddled on her horses.

It was Fern's way, whatever she did, to be playing out different scenes in her head. As she rode, she was Cathy to some as yet unseen Heathcliff, caught in a mysterious adult passion she so far felt only dimly. There was a driving, panting force in her nature, which must have expression, but she didn't know what.

'Strange girl,' they'd say about her, not being able to understand her dreaminess, her habit of not quite being there with them. 'Seems to lack imagination, but I suppose she's happy enough.'

She passed easily through school and exams, her fair and untroubled face giving away nothing of the tumults below. The summer she was eighteen she hesitated between modelling school and travelling for a year. In the event, she didn't have to choose. She was spotted at a county horse show by a photographer from the *Tatler*, who instantly recognised the sort of looks one of his top clients needed. That cool English fragility which was yet so durable was just the image for Hermes, whose up-market silk scarves and other accessories were beloved of the glossy magazine and county sets.

Fern became the face which looked out of *Harpers*, *Vogue* and *Country Life*, staring in porcelain purity, her mouth slightly parted, those green eyes suggesting an otherness which readers longed to possess for themselves.

It was very easy for Fern, who had spent her young life acting so many parts. And at this time she was physically every bit as innocent as she looked, floating on the fringe of London's fashion world without ever becoming touched by its passions.

Inside, though, she was a 22 year old turmoil, who really only ever felt alive when she was pretending. She suspected that the key to discovering her real self must be this thing called sex. She had to shake off her virginity. It was stifling her. But she couldn't do it as Fern, the cool English beauty.

No surprise then, that it was while she was playing a part that she willingly shed her cumbersome virginity. Her looks ensured her a succession of minor acting roles as well as her modelling work. One chilly morning at Elstree, during a television mini-series on the Roman Empire, her slavegirl tunic was roughly lifted and she was taken by a centurion, hastily and vigorously between scenes behind the set.

'Quietly!' was all he'd said. He smelt of the make-up stick.

Afterwards, she was in a daze. Why had she waited so long? She had felt like a woman with an itch whose hands are tied behind her back. This was what she'd been waiting for. The burning which had tormented her for so long was soothed. She had found the way to end her torture.

Fern set about sex with an ardour she hadn't shown since the days she first broke in a pony. She found there were times she wanted it gentle, times she wanted it rough, but there were few times she never wanted it at all. Yet somehow she avoided the reputation of being an easy lay. She did it by calling the shots herself. Very few men felt themselves the more experienced partner with Fern, and they were silently grateful for her attentions rather than indiscreetly boastful about their own conquests.

The men who took the edge off her lust never forgot Fern Sherwood. She could do things with positions, settings and clothes which gave you a hard-on months later. God knew where she got her ideas from. She looked so pale and unlikely, too ' the sort of woman who might compliantly open her legs for her husband while thinking about her shopping list.

'Doesn't seem interested in men,' said some who didn't know. 'Poor Fern, she'll probably end up a faded maiden aunt.'

It was while she was playing another role that Fern met Harry Willoughby. *Sighs in Summer* was the latest in a series of romantic novels to be televised and she was the obvious choice, on looks alone, for the virgin heroine, escaping her evil victorian guardian. The setting was Willoughby Hall, hired for the occasion.

The Duke, free of engagements, had wandered through the grounds to watch the film crew at work. And there he saw Fern, her face in perfect repose, gazing at the lake. Her slim body was encased in a tightly buttoned ankle-length dress and her blonde hair was ringletted. He watched, entranced.

She was pleased to be away from the studio. A new set always meant new possibilities, though there were few enough to be seen at the moment. The director himself was old news, the Victorian guardian was gay and Fern had had the only passable cameraman two days before. Tired of his sidelong way of looking down her cleavage during evening scenes, she'd coaxed and teased him into a lather, watching his boiling, quivering frustration as he had to remove, bit by bit, each layer of her complicated costume. The poor creature almost spent his load while tackling the final barrier, for even her drawers were genuinely Victorian – and crotchless.

'Who's in a hurry, then?' she'd cooed. And she had found it very funny. In those rare moments when her heat subsided and she found herself acting mechanically, she mused that men in the act of passion could at times be so very comical. How very uninteresting most of them were as people, after all. Fine, magnificently endowed beasts of the field, but dull human beings.

So when she saw the Duke, she was interested. He wasn't the sort to give a girl instant lust, but he had a quiet air of gentle strength which was attractive. And there was something else in his tall, slightly forward figure, which appealed to the caring side of her womanhood. She didn't spring at once, sensing it would be wrong with this man. Using her natural cunning, she became his friend as the filming went on, showing an interest in his house and estate. She even kept her hands off his staff, though the undergardener had a torso which made her weak at the knees.

It was a fortnight after the filming had finished that Fern found herself in the master bedroom at Willoughby Hall. Harry Willoughby was no virgin, though a strongly moral upbringing and a Spartan Scottish boarding school had left their mark. He'd had women, following his natural instincts, but orgasm had come in a rush of confusion and he'd never had his affections stirred. Until now.

That night, Fern, for once not role-playing, had gently, knowingly, sorted that out. Without embarrassment or shame, he had kept his pride in his manhood, encouraged by her frank thanks and enjoyment. He worshipped her from then. She had done what no other woman had done, making him feel good and right about himself – natural and strong. He decided that he couldn't live without her.

Fern was to be Duchess of Mercia, but her new husband insisted that she give up her acting and throw herself completely into the role of being his wife. She acquiesced. There would be all the fun of her new role and there would be children, too. She thought it worth a try.

But no children came along, and tests proved she was unlikely to have them. Nature, which had given her lust in plenty, had, by a cruel joke, also given her non-productive ovaries. Should they adopt? Harry Willoughby adored his Duchess, but he loved his family name and blood as well. He felt it somehow not right to pass the dukedom to anyone without a birthright in the Willoughby name.

The Duchess, reasoning that she had done the best she could in the circumstances, went back to her old ways. She kept her hands off her own staff, but there were constant relays of men. She picked them from the world of horses, from the fashionable London world where they owned convenient flats and hideaways, from any world which crossed hers. She once had the major of the local regiment, while she and the Duke were on a tour of inspection at the barracks. Swiftly and silently on a table in the map room, she made him take her all across Europe and the Mediterranean.

And her husband? She did love Harry Willoughby. The shocking realisation came to her one morning as she passed his room and saw him poring over one of his architectural drawings. What a fine man he was, and so handsome, really, in an understated English way. How good he was to her, never asking about what he must suspect. No, she didn't feel a passion for him any more, but she loved the man.

At that moment she swore to be true to him in every way except sex.

• • •

Martin Kingsley wished he could slink out of Willoughby Hall unseen. Surely any trained servant would realise he'd been wielding more than his pencil and notebook during the last half hour.

And why did the Duchess insist on accompanying him downstairs? She walked alongside him with such an aristocratic air that you'd think she'd merely tolerated his tiresome company and his tedious reporter's questions.

'Your coat, sir?'

The butler, Brunson, was waiting in the hall. Was his formal air as counterfeit as the Duchess's? Kingsley couldn't prevent the fleeting thought that perhaps Brunson was quietly awaiting his turn. Why did lust unhinge a man so?

How in hell's name was he going to say goodbye? A limp handshake would hardly suffice. He couldn't possibly take her in his arms, though the delicious animal tang of her was still in his nostrils.

'Thank you for having me' he rehearsed with a little inner chuckle. Oh, the randy bitch! Would she perhaps reply 'Come again soon'?

While he was still in this reverie, they reached the door. He stepped outside and, turning, saw the Duchess with a blue pencil in her hand. As he stood watching, she approached the plan of the house on the wall and, concentrating, drew a small cross in the fourth duke's dressing room.

Then, with a delicious laugh, she disappeared.

6

'Be-JAYZ-us!!!'

Neri Corinthian swept feet encased in calf-length leather boots from a desk littered with papers, letters and photographic prints and bounded to the window. Pointlessly, because in the afternoon of a dull March day the Manhattan light, strained through a thousand skyscrapers, wasn't much improvement on the neon strips inside her office, not even up on the 17th floor. But what she was reading in the latest issue of *Femthings* demanded that she leap to her feet anyway.

'Betsy – come here!'

For an Englishwoman, Neri made a pretty passable American. For a passable American she was close to a grade one New Yorker. Sure, the accent was a haunting marriage of two warring vowel systems – an accent that had men the far side of an airport lounge straining to listen, an accent which was no mean part of her seemingly effortless ability to seduce. But the energy, the colour, the sheer over-the-topness, seemed typical of her adopted city.

'Betsy, blast your big round eyes!'

The fact was that she was simply Neri Corinthian. Once you'd been in the company of this vibrant, fascinating woman for only five minutes you ceased to wonder where she might have come from. You were too overcome by the beauty of that strong-boned face and the vitality of that personality.

'You called, Miss Corinthian?'

'Hey, cut the false deference, dumbo,' she cackled with the hoarse laugh which could cut through the packed hall of a business convention. 'I don't pay you the best money on 54th Street to play the cute secretary.'

'I have some news for you,' said Betsy Clutmayer. 'Rates have been going up along the street.'

'Okay, for pay read interest. Who else has a more fascinating job and such a dynamic employer – and don't tell me anything about the President's personal assistant, I happen to know the job's boresville. You think George Bush brings in salami on rye with a can of diet coke for his secretary?'

'I'm more than grateful.'

'*And* remembers the tabasco?'

'It makes working for you particularly memorable, Miss Corinthian.'

Betsy Clutmayer, at 25, was all of fourteen years younger than her employer, but she'd long ago learned how to cope with her manic boss. It didn't do to take her seriously, not in her day-to-day round of badinage and idiotic make-believe. When it came to the real business, the photography, yes: then you had to get it absolutely right or there was a whirlwind raging round your head. That was life or death stuff, and it was money, big money. But otherwise you played your role in a never-ending game.

'Did you ever have a sister, Betsy?'

'Just twice.'

It was exhausting, of course. She couldn't imagine what it would be to live with this hyped-up woman, who not only behaved like a force of nature but dressed the part,too. Today her loosely curled raven locks fell onto the expensive cut of a crimson Adriene Vittadini cowgirl jacket. Beneath it, a long denim skirt, slashed to the thigh, revealed a stretching vista of thigh and calf above high ankle-boots with studded cuffs. Not many women of her age would have dared, but Neri Corinthian simply seemed inevitable.

'Twice? How can you have a sister twice, for Crissake?'

'I had two sisters once each, Miss Corinthian. It was easy. In fact,' she added, 'I still do. Would you like to know about my brother?'

As for the eyes, they were sensational. Betsy especially envied her those improbable irises, which glinted with a hue she could only describe as violet.

'Naaarh – brothers are out. I've married a few brothers in my time, and I haven't a good word to say for them.'

'In most states of the union, I'm led to believe, it's a legal offence to marry one's brother.'

'Other people's brothers, blockhead. I never had one of my own, thank God. Brothers are out and sisters are in. *My* sister is, anyway.'

'You have a sister, Miss Corinthian?'

Betsy thought she knew just about everything to do with her employer's personal life. After all, she wasn't the most reticent of people. She knew about the four husbands and she half-knew about the many lovers. She knew about the two children, which seemed a strangely conservative total for someone of Neri Corinthian's excessiveness. She knew her preferences in all sorts of areas, from men to take-out hot meals, from movies to colour coordinations. But she'd never heard mention of a sister.

'Do I have a sister, Miss Clutmayer? *Do* I? I have one helluva sister. Just take a look at this and wear sunglasses!'

'Shades,' Betsy corrected gently, holding the magazine to the light. It was open at a double-page colour spread, with some intercut pictures of buildings among the text on one side and the most gorgeous woman you could imagine dominating the print altogether on the other. The headline read THE MISTRESS BUILDER, which Betsy registered as a real no-no, horrendous taste, a bad breath job, and there was a sub-head: *'beautiful Brit who designs men's dreams'*

'And don't tell me it's a vile piece of journalese,' barked Neri. 'Do you think I don't recognise the stink of edited ham at five paces? Just get the gist of it. That's my kid sister they're writing about.'

She snatched the magazine back again. That was her little sister? Neri was too large-hearted ever to feel envious. Besides, she was a big fish in her own pond. But she had to admit Calla had class where she herself had pzazz. Even ten years ago, when she was a little lighter and her skin was tauter, she hadn't quite got that style, that polish.

'Would you say,' Betsy asked, 'that she's, uh, quieter than you?'

'Who ain't, baby, who ain't?' she demanded with an exaggerated nasal twang. 'But how would I know? I haven't seen her in sixteen years. Sixteen years!'

It was a shock to her system, that she did know. It made her feel queasy. For close on sixteen years she'd put the family out of her mind, even Calla whom she'd loved like a faithful pet. For all she'd known they were dead. For all they'd known *she* was dead. If she ever did entertain the slightest memory of them, they were frozen in time – which meant that Calla was for ever thirteen. Now here she was, staring out of the magazine, another successful woman in a man's world.

'Poor pose?' Betsy Clutmayer asked.

'Yep. And badly lit. See the shadow under the left chin?'

But to hell with the niceties. There were too many magazines clamouring in the market place for them all to have first-rate photographers. Neri was more interested in the text, crude though it was:

> *Bricks and mortar, stressed steel and concrete – these are the stuff of a typical man's world. But now a stunning Englishwoman has caused a stir in the hard-hat world of architecture.*
>
> *Calla Marchant, though still in her twenties, has a string of brilliant projects to her name. She's designed everything from luxury homes to office blocks, and she has one of the fastest expanding practices in the country.*
>
> *Says Calla, crossing one lovely leg over another: 'I think of myself as an architect first and a woman second.'*

'Do architects wear hard-hats?' enquired Betsy, looking over her shoulder.

'Course not. Do responsible journalists write about an architect's lovely legs?'

'*Lo mismo*, Miss Corinthian. Therefore this man is a creep.'

'You're a woman of discernment, Miss Clutmayer.'

She read to the end of the article, awestruck by her long-lost sister's knowledge and achievement. This was the real McCoy. This was roast beef with all the trimmings. This was major league. Where had she learned all this? How had she found the time?

Okay, face reality she told herself. It's sixteen whole years goddamit.

'Betsy,' she said.

'Yeah, I know. Online flight booking time.'

'Well I just might,' Neri mused. 'I've got a couple of free days, haven't I? Don't you think little Calla would be delighted to see me?'

• • •

Nobody could ever accuse Nerissa Marchant of being responsible. She'd been headstrong from the day she was born and she never saw any reason to behave otherwise. If you've the charisma which makes people inclined to forgive every lapse, why bother to reform yourself?

'She's quite dreadful,' they would say, and then add the fatal words: 'but you can't help loving her.' That was her trouble. Nobody ever could.

For her parents she was, of course, a perpetual trial. A younger, more flexible, couple might, by some effort of the imagination, have realised that her careless, flamboyant attitude was quite without malice and therefore needed only a careful tempering, a firm hand on the tiller. But Neri's parents were set in their ways and they fought her at every turn.

'When I'm older,' the young Nerissa would say with angry tears filling her eyes, her cheeks ruddy with rebellion, 'I'll leave home for ever and never see you again.'

It need not have happened like that. Despite her great flushes of emotion she was shallow in her affections. Her early boyfriends were swamped with adoration and then suddenly, inexplicably dropped. It was the same with the father of her baby girl, and if her parents had accepted what she had done she would probably have left him all the soooner and visited her mother and father from time to time. She could tolerate them well enough, all things considered. When they fought her over the baby, though, her impulsive, rebellious nature sprang up with bared teeth. She vowed never to speak to them again.

Nerissa discovered with something of a shock that she had no maternal instincts at all. For her it was no pleasure whatsoever to hold her infant to her breast, and she promptly substituted a bottle. She in every way resented this intrusion into her life. Whereas other women proudly wheeled their offspring through the local park in their new prams, she stalked stiffly along, prompted only by a vague sense of duty.

By this time she had ceased to feel anything for the father. Thank God she hadn't married him, she thought. That might have suggested a commitment. The conclusion she reached was the obvious one. He doted on his young daughter, therefore he could keep her. She wrote a brief note, emptied her bank account, packed a suitcase and her camera bag and bought a one-way ticket from Heathrow to New York. How marvellous, she thought, to create a new life in fourteen hours start to finish.

Some things don't change, though, one of them being the personality you're born with. Nerissa had the same waywardness as before, only now it had lost the restraints a closed society imposes on its members. These are understood restraints, mostly, not written out as a code, and they're often a mystery to outsiders. She liked not knowing the language of social etiquette in America. There were fewer rules in New York in any case, and those there were she didn't hurry to learn. Therefore she behaved more recklessly than ever. And, again, she was pampered and encouraged. She was outrageous.

'This chick is the end!' they would say. 'But I guess that's how they do it over in England, and she sure is cute.'

One night she found herself in the audience of a statewide television show. Jerry Corinthian's *Soapbox* was a populist programme, giving the common man and woman the chance to have their say about how they'd handle the latest White House crisis or lifestyle trend. The participants were chosen, as is usually the way, not by picking people off the streets at random but by canvassing pressure groups and specialist organisations. Nerissa, who'd picked up her photographic career again, had come along with some new friends from *Harpers* magazine, and their later excuse on her behalf (for people always made excuses for Neri, perhaps realising that she never attempted to make any for herself) was that she'd drunk rather too many camparis over dinner. Though how, as one wag queried, could you tell?

The TV debate ranged over the usual items of high controversy – drugs, abortion, religion in schools – with members of the audience getting excited and shouting out their trite comments. It was like a bear pit in there, Neri thought. The cameras must be making sense of it, because she sure as hell couldn't.

Jerry Corinthian was a man of about thirty, with a hooked, predatory nose, facial lines which suggested experience hard won and a close-cropped beard of jet black. She'd seen his programme before, but only now did she understand the anchorman's skill. Standing in the centre of the studio, clutching a lead microphone, he had only his wits to keep him and his programme from utter chaos.

She watched him closely. He seemed to have many more than the usual five senses. He talked a great deal, giving a kind of running commentary as the participants broke in briefly with their strident contributions, and he was all the time swivelling about, looking to right and left, listening for every intervention which might be promising. Since he was also wearing some sort of speaker in his ear, she couldn't imagine what mental turmoil he must be going through.

'The people are speaking,' he'd said, 'and we're being told that it's time to pull back our armed forces from the world's trouble spots – that's what the gentleman over there just told me. But now I'm getting some reaction, I think. Madam . . . '

'We shouldn't trust them damn Ruskies,' bawled a respectable looking blue-rinsed matron, beginning to put forward some hard-line ideology in comic cuts language. 'They don't change.'

Corinthian was listening, but you could tell he was about one-tenth involved – the one-tenth which was enough. The other nine parts of him were all busy with digesting sounds and expressions and instructions from the gallery.

'Point taken,' he declared, cutting the woman ruthlessly and swinging round to lower the microphone towards a young man sitting in a wheelchair: 'Now this is an American hero, a man who's suffered while taking up arms for his country, and I want to hear *his* view on this matter . . . '

It bowled relentlessly on, eventually turning to feminism. Neri was one of those strong women who, because they can get what they want without really trying, never offer themselves as champions of the movement. She was sympathetic, without truly realising what drove her sisters to wrath. She knew women were every bit as good as men – all right, she knew they were a damn sight better – so she didn't feel the need to stress the point. A man who got in *her* way had better watch out.

She was surprised, then, to find herself getting more and more incensed by Corinthian's line of questioning. Perhaps it was partly the anger of her friends alongside her, all of them waving like mad to get in front of that microphone, but she suddenly jumped out of her seat and ran down the aisle.

'Now this debate is really hotting up,' Corinthian joked, tugging the wire so that she didn't snag it in her haste. Close up, she could see a flicker of fear in his eyes. 'This lady just can't wait to have her say.'

They fought over the microphone, Neri prising his fingers away from it. He must have heard the noise it was making through his earpiece, because he let it go and she, gloriously, had the floor to herself.

'Could you dream up something more insulting,' she demanded, 'than a man standing in front of so many women asking impertinent questions about their relationships with men? Do you regard that as reasonable, Mr Corinthian?'

She tipped the microphone towards him, making sure that he couldn't grasp it.

'Well,' he said lightly, so that she had to admire his appearance of cool, 'I'm the guy they asked to do the job. You think you could do it better, ma'am?'

In a moment of clarity she seemed to take everything in at once. There were a couple of studio men just three or four feet away from her, but outside the camera's range, who looked ready to pounce but who knew that would make an utter shambles of their programme. There was a cameraman even closer who had a great smile on his face, as if to egg her on. And then, up high in the gallery, there was an army of men and women, among whom must be the producer and the director. There was a lot of heated debate up there, and one of the women was bent over a stick microphone, talking urgently. Presumably she was in contact with Jerry Corinthian, who was sweating heavily under the chin but who continued to smile like the seasoned professional he was.

'Tell you what,' she offered, looking to the audience for support. 'You ask the guys the questions and I'll ask the gals.'

Corinthian shrugged hugely and beamed broadly, playing for time. The audience seemed to think it was a great idea, and someone up in the gallery at least thought it was good damage limitation, because one of the studio hands knelt on the ground and held up a second microphone for Corinthian to use.

'It's a deal,' said the presenter, showing his pearly white teeth, which looked like his own at close range. She was rather taken by them. 'And perhaps we should make the introductions before we go any further.'

So the show had gone on – the Neri Marchant show as the papers had it the following morning. She'd continued to harrass Jerry Corinthian and to dominate the proceedings, and the programme came to an end in confused mime with the engineers fading the sound so as not to crash the ad break.

'That's Neri,' her friends said. 'You can't change Neri. And it sure was a laugh!'

• • •

Apologising wasn't her strong point. In fact she couldn't think when she'd last done it. Generally speaking there didn't seem much point. What was over was over, and life had to go on.

In this case, however, it definitely was not over. The fiasco had thoughtfully been preserved on video by one of her friends, and the following morning she was forced to sit through it twice, her head banging from the mother of a hangover, while they all roared and feted her and said wasn't she a scream.

The trouble was that she kept looking at the fixed grin on the face of Jerry Corinthian and for some strange reason it made her feel about the size of a cockroach. She tried to be a professional herself, and she knew that she had taken this man to the very edge of his abilities. She also knew, with a growing admiration, that he'd not fallen over that edge.

Perhaps that was why she was now ringing the bell of his house in Stillwater Hills, to tell him how she admired his competence. It would be better for her ego if she could. But motoring out from the city at lunchtime, cursing every crazy driver who even thought about cutting her up on the freeway, she knew this was going to be one of the nastiest moments of her life.

So why did she do it? The thought really didn't cross her mind.

'Oh,' he said, not bothering to smile. Perhaps he only smiled on camera, she thought. That would be reasonable, a conservation of effort. Did she squint her eye when she wasn't taking a photograph? 'You come for a screen test?'

'Have I –'

It took her ten seconds to know he was joking. He had this beautiful dry humour. Even when she realised it, and broke into a laugh that was full of relief, he only twinkled at her. But he did invite her inside.

'Jesus, what an acid-head I was,' she burbled, once the preliminaries were over and they were sipping fruitjuices by a picture window which gave views of hills and trees for miles and miles.

'It worked,' he said.

'Don't tell me that,' she protested. 'I've watched it twice on video. It gets worse every time.'

'Put it this way,' he said. 'I wouldn't want to go through that too often, Nerissa, but it got the show some great publicity and we averted disaster.'

'*You* averted disaster, you mean.' He had this way of caressing her name. She liked so much the way he spoke and the way he revealed a gigantic amusement without seeming to do anything at all. He had the trick of it. 'I could have ruined you.'

'My directors were ecstatic this morning. You've seen the press? Sure they wobbled a little last night, but directors are programmed to wobble.'

'How can I apologise to you, Mr Corinthian?'

'Don't call me Mr Corinthian,' he said, refilling her glass. 'Call me sir.'

She was more relaxed now, so it took her only two and a half seconds to know he was joking, and this time she fell about, and he joined in, and before you knew what time it was they were the best friends in the world.

That, in short, is how Neri Marchant became Jerry Corinthian's wife, and was to remain so for all of one year, ten months and eleven days.

• • •

It was easy to blame her work for the chronic fragility of her relationships. During her time with Jerry she got her first big breaks, so that she was Neri Corinthian professionally ever afterwards. She was in Paris on the August night Princess Diana and her playboy lover Jodi Fayed met their sudden end in an underpass crash. Three days later she was in Calcutta, grabbing the last pictures of Mother Theresa hours before she died. Then, a few weeks on, she was in Western Australia, firing off dramatic shots of the worst bush fires in a generation.

'The woman's got lucky timing,' the old hands said, and that meant they knew she was there to stay. Luck was something good professionals had. They were born with it.

But her rocky relationships were really the result of her own fickleness. She couldn't retain an interest in any man for long. With Jerry she made one particular mistake for the last time – she had another baby. Barney was a docile little thing, which was just as well in view of the insecurity of his surroundings. Both his parents were horrendously busy, neither had much time or thought for their offspring, and each was soon extremely irritated by the other.

That dry humour of Jerry's now appeared to be an ironic weapon to use against her. And he was convinced that her zaniness was a symptom of impending certifiability. They were no longer prepared to accept one another's idiosyncracies, and on the few occasions when they met for any length of time they fought like backyard roosters. They divorced when Barney was a year old, and this time she was the one left holding the baby.

No matter, she thought. She was earning good money and could well afford well-qualified child-minders. She set up home in a rented flat on East Sixty-seventh and used it like a hotel. The permanent resident seemed to recognise her when she flew in from an assignment, but maybe that look was simply an appreciation of the bright colours she wore. Barney showed an artistic bent from an early age and, because of the gaps between their meetings, seemed to be developing at a rate which would have bemused Picasso.

Her most priceless asset as a photographer was her versatility. Many of her contemporaries made names for themselves by specialising in a particular field – fashion, portraiture, landscapes, battle-zones – but Neri had built up a stunning portfolio in all of them. When an editor had a prestige project in mind, hers was the name he thought of. The second thought was 'Can we afford Neri Corinthian?'

Adrenalin enables work to be done. Its stimulus has other effects, too. She found her head easily turned and, although she knew the passion wouldn't last, she threw herself at any tempting relationship that came her way. No babies, she repeated to herself, strictly. However they may plead, no babies. Otherwise – well, what was a piece of paper? They both meant it at the time.

When Russia sent troops into Chechnya she shared an armoured car for fifty miles and a few hours with a Russian captain, Igor Galiullin. He was so dashing, that was the truth. And his sense of humour: why did she always fall for that in a man? It was, of course, a two-way affair. Igor was completely smitten by this tempest of an Englishwoman, who was absolutely not what one expected of her race and gender. They married months later in a Moscow registry, and knew it was a mistake as soon as the papers were signed. So they took themselves to their honeymoon dacha and drank and made love as if there were no tomorrow.

As there would not be. The divorce took a little time to go through, but the thing was understood even before she kissed him full-bloodedly on the lips and climbed into the Ilyushin that would take her away for ever. It had been a good, vibrant marriage, and there had been no babies.

Her third husband was a Brazilian writer whose picture she took while he was on a tour of the continent to promote what seemed to be an extremely complicated novel. She never read it. The newspaper reporter sent to interview Luis Lopez Morilla was very much in the way but refused to take the hint. Neri and Luis gazed at each other in a trance-like manner, she occasionally rearranging the spots and taking another picture, while the earnest intruder asked deep questions and interpreted monosyllabic replies as something deeper still. She could feel a marriage coming on and, anyway, she'd never been to Rio.

This was a longer-lasting affair than her Russian sojourn. She was able to arrange plenty of work in South America, and spent all of three months at the Lopez hacienda. They got on very well indeed, even to the end, but she was hopelessly bored. Large blue and yellow butterflies meant nothing to her, and if she heard another samba she'd self-destruct.

'We end friends,' she'd told him. 'We'll always be friends, Luis.'

'Si,' he replied, as deeply as ever.

When she married Mitsuri, her friends were convinced that she was after some kind of United Nations award. None of their friends had married a Japanese before. But then, Neri argued, none of their friends had spent six weeks with an incredibly civilised and witty Japanese while compiling a photographic essay about his country. Mitty was a translator and Neri was living off a healthy advance from Simon and Schuster. What else could a girl do?

'But why do you torture a man,' he was later to write, 'with dreams of what can never be?' He had poetry in him, she thought. She loved that cultivation in him. 'I cannot believe that you meant to harm me.'

Mitsuri had loved her more than anyone, and he wrote for three years before he could resign himself to his fate and agree to the divorce. The tragic tone of his beautiful letters at last began to affect her. She wouldn't change her mind, of course, but she did question whether she had been entirely fair. She was unhappy about his sadness. She also found the stream of letters disquieting. In this way she came to another irrevocable decision: not only no more babies, but no more husbands. Even Neri had finally had enough.

• • •

'I've had a recurring dream,' said Barney, who was ten years old and sounded fifty. 'You have this suitcase . . . '

'This very one?' she asked, throwing a few packs of tights into it. There was a law about tights, she thought with a grimace. However many you took, you always needed one more.

'Any one, but I guess this one. Isn't this the one you always use?' He frowned at her. How could a ten-year-old frown at his own mother? 'In this dream everything gets swept up into the suitcase, every last bit of rubbish, and the house is tidy again.'

'I don't think I like this dream, big guy,' she said. 'Isn't the house tidy while I'm away?'

'It's pristine, momma.'

'It's *what*? No – I heard you. It's pris-tine. Splendid. Good for Adeline, sweet, sweet Adeline. So what does that make your dream?'

'This is one I'm not following, momma.'

'Listen, Barney, dreams aren't just dreams. Dreams are for real. They mean bad thoughts and hard wishes. You follow that?'

'This is the Freudian lecture, is how I read it.'

'So the place is normally clean. I mean pristine. But in your dream I'm ridding the universe of chaos when I scram. Therefore, if you'll forgive my paranoia, you blame me for all the dirt and confusion in your life. Answer that, crumbum.'

'It's hard, momma.'

'It's more than hard,' she said. 'It's cruel and vindictive and wounding.

67

On the other hand,' she added, 'it means I don't have to feel bad about going. At least you can get the place sorted.'

Why had she never been curious about her sister? she wondered. It was exciting to think that while she, Nerissa, had been going for gold on one continent, Calla was kicking up a storm in another. They would have so much to talk about. They'd pick up where they left off. Or at least, she corrected herself, just before where they left off.

'And when do I get to see this mystery aunt?' Barney enquired, sounding a little miffed. He picked up a strand of black cotton which had fallen from the suitcase and carried it delicately to the trashcan. 'Don't aunts like to meet their nephews these days?'

'I'll warn her first,' Neri said.

She'd read the magazine article several times, and she sensed something in it which she had to admire. Determination. She was pretty unshakeable herself when the situation arose, but there was clearly a single-minded quality about Calla which it must be awesome to encounter at first hand.

'Gee, thanks,' Barney replied sourly as the phone rang. He went to the suitcase and rescued a dangling bra strap. He liked order.

'Hi, Betsy. You what? But doesn't Krostow know I have an agent? He says who needs an agent when friends get together . . . Yeah, put him on.'

She swung her legs onto the sofa, kicked off her boots and lay back with the receiver tucked between shoulder and chin. She felt a change of plans coming on. Other people might have found this disorientating, but Neri Corinthian wasn't other people. She *enjoyed* uncertainty. There would always be a time for everything you wanted to do.

'Look, Mr Krostow, I was about to fly to London, England. The plane leaves two hours from now. Further than that, I normally talk this kind of business through an agent.'

The smile on her lips suggested self-satisfaction.

'But with that kind of offer, Mr Krostow, who needs an agent? I'll be out there in the morning.'

Barney sat on the end of the sofa: 'Aunt Calla remains a mystery,' he said, as if reading off a book title.

'Alas, the fast buck takes priority,' she replied. 'One of life's harsher truths. But it's merely a pleasure delayed, Barneykins. She won't escape me that easily.'

As she padded out of the room he picked up her boots and positioned them side by side next to her chair. Then he collected the telephone and replaced it on the table. Why me? he asked himself. Why don't other guys have a mother like mine?

7

Jason Andover didn't much like being taken for a ride in either sense of the phrase, and right now he had the feeling both were applicable.

'I've changed my mind,' he said.

Calla was at the wheel at they drove through Notting Hill Gate. It was an evening early in April and it was already dark. He stole a glance at the high-cheek bones and well-defined features which even now, years after they'd first met, had that disturbing ability to make his heart beat faster. How she had blossomed, his Calla – without growing essentially different, but becoming stronger and more lovely, more like herself. She was just back from a business trip to Paris, and while she was away he had felt cut off from the living world.

Sitting in the passenger seat was no blow to his pride. Jason wasn't one of those men who need always to be in control in order to convince themselves that they fit some macho stereotype. But nowadays he was too often incapable of driving. Most of the time he fought off the temptation, but he missed hurtling along lanes and motorways alike at high speed. That had been one of his greatest pleasures.

'Stop, please.'

She ignored him, and that told him his sixth sense was functioning well. If they were making for a mystery party, why wasn't she dressed the part? Not that Calla needed bright clothes and make-up in order to draw every eye in the room, he thought. Perhaps she was giving the other women a chance. Nevertheless, he reached across and held her forearm, so that she was forced to swerve.

'I asked you –,' he began, in a harsh voice she wasn't used to.

'If you refuse to come,' she said firmly, shaking off his hand, 'we're finished, Jason. Read my lips. *Finished.*'

A chill ran through him. O, sweet Jesus, he thought, it's come to this at last. I've seen it coming, and now it's here. His teeth bit into a finger, drawing blood. Without a doubt, she meant it. He knew her resolve. He knew this wasn't a game. But it was an unbearable possibility. Calla was a perfect precious thing which somehow gave his life colour and impetus.

'I'm your plaything,' he drawled, waving a complaisant hand as if he hadn't a care in the world.

Those years ago, when he found her by Cleopatra's Needle, she had been the innocent, the one in need of protection. How much had changed in that time! Now he so often felt the dependant one. He needed her. Did she need him? He stole another glance and thought how strong she was.

They drew up outside a Georgian detached house set back from the road. A lighted window showed a drawing room with people in chairs, chatting.

'Not exactly jumping, is it?' he said. 'It's crying out for us, angel, to liven it up.'

'It's not that sort of party, Jason,' Calla replied, turning to him at last. 'Jason, promise me you'll stay for a while. Give it a chance.'

'Fascinated,' he grinned, though still feeling hollow inside. 'What kind of gathering can it be? China cottage collectors? Undertakers and their apprentices? Or a really wild gathering of vegetarians? Should we have brought a bottle of barley water? I *am* looking forward to this!'

'Just promise,' she said in a dangerous voice.

'Okay, I submit. I promise.'

A tall pale woman came to the door, and it was obvious that she and Calla had already met.

'Jason,' she smiled, offering a limp hand. He followed them inside. 'You don't have to talk if you'd rather not,' she said over her shoulder. 'Some people prefer simply to listen on their first visit.'

What in God's name, he wondered with a little squirm of alarm, had Calla brought him to? Had she come under the influence of some strange sect? Perhaps all these people were waiting for a fat berobed guru to appear in a white Mercedes and work them up into a frenzy. He did recognise one or two faces – in the corner sipping orange juice there was a model well-known in the pages of one of the magazines he did art reviews for. And, although she looked very different without her make-up on, there was no doubt that that was the editor of *Chic* who was in deep conversation with a dark chap by the fireplace. She, too, seemed to be drinking nothing stronger than fruit juice.

'Darling,' he murmured, 'what are you up to?'

She looked him straight in the eye with an expression which was at once loving, exasperated and utterly determined: 'It's a meeting of Coke-Anon. You're going to sit through it, damn you, every last minute.'

Her violet eyes never left his face for an instant. Scanning that face, that darling face, she saw only too clearly the changes which had overtaken it. Oh, it was still Jason, a face which could light up with sudden humour. But it was thinner, gaunter than before. His eyes, which had always seemed to twinkle with mischief, were now burning bright, far too bright.

'It's a self-help group. They meet in each others' houses and talk about their problems.'

Jason opened his mouth for a witticism, but none came. At this moment she hated herself for what she was doing to him. It was bitter medicine, and she was forcing him to take it. But there was no other way. Unless he could beat his addiction, it was all over. She couldn't live with this slow suicide of the man she once knew.

'Cosy,' he said, his voice unusually harsh.

'Try it,' replied Calla, in tones which were more commanding than pleading.

'Obviously quite the place to be seen,' he said in a heavily satirical tone. 'The last time I ran into our model friend Peta she was snorting the stuff through a rolled ú50 note off her Gucci handbag mirror. Very elegant, I thought.'

Stay, please stay, Calla was silently urging. Give this a chance. Give *us* a chance. I swear it's all over if you go. I swear it on Mother Angelica's bible. I swear it by everything holy. I swear it by the love I have for you, Jason Andover. Don't throw it all away.

'Jason!' The unmistakable voice of *Chic*'s famous editor rang across the room. Ella Lepard was moving towards him as quickly as her leather trousers would allow.

'I knew we shouldn't stay,' he murmured to Calla, before charmingly kissing La Lepard's much-bejewelled hand. 'The places we meet,' he smiled ironically.

'I'd no idea, honey,' she said, her miss-nothing eyes hungrily taking him in, 'that we shared this interesting problem.'

When Ella Lepard had been in newspapers, she'd been known as the Barracuda of Fleet Street. It was quite a title when you considered both the number and the class of the contenders. Several nervous editors on the Daily News had tried to tone down her scathing column, in which she savaged her prey with whiplash prose only just the right side of libel.

But the Barracuda had known her readers better than any editor. She knew what they liked and she knew how to dish it out. The column stayed and so did she, while editors came and went. Passing 45 in a world where youth rules, Ella Lepard had grown almost into a parody of herself.

She was rarely seen without the blood-red finger nails which her victims imagined as talons. The tan was sunbed permanent, no matter how deep the lines on her face, and the jewellery, like the prose, was completely beyond the bounds of the commonplace. Blonded hair was worn in that deliberately careless style which took ages to perfect, and the glasses were perpetually stuck on top of her head.

The Barracuda had two weaknesses – adulation and money. Well, yes, there were toyboys too, but unlike the money, they didn't gather interest with age. She never kept them long. Plenty of her friends were grateful for her cast-offs.

It was one of her weaknesses that took her away from newspapers. A huge American magazine corporation had bought the ailing *Chic* magazine and offered Ella Lepard a blank chequebook to turn it round. It meant the end of one of Fleet Street's legends and the beginning of the greatest success story in magazines.

Turn it round she did. And how! The *Chic* offices were briefly known as the abattoir as she sent everyone packing except the company which replaced the washroom linen. The result was glossy, outrageous and expensive. *Chic*, in a word. That blank cheque was written in Ella Lepard's sweat, no doubt about it.

But something was missing. It was the adulation. The transatlantic variety, which came in dollars and a Manhattan flat for a perk, just wouldn't do. The Barracuda needed the kick, the sheer high she had got from writing her column of witty venom against the clock on the wall of a grimy daily paper and knowing more than three million people would buy the paper to read her.

She'd grown bored, and in the magazine world boredom is alleviated by parties and title launches, where cocktails and cocaine go together like bread and butter. In spite of the hard-headed common sense with which she had berated those unlucky enough to appear in her column over the years, La Lepard had started to snort cocaine.

And so here she was, one of the glitterati in a less than glittering situation. Calla knew, from Jason's own riotous account, that she had once tried to add him to her toyboy ranks. She was the sort of highly coloured and exotic creature Jason loved to send up. He'd perform imitations for weeks after this, Calla knew. Or, at least, the old Jason would have done.

'Unless I'm being tactless,' Ella Lepard added with mock concern. 'Are you perhaps here to give dear Calla some support?'

Calla, smiling sweetly, paused for just the right length of time before saying: 'I'm sorry. I'm not much good with faces. It's Ella Lepard, isn't it?'

The smile in return was just as sweet, but only an innocent would have trusted such sweetness. The Barracuda drew on her long cigarette: 'Visited any wonderfully fascinating building sites lately, honey?'

'Oh, a few,' replied Calla. 'I can recommend some excellent hunting grounds if it's rough trade you're after.'

'Do they come with your personal star rating, Calla, my dear?' inquired Ella, without pausing for breath.

'Thought you liked to test-drive them all yourself, Ella,' Calla casually remarked, hearing with some satisfaction the click of irritation from the Barracuda's mouth.

Jason beamed. His Calla had won that round, no doubt. Very entertaining it had been too.

The tall, pale woman was standing up now, her hands resting on the table, clearly waiting for silence. She had the practiced, desperate smile of someone who fears rejection: 'I'm Meriel Boon,' she said gently.

'What's this?' asked Jason. 'The cabaret?'

'For shame, sweet thing,' murmured Ella. 'It's the sermon, and guaranteed to put the fear of God into you newcomers. Don't forget to put something in the collecting plate as you go. If you don't your nose will collapse.'

Silence fell: 'You're all very brave,' said Meriel Boon. 'Those of you who haven't been to one of our little meetings before may be wondering what you've let yourselves in for. I can assure you that hundreds of people before you have wondered the very same thing, and they've gone away with new hope.'

'I'm afraid,' Ella Lepard whispered hoarsely into Jason's ear,'that there is sometimes the smack of a revivalist meeting.'

'This evening, without further ado, I would like to introduce to you a leading American expert on cocaine and allied drugs, Mr Milton Freeborn. Mr Freeborn works for the Drug Enforcement Administration in Washington DC.'

'Rather sounds,' ruminated Jason, 'as if the stuff's become compulsory.'

'He's currently in this country to advise the Home Office on appropriate measures in the fight against drug abuse.'

As her guest speaker rose to his feet they heard her say earnestly: 'As tough as you like, Mr Freeborn, please. Don't spare them.'

Jason quickly moved to a chair closer to the door: 'In case I feel sick,' he smiled at Calla. 'I'm still here, aren't I? Stay cool.' But she found her anger rising. She found herself thinking of the trip she'd recently made to Paris, and when she remembered what had happened there she reacted bitterly: is it worth it? Why go through all this when there's an alternative? And this made her more angry still.

Mr Freeborn was an angry man too. He'd seen the evils of drugs at work when he was a New York cop on the 42nd precint. He'd seen the depths to which human nature can sink when in need of a fix. And he'd seen the money-men behind the misery.

Now he got angry to order. There was more than a touch of evangelism in Milton Freeborn as he visited groups like Coke-Anon during his stay in Britain. By and large these were well-off addicts he saw before him – not kids who'd had it rough on the streets of life, but those who'd been brought up behind its curtains and up its gravelled drives. In short, these were people who should know better, who had deliberately brought themselves to the levels of kids who'd never had a sniff of their education, their possessions, their designer clothes.

He was a big man, with that iron grey hair and craggy face you see on Americans whose convictions have been born out of hard experience. And hard experience was what he was about to hand out. He thumped his beefy hand into his palm and began.

'Feel okay?' he growled. 'Feel pleased with yourselves for getting along to this nice house tonight? Enjoyed your chat? That's swell. I'm real happy for you.'

He paused, long enough for Jason to murmur: 'Something tells me he doesn't exactly mean that.'

Freeborn took a breath that seemed meant to last him some time: 'Let me tell you something. Whatever's motivated you to come here, you haven't even tasted the horror of what you've started in your nice sociable parties with your elegant drinks and your elegant coke habits.

'I read a case in one of your English papers. The son of a lord who had a cocaine habit. That habit was costing him five thousand a week. Pounds sterling. Quite a lot, even for a lord in waiting. What did he do when he ran out of cash? He sold his blackberry to pay for his next deal. Whad'ya think? Poor guy. How my heart bled for him!

'Now some folks don't have blackberries. That might come as a shock to you folk. But I figure that even those who have them can only sell them the once. And what do you do next time you need a few grammes? You sell something else.'

There was a feeling of uneasiness in the room. Calla saw Jason exchange looks with Peta, the model, a leggy blonde creature with a snub nose. They smiled conspiratorially, as if to say that they weren't really listening.

'What do you sell? Your car? Your house? Maybe that expensive Rolex Oyster on your wrist? When you've hocked your wedding ring, what have you got left? Believe me, cocaine's not a kind creditor. You go on paying – even when you've lost your job to your drugs habit.

'And that's when you find yourself on a level with those kids who've only ever seen a portable phone through a shop window. Those kids whose idea of a house is a condemned appartment in an overcrowded block, or the driest shop doorway they can find. What do *they* sell?' Freeborn paused for effect, though apparently not for breath.

'Other people's blackberries?' hazarded Jason, with a studied insouciance.

'Themselves!' Freeborn exploded. 'They sell themselves, because there's always a market for the human body. And you're in that market.

Sure, you may be only window-shopping right now, strolling round and looking at the wares for sale. But you're in there where body gets sold like meat.

'Whether it's your body which ends up abused and torn, or whether it's somebody else's, you're responsible. You're responsible because you keep the dealers alive and fat. You keep their stinking trade alive and fat. There's a stink attached to you, whatever fine scents and fancy clothes you cover it up with.'

Peta winked at Jason, who showed the tip of his tongue through barely parted lips.

'I've seen horrors, my friends. My fine, pampered friends. I've seen horrors which would make you sick. Horrors which you feed. I've seen new-born babies spasming and convulsing and dying because their mothers are addicts. And that's why the likes of you make me sick.

'Listen! I have seen boys and girls – kids who should be at high school – degraded into cheating, stealing and prostitution. I have seen children whose bodies have been used by depraved adults as if they were rag dolls. Believe me, venereal disease and busted skin is the least of their worries. I have seen children with AIDS, doomed to die because they sold their body to sodomy for the next few grammes. A heroin addict needs at least £100 a day. The first thing it costs is self respect. The last thing is life itself. Drugs don't let you go until you're dead.

'But you can't quite believe this can you? Here in your comfortable lives, what has any of this got to do with you? Well I've got news for you. It might be a while coming, but it's round the corner, waiting. You think you can always get treatment when you want it? If you've got any money left by then, sure. How does six thousand pounds a week as a private patient in one of your English clinics grab you?

Maybe, Calla thought, that wasn't big money for some of those here tonight. But nobody was smiling any more. And she herself, however much she'd known before, felt sick to her stomach.

'Let's look at your friends, shall we? You know, the ones you fund, the ones you keep in cars, yachts and houses. Who *are* they? Are they the sort you'd want in your house, at your dinner party?

'Your friends the drugs barons get an annual worldwide income from you of two hundred and seven thousand million pounds. That's £50m every two hours six minutes. Believe me, these guys don't pay taxes. Most of you use cocaine. That comes mainly from Latin America. Now I'll tell you something. One of Bolivia's cocaine traffickers offered to pay off – personally pay off – his country's entire foreign debt to the US if his son was released from American custody. That debt was around £2.5 billion. You're the mugs who make that possible.

'Couriers carry coke through customs in their own bodies. the stuff you very nice people sniff has been put in a condom and swallowed by some guy. It's delivered a day or two later, over the john. Others bribe women to carry the stuff in their vaginas. Sometimes these condoms break and release the drug into the carrier's sytem and the carrier dies. What a shame. Who cares? Not the drug barons.

'So you're making some nice guys real rich. Proud of yourselves? You're degrading the youth of the world into prostitution and death. Proud of yourselves? You're fucking up your own lives. You make me very angry and you make me very sick.'

Freeborn paused for breath, but nobody relaxed. He had the room in the hard-skinned palm of his hand. Calla stole a look at Jason. His face was expressionless. His usual satirical look was gone. Even Ella Lepard looked serious. She hadn't once pulled on her smouldering cigarette while Freeborn spoke.

When he started up again, it was in a calmer, softer voice as if he had exorcised himself of his fury. 'You English embarrass easy, I know. And some of you have come along tonight because you're worried. Not about yourselves, but about someone you love who's snorting coke. I want to talk to you people now.

'It might be your lover. It might be your child. Here's how you know. Here's how you look out for it.

'Soft drugs. I hate those words. There are no such things as soft drugs. If a member of your family uses cannabis, do something. Young people keep being told by their pop idols and even, lord help us, by politicians, that herbal cannabis is no worse than an alcoholic drink or an ordinary cigarette. Friends, cannabis is much more dangerous.

'The mind-affecting substance in cannabis is called THC. It's increased fifty-fold since the 1960s, when we were sold the lie of 'harmless drugs'. Fiftyfold, for Crissakes! Imagine a bottle of rum which served 1,650 drinks instead of the normal thirty. That's what a fifty-fold increase means.

'Alcohol leaves your body system within twenty-four hours. Cannabis lingers for a week. It's a small step to coke, to other stimulants and to narcotics. There are *no* soft drugs.'

As he launched into a description of likely addicts, their symptoms and their habits, Calla remembered Jason as he was at the beginning – idly smoking the occasional reefer, being his attractive, witty self and making her fall completely in love with him. In those days she had failed to spot the warning signals which now seemed obvious.

She had tried it herself on the odd occasion, but Calla's nature was too impatient, too passionate. She wanted highs and she got them, but from the fizz of being creative, from fighting her corner in boardrooms, from designing buildings and watching them take shape in front of her eyes. Where Jason was reflective, she was active. Where he watched, she took part. There'd been an electricity in their differences in the early days. Was there anything now but irritation and a lingering concern which was destined to die?

He had turned to cocaine two or three years ago. Calla was ashamed to realise that she could not remember exactly when. She should have been aware, she knew. But she'd had her own projects, her own battles to win and, dammit all, he should be able to take care of himself, shouldn't he?

Shouldn't he?

She had found the tell-tale signs of a user on his desk. Jason wasn't the type to bother hiding the cut-off straws, the rolled slips of paper with the white powder clinging inside. He kept the stuff, with typical aplomb, in an antique ink stand. The second bottle, meant for sand to scatter on wet ink, was full of the white, bitter-tasting crystalline powder. She had wetted her finger and dabbed the stuff on to her tongue.

'Happy powder,' he'd laughed, 'and harmless.'

He'd told her, as drug-users often do, that it was a party drug, a fun thing for the casual user. There was no danger of addiction. But he had never offered her any. He knew more about the danger than he would admit. He might ask Calla to love him in spite of his weaknesses, but he wanted to protect her from the same fate. At parties, she would see him mingle with the snorting set, returning to her bright-eyed and euphoric. The effects of coke were felt within three minutes.

'It makes me feel exhilarated, my Calla,' he would say. 'You're always berating me for not being a go-getter like yourself. With this stuff I get the biggest go available for the getting.'

But what Calla could see was a lover who was troubled by insomnia, who had lost his appetite and who was hell to live with during those periods of clarity when he could see it, too.

Milton Freeborn was still scaring the hell out of his audience: 'More than fifteen million Americans have tried cocaine. They're victims of a glamorous myth which dates from the 1920s. Remember the Lost Generation? Cocaine has a spurious glamour, a killer glamour. Believe that myth at your cost – the cost of ruined lives, ruined health and death.'

The fist smashed into the palm again: 'Fight it!' he growled, and strode out of the room.

'What an exit,' remarked Jason lightly, a fragile smile playing on his lips. 'I fear an encore.'

He was trying to joke, Calla observed, but he was pale with shock. There was a sheen of sweat on his forehead. That was the effect Milton Freeborn liked to have.

• • •

Calla remembered Paris. To be precise, she remembered Philippe Beauvoir and wondered, with a yearning which surprised her, whether he would ever be more than a memory.

Her face and throat flushed with an inner heat as she relived the moment the sensation had first hit her. She was standing in the Cour Napoleon of the Louvre on one of those tangy spring afternoons which make Paris seem like the only desirable place on earth. She was unaware that even here, in the heart of a city where the chic is almost commonplace, she was drawing attention from all round.

What was claiming *her* attention, ostensibly at least, was the enormous glass pyramid which now stands in the middle of the formal square – still the most controversial structure in a city where buildings are accustomed to shock. Pei, of course. Sino-American. And damn good.

She was enraptured by its simplicity, its sheer nerve in bringing light and playfulness into such a severe setting. Three mini pyramids stood about it, and reflections flickered between them like a lambent flame. Fountains sprayed softly into flat triangular basins, which were large and calm, catching the lights of the glass.

It was then that it happened. She saw Philippe Beauvoir through two layers of glass. Her eyes rested upon him and refused to move away. During the last three days her feelings for him had changed from those of a colleague eager to see and learn as he led her around his magical city. But she hadn't been quite sure of how much they had changed until now.

Calla couldn't help but be aware of her own power over men. She was used to it, liked it. But now, regarding him from what she thought was a safe distance, she recognised with a throb that Philippe had an unsettling power of his own.

Here in the sunny square, where hundreds queued for their dose of culture in the galleries of the Louvre, there was only one picture Calla wanted to gaze upon – Philippe in the frame of the Pyramid.

He was very French. Not (she smiled at the memory) in the self-conscious style of that young man she'd seen last night leaving the Hotel Crillon in the Place de la Concorde – wearing a black silk suit and carrying a Louise Vuitton manbag. No, there was nothing foppish about Philippe, but there was a great deal of Gallic attractiveness all the same.

He was tall, with heavy and full eyebrows. His hair was dark and curly with a slight greyness at the temples. Now that it was late afternoon a swarthy shade of stubble coloured his face. A good quality cotton shirt was tucked over a flat belly into beautifully cut trousers. A Hermes scarf was tied cravat-style round his neck. He cared how he looked, mused Calla. But not too much.

She swallowed hard. She'd had temptations before of course. She was the sort of woman, the sort of challenge, who attracted high-powered men. When Calla walked into a meeting, it crackled with excitement. She was a puzzle, a lovely walking contradiction on high heels. There was an undeniable come-on about her, coupled with a clear beware sign which men found incredibly arousing.

Oh, she knew it all right. And she wasn't ice. There had been men who made her look twice – married men who would have been discreet and single men who would have been thrillingly indiscreet.

Calla was no girl – she was a woman of passion. And she took her passion to bed with her, where she was imaginative and abandoned. Jason felt he could watch her face at that moment forever, when her neck muscles were taut and her head thrown back as she was taken with those repeated waves. Only he, Jason thought with pleasure, had seen that delicious giving moment when her eyes finally shut the world away and she entered the realm of pure sensation. There was a touch of the wild about Calla.

So when she walked into those rooms of men, she knew what they were thinking behind the civilised uniform of their dark suits. And she gloried in her desirability. When she said no it was because she wanted to. No-one would ever say Calla Marchant had slept her way to the top.

Men thought of her as both aloof and intensely wantable. There were her bold violet eyes, to be sure, and there was that lovely face. But above all, there was that body and that crackle of excitement. They wanted to see its unrestrained fullness, the passion which breathed under each contour of her clothes. And they wanted to master it.

She had wondered, on this last afternoon of her trip round Paris with him, whether Philippe had felt that crackle. When, suddenly, his eyes met hers through the walls of glass, she knew the answer to her question.

'Beautiful and very daring, n'est-ce pas?' he had said when they first arrived, looking through the pyramid and down into the basement lobby where the crowds came into the museum. Now, returning to her side, he said simply: 'The best buildings, I think, are like human beings, born out of passion.' She hardly dared to meet those eyes with hers for fear of what he might see.

It had been a wonderful three days. She had her old friend Bunny

Simkins to thank for putting her in touch with Beauvoir, one of the architects involved with the remarkable La Villette project on the outskirts of Paris.

Architecture was an intensely competitive world, but he was truly fond of his old pupil. If his own thoroughgoing traditionalist approach didn't win the day, well, he'd like to see his bold young friend at the top of her profession.

'I must warn you, Calla,' he said, 'that competitions are ridiculously expensive. I've known architects who've ruined themselves in the process. You can spend a fortune on them and have absolutely nothing to show for it.'

'I'll take that risk,' she'd replied boldly, blindly.

'If you're really determined, Beauvoir's the man to see.'

He believed Philippe, whose father he had worked with, would help Calla see how a team of inspired Frenchmen had managed to temper the limitless flight of the imagination with a durable design for living. It was in La Villette that Calla had first seen what made her guide a real architect, a man who could make visions solid. He had stood on the spot he claimed was the centre of the 87-acre park and said: 'Calla, can you imagine canals, abattoirs and meat markets? That was what we had here. And now you look.'

She did look – at the theatre, the concert hall and the exhibition centre created from the 19th century market hall. She looked at the science and industry building, reflected in its own moat.

'And they say old and new styles cannot mix,' said Philippe in that accent which was already beginning to rouse something within her.

He watched her changing face as she saw La Villette's trademark, a polished steel sphere 36 metres in diameter set in its own pool of water. It reflected the buildings and their surrounding skyscape. She gazed in silence for a couple of minutes. Imagine being given such an opportunity as this. What a chance to leave your mark on the world!

'Obviously influenced by the Pompidou centre,' she said, pointing to the external lifts with views over the park. 'But who'd have thought to surround a futuristic place like this with a moat?'

'An architect, Calla. An architect with new thoughts,' Philippe replied.

It was new thoughts which were troubling her now as she tried to sort out what these three days had done to her. She had seen so much in this city where powerful men had always sought to secure their immortality in stone, brick and concrete. Philippe had shown her everything.

It all came before her now in a jumble of recollection. There was the remarkable inside-out Pompidou Centre, the lofty Montparnasse tower rudely interrupting the celebrated skyline. There was Valery Giscard d'Estaing's loving restoration of older Paris buildings. And there were Mitterand's wonderful, controversial pyramids and his defiant arch at La Defense where new towers were still springing up.

Philippe had taken her to the top of the Arc de Triomphe to see how the city radiated out like a star beneath them. 'This was Napoleon's dream, this arch,' he said. 'He was an emperor in every way. An emperor of men's hopes and aspirations. An emperor in war. An emperor in amour. A great lover of the world.'

But Philippe was talking again, in the here and now, in this square with the light and the water and the people. Calla looked at him and felt that – quite simply, but violently – she wanted him. Oh, not merely for his body, but for his passionate soul. She wanted to feel, to taste the very essence of this man who could talk about buildings with such feeling and with such fine intellect. Wouldn't he himself prove a veritable emperor in bed?

He was staring into her eyes as if for the first time   startled by their hue: 'You suit this place, I think. It is for you the light plays on the glass and the water and the flesh.'

Then he slipped a hand under her elbow and guided her through the crowds and under the arch which leads to the Rue de Rivoli. She made no effort to shake away his hand. She walked with him quickly and decidedly.

They said nothing until they reached the Ritz in the Place Vendome, where Philippe led her through to a Louis XV salon.

'Tea, I think, with separate hot water as you English like it. We are both rather thirsty?'

Calla was thirsty, it was true, but she wasn't sure that tea was the answer. She would rather be quenched by the long lean form now leaning towards her in his chair. She felt some emotion deep within her crying for release.

'All sorts of styles here,' Philippe was saying. 'A medley of rich convictions. It's the place for you. I'm told the hotel bedrooms are the height of rococo splendour, their bathrooms wonders in marble.'

And how easy it would be to drop the hint, to lower the eye, and to find herself with Philippe in one of those ornate bedrooms! She had rarely felt such an urge towards the forbidden. But no, she thought, she mustn't, she couldn't. Poor Jason, suffering alone – he needed her strength. She was the strong one. She wasn't the type to be a victim of her own wayward hormones.

'If only I had the time,' she said, watching him closely to observe whether he understood. But he only shrugged, and smiled gently.

'I've detained you too long,' he replied. 'Forgive me.'

'No, no –' But it was impossible to put matters right, to let him know. Instead she thanked Philippe with proper English politeness and stood to leave.

'Au revoir?'

'Au revoir.'

He watched her walk through the magnificence of the salon, putting it to shame with her own. Then he sat back and gazed darkly at the half-filled cup she had left behind.

Outside, she took a cab to her hotel and had it wait while she checked out. It sped her through the outskirts of the city to Charles de Gaulle airport – another of those whacky French buildings. But she hardly noticed it. Only over the grey channel did she bite her lip and wonder why in hell she'd walked out.

• • •

The Andover family fortune had begun with Jason's grandfather, Forsyth Andover. Between the wars, he had taken on a rundown brewery in a small Oxfordshire town and built it up. From a small row of huts and cramped barrel yard, the business had grown until the smell of hops hung over Boxstead and greeted visitors with an aggressive pungency as they approached the once sleepy market town.

Forsyth had all the shrewdness and vision a self-made man needs. He also had the nerve. No business partner would have gone along with his mad idea of taking on a chain of low-profit rural pubs. That was where the vision came in. The county brewery, Oxon Ales, was being swallowed up by one of the huge multiples, Vass, which reluctantly bought the pubs because they were in the same package deal as the brewery busioness they really wanted.

Vass were only too pleased to let the millstone round their massive neck go cheap. They had accountants, directors and wise men to shake their heads and advise against trying to make a go of the pubs.Forsyth had only his instinct and that told him to go for it. The pubs needed flair and finance. He had both. He foresaw increased rural prosperity would come with increased farming mechanisation, by now underway after the engineering revolution brought about by the second world war. He foresaw that more and more cars meant more and more visitors to the countryside.

Soon it was his turn to fight off buy-outs and merger proposals. He did so with the help of his only son, Robert, now coming into the business, and learning it the hard way, from the brewery yard up. He was a different character from his father – every inch the businessman old

Forsyth was, but without his father's sentimental streak. The same shrewdness was there, but there was a steadiness in him too, which was vital in the second generation.

Robert Andover married well – his wife Sarah was everything he could never be. His family's money was still a generation too recent to buy that sort of refinement for itself. Sarah was a dean's daughter, wooed from the Cathedral Close by the persuasive and persistent Robert. Her marital home was the Manor at Boxstead, which Robert had refurbished to her requirements. Sarah was like something from another world. Fine-boned, delicate and artistic, she was quite unfitted for business and hardly understood her husband's day to day doings. She loved her paintings, her antiques and her Robert. What else should she do?

Even their hobbies were worlds apart. Robert went in for high-risk, high-cost sports like power-boat racing, which left his wife cold. She would worry for her husband when he was throwing himself into these adventures, and one of her great sadnesses was that he was later to take her much loved first son, Jason, with him. But all that was still to come.

Jason was born out of Sarah's love for Robert. She was no earth-mother. Sex and natural processes such as childbirth could never move her as an adagio or an El Greco could. She was too fine, too fragile for this usage. When Robert's demands on her sexuality lessened, she accepted it with relief, never asking herself the uncomfortable question why.

When she found herself pregnant with Patrick, she vowed he would be the last one. She loved her three-year-old Jason to distraction, but nothing could blot out the pain and the mess of childbirth. Its indignity was too much for her. She had herself sterilised soon afterwards and tried to love her new baby as she had doted on the first. But where Jason had adored her in return, Patrick was a difficult and querulous child.

'All the manners came out with the first one,' the nanny would say, as this small dictator exercised his power over his nursery kingdom. Torn with guilt at her lack of love for him, Sarah gave him his wilful head. Robert was simply too busy to notice his younger son's increasingly domineering nature. Things were happening in the brewery world.

Robert predicted the vogue for real ale years before it happened and realised there was money to be made out of the old-fashioned brewing business which technology was rapidly discarding in favour of electric pumps, strangely fizzy brews and juke-box pubs. With his retired father's help, he dug out the long-forgotten recipe for the original Boxstead ale, christened it Forsyth's Old Particular and sold it in ancient looking bottles.

Meantime, he was diversifying into other areas. He bought into major hotel chains, he operated airline catering franchises. He foresaw the

British turning in their thousands to wine at their meal tables both at home and in the massively expanding restaurant market. So he gained a controlling interest in a vineyard in Alsace. The Andover name became familiar on the Stock Exchange.

Home was a haven from all this, where Sarah raised the boys with the help of nannies and made the place sweet with paintings and piano music. Robert had a mistress of course, in a London flat, for his ever more frequent trips to the capital, but his family always came first.

Then came the big money. Forsyth was dead when his son sold off the business to which he had given his life. He would have hated the loss, but he would have appreciated the poetry of the manoeuvre. Vass Breweries bought Forsyth Ales for £7.5m, only 25 years after selling the pubs to Forsyth Andover for a few thousands.

Robert expanded his wine empire and other interests. Life was good. Sarah was building a well-respected art collection. The boys were down for Rugby School. The mistress was content and discreet.

For Jason, it was a charmed boyhood. From his youth, he was able to look the world in the eye without fear. Everything he touched he seemed to find easy. He inhaled music and art from his mother as easily as he had taken her milk as a child. He took up the violin while at the local prep school and mastered it with none of the ear-splitting noises made by most novices.

The music and the art were nothing to Patrick. The fantasy games which had delighted Jason left Patrick cold at the same age. Even as little more than a toddler, his pleasures were orderly and cruel. With a child's bucket and spade he would scoop up stinging red ants from the roots of plants and carry them carefully over to a black ants' nest. Then he would watch as the black ants defended their territory and the two armies engaged in battle.

As the years passed, the differences between the brothers became more pronounced. Sarah became slightly frightened of her younger son, but was charmed and happy when Jason was pronounced a gifted child violinist. Robert was less charmed, but finally came round to the idea of extra coaching for the boy when he entered Rugby School. After all, one son in the family business would be enough and Patrick seemed the likelier lad. Already he was showing the Andover determination and will to win. And Robert was secretly gratified to have produced such unexpected artistic talent. After all, he could afford to be generous. He was proud of both his boys.

At school, Jason, fulfilled his promise on the violin. He loved art but he was an elegant sportsman, too, excelling at cricket and sailing, in which his wiry strength assured him of success. He was the sort of boy who managed to scoop prizes both on the field and in the form-room without collecting his classmates' resentment.

A visiting violin virtuoso was appalled to see the young man he had applauded for a masterly rendition of Paganini facing the bowling in the First Eleven the same afternoon.

'His fingers!' he had almost pleaded with the headmaster. 'Those precious fingers!'

But Jason merely laughed it off. He liked his cricket. He enjoyed the harmony of his own body as he enjoyed the harmony of a piece of music. He liked to feel it stretching, working, achieving. This was common ground with his father, too. Jason loved the 'high' of power boat racing. He lapped up the sensation of speed and daring.

He was chosen for the National Youth Orchestra, and after one season he became leader while he was in the sixth form at Rugby. When Jason bowed to applause at the end of a performance, hundreds of girls would clap all the harder at the sight of that soft hair flopping forward. How they longed to brush it out of his eyes!

Patrick arrived at the school while Jason was in the Upper Fifth. The worst in the English public school system fostered the worst in him. He already had the will to win. The sheer competitiveness of the place simply gave him the will to win at any price. He had a flair for mathematics and was the only boy in his year to have the *Financial Times* delivered.

He studied enough to get by in form, but Patrick knew what he really wanted. He wanted to win and he wanted money. He studied the paper's share columns with just that in mind. For him, school was a necessary prelude to the real game of money in the City. That was where he could really prove his flair for winning.

Here in the narrow confines of the boarding school, that ambition found an ouitlet on the sports field in games like rugby and hockey. Patrick was big and strong, but he was subtle too, and he perfected the art of the difficult-to-prove dirty manoeuvre. He was wicked in the scrum.

That summer holiday while Jason waited to start his Upper Sixth year, he found Patrick going through his mother's art and antique collection making notes.

'Feeling okay?' Jason asked lightly. 'A sudden rush of culture to the head? Like the Canaletto, do we? Or is it the Turner sketch which has caught your eye?'

Patrick gave him an unfriendly look: 'Paintings and antiques are a vital investment hedge against tax and inflation. It's only sensible to have an inventory,' he said.

'Christ, your'e a cynic, my young brother.'

'What are you driving at?'

'As Oscar Wilde put it, a cynic is a man who knows the price of everything and the value of nothing.'

Patrick looked nonplussed: 'I don't understand,' he said. 'What's the difference?'

In spite of his musical gifts, there was a time when Rugby nearly closed its doors against Jason. He was a natural leader among boys. They liked his ease, his ready, if lop-sided, smile. But some of the places he led them to were not entirely to the school's liking. There were half-day holiday forays to the local girls' school. Jason was seen at the wheel of a hired car with a sixth former of that school at the wheel. Reports were filed and warnings issued.

'I'll be good, ' Jason promised his housemaster, hardly pretending to be contrite. He knew full well that with the prestigious G.D. Clerkwell violin scholarship to London University in his pocket, the school was unlikely to let him go, whatever threatening noises they made.

At university some irksome restraints were shaken off. Not that Jason waited that long to solve the mystery of what not-so-little girls are made of. After that discovery in the summer house of Boxstead Manor with an obliging local girl, he pursued his investigations at university with eagerness.

Jason liked girls, but his passion was for his music. The more exposure he got, the more acclaim he received. He was tipped to be a notable orchestra leader at a young age. It was an intense devotion to his craft which had won him such a promising future.

He found release from the musical demands on his spirit in the animal tussle of man against the elements. He was his father's regular team-mate in power-boat races. 'He's got everything going for him,' friends would say. He was, as American colleges have it, the one most likely to succeed.

That was until the incident one October day which was to change his life for ever.

• • •

When the stakes are high and the competition is fierce there's a tight, reined-in atmosphere in powerboating which is more intense than in any other sport. It's something to do with the risks involved at incredibly high speeds, but it comes especially from the unpredictability of the elements, which can wreck a team's chances even when it has done everything right.

Robert Andover stalked the quayside at Cowes, watching his rivals tending their boats, repeatedly gazing out to sea as if he could read every rise and fall of the swell. He was also keeping an eye on his sons, frowning upon any sign they gave of fraternising with the other drivers.

'Don't tell them a damn thing,' he commanded gruffly. 'They'll pick your brains and learn your secrets. Let them be worrying about what you're going to do to them out there.'

His diesel-powered *Andover Ace* was a gleaming 41 ft monohull, cobalt blue with broad crimson streaks. He was proud of it. Its Seatek engines gave it speeds of well above 100 mph. The hull had been designed by no less a man than Fabio Buzzi. That meant class. It meant Andover was a prime contender for the European Championship. He coveted that title.

'Hey, Roberto! You seen those waves?'

The Italians were here in force, and Stephano Bianco, who now strolled across to the Andovers' boat with a broad smile on his face, was one of their best.

'Huh?'

'They're forecasting up to five feet. Very nasty. Can your bambini cope with that?'

'They're not bambini, blast you Stephano. They're grown men. They'll give you a hiding all right.'

Andover's confidence in his sons was genuine. He'd taught them everything they knew and he'd put them through their paces in tough conditions. True, this was the trio's first competitive race in the very top flight, but there had to be a first time. Jason was twenty, Patrick a strong, bull-like eighteen. He judged that they were ready for it.

'You seen, Roberto, what Contadini's done to his cat?'

'Yeah, I've seen.'

Luigi Contadini was the reigning champion and still the favourite, but the choppy conditions were bad news for his catamaran, the crimson coloured *Viola* . It could wallow. Andover had watched him removing the stabilising wing in order to increase his bow angle. It was a stupid thing to do, in his opinion – too bloody risky. He himself was always careful to calculate the odds.

'A bold idea, eh?'

'Crazy.'

They stared at each other wordlessly for some seconds, uneasy.

'So good luck, Roberto.'

'Good luck, Stephano.'

That's how it always was in the last minutes before a race. The drivers verbally fenced with one another, seeking a psychological advantage while at the same time respecting the skill, the bravery and the sheer bristling competitiveness of their rivals. It was unreal. Afterwards they would be friends again, but now they were like zombies, automatons, their feelings frozen by a kind of fear.

'Time to go, boys,' Andover said.

Jason and Patrick were relieved to be on their way. This amount of pressure was new to them. They settled into their seats, strapped themselves in and tugged the deep blue helmets onto their heads. Their father took the helm and Jason started the engine. They nosed out of the harbour and towards the starting point. There was a strong breeze blowing and the sky was a dirty grey.

'You happy?' Andover asked.

They nodded. It wasn't a word either would have used to describe their feelings right now. They were edgy, strung up, raring to be off. Instead they rocked to and fro in the turbulent water, their hearts pounding. There was nothing worse than this expectant calm. When they looked around them they saw a fleet of brilliantly-hued torpedo shaped boats, every one a thing of beauty and precision engineering. And they saw grim, screwed-up faces under the colourful crash helmets.

'We're going to enjoy this,' their father assured them, a gleam in his eye. 'This is going to be one helluva race.'

There's no noise like the abrupt revving of supercharged powerboat engines in the moments before the start of a race. During those vital last seconds you're aware of the searing roar; of the smell of the fuel; of the sudden violent motion of the boat as it settles into its 'go' mode; and, most of all, of the agony of aching desire within you to open the throttle and to surge forward so fast that you head snaps back and your brain almost blacks out with the shock of it.

They screamed towards the Needles in a blur of billowing white water churned to a fury by the biting propellers. It was violent, noisy, chaotic, but Jason gradually began to make sense of the race. He was thinking again, reacting on the instant as they hit new water. The *Andover Ace* was ploughing through the waves with great style, its nose above most of the turbulence, and they were running near the front of the field.

Now the wind strengthened and there was rain in it. Throughout the 18-mile Solent loop they kept the leaders in sight, but as they swung towards Anvil Point and Portland they were visibly losing ground. Jason observed his father's technique with a growing admiration, seeing how he time and again adapted his tactics to make the best of the worsening conditions. His brother, he noticed, held himself taut with a furious concentration.

Crews have a choice of routes in the Cowes Classic. Opting to skirt the coast, their boat sheltered from the rough northerly wind, they streaked towards the halfway marker at Torquay in sixth position. Bianco was out in front in his pink dayglo monohull *Senorita*, bombing across the sea as if it was flat as a millpond. There were three Italians in the first five, among them Contadini's *Viola*, which was running much better than he could have dreamed, just off the pace.

'Change of plan!' Andover shouted to his sons over the din as they refuelled at Torquay.' They'd clocked 117 miles in 98 minutes, but it still wasn't enough. 'Going back we'll leave the coast and take the direct route across Lyme bay.'

'Dirty water,' Jason warned. 'They're falling like ninepins out there.'

Several boats had already retired with blown engines and flooded intakes.

'Yep. But we save twelve miles that way. They won't be expecting it. We have to try anything we can.'

Patrick screwed up his eyes: 'We'll pulverise the bastards!' he mouthed venomously. 'They won't know what's coming to them.'

It was the roughest ride Jason had ever known, ploughing through the slapping water of the bay, but after only twenty minutes he knew his father had made the correct decision. They were closing fast on the leaders, and by the time they re-entered the Solent the white spume of the nearest boats was spattering against their visors.

Jason, feeling the excitement of the chase, stole a glance at his brother – and saw a face transformed by wild passion. His lips were set, his eyes were narrowed into slits, the vein at his temple stood out a dark and throbbing blue. It was somehow a frightening expression, but Jason was too busy to give it further thought.

Before they reached the Gurnard marker, *Andover Ace* had passed two of its rivals and another had dropped out with mechanical problems which left its crew waving their arms in anger and frustration as the other drivers hurtled past. Now there was a three-way duel for the race, with Bianco and Contadina neck and neck out in front.

Andover, having coaxed his boat through the treacherous chop and swell, now ordered the throttles to be fully opened in the calmer water towards the finish. All the time he was making deft signals which his sons interpreted into manoeuvres as if by instinct. They were a few hundred yards behind the leading pair and gaining fast, gaining fast enough perhaps to steal it, but they were coming up between the other boats and the gap between *Viola* and *Senorita* wasn't big enough.

Now Andover had to make a lightning decision. He could change direction and try to overtake the other boats on the outside, or he could wait for that gap to widen and power through between them. He gave the signal: they were going through if the chance came. To go outside would lose vital seconds and the finishing line was already in sight.

'Jesus!' Jason thought as they buffetted through the wake of the other boats. 'This is too damn close!' And he saw his father signal urgently to Patrick, who had control of the throttle. The speed came back, but not by much, by about as much as if Patrick was giving the impression of obeying his father but was refusing to go the whole way, to ease right off, to bide his time.

At this very second the *Viola* blew up. Where Contadini had lowered the aft end of his tunnel in order to raise the bow, a huge spume of water was forced up through the deck. The speeding catamaran slewed drunkenly, swung instantly into a vertical position and began to sink.

From the cockpit of the *Ace* they could see only a frothing whirlpool of white water, with the huge cat's twin hull thrown up within it. Andover signalled frantically, but they came on faster and faster. Jason realised to his horror that Patrick had opened the throttle full out, seeking to plummet their boat through the gap which had been too narrow only a moment before and which now wasn't measurable at all in the violent flurry of churned sea.

Andover was gesticulating angrily, urging his son to hold off, but there was a manic intensity now on Patrick's face, something almost inhuman in its ferocity. Jason threw himself across the boat to seize the throttle, but his brother struck a forearm across his eyes so that he slumped back into his seat.

Then they hit. The *Ace* smashed into the upturned hull of the stricken catamaran and Jason lost all sense of time and space as he was hurled high into the air and down into the water. He shook his head clear. He saw first the crew of the *Viola* – three bobbing helmets – and then, as he twisted in the water, a figure lying flat on the surface, supported by his lifejacket.

'Father!'

He swam powerfully to the floating man, taking in at a single horrified glance the deep gash on the forehead, pouring blood, the pallor of the skin, the slackness of the body. At the same moment he realised that his brother hadn't resurfaced at all.

Jason dived under the boat, making unerringly for the spot where he knew Patrick must be. He must have become snared in the straps when the *Ace* keeled over. Jason fumbled blindly at the cockpit area and his fingers found a leg encased in waterproof material. It was kicking with a wild desperation.

He grabbed it and tugged unavailingly. Aware that he had only a few seconds' breath left in his lungs, he swam in as close as he could get and began to tear blindly at anything which might be restraining the body. The panic seemed to give him a superhuman energy. He was aware of the body shifting and then there was a searing pain in his left wrist. Something inside had gone, he knew, but at the same moment Patrick slid away from the boat, rolled over and rose, hands clawing, to the surface.

Afterwards there was the noise and confusion of the rescue operation, the throbbing pain in his arm and, at the back of everything, like an organ chord that reverberated for ever and ever, the dull, dreadful certainty that his father was dead. In a merciful daze, he was aware of comforting his mother and of having his injury treated, knowing already what the doctors weren't to confirm for months, that something irreparable had happened to the tendons inside his wrist so that, though it was in all other respects normal, it would now always lack the flexibility for him ever to become the supreme violinist which destiny seemed to have marked him down for.

That evening he visited the hospital where Patrick lay recovering from his ordeal. He had suffered concussion, three cracked ribs and minor lacerations, and he'd been in a state of shock. He was still under sedation when Jason entered the ward but, hearing his brother announced, he forced himself into a sitting position, pulling on the rail of the bedhead with a grip which turned his knuckles white.

'Well, Jason,' he demanded. 'Did we beat the fuckers?'

8

Grant Locke spent the train journey to the west country with two women on his mind, all the while doing his best to fend off a third.

He felt rather guilty about Dulcie. There she was – indeed, *here* she was, sitting next to him and pressed up rather close – an attractive woman in her mid-thirties, a damn good secretary, a confidante, a clearer up of his personal problems. Where would he find a better employee or, for that matter a better companion? They got on very well. She didn't stand for his Yorkshire bluntness and he allowed her, within reason, to organise his life. This had seemed to Locke a very satisfactory state of affairs. Just lately, though, she gave signs of wanting something more.

'Shall I book us into a hotel for the night?' she'd suggested chirpily when fixing the Charlesbury trip, and he'd wondered if he was imagining that edge to the voice. 'It's a long way.'

'There's a saying where I come from . . . ' he began – and, as usual, she guessed which one it was before he could repeat it.

'Time's money,' she sang.

'Too bloody right,' he replied, as he always did. 'We'll get the late train back.'

He felt guilty because he knew he'd encouraged the closeness between them. Of course it was nothing improper, just the kind of fond relationship that so often builds up between a man and his secretary when they're much of an age, both attractive and much thrown together. It was good to exchange little smiles in front of a stranger, to share the occasional private joke. It was pleasant that their hands touched from time to time as they exchanged files. It meant nothing very much.

But now Dulcie seemed – well, the phrase 'on heat' came to him, but he cast it aside as offensive. She was nothing if not the model, well behaved employee. He respected her. Nevertheless she'd seemed perpetually flushed these last few days, as if in a light fever, and her manner was that of someone who seems always to have something she's about to say but can't quite express. This was unsettling. Locke knew that he musn't succumb, for both their sakes. Something would go wrong eventually and that would be disastrous. How to get her off the boil, though, was a difficult question. When he felt the light touch of her fingers against his he quickly removed his hand on the pretext of scratching his cheek. He wished they weren't alone in the compartment

They passed a small village which he thought he recognised, and then he saw, with a jolt of pleasure, the villa he'd designed there for the dog food millionaire Harry Stretch. It was plure play, but it met Locke's requirements of being small scale. *Human* scale, he called it. There were pitched roofs of weathered tile, a walled garden and an ornamental pond with stepping stones across it.

'I think I might nap for a while,' she announced, and before he could reply she had closed her eyes, inclined her head and rested it on his shoulder. She began to nestle.

He returned to his earlier thoughts. One of the women on his mind was, in fact, poised on those precarious stepping stones of life between childhood and womanhood – his daughter, Malibu. Sixteen rising seventeen, she was about to throw herself upon the world. The world, Locke thought, had better watch out.

Careful not to rouse the dozing Dulcie, who pressed into him as if he was a wellsprung mattress, he extricated Malibu's letter from his top pocket with his one free hand and shook it open:

> *Dearest Daddykins,*
> *Otiose manifestations of affection, and likesome suprafilial*
> *wotsits.*

He smiled, despite himself. A man who spurned the fanciful in his own life – indeed, who prided himself on down-to-earth northern grit – he couldn't but be proud of his daughter's imaginative flights, even when he realised that they were the most ridiculous balderdash. Where did she get that overcharged playfulness from? Actually he knew the answer to that, but he liked to think that there was some creative verbal impishness in himself which his bluff manliness refused expression. Grant Locke was the least impish of men, just as he was among the most rogueish.

> *Hypergrievous though 'tis t'admit, yr angelic offspring has perforce*
> *to declare her desire, nay passion, determination, grossest*
> *proclivity, to flee the godawful gaol in which she lies incarcerated*
> *at firstest opportunity.*
> *The reasons, some of which heartrendingly rehearsed heretofore,*
> *include:*
> *Item:– Miss Cooper is a beastly dragonette who breatheth fire*
> *Item:– Yr angel's noddle is a-bursting with knowledge useless*
> *as a comb on a bald man's pate*
> *Item:– Said angel is a-quiver on threshhold of Experience,*
> *Wisdom and a Brave New World*

It was one thing for a man to enjoy tussling with the world, the flesh and the devil, Locke thought, but quite another for his daughter to get involved in the sweaty wrestling-bout of life. He didn't have a romantic view about women, but he was solely responsible for Malibu, and he'd begun to realise that a few facts would soon have to be faced. Malibu herself was hardly in a position to face them.

As she herself had said rather more than once, you can't give a girl that kind of name and then expect her to become a dutiful housewife or a compliant secretary. It wasn't that Malibu had any improper ambitions, rather that she didn't recognise any limits to what she might eventually do. Since she wasn't the academic type, she might be in for a bitter disappointment.

On the other hand, Locke had to admit, anyone with Malibu's spunk and individuality, with that as yet undirected flair, had to have a fair chance of making her mark. Where she was concerned, he was a very soft touch himself. When she was home from boarding school he did find her exhausting, if utterly delightful. When she was away he almost worshipped her.

Prompted by her teachers, he had tried to encourage her to stay on at school. They thought she had potential, even if her record had been pretty wayward so far. She was an honest, open-hearted girl. She might grow out of her silliness. But her letters revealed that she was adamant, and Locke knew he hadn't the heart to insist that she stay on.

> *Might a loving, caring fatherkins help his doting angel find a primrose path in acting or tv work or any dashed thing that's not goddam boring like computer programming, bank clerking, stock-taking, lathe-turning (whatever that is), egg-packing, insurance, shop-working & WHATEVER KILLS THE SPIRIT!!!!!*

What was he to do? He should have been prepared for Malibu's declaration of independence, but he had refused to think about it. Now he had only a few months to come up with a plan. By the time summer came she would have thrown off her chains.

At this moment Dulcie slid across him and a hand came to rest on his thigh. She breathed deeply. Locke hardly dared breathe at all. He gingerly took the sleeve of her coat between his fingers and lifted her arm away. Her head burrowed into his chest in compensation.

The second woman on his mind he knew he shouldn't be thinking about at all. If he was to count Calla Marchant among his conquests he would have to spend time and energy on the project, and it was time and energy he couldn't really afford. The Duke's development at Charlesbury must, of course, be paramount. Locke felt confident about winning the contract, but that was force of habit: it was his way to expect success, and it had to be admitted that he wasn't usually disappointed.

Romantically his track record was more uneven, however, and Calla Marchant was a far from ordinary woman. It was sheer madness, but he hadn't been able to keep thoughts of her at bay since that evening at Willoughy Hall. How explain the effect she had on a man? It made him feel vital, that was the trick of it. It was as if she sucked up all the energy of the universe into that curvaceous frame and dispensed it little by little to whoever came into her ambit.

He knew that he had to have her.

• • •

The more sensitive of us have that precious knack of 'reading' other people – of discerning deep veins of character in the lines of a face glimpsed for the first time only a few moments ago. Understanding a building in the same way is a much rarer gift, while it is given to a mere handful of individuals to be able to fathom the secrets of a whole town after no more than an hour's stroll around it.

Grant Locke was one such individual. As he wandered the streets with his secretary at his elbow, taking notes, he noticed its outward dress and the agelines on its weather-beaten face, but he also quickly fathomed its history, its habits, its humour. He divined what made it tick.

'Neighbourhood pockets,' he dictated to Dulcie. 'Not a bad phrase, eh? It's a small town, but it's already fragmented. We'll keep that.'

Charlesbury, like most English towns, had changed with the times. That was what Dulcie insisted on telling him. She'd bought the guide-book. It had been a stronghold of the conquering Romans, an obvious place to choose because, as the guidebook said, it lay at the centre of major trade routes, because it had its own river, the Ower, and because the sea was less than twenty miles away to the south.

'To hell with ancient history,' snarled Grant Locke, who was famously impatient with it. 'I don't intend to base my plans on a barracks block. The Romans, Dulcie, were cruel, aggressive bastards.'

'Do I include that in the notes, Grant?'

The same guidebook, according to Dulcie, reported that Charlesbury declined when the Romans left in the early fifth century, recovered some of its status as a commercial centre in medieval times and flourished as never before in the Georgian period, thanks to its thriving agricultural community. Harry Willoughby's forebears had arrived when land was still cheap and had built their mansion on the further bank of the Ower, at a safe distance from *hoi polloi*.

Strolling down the high street, she was most aware of the Georgian legacy. There were fine, porticoed buildings in brick and stone. The town hall had large pillars at its entrance. The court house had a classical frieze along its facade.

'I agree with Henry Ford,' Locke countered aggressively. 'History is bunk. In architecture it is, anyway.'

'Forgive my ignorance,' she said, 'but isn't that exactly the opposite of what the Duke believes?'

'Of course it is. The Duke believes we last did things properly the day before yesterday. That's what reactionaries always believe – whether they're talking about motors or music or manners or morals. It just so happens he likes the buildings I design in spite of himself.

'Anyway,' he added, 'he's the last person to judge. Architecture and town planning are all about power. The Romans had power, so they stamped their boots all over Charlesbury. The Duke also has power, which is why he's planning to do the same – though in a much gentler way, of course. Harry's a gentleman. That means he wields his power without realising it. It's the most dangerous form of power there is.'

Their tour of the town was almost over. The railway station was in sight. Dulcie had snatched a glance at her watch and was wondering whether they had almost missed the last train. Locke knew what she was thinking, and he also knew they had another half an hour. He was sorry in a way. She was a shapely little thing and the experience would have been very sweet.

'And who calls the shots here?' he demanded. 'Apart from the Duke, that is.'

She was thinking how heated he became sometimes. There was a suppressed anger never far below the surface.

'Not your working classes, however rich they're supposed to have got these past few years. We've seen their cramped council houses on the outskirts. That's where they put the working classes – until the centres decay. Then they're allowed to camp in the ruins.

'Most of them have come in from outside, looking for jobs: they're factory fodder. And as for the genuine locals – well, they're mainy living in substandard cottages with damp bedrooms.

'It comes down to money, Dulcie. Filthy lucre. The money which the bankers and their cronies have got coming out of their ears. They've taken over the high street. The money of the national store chains. You've seen that monstrous Sixties shopping precinct with its squared-off buildings, its windowless squalor. And the money of the City brigade who've bought up all the olde worlde properties for miles around. What chance has the common man got against that crowd?'

'And the power of the architect?' she asked provocatively. 'The power to change all that.'

'Rubbish. Pure, unprocessed excrement. That's the kind of baloney people like Darl Pannick feed you with. They think they can change the world with a blueprint. Sure, we can make little alterations if we're lucky, but we're just fleas on the sleek fur of the powerful.'

They stood by the station, looking across at the land on which the Duke's new community would spring up. There were undulating fields, with a few sheep barely discernible in the dusk. A small stream, a tributary of the Ower, ran under a wooden bridge.

'And soon,' she said, 'all this will be churned up and the bulldozers will move in. I wouldn't like to be one of the locals.'

He grinned: 'Reminds me of a saying where I come from . . . '

'I know,' she said. 'Where there's muck there's brass.'

• • •

He had learned his anger at his father's knee. Not through emulation, but by observing a meek acceptance of poverty which disgusted him.

Home was a back-to-back in Dewsbury, the Yorkshire woollen town. The factory where his father worked was one of dozens. There were dozens of other employers who paid their men as badly, and there were tens of thousands of other men who came home sheepishly with barely enough to keep their families provided with scrag ends of meat and bruised vegetables bought cheap from the barrow at the end of trading. Even this existence was threatened as the clothing industry was squeezed by cheap imports, and first one mill and then another sold its insides wholesale to China and other even cheaper-labour countries.

But the other men raged, didn't they? The young Grant Locke knew they must. His father didn't.

'Why don't you ask for more money, Dad?' was his innocent question before he was old enough to understand the ways of the world. 'Why don't you tell them we haven't enough?'

And even though he was a naive child, he knew there was something craven and despicable about the answer he got: 'The Lord will provide, my boy.'

The Lord singularly failed to provide during the years he was growing up. He had two younger brothers and three sisters, and his mother was worn to the bone with caring and worrying. She didn't complain either, unless tears counted as some sort of criticism of the divine order of things, but Grant didn't expect her to. It was his father's job to put things right. He thought men had a duty to look after their families.

As soon as he was old enough he found work for himself. At first it was helping the local butcher. He worked as many hours as he could and gave the cash to his mother with pride.

But there was the anger, too. He made sure to present the money in front of his father. He meant it as an indictment. If his father was unable to provide enough, his son would show him how. He looked into his mother's face, willing her to understand, but she only smiled and ruffled his hair.

'Keep some for yourself,' she urged him, but he refused. It was a matter of principle.

They were a devout chapel-going family, and young Grant rebelled as if he were being asked to make a pact with the devil. Which is what he thought. The devil of mildness and meekness had taken over his home. This devil prevented any kind of improvement in his family's condition.

Once in his middle teens, he naturally gravitated towards political groups of the left. Anything offering change had to be grasped with both hands. He attended meetings of the Labour Party and the local Communists, and he distributed pamphlets around the town.

'Don't bring them things in this house,' his father warned him. 'We're not political in this family.'

'Not doing anything at all is a political act,' he replied scornfully, sure of himself in his young manhood. But he obeyed out of respect for his mother.

He was a good scholar, if inclined to be somewhat unruly, and he carried both his brains and his rebelliousness through the local grammar school. The beligerence he had acquired at home he took into the outside world with him, and it soon became a habit he couldn't break. If something was insisted upon, he wanted to know why it shouldn't be otherwise. If anything was forbidden, he demanded to know why he shouldn't do it.

'You'll never get on,' his father said, 'if you can't learn your place.'

'I'll be my own master,' he replied.

By the time he was eighteen, and bearing a clutch of 'A' levels, he was thoroughly his own man. He was working in a factory, as a draughtsman, but he knew his destiny was in his own hands. He studied at evening classes in order to increase his qualifications, for qualifications were a route to power. Grant Locke didn't intend to be any employer's plaything. He was a jaunty individual, stockily built with broad shoulders which met the world with a swagger. After you'd met him you didn't forget the experience. He had presence.

After about six months in the job there was unrest among the men over conditions. Grant, though he knew they were right, felt himself demeaned by joining in their protest. This gave him a sleepless night, worrying his conscience.

'You're for us or against us,' the shop steward said sharply. 'And the lads think it's against.'

'It's for,' he said. But he knew that what he hated was their habit of subservience. They would never face the management man to man and ask, with their dignity, for what was reasonable. They always had to hide behide their union to preserve their them-and-us mentality. They knew they'd never be on equal terms with their employer. Grant couldn't abide that attitude. It reminded him of his father. He *would* be equal, one day.

When he was twenty and had passed his examinations he left Dewsbury and took a job with a large architectural practice in London, renting a seedy terraced house in Shepherds Bush. He didn't pretend an emotion he could not feel. He left his mother with a sadness but his father with relief. It was goodbye to all that kow-towing to authority.

Now he was a young man in a hurry. He learnt everything he could as rapidly as possible. He read books and he asked questions. His employers began to take notice of this rather headstrong newcomer, who had the unusual combination of keenness and, at times, absolute bloody-mindedness. For Grant Locke didn't much care what people thought of him. He dressed casually, allowed his northern vowels to reverberate through an office of polite southerners and said what he thought. His saving grace was that he had an undeniable talent.

Women took to him without quite knowing why. He wasn't good looking, though that sharpness of eye made it plain that a little devilment was on offer. He never went out of his way to flatter – that was another form of subservience as far as he was concerned. Indeed, he never seemed very interested in what women had to offer. Take it or leave it, seemed to be his philosophy.

This off-handedness in one so obviously talented and knowledgeable was, of course, irresistible. He had no problem attracting women, and when they knew him they liked his ironic sense of humour and his self-confidence. They felt safe with Grant Locke, but not *too* safe. He was exciting in an undemonstrative way. He added spice to life.

For his part, he enjoyed a relationship with a woman, but he felt a strong desire not to be trapped by one. He was his own man and meant to remain so. Once he had lived with a woman for a few months he began to feel restless. He would precipitate some sort of a crisis which could have no end but separation, although in most cases, and strangely, they would remain friends afterwards. He could be brusque, his tongue was sharp, but he had a gift for friendship.

He was also lucky. When he was twenty-four the woman he was living with misread her calendar and got pregnant. Furthermore, she insisted on going ahead with the birth. This seemed, at the time, nothing short of a disaster. Malibu was a noisy, unpredictable baby, but that wasn't the point: he hadn't wanted any kind of baby, however angelic.

Here, though, his luck turned. His lover's parents gave her a sizeable cash sum – her dowry, he jokingly called it – at a time when property was still relatively cheap. They bought the house he'd been renting, and the young architect transformed it. Within a year he'd sold it for a large profit and bought two of the other properties in the terrace. He was on his way to big money.

Malibu's mother didn't stay, which caused Locke no great pain. As for Malibu herself, he simply shrugged and got on with life. To complain would have been to show subservience, to have played them-and-us with fate. He could afford child-minders and, anyway, he enjoyed being with his daughter when he wasn't designing other people's buildings or developing his own.

Without meaning to, he'd very soon earned a wide reputation for rescuing small areas of decaying cityscapes – areas such as his own first terrace. He was the philosopher of 'think small' architecture, vernacular architecture, helping the common man and woman to live in their own communities but in better designed housing. He campaigned to save run-down squares from the bulldozer.

What he was really doing was proving a point to his father. Never mind that his father was now dead, Grant Locke was proving that you could be working class and proud of it, that you could live in decency and look anyone else in the eye. He was still working class himself in his mind. He didn't want to escape it, he simply wanted the ordinary man and woman to be accepted on their own terms. In this way he was feted by the establishment but felt that he was carrying out a rebellion.

There was no reason why a gritty, down-to-earth lad shouldn't prefer classy ladies, of course. Locke's taste was for the exotic, the volatile, the feisty. He enjoyed drama. He could handle it. Consequently his relationships tended to be unstable and short.

'My father,' Malibu would instruct her friends, 'has more women than a tomcat has fleas – and they make him just as jumpy.'

It was true, and he liked it. It was good being an unrepentant tom. And when he began casting glances at Calla it didn't trouble him one bit that he might be playing with fire.

9

Fern Willoughby was in a typical attitude of repose, leaning against her Land Rover, hands deep in jodhpur pockets and surveying the fine English landscape before her. She was in the surroundings she loved. There was that distinctive cocktail of smells her fine nostrils adored – horse flesh, horse sweat and hay. She breathed a contented sigh, which hung visibly in the early morning air.

It was Badminton, the top trials of the season and the hub of the competitive horse world.The mad chases of the fox-hunting season were all forgotten: three-day eventing was an exercise in discipline and skill. Fern loved the hunt ' the headlong dash across crisp countryside, kicking up the fallen leaves and jumping over hedges to goodness knows what beyond – but she had other priorities just now.

She was a top-rate horsewoman, one of the best in a country which produces some of the best in the world. She wanted more than anything for this to be *her* season and she believed that at last she had the horse she needed. She'd named him Centurion. He was a gelding, but Fern's robust sense of humour made this remembrance of her first lover irresistible.

All around her were the delicious sights and sounds which herald a new event. Horses were being walked to prevent the stiffness which bedevils them on chilly days and to keep the highly-strung ones calm. Competitors in various stages of riding dress struggled out of comfy quilt waistcoats and into black riding jackets. Friends and rivals who hadn't seen each other since the last trials exchanged loud greetings in voices accustomed to hallooing across the acres.

'Fern!' cried a tall woman, leading a lean, long bay, which bore a striking resemblance to its owner. 'It's been a bloody age!'

This was Virginia Fripps, whose language was stable-like, but whose horsemanship was beyond question. She loped over to the Duchess, her overbite extended in a grin: 'Who's your mount? Are you still on MacCreadie?'

'No, Ginny. It's a surprise packet this year,' Fern replied, hardly stirring from her position, but running an active eye over the bay. 'Pugwash looks fit.'

'Fit, but hellish nervy this morning. Ralph reckons it's something in the oats.'

'Oats? He should know, I suppose,' murmured Fern. Ralph Fripps was quite an expert on one particular sort of oats, she had reason to remember. That was a couple of seasons ago at least, but loose boxes had never seemed quite the same to her since Fripps in flagrante.

'Must go,' said Virginia, choosing not to understand. There was a good deal of this not quite understanding in the horse world, and for good reason. 'Better walk round this bloody course first. See you after the fray, eh?'

Fern hoped she'd been right to bring Centurion. He was young, hardly seven years old, and had been trained for only three years instead of the usual four or five. But if he was to shine anywhere, it was in the wide open spaces of three-day eventing. He was too big, too long, for the indoor jumping events – couldn't turn soon enough in those tight spaces to approach the next jump at the right speed and angle. Those short, springy Australian horses were hard to beat in conditions like that.

He was a good-looking beast, almost black. Training him hadn't been easy. He had great spirit and a damnably soft mouth. He would respond to the slightest movement on the reins – the Duchess always treated reins as if they were of silk – but he had character, a mind of his own.

She had managed to harness his spirit for jumping and cross-country without, at the same time, breaking it. That was one of her greatest skills. She made her horses think and she instilled a vital trust in them. As for that exercise in equine ballet, dressage, Centurion's responsive mouth proved a wonderful compensation for his weight and size.

Fern was optimistic about her chances during the first two days of the programme, but she was keenly aware that the Germans, those almost unchallengeable experts in the art of dressage, could ruin her chances. She needed, therefore, to build a good lead in the showjumping.

Her husband, in his typically even-handed way, thought she had a good chance of being placed in the first three: 'German riders on German-bred horses,' he remarked to her. 'Damn difficult to beat in dressage. Fancy French business, anyway, dressage.'

She knew Willoughby was a good judge of such matters, but she rather objected to this assessment of her prospects. It made her even more determined.

'Just watch me!' she thought, and felt rather like a schoolgirl for thinking it.

She wasn't competing for the money, of course. The first prize at Badminton is a mere £50,000 – peanuts compared with the £250,000 it costs to buy a first class eventer, even before you start to add on all the extras. It certainly meant very little to the Duchess, whose habit was to give her winnings to her favourite charity, Riding for the Disabled. She was here for the buzz of competing, for the thrill of winning, for the sheer physical and public mastery of the beast beneath her. It was a buzz that took a long build-up. Merely qualifying for Badminton means years of success in lesser events.

Harry would be here too, to watch her, and that was a comfort. For all her physical infidelity, Fern needed the support of her Duke, relied upon the strength of his infinitely superior moral character to see her through.

Now she detached herself from the side of the Land Rover and began to unbolt the loose box. Her groom, Seamus, would be back soon with his opinion of the course. It would be a laconic opinion, for Seamus was the least talkative Irishman ever. The gift of the blarney had passed him by, but he was instinctive about horses as only his countrymen can be.

'He's a daycent mount,' had been his opinion of Centurion from the first. He regarded Centurion as the finest of all in the Willoughby stable. MacCreadie was past his best, he said. Trumper was a fearless hunter, but hadn't half Centurion's brains.

Fern led Centurion out, looking at him with an eye in which love and knowledge mingled with a craving. She had plaited his mane herself this morning while Seamus did the tail. His tautly muscled neck now streched out towards her, nuzzling into her shirt, the warm breath rising from his nostrils.

'The usual,' said an Irish voice behind her. Seamus was a small wiry man who looked strangely out of place anywhere away from horses. There was permanent grime under his finger nails and his curly hair was quite out of control. Strange how grooms could never practise their art on themselves, thought the Duchess.

She fixed him with an enquiring look, as if hoping to extract a rather fuller opinion.

'It's an Olaf Petersen course,' he elaborated, shaking his unruly head. 'And it's the usual.'

'I'll take a look first and walk him round later,' said the Duchess. Seamus was the only member of her staff who never addressed her by her title. But she didn't mind. From his sinewy wrists to his battered old boots, he was more at home with horses than with people.

She'd often wondered, of course, what he might be like in bed or, more to the point, in the hayloft. But sampling the staff was against Fern's own unwritten rules and she'd refrained from testing his mettle.

He was right about the course. It had the Petersen hallmark of being practically nothing but poles at every fence.

'Blimey!' The familiar Lancastrian voice of James Thornton fell boomingly upon her ears. 'What do you make of this one, Graciousness?'

Thornton loved to de-bunk titles, but it was all good humoured. Nothing, after all, could be quite as absurd as the title he won year after year for jumping at the Great Yorkshire Show – Cock o' the North.

'It's about time,' he stormed in his mock-serious manner, 'that these

Germans were told there's more to life than ruddy poles. Where's the imagination? What's wrong with fences, gates and walls?'

Fern grinned: 'Not too tough for you is it, Jimmy?'

'Even a Duchess,' he replied waggishly, 'can have her bottom smacked. But it's tough, all right. Precious little opportunity for flukes or beginner's luck.'

There was a marked difference in Fern as she walked about the course. She loved these early exchanges with other riders, the brisk greetings and the badinage. Her step had quickened. Her expression had grown more decisive. Those lazy green eyes were lazy no longer. She could sense competition in the air.

The place was filling up now. In the stands she could see mingling together the horse-mad little girls with their competitive mothers, the diehard, travel-anywhere fans of the riders and the truly knowledgeable followers of equine sports. Beyond, in an exercise ring, riders were putting their mounts over jumps, while others cantered in the wide acres of the Badminton estate.

'Fern Willoughby!' exclaimed a red-faced man wearing the blue and gold badge of an organiser. He carried a walkie-talkie set. 'So it'll be a good Badminton after all, by Jove!'

'You've said that to a dozen women already this morning, Mr Jaggers,' she laughed.

'But this is the first time I've meant it,' he insisted, pausing in his tour of inspection. 'How do you like the course?'

'Tough but fair. It'll sort the men from the boys.'

'No comment,' he replied, unable to prevent his eyes roving along those high buttocks fighting against the constraint of her jodphurs. The radio in his hand suddenly crackled and came to life, and he held it close to his ear. She made out the words 'public' and 'car park'. 'Alas,' he said, 'duty calls. Make sure you win, now.'

'I'll be giving it a damn good try, Mr Jaggers.'

Oh, the wonderful, stimulating atmosphere of day one at Badminton! There were stalls selling everything from Barbours to pocket flasks. Judges and show organisers walked around in their unofficial uniform of tweeds and twills, carrying shooting sticks, wearing checked hats or trilbies, examining the courses and chatting to the competitors. Sponsors wearing painfully new country gear bought specially for the occasion tried to look comfortable and at home.

Yes, sponsorship provided the big money these days, she thought. Fern had had offers in plenty from a wide range of enterprises – everything from electronic giants to food corporations. But she'd turned them all down. She didn't need the money and she certainly didn't like the idea of being associated with banana-flavoured drinks. The Duke was prepared to let Fern run the best stables his money and her skill could produce. It was in some way his compensation for her childlessness.

She knew most people in the horse world, and everybody who mattered. Since giving up her acting career it had become even more her stage. She liked the theatrical side of it all, the thrills and skills of public display. And it was the one area of her life where she risked everything on her own talents.

'I see Jarvis is back on Bloody Mary,' said the toothy Virginia, appearing from behind a coffee stall. 'Spent the last season in Germany. Must be in with a good chance.'

'As good a chance as in the European at Rotterdam?' smiled Fern. Jarvis had hopelessly misread the course that day, and even an almost flawless dressage couldn't redeem his poor showing in the jumping.

'He won't make the same mistake twice,' was Virginia's verdict.

As she saddled Centurion and headed for the acres reserved for exercise, Fern felt the old urge come through her. As in her young days on the Cornish heaths, she felt that she could ride forever. There was nothing she couldn't do while she could master her black mount. She loved to feel that smooth motion beneath her quickening to a canter. Even, so even. And yet so exciting.

'This time,' she whispered into Centurion's ear, 'is our time. Trust me.'

The ground rushed beneath the horse's feet, but Fern knew better than to tire him out. What she was doing was giving him the same feeling she had. The two would be working together, reacting together, breathing together. Their minds must be in tune. After a short while she slowed him to a trot, then walked him back to the course.

'We'll make them stare, won't we, Centurion?' she said, as she leaned forward in the saddle, to pat his shiny neck.

Harry Willoughby had arrived in time for the start of the jumping, and his expert eye had already assessed the difficulties of the course. He would be joining Fern tonight at Oakwell House, where they'd be guests of their friends, the Mason'Foxes. The Hon Marion Mason-Fox, sitting with him now in the Members' Enclosure, was joint mistress of the local hunt, and the Duke was a regular visitor during the season.

'No chance of a pre-off chat with Fern,' he said, watching the first competitor complete his round with four faults, 'thanks to these damn drug regulations.'

'It's the power of filthy lucre, Harry,' replied the Hon Marion, shrugging plump shoulders. 'Once they let the sponsors in, corruption was bound to follow. Where there's money there's foul play.'

'I suppose you're right.'

'Of course I am. It's human nature. I daresay it's the same in the world of architecture these days, what? God knows what depravity your Charlesbury scheme will foster.'

The Duke knew his dear friend too well to rise to her bait. He knew that she regarded his development plans as the thin end of the wedge for country landowners. Before you knew it there'd be new towns springing up all over the place.

'You'll have a chance to judge, I think, Marion,' he smiled. ' I saw one of the likely contenders for the Charlesbury project hanging round the sponsors' tent. I'll introduce you later, if you like.'

'Oh, I rather think not, Harry, thanks all the same.'

Willoughby had in fact been surprised by the sight of Langton Meredith at Badminton, but he'd scarcely had the time to think about it. And now any such thoughts were dispelled by the sight of Fern coming into the ring as number seven. There were no clear rounds so far.

What a fine figure of a woman his wife cut on a horse, he thought. That was what he always thought. The uncomfortable truth was that, however her appetite for him had declined, the Duke still wanted his Duchess body and soul. He watched with absolute concentration, almost jealous that all these others should see her too.

Her fair hair was looped under her hat. The green eyes sought out her Duke just once and then were blind with concentration.

There are different sorts of rider. There are the natural ones who seem to have total affinity with the horse and are without fear. The moors and the wide open spaces are for them. There are the masterful ones for whom riding is a battle of wills between horse and rider. They can come a serious cropper on their own arrogance.

And there are those like Fern Willoughby, for whom riding is a partnership, like dancing or making love. For them it's full of power games and tenderness, harmony as well as command.

Fern was in charge, but she never forgot that the beast beneath her could kill her with a single hoof, could run faster than her and jump higher. Hers was a passion for horses as something other, not as an extension of herself.

The bell went and she turned Centurion into the first jump.

'Nice,' remarked Marion approvingly. Like so many country folk she appreciated finer points she would have been hard pressed to have explained. You *knew* when a rider was in command.

Fern was taking it in leisurely style. The first round wasn't against the clock. She knew that rider's nerves passed along the reins to the horse like pulses on a plucked string.

'Clean pair of heels,' said Marion as jump succeeded jump. She was unaware that the Duke was quite oblivious to her. He had eyes only for his Duchess. He saw how, at the corner, she shortened the reins for the approach to the highest jump on the course.

Centurion left it so late you could hear the cognoscenti in the Members' Enclosure draw in their breath. Then he pushed on his mighty hind legs and lifted clean over it. Fern raised herself in her seat to lean forward and pat her mount's neck: 'The rest is easy, soldier boy,' she whispered.

'Walked it,' was Marion Mason-Fox's singularly inappropriate comment as Fern trotted Centurion out of the ring and the plummy-voiced commentator announced: 'Clear round'.

It was as if Fern and Centurion had broken the spell of the Petersen course. By the end of the round, there had been two more clears. Thornton had judged and cajoled his way round without faults. And Irishman Willie Gorman took Londonderry Air round clear with a jaunty devil-may-care style and at break-neck speed.

Harry Willoughby knew better than to talk to Fern between jump-offs. Those green eyes he loved would be far away. So he eased the almost unbearable tension by a chat with Langton Meredith, who had somehow made his way into the Members' Enclosure.

Meredith knew better than to push. He was prepared to be seen moving around the gathering and bide his time until the Duke noticed him. He didn't look out of place, dressed impeccably as usual and consulting the programme and the result listings with the air of a man genuinely interested in three-day eventing.

'Meredith,' he said politely. 'Hope I'm not disturbing you?'

Willoughby shook hands. Actually, he was pleased to find diversion from Marion's hearty commentary on each rider. Pleased, too, to have his attention drawn away from his no doubt suffering wife to other, less harrowing, projects.

Meredith feigned surprise with absolute success. And in that hissing way of his, he complimented Willoughby on his wife's equestrianism.

'Kind of you to say so.' The Duke was not the sort to discuss his wife with other men, which all things considered was lucky for her. 'You're here with one of the sponsors?'

The architect smiled his assent: 'A regular contractor of ours. Likely to be in on the Charlesbury project if we get it.'

'Indeed?' The bell went for the second round. 'Are you here for the three days? We must talk tomorrow. Dressage is a frightfully dull business – French idea now taken over by the Germans, you know. Might as well put a horse in ballet shoes and be done with it.'

Meredith laughed politely and nodded. Tomorrow would do.

The second round of the show-jumping was against the clock. It was Fern, Thornton and Gorman. The jumps had been raised during the break and the course examined by the supervisors.

Gorman went clear again, the luck of the Irish holding as no fewer than four poles rocked in their cups and settled back into place. Thornton's usually good-humoured craggy face was grimly set as he collected eight faults and found himself behind in time as well.

The crowd was with Fern. Maybe because she was the only woman left in the contest. Maybe because she felt they were her audience and she wanted to put on a show.

Halfway round the course she was still faultless but behind Londonderry Air on timing. She decided to give Centurion his head, slackening the reins to let his strong neck go forward. The look of concentration on her pale face was replaced by a flush of animation.

The risk she took paid off only in part. She ended four seconds behind the Irishman, but with four faults. They were collected as her fully-stretched animal brought his hind legs back rather low and knocked a pole off on the last jump.

She was at the top of the field, still in with a damn good chance. And there was compensation in the gasp from the crowd. At least she was giving them a show, thought Fern Willoughby. She enjoyed giving a show. And there were two more performances to go.

'Hardly ever seen her look so alive,' remarked the well-meaning but tactless Marion to the Duke. Sadly, Harry Willoughby reflected that this was probably true. How he wished she could win. His wife deserved a triumph of her own.

● ● ●

That night, at the Mason-Foxes' rambling and delapidated Gothic house, the Duchess found herself annoyed by the man who ran Rupert Mason-Fox's highly successful stud farm. She'd noticed him before, but tonight her nerves were on alert for the competition and she found him intruding into her thoughts.

On the face of it, he was pleasant enough company for a horsey country evening. For all her apparent fragility, Fern wasn't one to shrink from the details of mare-covering. In these circles, it was as common a topic of dinner conversation as the performance of the stock market and the unpredictability of the weather. It was the way he injected an almost unbecoming heartiness into everything which set her teeth on edge, his glossy brown eyes lighting up in a face beaten to a leathery ruddiness by long exposure to the elements. And it was the way she sometimes caught him inspecting her knowingly – as he might look at a mare in heat, she kept thinking. Well, he could think again, whatever he might have heard. The last thing she wanted was Ivan Durrocks pawing her. Her pale flesh quite shivered at the thought.

Harry Willoughby knew better than to expect much more than mere affection in bed from his wife that night. A woman entirely occupied by the passion of the moment, she had energy for little but the trials during these three days. In any case, he had grown accustomed to waiting for the first move to come from Fern. She ruled the bed just as he ruled everything else.

'You don't have to watch tomorrow,' she murmured, on the threshhold of sleep. 'I know how you hate dressage.'

'Of course I'll watch. I'll watch every moment.'

Her fingers briefly found his: 'You're a sweetie, Harry,' she sighed, as she dropped into her slumbers.

He was, however, much relieved the following morning to be diverted by some sensible talk with Langton Meredith while the dressage went on. Meredith was as keen to pick up the Duke's latest musings on the nature of architecture as he was to float, in the most circumspect way possible, his own ideas for Charlesbury. He was nothing if not shrewd.

'Sensible chap,' the Duke remarked to Marion and Rupert. 'Willing to listen as well as talk.'

'Well turned out,' said Marion as if she were commenting on a horse and carriage team. 'Thought architects were usually arty chaps.'

But the Duke had already ceased to listen. He had Fern in his binocular sights again. She was a long way off, but he got her in focus and gazed with pride. She was fixing her hair in the blonde net which kept it in place for the exact art of dressage, while Seamus, with unusually clean hands, made sure her tailcoat was free of fluff.

'Tell me about Durrocks, Seamus,' said the Duchess, who had been unable to get those appraising brown eyes out of her mind. Seamus would know. He talked to the grooms and the stable girls.

'A hard man,' Seamus shrugged. 'Tells the lads he knows what they're thinking. And he does'

Fern nodded slowly, apparently preoccupied with the exact angle of her hat.

'Shall we bother today?' joked Thornton, striding past at this moment.

'Feeling faint-hearted, Jimmy?'

'If it went on sheer beauty, your Graciousness, you'd walk it,' he offered gallantly. 'As it is, the Krauts will dance it.'

And they duly did, however much Fern demanded of Centurion,

reining him in with a fierceness the beast had never encountered before. 'Every point counts,' she kept telling herself. 'Don't even think about what the others are up to.'

Of course she knew that Thornton was right. The Germans came in first and third with Jarvis in second place, a tribute to his German spell.

'Fern's in fifth,' the Hon Marion's voice rang through the Member's Enclosure, giving Willoughby a sinking feeling. He'd watched his wife with fists nervously clenched and had tried not to notice how well the Germans were doing.

'Damn!' he said irritably.

'But that's all right, Harry,' Marion drawled, coming up to him and putting a consoling arm round his shoulders. 'If she does a good cross-country.'

'Not sure I can stand the tension,' he replied.

Neither of her main rivals from the first day did any better than Fern in the dressage. Gorman's Londonderry Air gave the distinct impression he thought such stuff was nonsense, occasionally giving an extra step or two, which looked like an Irish jig. And Thornton quite simply could not be graceful if he tried. He always felt foolish in dressage and his strong, mature mounts weren't the sort to have much truck with such a refined sport.

It was a restless evening for Fern. She was tired from the concentration of the dressage, and she felt edgy, irritable. She noticed with annoyance that Durrocks's hand hovered slightly over hers as he took her glass for a refill. Presumptuous shit, she thought. She overheard her husband say that Marion had extended an invitation to Langton Meredith, the architect, for tomorrow night. More socialising, she groaned to herself. Why couldn't she be left alone?

But she woke the next morning feeling better. Once again the atmosphere at the trials was of thumping hooves, saddle soap and joyous neighing. Tail coats were exchanged for sweat shirts, hairnets for pony tails. This was the life!

This, she knew, would be a proper day's sport across an adventurous and imaginative cross-country course designed by Captain Mark Phillips, a Badminton winner four times over. It was a big course, just made for the likes of James Thornton, but she found him in a resigned mood. His dressage showing had been so lamentable that he felt he had little to hope for.

'Unless Ginny Fripps will come home with me tonight, I'm a broken man,' he sighed.

'Don't,' she told him with a grin, 'be a bloody ass.'

Pacing up and down the Members' Enclosure, the Duke worried that some of the more treacherous jumps might unseat Fern. He had the highest regard for her riding abilities, but he had all the concern of a lover for her too.

'Wish I hadn't come,' he told Marion.

'But you *always* say that, Harry. And afterwards you're always glad you did.'

'Hm. Usually the stakes aren't so high,' he said, unanswerably.

Fern had no concern other than winning as she threw herself across Centurion. She leant forward to pull his silky black ears: 'We'll show them, my soldier boy,' she whispered. 'Please!' she added, for good measure.

The horse shook his mane, now free and unplaited, as if he too felt the thrill of it all. Most of the toughest fences, Fern knew from walking the course, were in the first half. There were fewer of them in the second half, too. That would be good for a gallop to make the time up.

Her nerves were tensed like the horse's. Her supple body, like his, was in competition shape. You can't enter Badminton in anything less than top condition, not if you're serious. This, she knew, would be a hell of a test for them all.

Willie Gorman rode in typical fashion, letting Londonderry Air inhale the electric atmosphere and go like the wind. With his usual luck, he escaped the penalty of too great a speed in the early part of the course. But over the later jumps both horse and rider grew careless. Water splashed up from the moat, a brick was knocked out of a wall.

Poor Ginny found her long and lean mount in a long skid as she cornered too fast from the gate. He refused the next jump and simply went round the one after that. She couldn't stop him. Marion Mason-Fox, watching the action through her field glasses, whistled long and low.

'Fripping awful,' she said, and bayed with laughter at her own joke.

Jarvis on Bloody Mary was miles outside the time limit and collected 20 points for a refusal. Two riders were thrown and three eliminated, including one of the Germans. Thornton, having decided with practical Lancashire good sense not to risk his horse's precious limbs in a contest he could no longer win, took it steady and ended clear with a time penalty.

Of the six horses home within the time limit, Gorman's was the best score so far. Only Fern, her placing decided by her surname, was left to jump.

'That coffin's a bugger, Fern,' Thornton warned as she prepared to set off.

The coffin was an aptly named jump ' a tricky three-element job, difficult at the best of times and made more so by the muddy ground.

'How do I tackle it?' she asked, psyching herself up for anything difficult that came her way.

'Just don't be scared of it.'

The flag came down. Fern's fair hair bobbed behind her in a pony tail as Centurion set off with a start. The horse was jumpier than she'd realised, but she sat him.

Through the flying mud and the wind, she rode like a woman possessed. Every eye was on her and she knew it. She had rarely felt better, higher. She was on the Cornish heath again, with the wind in her hair, with a low mist swirling in the gorse and the dark shape of a ship out at sea. She and the horse were one, as it always was in those days. She felt perfectly balanced, and it was as if she was in touch with every sinew of her mount, guiding him, coaxing him, forcing him. Was there anything she couldn't do today?

The Bank, the Maltings Wall, the Breaker and the Moat were all behind them. Centurion was running with victory in his nostrils. He was going unchecked for the Coffin and she was *not* scared.

'She'll hit the first element if she doesn't pull him in,' cried the Hon Marion. 'Oh! Good gel!'

Fern had taken up the slack in the reins just in time and Centurion had cleared the notorious jump. But his stride was broken and Fern knew it was all down to sheer speed in the second half. Dare she let him have his head to beat the Irishman?

She answered with her body, leaning forward and lengthening the reins: 'Go, Centurion! Go!'

There are a few precious moments in life when mind, body and spirit are perfectly harmonised. Expert horsemen and women may, if they are privileged, know that even rarer sensation of feeling that harmony extended to the animal they are riding. It's an experience which ever afterwards colours a life with an almost religious glow, and Fern felt it now.

They galloped together, horse and rider sharing power and need, straining for speed, kicking up great clods of earth, clearing the obstacles as if they had wings.

'Ruddy clocks running fast,' the Duke muttered, watching the vital seconds ticking away. 'God, I can't stand it.'

'Faster!' urged Marion, despair in her eyes.

But James Thornton, who had come to join them after his own ride, took in distance and speed in one professional glance: 'Break open the champagne,' he said. 'She's right on course.'

On course by all of three seconds, in fact, and she felt as if she could have gone on riding and jumping for the rest of the day and all through the night. The gold at Badminton, for mercy's sake! The very best prize there was! Fern reined Centurion in and sat trembling in the saddle as they all came clamouring about her.

Yes, she was trembling. It was the strangest sensation, a mingling of happiness, released tension, exhaustion – she didn't really know what it was. But she allowed Harry Willoughby to help her down, and she wept like a child into his shoulder.

'Bravo!'

'Congratulations, Graciousness!'

'Wonderful ride, darling!'

Everyone wants to applaud a winner, to somehow share in all the excitement and joy. She made her way to the rostrum slowly, cheered and embraced and back-patted all the way, so that she thought it would never end and would have been happy if it were indeed so.

That night there were celebrations at Oakwell House, with everyone in full fig. The interviews could wait until tomorrow. Tonight was for friends and intimates from the world of horses – though Langton Meredith was there, too, and obviously getting on famously with the Duke.

Fern was still strangely high, her pale green eyes unnaturally bright and seeming to reflect the emerald evening gown she wore. She had her gold medal, she had the virtual certainty of a place in the British Olympic team, but the adrenalin still coursed through her veins. It gave her a panting, rapacious air. She moved through the throng with a vibrant, glowing energy. She was like an animal with a hunger no amount of red meat can satisfy.

At last she could stand the agony no longer. She slipped from the house and out to the stables, flinging open the door so that it shuddered on its hinges. Ivan Durrocks, communing with his horses, never had a chance. He was prey, and he was about to be eaten alive.

Half an hour later, sitting breathless and trouserless on a bale of straw, still wearing his tweed jacket, shirt and tie, he was wondering what exactly had happened to him after the stable door swung shut. He'd been thoroughly punished, that he did know. Screwed, in a word. Savaged. And he would never forget her triumphant horsewoman's yell as she sat astride him, riding, riding, while his fingers played in the bush revealed by her hoisted gown.

10

'Pepito, you creep!'

It seemed to Neri Corinthian that she spent her life calling out to people who either ignored her or took so long responding that it amounted to the same thing. The reality was that people found it quite impossible to ignore that vital presence and that nobody could have reacted fast enough to satisfy her insatiable demands of the universe and the multitude of hapless creatures it contained.

'Senhora?' came a voice offstage – which meant somewhere down the hotel corridor.

Of course he didn't understand what a creep was. His English wouldn't go far beyond such essentials as 'Martini' and 'carry your bags?' and a warm 'thankyou' when he was tipped. But even if she'd known the Portuguese expression for the same general idea she wouldn't have used it. She needed a favour of the man. No, she needed *two* favours: one was that he hurry his legs along that expensive Persian carpet a little.

'Carnival,' she said slowly as he trotted through the door of her suite. 'Car-ni-val. Si?'

Yes, he understood. So far, so good. But if you were paying top rate at the Copacabana Palace, she reasoned, shouldn't you demand multilingual porters, maids and bellboys? No, Neri Corinthian, she answered herself. As if having once being married to a Brazilian wasn't enough (and on reflection it was quite enough) she'd seen plenty in the past few days to know that the gloriously rich trappings of this gaudy city hid a pall of poverty, ignorance and disease. Any money these people could pick up, good luck to them.

'I want ticket,' she said firmly, using the pidgin-English and the loud voice which both Americans and their transAtlantic cousins resort to when addressing the natives. 'For Carnival tonight. Tonight, yes?'

'Nao, señora.' A slow, extremely sad shake of the head. It was going to be difficult. Unless, of course . . . Neri knew this conversation backwards, in any language or none.

'I pay,' she stated. 'Money OK. Dinero.'

No, that was Spanish, for Columbus's sake. She rubbed thumb and finger together.

'Look.' She held out the guidebook. 'Pasarela do Samba stadium.' Damn the Portuguese language and damn the man who invented the samba. 'Tonight. Tick-et.'

'Nao ha neñhumas, señora.'

'Whatever that means exactly, Pepito,' she growled, 'forget it. Here's an advance.' She took a wad of colourful notes out of her handbag and thrust them into his hands. 'Im-por-tant, si?'

'Sim,' he replied, as if correcting her abuse of his mother tongue. 'I try.'

'Yes, you try little man,' she called after his retreating form. She wasn't used to being defeated and this *was* pretty important. Come to that, she wasn't used to having to rustle up tickets, whether for airline seats, hotels or any blasted thing. That was usually fixed by the kind of prestigious magazine or newspaper she worked for. With the Rio Carnival, however, none of the usual rules applied. Sure, *Vogue* had got her out here without any problem. Neri Corinthian and Conde Nast knew each other like an old married couple. They'd set her up in the best hotel in town, with a view right along the most famous stretch of beach in the world. After that, though, she was having to hassle.

She was just enjoying that view down to the beach, when the room telephone rang. A pity to drag herself away, she thought. She was watching beautifully muscled young men jogging along the handsome broad promenade with its wavy decoration of black and white paving stones. Others were doing press-ups in the heat of the afternoon, while graceful mulatas strolled by wearing bikinis so brief they might have been wearing nothing at all. The place was a hymn to grace, relaxation and the pleasures of the senses.

'Hello,' she barked into the mouthpiece. 'Is this a conversation I need?' The response to this was an appreciative chuckle whose owner she recognised immediately. 'Luis, you dog! How did you know I was here?'

'Through the Carioca grapevine, my angel.'

'Well, the answer's No, my darling. I have work to do. And, unlike creative artists, I have a deadline to meet.'

'You think I have no deadlines?' protested the third of her four husbands. 'How do you imagine I have a new novel published every two years if I don't work with discipline?'

'Ghost-writers, I shouldn't be surprised. And don't splutter in my ear like that, Luis. I never did connect those great sprawling South American fantasias of yours with the man I used to iron shirts for.'

'When did you ever iron a shirt in your life, woman?'

'Metaphorically.'

'Ah, you have this skill of ironing shirts metaphorically?'

'Call it magic realism, Luis,' she cackled. 'Stop badgering me for Crissakes! All I want to tell you is that I'm busy. You won't know what I mean because you always managed to keep me away from work on that wretched cattle station of yours, but I do earn a few dimes now and then snapping pictures with this little camera I have.'

'So you don't want to see Carnival?'

God rot his little word processing fingers, she thought. Neri Corinthian didn't enjoy being upstaged, whether conversationally or in any other way. It was even worse being upstaged by an ex-husband.

'You loathe Carnival,' she told him. 'You'd do anything to get away from it. You've not been to Carnival in twenty years. I know this, Luis.'

She also knew that one year, inexplicably finding himself in the city at Mardi Gras, he'd taken the extreme step for an atheist of entering the religious retreat which the Archdiocese of Rio organises every year at this time as an antidote to Carnival.

'My skin indeed crawls at the thought of it, Neri, but I have work to do, too. You don't know that I write for *O Globo*?'

'Any newspaper which encourages your wordy effusions, Luis, wants its collective head examined. It must also have a hell of a lot of spare space.'

It occurred to her, as she was enjoying putting him down, that perhaps this was a little unwise. He might, after all, be able to help. Not that she wished to lose face.

'You got tickets for the stadium?' she asked abruptly.

'Naturally. You're not telling me that you have problems in that direction?'

'Naturally not.' She began thinking damage limitation. 'Anyway, if we went together you wouldn't go home afterwards. That's what you're like.'

'That hurts, Neri.'

'It's what men are like, period, Luis. And it's what you're like especially. I have a good life now. I have no complications. That's how I like it.'

'Bravo.'

If she had wanted to see him again she would have rung him before she left New York. He would have arranged for his chauffeur, Miguel, to be waiting at Galeao International. Very cosy and very suffocating it would have been, too. Neri didn't enjoy being adored.

Instead, she had relished being alone in the wildness of Carnival. She'd arrived on Thursday, and already the spirit of the great event was in the air. She repeatedly ordered her cab driver to stop so that she could leap out and photograph small groups rehearsing their part in the grand procession.

It was, to her surprise, meticulously organised, with the director of each little platoon blowing a whistle to keep his dancers in formation as they advanced to the beat of drums. It took a fascinated Neri three hours to reach her hotel.

On Friday the streets had been transformed by the sudden appearance, like mushrooms after a shower, of flimsy kiosks selling masks, paper hats, streamers and confetti. Along Avenida Rio Branco, the business centre of the old town, Neri watched workmen feverishly erecting wooden barricades in front of the plateglass windows. Other people, meanwhile, were putting bright decorations up – gaudy rosettes, bunting, fluttering flags.

That evening she had seen the first parades through the streets, more noisy and extravagant than any she had ever seen, and there were more on the Saturday. But wait until Sunday, she was told. That's when Carnival erupts in all its full, outrageous glory.

Today was Sunday: 'Of course, Luis, you could promise to be on your best behaviour, I suppose.'

'I could, my angel. I shall.'

'Whoa! Let's not rush into things here. What exactly are you proposing?'

'An innocent evening, I assure you. A drink before we leave, perhaps. Back in time for your beauty sleep.'

There was a sharp rap on the bedroom door. She covered the mouthpiece with the palm of her hand: 'Come in.'

'Shall we say seven o'clock?'

Pepito, blessed creature, came quietly into the room holding a ticket. He gave it to her and stood waiting. Neri reached for her bag and gave him a few more notes. Still he waited. He looked honest enough, she thought, and the inflation of the cruzeiro was a joke. She kept giving him notes until he smiled, nodded and turned on his heel.

'Seven thirty then?'

'No, Luis,' she said forcefully. 'It's a bad idea. Don't waste your precious time on me. I shan't be able to give you the least bit of attention, and you know how you do crave constant fussing. It's the child in you.'

'Cojones!'

'That's Spanish, Luis. I understand it.'

'I'll call for you at seven.'

Damn, she thought, as she put the telephone back on its rest. That's what comes of indecision. That's what comes of nearly ignoring a well-tried maxim – never turn to an ex-husband for help.

Now, blast him, she'd have to get showered, dressed and ready and be out of the hotel before seven o'clock.

● ● ●

There's no event in the world as colourful, as throbbing with energy, as the Carioca Carnival in Rio. More than half a million people – men, women and children – deck themselves out in the most beautiful, outrageous costumes they can make or buy and they sing and they march and they dance for hours and hours until night becomes day. Then they sing and march and dance again for days and days and days.

In their blood the genes are Indian, European and African, and this spicy stew creates the fluid grace, the lovely light tan skin, the lustrous eyes of the typical Brazilian, male or female. This lucky breed will look ravishing, desirable to the opposite sex or to both, whether in skimpy swimwear, elegant evening attire or even something casual slung over slender shoulders and revealing the curve of a waist, the sleekness of a thigh. But the ultimate in sensuous extravagance awaits Carnival, when these beauties come encased in vivid ostrich-plume headdresses, shimmering sequined drapes, rhinestone collars and belts which glitter with sequins.

Neri's ticket gave her a coveted place in a VIP booth, but she was forever rushing out of it to take a picture close up. Just when she thought she had quite enough in the can (for how could she expect anything better than what she'd already filmed?) along would come, twisting and drumming and clapping, yet another incredibly turned out troupe – indeed, nothing less than a fancy-dress army.

'This is all one act?' she enquired, unbelievingly. She'd been told that the different samba schools had their own complete parades, with dancers, bands and floats. What she was watching pass slowly before her rounded eyes certainly had a common theme – the sea, with ships and sailors and mermaids and enticing grottoes and human waves and much, much else – but it had already been going on for more than half an hour and the end wasn't anywhere in sight.

A local behind her laughed, showing gleaming white teeth: 'This one is quite good,' he said, speaking a faultless American English, 'but it won't win. There'll be better ones.'

'You watch the crowd,' his wife advised Neri. 'You see how much they cheer and then you know.'

How the hell they could cheer any louder, Neri thought, was darned hard to imagine. They were packed into the stadium, standing shoulder to shoulder and swaying with the beat of the passing bands. They were drunk – some of no doubt on *batida*, that ruinous concoction of rum and lime with ice, but a good many more on straightforward animal excitement. There was a palpable joy rocking round the stadium. You could hear it, see it, smell it.

'But excuse me.' A small, swarthy, balding man with some kind of European accent shifted himself a little closer. 'You talk of winning. This is a competition?'

'Oh naturally,' the Brazilian said. 'These people would kill their grandmothers to win.'

'And how do you judge?' the other persisted.

The Brazilian shrugged and averted his gaze. If that's not the crummiest question I ever heard, Neri thought, I'm the Sheikh of Baghdad.

'They weigh them before they start,' she said in a helpful tone of voice. 'Then they weigh them again at the end. The gang who've sweated hardest get the prize.'

'Really?' he asked. 'No, no, that can't be right, I think. I suspect you're pulling my leg.'

She laughed hoarsely: 'You think I can get down that far?'

Another samba school at last came into view. It was led by a huge float which depicted the Brazilian flag. Neri thought that it fluttered in the breeze until she saw what caused that rippling effect: each colourful band of the flag was composed of a dozen brown-skinned girls under a canopy of richly-hued feathers.

'I shall explain,' said the Brazilian woman. 'The first float sets the theme, yes? This one depicts our country's Independence. Behind the float come the officials of the school – those serious gentlemen in suits who are bowing rather too much.'

'They're bowing to the jury,' her husband pointed out. 'So perhaps it can't be too much.'

'Then you see the *porta-bandeira*, the girl standard-bearer, who wears the fine lace dress from the 18th century. And with her is her escort, who dances like a whirlwind. All these things are obligatory.'

'This is all traditional,' threw in her husband. 'It's been this way for more than seventy years.'

'Ha!' laughed the European mirthlessly. 'Seventy years can be a tradition? I laugh at that, rather.'

God help me, Neri thought, I shall brain this guy if I don't move. She picked up her camera and took a few shots of a jazzily attired percussion band, madly improvising on a curious set of improvised instruments. She'd never heard such a medley of sounds in her life.

She remained close to the procession for a while, not bothering to take more pictures but soaking in the sights and the sounds. Perhaps, after all, there *was* something about the rhythm of the samba. A group of young girls shimmied by, waving parasols, and they were followed by a swarm of tiny tots, grinning all the way between their ears, jogging up and down to the beat, their costumes brilliant reds and greens and yellows.

In and among this vast cast of players flitted the platoon leaders, keeping the marchers in step, the musicians in tune, the singers in time and in key. Each school had written its own song and the crowd seemed to know it off by heart. They raised their voices as if in an exotic hymn of praise. Some of the poorest people in the world had created this unforgettable spectacle, Neri remembered, magically transforming despair into glory.

'Oh, my God!'

She had been giving herself up so completely to the sensuousness of Carnival that she hadn't noticed Luis until he was almost upon her. He was picking his way towards her, that she was sure, even though the size of the crowd made his progress very slow. An evening with her ex-husband she could not endure. Why the hell *should* she? What were the divorce laws for if you had to spend the rest of your life fending these tiresome creatures off?

Shouldering her camera bag she hurried back to the booth and accosted the swarthy European: 'If it's not too late in our relationship to ask,' she said, 'would you mind telling me your name?'

He stared at her, perplexed.

'N-a-m-e,' she spelt it out. 'Or aren't names a tradition where you come from?'

'I'm Pannick,' he replied. 'Darl Pannick.'

'Ha! Did I ask your name? I asked your name. And what did I get?' She laughed merrily. 'I got your name! Darl Pannick, for Crissake! Where did they give you *that*?'

He only frowned.

'No, it doesn't matter. This matters: we're together, yes? We came here together and we're going back together. Do you follow me?

'You *don't* follow me, but I'll explain in due course. Right? You Darl Pannick, me Neri Corinthian. Yes? Like Tarzan and Jane. Am I talking to someone from another planet, for sweet Jesus?'

It seemed that she was. Nevertheless, as Luis approached, Pannick allowed her to slip an arm through his and to puff a little blow at his temple in an obvious demonstration of affection.

'Hello, darling,' she cooed to the third of her four husbands. 'Meet Darl. An old friend of mine.'

'Boa noite.'

'No, darling, Darl's not one of yours. He comes from somewhere fascinating where for some mysterious reason they don't speak a word of Portuguese.'

The two men shook hands, dumbly. Neri Corinthian in this mood (well, in any mood, actually) didn't leave a man much room for interruptions.

'And Darl is just taking me off to dinner.'

'Bravo!'

Perhaps bravo, she was thinking. Perhaps a frying pan and fire job. But all she needed, please Lord, was to get outside and escape. She leant forward to kiss Luis on the cheek, noticing how warmly his hand pressed hers. Why didn't men understand the word *finito*? she wondered.

'Adeus, Neri.'

'So long, Luis. Keep embroidering the yarns. This way, Darl baby.'

As he dutifully followed her through the crowd she heard him say, she hoped not too loudly: 'Sorry, but what was your name again? I didn't quite catch it. Nellie, is it?'

• • •

If she heard about one more wonderful, innovative modern building, she told herself, sinking her teeth into the sweetness of a *baba de moca*, she would pour the remains of the Madeira over the man's head. She savoured the separate flavours running over her tongue – syrup, coconut milk and cinnamon.

'And the very same Oscar Niemeyer also built the magnificent stadium where you and I met this evening.'

Then she would hit him with the bottle for good measure. Come to think of it, didn't the stadium count as one more building he'd mentioned? She reached her hand stealthily across the white lawn tablecloth only for him to pounce first, seize the bottle and fill her glass.

'Darl, baby,' she laughed, 'you don't know what a close call that was.'

'Escaping from your former husband?' he asked, topping up his own glass. ' I understand completely.' He sniffed the wine appreciatively, with the air of a man who knew what his nostrils were telling him. 'You're by no means the first lady for whom I've rendered that service.'

'Is that so?'

But yes, she could believe it. There was, after all, more to this guy than she had first imagined. Much more. The architecture, true, was beginning to drive her half way to the funny farm. If put under hypnosis, she reckoned, she should be able to describe, draw and evaluate every last building in the city of Brasilia. But she would never have been enticed here, however stunning the rooftop view over Ipanema beach, if she hadn't found something fascinating in his combination of awkward, innocent earnestness with a kind of shop-soiled worldliness. She'd wanted to find out more.

'Well?'

'Well *what*?'

'Spill the beans, you teasing fart!' she exploded with a guffaw, so that coiffured heads turned towards them. 'Don't sit there picking at your plate like a fastidious parrot. Bring on the runaway wives!'

He was a man who had improved with age, she thought. The skin had grown leathery, with deep creases where he laughed and frowned, but it was still vital. She thought it would be warm to the touch. His voice had descended the register and gave a comfortable grainy sound. And if he was small, much shorter than she was, it didn't show across a restaurant table.

'I'm not a man to divulge secrets,' he said quietly, but smiling. 'And how could I tell so many stories when the meal is nearly over? I can think of at least six examples.

'Although,' he added, pushing his plate away, 'only four of the ladies were still married at the time. Would you like coffee?'

He couldn't have been more teasing if he tried. *Was* he trying? Neri was beginning to think that there was a deep streak of know-how in Darl Pannick which he took great care to conceal. She certainly couldn't resist prolonging the evening a little while longer in order to pump him for stories.

'And two cachacas,' she added, as the waiter took the coffee order. Pannick raised his eyebrows. 'Rum,' she explained. 'You'll like it.'

What she didn't explain was that this Brazilian speciality was made from sugar cane and was incredibly strong – ideal for loosening the tongue.

'You're a dark horse, Darl,' she grinned. 'Tell me, are you married?'

'I have been.'

'Once?'

'No,' he said, lowering his eyes with an expression of shame. 'Four times.'

'Hey!' she bawled, thumping the table with a fist, then reaching forward to take his hands in hers. 'No kidding! Really four? Then *snap*!'

● ● ●

'It was Lucio Costa who designed the city,' he was explaining. 'There was this grand competition when Brasilia was only a wonderful, abstract idea . . . '

You, Neri Corinthian, she was accusing herself, are the most blind, stupid, bird-brained, cretinous clown that ever clicked a Minolta. Consider the evidence: One, despite more experience of the matter than it would be decent to admit, you thrust yourself into the company of a complete stranger of the opposite sex. Two, on the strength of a man having had four wives you invite him to your hotel room. Is this the action of a sane woman?

' . . . and Costa won it, lucky fellow. Made for life! Another notable figure was the landscape architect, Roberto Burle Marx, who created . . . '

Three, you pump practically neat alcohol into his veins to get him talking. And then what in God's name does the bastard talk about?

' . . . an illusion of naturalness among the concrete. But Niemeyer was the presiding genius. Everywhere you meet his buildings. You've seen pictures of the cathedral dome, perhaps? It's a clever deceit. Most of that vast structure is under the ground . . . '

She stood up. 'Keep talking, Darl baby,' she said, making for the bathroom. 'I can hear you.'

Can I hell? she thought with a chuckle, pulling on the light cord so that the extractor fan whirred into life. She sat on the lid of the toilet pondering what to do. There was the sarcastic approach, but she was sure it would pass over his head. She was dealing with one of those monsters, an intelligent man with no sensitivity to language. There was the weepy approach. Momma's so tired, headache, something awful happened back home. But the man would probably alert the entire paramedical services of Rio de Janeiro. He was an enthusiast. Or there was the violent approach. Shout very loud, throw open the door, grab him by the hair. Maybe that was the best plan in the circumstances.

The crazy thing is, she thought, opening the door and bracing herself for action, is that I *enjoy* architecture. I like going round buildings. I've photographed hundreds. Just skip the earnestness, baby.

"And I can't possibly do business,' he was saying, his flow unchecked, 'with a man who deals in drugs.'

'You *what*, Darl?'

'With this Diego Morais. He's a corruptor of the world's youth.'

'No, no, start again. I missed the details.'

Shit, why was she such a sucker for gossip, dirty stories, bad news? *Get the man out!* something inside her screamed.

'Who's Diego Morais?'

He shook his head, jumped from his chair and opened the fridge. It was incredibly well stocked.

'More cachaca?' he asked, taking out two miniatures. He poured them and handed her a glass.

'I think I've perhaps been speaking too much,' he said. 'You're tired.'

'Tell me about Diego Morais.'

'You're being polite, Neri. Enough of this architecture. I know that it's a passion with me. I've seen a world without proper housing.'

'For God's sake,' she shouted, rising to tower over him, 'I genuinely, honestly, cravingly for Crissakes want to know about blasted Diego frigging Morais!'

'Okay, okay.' He sat down on the bed and took a sip from his glass. 'Okay.'

There was experience in the lines of that face, she mused. Forget the surface babble, the apparent naivety, this man had been around. He'd suffered. He was the kind of man who couldn't be trusted to cross the road alone but who knew things the average man and woman hadn't dreamt about. She sat next to him and took a good swig from her own glass. Lord, it was sweet!

'Diego Morais,' he said, 'is one of the richest men in Brazil. No, one of the richest men in the subcontinent. He has more wealth than his country has debts. This means that, among other things, he has land – vast areas of it.

'Brasilia, as you know, is a new capital city, created out of the wilderness only fifty years ago. Morais owns most of the land around it, and he has plans to develop it. I mean grandiose plans. Rich people are never content with what they've got, haven't you found it so? He needs architects. I have a certain reputation, and therefore he invited me to Brazil to inspect the land and to discuss what I might do with it.

'I can assure you, Neri, that I came full of optimism. It seemed to me a great opportunity, perhaps the greatest I shall ever have. But then I learned the story of Diego Morais, which is why I shall have nothing to do with his scheme. Nothing at all.'

'He's a crook?'

'An inadequate word for scum like him. He traffics in cocaine. That's where he made his fortune. That's still the basis of everything. Do you think I could design buildings which have their foundations sunk into human corpses, wasted lives?'

He scowled with disdain. Darl Pannick was, she thought, rather a noble figure after all. She'd met more than a few dull moralists in her time, but this fierce declaration of principle was something else altogether. Damned admirable. Rather attractive. How positive it was, clearly distinguishing black from white! Why did her own energies never turn in that direction?

'A top up?' she suggested, sliding from the bed and kneeling to open the fridge door.

God, what a glorious mess her life was! One day in New York, the next in Rio, probably the next in Tokyo or Delhi or Prague or wherever some editor with fancy ideas and a big cheque book wanted to send her. She loved the mess, the not knowing where she'd be or what would happen to her. Sure, it made for problems. With Barney, for instance:

that kid treated her like some inadequate who occasionally stumbled into his life and who he was vaguely, irritatingly responsible for. But the sense of adventure more than compensated – for ever new places, new people.

'Uh-huh?'

She felt a hand grasp her shoulder and there, leering above her with a bright twinkle in his eye, was a Darl Pannick who had obviously decided that it was away-with-dull-care time. He'd taken off his jacket and loosened his tie but, more to the point, she saw with a sensation rather greater than surprise that he'd slipped off his socks and shoes and, for good measure, dropped his trousers, too. While she was still taking this in, his free hand grasped the tab of her zip and split the back of her dress open right down to the base of her spine.

'Bejayzus!' she said simply.

'Don't think I don't know,' he grinned, expertly freeing the dress at the shoulders so that it slid down the length of her body, 'what you've been up to all evening.'

'You *do*?'

'How you've been teasing me.' The slip was next to go. It shimmied over her flesh. 'Your little game.'

'Game?' she enquired. 'And may I point out, Darl baby, that my thighs are killing me.'

He laughed, spun her round and lifted her up. She saw the huge swelling in his underpants, the black hairs coating his legs.

'How you string me along,' he said. 'How you insist that I keep talking about these buildings.'

'I insist?' The room was warm enough, but she did feel kind of uncomfortable standing in front of him in bra, panties, tights and high heels. She kicked the shoes off.

'Do you think I don't notice how, every time I pause or try to change the subject, you persuade me to keep on talking architecture? All the while that I'm throbbing with desire?'

'Now hang on, Darl baby – '

'That we're both throbbing with it, Neri.'

He yanked his tie over his head and ripped off his shirt to reveal a chest matted with the darkest hairs she had ever seen on a male torso, even including a few prodigious examples in the New York zoo. He was a little satyr! She found herself looking for his trident and tail.

'Is that so?' she asked, narrowing her eyes. Life's glorious mess! Neri Corinthian made an adventure out of anything, that's what they said. And they were damn right.

'You gotta catch me first!' she yelled suddenly, and made a sprint for one of the large armchairs at the end of the room. He gave chase, scurrying after her, squat legs pumping, feet pounding on the carpet.

'Ha!' he cried, breathing heavily.

As he came round the back of the chair she was away again, this time leading him a merry dance round a standard lamp. He was gaining on her, but she leapt nimbly over a glass coffee table, her long legs clearing it easily. Pannick's feet skidded on it as he jumped, and it turned over with a crash.

Jeez, it was a long room! She didn't know when she'd had such fun since the assault course in her old school gym.

'Nearly!' he gasped, as she skipped behind a sofa. 'But not quite!' she panted triumphantly.

What a man he was, after all. Neri liked spunk. She liked energy. She liked humour. And here it was in abundance. What larks! '

'Geronimo!' he bellowed.

She laughed hoarsely and slowed her pace. Of course she knew that, for all these fearsome war-whoops, Pannick was a gentleman – she'd never tolerate a man who dared try to force her. She could end the game here and now, *finito*. Oh yes, she could easily do that. But she eluded his grasp yet again, hearing his breaths coming more heavily now.

As she skirted the armchair for the third time she slipped and fell to her knees. Pannick made a grab for her ankles and then, ever so slowly, regaining his breath, reached to the top of her tights and began to pull them down. He gave a little contented murmur and she chuckled. She turned on to her back as his hands tugged the material over her thighs, then past her knees. As the tights came off completely he bent low and kissed her toes.

'Bad move, sucker!' Neri yelled and, scrambling to her feet, raced away down the length of the room.

'Come back, you witch!'

It was a more leisurely game of cat-and-mouse now. They were both gasping for breath. She stood behind the sofa, feinting to go this way and that. He perched on the balls of his feet, the dome of his head soaked with perspiration. Suddenly, he threw himself forward and over the back of the sofa, but he'd misjudged the strength of his leap and finished on his head, feet stuck in the air.

'Ole!' cried Neri, and, seizing the elastic of his pants, tore them off in one movement.

'Yeeeow!'

He rose slowly to his feet with tears in his eyes. *Homo erectus*, she thought. Why am I such a sucker for this species? Why could I never resist its horny charms?

She padded away with a glance over her shoulder. No, he wasn't about to give up. He was pacing after her now, rather than running. It put her off her guard, rather. She was too slow going round the standard lamp, and he managed to seize her foot and trip her up.

This time he came closer to her, folded himself in behind her and, with one leg flung across hers, reached for the clasp on her bra. This man had had plenty of practice. The garment was off in three seconds flat. Well, she mused with pride, not so very flat. Her breasts stood proud, the nipples hard and thrusting.

'Submit?' he asked.

'Like hell!'

She was off again before he even guessed that the battle wasn't yet won. Round the sofa they went again, and round the lamp standard. But now she was handicapped by her own ample breasts, bouncing in her flight. He finally closed on her when the only piece of furniture she could reach was against the wall behind her – and that was the bed. Neri threw herself upon it, extending her limbs in a gesture of surrender, breathing deeply.

He tumbled after her, lying on his back, his chest rising and falling: 'Submit?' he asked again.

'I submit.'

To her great surprise he was among the tenderest lovers she had ever known. As they recovered their composure and lay warm and glistening from the chase, he slowly ran a finger between her breasts and down into the softness of her belly. With the flat of his hand he rubbed gently in a circular movement, seeming to draw all her feeling into that one spot. He soothed her with fingers which spoke of knowledge of the flesh, and of the exploration of more knowledge yet to come.

He slipped his hand inside the material of her knickers, pulling and coaxing so that, as she arched her back in compliance, they slid down her sleek thighs and away down off her feet. She closed her eyes and felt his lips mumbling her nipples, one by one, moving against flesh so hard it must surely crack. The smell of him was good, too, infusing the salty stench of their sweat with a musty tang. She nestled her nose into the skin over his ribs and sucked the aroma into her nostrils, greedily.

It was slow and oh, so sweet. She felt, and yielded to the feeling, as if she were being prepared, nerve by nerve and cell by cell, for the ultimate sensuous feast. Each course, delicious in itself, only increased her appetite for the next. She wanted to move on, urgently, but he knew better, holding back the eruption of that pleasure even as it intensified. He pleasured and teased, teased and pleasured. And so it was that she came ravenous to the feast, clamorous, frenzied, loudly demanding.

Afterwards, as they lay back, quietly panting, she asked him (thinking, *What in God's name am I starting here?*), 'Did you ever, in London, come across an architect called Calla Marchant?'

'I did,' he said. 'Only recently. A striking young lady.' And with eyes, he nearly said, very much like your own. But women didn't appreciate that kind of comparison. 'She has, I think, a growing reputation.'

'You think she's good?'

Pannick grinned: 'Please, Neri. No more talk of architecture. You're becoming obsessed.'

He nuzzled his nose into her solar plexus and began to surprise her all over again.

11

Perhaps it wasn't such a bad assignment after all, Martin Kingsley was beginning to think. You weren't expected to file copy every day and you did get to romp with randy duchesses and eat at the Groucho Club.

Today, at any rate, he was at Groucho's. It was the number one private club for media types, but these were generally people on a far higher plane than himself. Stars, not hacks. Looking about him now, he could see Will Self with a crowd at one table, Damien Hirst holding forth with Melvyn Bragg at another. As an outsider he would normally curl his lip when talking about these pretentious folk. Now that he was, briefly, one of them he felt pretty chuffed.

Quite why Langton Meredith should be a member, he couldn't tell. The place wasn't exactly bursting at the seams with architects. 'Pick me up at the RIBA and we'll take a cab to my club,' Meredith had suggested on the telephone. Kingsley had imagined a dull, cavernous sort of place with faded blueprints on the walls, and Meredith had kept him guessing during the short taxi ride from Portland Place to Soho. He'd had a self-satisfied little smile on his face as they turned into Dean Street.

'Sorry if this is a bit tedious for you,' he said. 'I suppose you eat here practically every day.'

'Well, no,' Kingsley replied, recovering his poise just in time. 'Not that often, actually.'

So what was this meeting about? One axiom he'd never had reason to doubt was that there's no such thing as a free lunch. Meredith wanted something. That, in turn, put Kingsley on his mettle. No journalist wants to be used. If a story's worth running, it's because he's evaluated it for himself. He's the one who understands news values. Therefore he's on guard for the smart con, knowing that the world's full of shysters who thrive on any publicity they can get. That's how journalists have earned their reputation for being cynical. It's the attitude they need for survival.

Over a preliminary drink, while they munched nuts and the largest olives Kingsley had seen in all his life – 'Something of a speciality here,' Meredith murmured, 'as you probably know' – they still made polite conversation about the weather and the state of the roads.

During the first course Meredith turned the conversation to Fleet Street – 'So called. I practically wept when the *Express* crossed the river and there were no papers published there at all' – and over the Dover sole they discussed the latest scandals, political and sexual.

Towards the end of the main course, right on cue, the architect threw out a casual remark about Kingsley's current project.

'Are people being helpful?' he asked blandly.

Which means, Kingsley thought, interpreting effortlessly: 'Are the rest of the buggers bending your ear the way I'm doing now?

'They're all playing for high stakes,' he replied. 'It makes them cautious.'

What he didn't intend telling Meredith was just how nervously everyone seemed to be behaving. Kingsley had begun to discover what a crazily hypercharged world he'd blundered into. When he took the story on he thought it was a dry subject, all planning laws and local authority reports – he'd have to learn to understand red tape and statistics.

But the British architectural world was in a state of ferment right now, with modernists and traditionalists at one another's throats, and the Duke's Charlesbury scheme had brought the issues involved to screaming pitch.

'Understandable,' Meredith said. 'And I don't suppose any of the major practices can avoid taking part in the competition, whatever their reservations.'

A poor effort, that one, Kingsley thought. Interpretation: Will you please tell me who my rivals are going to be?

'What kind of reservations?' he asked, deciding to put the pressure on the other man for a change.

'Oh, I'm not sure, you know, that all of the best qualified firms see eye to eye with the Duke in every respect.'

Smarmy bastard, Kingsley thought. As far as he could tell there was hardly an architect in the whole country who saw eye to eye with the Duke. Sure, quite a few enjoyed his restatement of classical values, but he hadn't met a single one who didn't worry about his Little England, back-to-the-past mentality.

Meredith organised the pudding and coffee: 'Anything I say today is off the record, okay?'

So the man wasn't after publicity for himself. Therefore today's target must be the opposition. He was about to spill some dirt, but wouldn't take responsibility for it.

'Sure.'

Couldn't launch straight into it, of course, Kingsley knew. Too crude. There'd be a diversionary tactic first.

'Just seen Melvyn Bragg over there by the window,' his companion said with fake surprise. 'Have you been watching his latest series? Wish the fellow would get himself a decent barber, but otherwise a great performer, eh?'

They were stirring their coffee when he began again: 'I like what you're doing, Martin. I think your newspaper's got vision.'

Jesus, Kingsley thought, he must really be desperate if he's trying that kind of flattery. He sipped his coffee, enjoying the pungent aroma as the steam rose up his nose. He was damned if he was going to say thank you.

'If I can be of help,' Meredith continued, 'I'd like to work with you as much as I can. As you'll appreciate, I have many a great many contacts in the architectural world. I know the business and I know the people.'

'What do you have in mind,' Kingsley asked abruptly.

'Oh, not money, Martin. Don't misunderstand me. I'm far from wanting any financial gain. It's just that, if you'll forgive me, this is a difficult area for the layman.'

That's right, Kingsley thought. Don't trust the amateur. The cry of the professional through the ages. And then the amateurs – that's the rest of us – find we've been screwed crosseyed by these effing pros.

'Let's just say, Martin, that I'm available whenever you need any background. You know where to find me, and I'm contactable at any time.'

'Thanks.'

And now the punchline. There had to be punchline. He allowed the waiter, obeying his host's gesture, to top up his coffee. One, two, three . . .

Meredith laughed awkwardly: 'To prove that I know the people in my profession inside out,' he said, 'here's a little something for you. It may not be in your line, you probably won't want to do anything with it, but do check it out.

'You've come across Bunny Simkins?' he asked.

'Met him last week,' Kingsley said. And how unlike the rest of the breed, he thought. Relaxed, open, generous. 'I liked the man.'

'Yes, yes, charming,' agreed Meredith, playing with his coffee spoon. 'He's a first-rate architect, I don't think you'll find anyone to disagree with that. Most charming.'

There was a silence, and Kingsley let it spread. Some of his best stories came from indiscretions when people frantically tried to fill awkward silences. Not that Meredith's indiscretions would be anything but prepared.

'It's only a pity, isn't it, that he hasn't found fulfilment in his, er, personal life. You know what I'm referring to, I take it?'

Damn it, of course he didn't know. And, yes, he wanted to know. That was human nature.

'No, I don't.'

'Well, please don't just take it from me, Martin. Check it out. You'll find something a bit distasteful I'm afraid.

'I'm not trying to play God here, or to make grand moral judgements. If grown men like the company of young boys, that's their problem as far as I'm concerned. But sooner or later it's going to become an issue, if you see what I mean.'

You unprincipled bastard, Kingsley thought. Of course I see exactly what you mean.

'Good heavens, look at the time!' Meredith exclaimed, waving his wrist near his face. 'Must get back to the office. I've so much enjoyed your company, Martin. Keep in touch!'

• • •

Eaton Square is one of those tiny pockets in the dirty great overcoat of London where most people would like to live. Even those who swear they hate the noise and bustle of the capital, those who tell you how the quality of life has gone downhill faster than a sewer rat into one of the city's drains, will shrug their shoulders and admit that there is an indefinable something about Eaton Square.

It's not really indefinable at all. There's space and light, there's a central garden with trees where the non-residents aren't allowed to set foot and there are large terraced buildings which are beautifully proportioned in the Georgian manner. Even the traffic's mannerly here.

People who commute to London every morning and say they're glad to see the back of it every evening, people who say they can never imagine living in the great metropolis, make an exception of Eaton Square. Living there would be different – if they could afford it.

For of course you need money to live in the square, plenty of money. Wealthy businesses and foreign governments are in possession of much of it. Extravagantly well-heeled individuals spread themselves over the floor of a single house and pay through the nose for the privilege.

The Duke of Mercia owned a whole block and lived in one end of it when he was in town. In keeping with the square and with the Duke himself, the entrance was understated: a black six-panelled door under an elegant spider's-web fanlight with glazing bars of cast lead. You climbed a flight of four steps to reach it, and then you rang a bell. If it was a sunny May morning and the birds were singing in a big blue sky, you felt pretty damn good.

'Think big and think wild,' Calla recited to herself for about the ten thousandth time in her life as she waited for the door to open.

A secretary led her into an airy vestibule where a tall arched window spattered light onto red tiles. At least, she thought, she wasn't gate-crashing this time. There were water-colour paintings on the walls and, left alone, she stood close to examine them. They were a mixture of town and country scenes, and she recognised views of Willoughby Hall and of this house in Eaton Square. Presumably they were all of properties owned by the Duke.

'Miss Marchant.'

Harry Willoughby had hesitated for a few seconds before making his presence known. If asked, he would have said it was so that she had a chance to see him first, to prevent any embarrassing element of surprise. That was what his breeding dictated. The simple fact was that he had enjoyed gazing upon this strikingly beautiful young woman in the vitality of her prime. It wasn't lust, or certainly not admitted lust. Willoughby didn't allow himself to feel that way about women. He'd been brought up to think it distasteful, and that was how he did regard it. But it didn't escape his notice that she had a combination of looks and figure and bearing which only a eunuch could fail to admire.

'Your Grace.'

And also, he thought, taking her hand, wonderful eyes. Because he wasn't harbouring lustful thoughts he was able to gaze a fraction longer than might otherwise have been the case, and Calla caught that attraction. Fifteen-love to me, she thought, suppressing a little smile. She certainly hadn't come here to be intimidated (that Chanel suit with its black and white dogtooth top made exactly the forceful statement she wanted) but the Duke's lingering glance made her bolder.

'Let's go to my office,' he said.

Anything less like an office it would have been hard to imagine, but it did contain a leather-topped desk with a telephone and piles of paper and was obviously a working area. It was a large room, with broad sash windows, delicately patterned pale green wallpaper and a broad frieze with classical decorations.

They sat in deep leather armchairs a few feet apart and the Duke rang for coffee: 'What can I do for you?' he asked, with the pleasant smile of a man who is graciously giving you his time but only so much of it. Half an hour, to be precise, although seven minutes of that had already gone.

'I owe you an apology,' she said.

He raised his eyebrows. What is it about the English upper classes that can so effortlessly suggest aloofness, condescension and a cool detachment? Those eyebrows were saying that Harry Willoughby really couldn't think what she was talking about. Or, if he did remember, it was of no concern whatsoever. Life had moved on. How could such a petty thing signify one little jot among all the important business he had to deal with? Fifteen-all, she conceded.

'I'm afraid,' she lied blatantly, 'that I misunderstood the nature of your event at Willoughby Hall.'

Eating humble pie had never been Calla Marchant's scene, but there was a time for everything. She wasn't exactly wearing sackcloth and ashes, she had to admit, but she'd come to play the role of the repentant sinner for all she was worth – and it was as calculated a piece of behaviour as the gate-crashing had been in the first place. It was her only conceivable excuse for arranging to meet the Duke face to face.

'I'm not in the habit of barging in on other people's parties.'

He smiled: 'That, I'm sure, is their loss, Miss Marchant.'

An elegant reply. What was going on in that ducal brain? Probably he was thinking of his next board meeting or of some high matter of State protocol. This grand scheme for Charlesbury, Calla thought, had come five years too soon for her. Yes, she was the up-and-coming architect, but she knew that her track record was a short one. The Duke owned stables. He knew all about bloodlines and how it was best to trust in proven quality.

'And as far as I'm concerned,' he added generously, 'the matter is forgotten.'

In came the coffee. Willoughby gazed reflectively out of the window as his guest was served. It was a fine morning and the company was exceedingly pleasant. Yes, most exceedingly pleasant. He rather wished that he had more than fifteen minutes left to enjoy it.

'Mind you,' Calla broke into his reverie with a suddenness which startled him. She waited until he turned, fixing him with what she knew was a distinctly saucy smile. 'I did wonder why I hadn't been invited in the first place.'

His lips were a joy to watch, she thought. They gave perfect expression to the turbulence within him. Of course, her remark was preposterous. It was rude, uncouth, ill-mannered, terribly bad form and all that tosh. How dare she question the guest-list of the richest duke in the kingdom! But if you're going to behave badly, she told herself, make sure you do it determinedly and with no end of style.

'Did you?'

It was the perfect non-committal reply, banging the ball back into her court with heavy top-spin. But she wasn't fooled. She had seen those lips. She wasn't about to be thrown out on her ear. Harry Willoughby had registered the insolence of her remark, but he'd responded to her sassiness, too. The game, she thought, was neatly poised.

'I'd hate to believe,' she continued, with the merest suggestion of a wink, 'that any architect might be handicapped by her sex.'

'Her *sex*?'

'By the fact that she's a woman.'

'Ah, I see.'

Dammit, she thought, he's blushing. A little worm of an idea sneaked into his brain for a second, I do believe.

'Certainly not, in my own case, Miss Marchant. I must admit that very few women architects have been brought to my attention. Indeed, I do believe that you are the first. But I can assure you that I have no prejudices whatsoever in that direction.'

She sipped her coffee. She had already achieved her main objective of forcing herself into the Duke's presence and making sure she was someone he didn't forget. Thirty-fifteen to me, she calculated. Dare she push it further and mention Charlesbury? Aw, go on! she urged herself. Sock it to him!

'And when it comes to your new development, would a woman architect be considered suitable?'

He frowned, stood up and went to the window, hands clasped behind his back. It was a little while before he spoke.

'Forgive me if I seem somewhat reticent, Miss Marchant. I'm most concerned not to show favour, or the reverse, to any individual before the close of the competition. I do intend it to be a fair and open competition.

'I shall only reiterate what I said at Willoughby Hall in February. That was, I do believe, after you had left.'

Okay, she thought. Thirty-all. He obviously couldn't resist it. And who could blame him? What an unforgettable exit that had been.

'Whoever I choose to design my new community at Charlesbury will need a wide range of skills – technical, financial and social skills, to name but three. It will have to be a remarkable plan, and I'm looking for a visionary architect to devise it and carry it through.

'Does that answer your question?'

Had be been a little *too* plain-speaking? he asked himself. He had no wish to be cruel. In fact he very much took to this attractive and spunky young woman. He'd hate to send her away unhappy.

Calla declined to flinch. Was that 40-30 to the Duke? Well, to hell with the scoring! This was only a practice game. She was still in training and getting better all the time. She had until September to be match-fit.

'I suspect that we may interpret the answer in different ways, your Grace,' she replied with a smile, rising to leave. 'I'm delighted to hear that the competition will be truly fair and open.'

'Naturally.'

He showed her to the door himself, reflecting that half an hour had passed with unusual and highly regrettable speed. She was a highly competent architect, he was thinking, but so very young. After her unexpected visit to Willoughby Hall he'd made discreet enquiries. She certainly had talent. No, that was an understatement: she was bursting with talent. But the experience he needed? That wide range of skills?

'I've enjoyed our meeting, Miss Marchant. Thank you.'

He watched her clip down the steps and cross the road to her car. To his discomfort and shame, what stuck in his mind as he closed the door and returned to his office was not her architectural credentials but that wonderful pair of legs.

• • •

They'd never been quite sure of Harry Willoughby at his hardy Scottish boarding school.

'Willoughby is troubled by ideas,' remarked his housemaster in the staffroom.

He was wrong. Willoughby was delighted by ideas. And if the school wasn't sure about Willoughby, *he* wasn't sure about the school.

He wasn't sure that cold showers were necessarily good for the soul. He wasn't sure that unquestioning obedience was necessarily a good training for later life. And he wasn't sure that team spirit wasn't another name for keeping the less fortunate out of your club.

'Doesn't like rules, that's the problem with the future Duke of Mercia,' said the commanding officer of the school cadet corps. And yet it was difficult actually to catch him breaking any. There was just something about that rather aristocratic look of ever-so-slight surprise which made those who lived by rules feel rather silly.

It was Harry Willoughby's bad luck to have more originality and more sensitivity than was good for him. He wasn't quite an intellectual, and no true artist would have called him an aesthete, but in these surroundings he looked very much like both. He asked questions when he was supposed to accept the status quo. He was interested in drama and paintings.

At home it was much the same. During the school holidays at Willoughby Hall his father, fully 30 years older than his still strikingly lovely mother, would attempt to instil in him the high seriousness fitting for a young man who would one day take on great responsibilities. The old Duke wasn't fond of some of the ideas his son had picked up from God knew where.

'Rubbish!' was his perpetual cry as he tried, without the slightest success, to talk young Harry out of some preposterous notion. 'Can't be so!'

The Duke's concern was to give the lad a firm grounding in the vast enterprise which was the Willoughby Estate. 'Educating Harry' became his great passion. He took the lad to the Estate's offices in London, which administered the entire interests of the Dukedom, from farms to investments, from grouse moors to a chateau in France.

'Built up over many generations,' he told his son, 'and capable of being frittered away in one. Take heed.'

He'd have been horrified to watch young Harry performing in the school debating society. Here the rather diffident young man came into his own. Whatever his personal feelings on a subject, he seemed able to debate both sides of any question. Or more.

'Willoughby can always find a dozen ingenious arguments in favour of any proposition,' his head of English remarked. 'And he's quite capable of demolishing every one of them just as effectively.'

He fitted in well enough at school. Willoughby really wasn't a rebel. He played sport to a reasonably high standard and he passed exams without much trouble. 'A good egg,' was the general opinion, 'even if he does keep himself to himself.'

He wasn't clubbable, that was another problem. He hated being made to conform to a stereotype – which is what the cadet corps CO really objected to. Harry Willoughby didn't much like the sons of the upper classes. He didn't fit. He found their prejudices obnoxious. He thought they were philistine. 'If this is Society,' he thought, 'count me out.' But he knew he couldn't count himself out of it for one minute.

How he hated the mob instinct! Where this part of his makeup had come from he couldn't guess, but he was a fierce champion of the individual, and especially of the underdog. He was incensed by injustice, and in the hothouse atmosphere of a British public school he found plenty of it.

'He has a tendency,' one of his end of term reports remarked, 'to champion lost causes.'

What this meant is that he couldn't stomach the brutish, half-condoned bullying which is part of British boarding school life. It made his blood boil. He would find himself, violently angry, stepping in to protect the victim. Then he would quickly disappear, embarrassed by any show of thanks.

Although he was generally liked, few of the other boys would have claimed to know him. He was too detached, a bit of a dreamer. There was something intensely private about Harry Willoughby, as if he was a visitor from another world. As, in a way, he was.

What does a teenaged boy think when he surveys the huge estate in the country, the wild moor in Scotland and the chunk of real estate in Eaton Square which will all be his? Harry Willoughby accepted that he held it in trust for future generations, but he also longed for something more. His young man's vitality bridled at the restrictions of his life. Not for him a life of shooting and fishing, though he enjoyed them both well enough. Not for him a life of petty housekeeping – restoring a wing or a summer house when they deteriorated, keeping a weather eye on the estate.

How excruciatinly boring! How unfulfilling!

Dear God, he thought, there had to be something more, something which would use all his energies and his bright dreams.

'Not a problem your ancestors ever had, sir,' Molly the old cook remarked as the young heir sprang one of his occasional visits on her kitchen – 'for cake and chat' as he always put it.

'There was always another pretty girl round the corner in them days,' she added. 'Or in the kitchen, as I remember. Always a new horse to buy, a new bishop to entertain. And London! Well, as you know sir, there were so many parties at the Palace . . . '

Parties at the Palace still demanded the attendance of the Duke of Mercia. The family was part of the royal circle. 'Why can't I be like other men of my class?' the young Duke-in-waiting asked himself. 'Why do I find this scene stuffy and tedious? Why can't I get pleasure from nodding and bowing and cutting ribbons at opening ceremonies?'

There wasn't enough in life for Harry Willoughby, that was the truth. He left the Gothic towers of Glenstone knowing he must find some spice to add to the heavy ducal banquet which was spread before him. He mustn't simply inherit, he had to make his mark.

And then, as if in answer to prayer, he found himself in the magical surroundings of Cambridge. It was bliss. One morning, in a dawn mist, he danced deliriously by the banks of the Cam, thanking his lucky stars. He was suddenly happier than he'd ever been in his life. The very air seemed fresher. It was another place of privilege maybe, but the University encouraged people to *think*, damn it! Better still, that was the whole point of being there. He felt drunk with freedom and, especially, with a new hope.

Something else struck him, too. For the first time in his life, he met people whose lives were utterly different from his own. The working classes, true, were still having trouble shouldering their way in, but – incredibly – many of these students had mothers who actually worked, sisters who didn't put in a few hours at Sotheby's and fathers whose names weren't to be found on any list of directors.

And there were girls, too. Everywhere – on bicycles, wearing Laura Ashley dresses, reading books on the banks of the Cam. They simpered less than the cousins he had known. They had opinions. Most of them were intelligent. They occasionally drank too much. And they had sex.

Harry Willoughby had sex, too, but here his background and his great responsibilities got in the way again. The sad truth was that, though Harry Willoughby was born and bred to be a Duke, he was attracted to the sort of girls who would never be accepted as his Duchess. He liked a bit of spirit. His nose picked up the scent of danger, of forbidden fruit. He wanted girls who were a bit of a laugh and a tiny bit naughty.

If only he were a true rebel, he would have followed his instincts. But he was his father's son, and he resisted. He dutifully dated girls of 'the right sort' and occasionally coaxed them into bed. But after the thrill of his first few conquests, he found them unexciting.

'Trouble is,' he explained to his friend Andy Morris, 'they've got "the right sort" stamped all the way through them, just like Brighton rock.'

With his male friends, of course, he could pick and choose as he wished. Willoughby didn't mix with the public school crowd. They'd begun to seem unreal. He took up with people who shared his spirit of adventure, who wanted something new from life.

Andy Morris was a left-wing zealot. He was going to change the world. He was a crinkle-haired ex-grammar school boy with an explosive temperament and a laugh to match. Next to the calm and measured Willoughby, Andy Morris was like a stocky, powerfully- built windmill. Willoughby only smiled where Morris roared with laughter. He questioned where his ebullient friend declaimed manifestoes. He admired girls where Andy boldy engaged them in conversation.

They were an unlikely twosome, but they shared a zest for life. In Willoughby's case it was carefully hidden, covered by his formal manners and suppressed by that call to duty, but they shared the thrill of exploration which only young people can know. Something better was coming. For Morris it was the dawn of a new socialist era.

And for Willoughby? Something equally democratic, but a little more tangible.

It was a visit to his friend's family during the long vacation which was to open his eyes to what later became his main obsession in life – people and the buildings they live in. It was an experience he was to remember all his life.

Willoughby's days had been spent among the privileged classes, among their money, their manners and their mansions. Home was the late eighteenth century classical beauty of Willoughby Hall and the acres of its estate. The Victorian walls of Glenstone had been built by the rich in a different but equally splendid style. At Cambridge, he'd enjoyed ivy-mantled quads, chapels and dining halls where the sons of the rich had been sent for hundreds of years.

Now, with Morris, he saw the other sort of home, the other sort of estate. His friend's father was an over-busy, chain-smoking GP with a practice in the heart of Birmingham, a once great Victorian industrial city now made ugly by the twentieth century homage to the motor car. Massive flyovers and car parks drove the people underground into subways. There was a shopping centre called the Bullring which seemed to signify, he thought, the death of the human spirit.

The differences in home life didn't surprise Willoughby. He was sensitive enough to know that he'd led a remarkably luxurious youth. The meals cooked by Mrs Morris herself, the queue for the bathroom in the morning and the proximity of the neighbours he could take in his stride. After all, this was a respectable, middle-class home.

The shock was outside its walls.

With Dr Morris the next day he visited estates of system-built flats. They'd been put up only fifteen years before, made of pre-cast concrete, with thick ropes of copper holding them together. Already they were ready for demolition. Concrete walkways in the sky were ill-lit and covered in graffiti. The lifts were out of order and the staircases stank. The concrete slabs sometimes dropped off the outside because the copper corroded.

Inside, conflicting smells greeted Harry Willoughby. One was soapy, the other rotten: 'They're all the same, these places,' the doctor said in a matter-of-fact tone of voice. 'Plagued by a black mould, because of the damp. Covers everything. The housewives use carbolic to get it off. Six months later it's back.'

The memory of that day stayed with Harry for ever. Why hadn't he known? The warm stone walls of Cambridge couldn't expunge it. Like the black mould, it kept coming back. He had discovered another, grimmer world, far outside his own.

That was why, when his father died early in his second year at Cambridge, he knew what he was going to do.

'It's farewell to wild dreams of the future, old chum' Morris said with a sly grin, 'and back to harsh reality.'

They were strolling through the Backs on one of those mornings when Cambridge seems like a universe on its own, spinning amid blue skies and the corn fields of some of the richest farming land in England.

'Nonsense!' he replied, thinking how like his father he must sound. 'Wild dreams are just what money might be able to buy.'

Shortly after his visit to Birmingham, he'd been touring the Willoughby estate and had noticed the appalling condition of the tied cottages in which his father's tenants had been living. Wasn't that just another form of deprivation? Now, returning to Willoughby Hall as the owner of everything he surveyed, he toured the cottages and spoke to his tenants. He consulted architects and builders.

'These people need proper bathrooms, damp courses and new roofs,' he told a meeting of the Duchy officials at the London offices. 'I'd like the work carried out as quickly as possible.'

There was an uncomfortable silence, broken by Jenkins, the Willoughby estate manager and a man with the face of a weasel and the voice of a rasp: 'I think your Grace will find they don't like the idea.'

'But I spoke to them. They need these things.'

'With respect, sir, I see these people almost daily. They like to be agreeable to you, but the truth is, they want to live the way they've lived all their lives. The one thing they would hate is disruption. You'll end up paying a million quid for ingratitude from the lot of them.

'In fact, I've a letter here signed by most of those on the Willoughby estate itself, asking for the work not to be done. It's a bit scruffy and not very well-spelled, I'm afraid, but as you can see, it's clear enough what they mean.'

Willoughby read the letter, agreed that the matter of the improvements should stand over to the next meeting and journeyed home a puzzled and rather uneasy man. He felt he was being made a fool of by somebody, somewhere. And he was damn sure he was going to find out.

He found out.

'Harry,' his mother greeted him on his return. 'I've had two of the girls from the cottages over here weeping their eyes out. They've heard you intend doing up the cottages, selling them off and forcing out those who can't afford to buy. They're stupid people, my dear. Sort it out. I can't be doing with all these tears.'

Cunning little shit! thought Willoughby. But why's he done it?

A few days later he called the estate manager to his office.

'I don't know how long you've been robbing my father, Jenkins,' he said icily, 'but you've had your last penny from this estate.'

'Don't understand, sir.'

'In which case you may take the matter to the courts if you wish. You'll probably deny that you and a certain local building firm have been raking in cash for work that's never been done on the estate cottages. Spare me the explanation. I know the facts. Now get out.'

'But your Grace . . . '

'Simply get out, Jenkins. Now!'

He'd been surprised by his own resolve. He learnt in that moment how rigorous he could be when it was a matter of making dreams come true. And it inspired him to carry on in a similar vein, with further schemes to improve his estate.

Architecture became his passion. He'd always been interested in buildings, to be sure, but now they became a symbol of how society treated its members. Willoughby was supporting the underdog again, and he was doing it in the most level-headed way he knew.

It became a crusade. He read everything he could on architecture. He took pictures in the towns he visited. He talked to architects and, most important of all, to the people who lived and worked in their buildings.

'Quite nutty, of course,' outraged architects would say when he savaged one of their designs.'Doesn't understand a thing about it.'

When the idea for a new Charlesbury came to him he knew the reactions would come fast and furious from all directions. Harry Willoughby could take that. He was used to being called a dreamer, and he didn't give a damn.

It was one hell of a dream, after all.

12

Becoming the greatest architect of your generation wasn't exactly a piece of cake, Calla decided ruefully, swerving to avoid a bus stop which seemed to have moved several feet into her path, whatever an Einstein might have to say about the possibility. If it was a shade easier she certainly wouldn't be driving home from the office at three in the morning, her vision playing tricks with her.

'You can turn everything off, Adam,' she'd told her personal assistant at six o'clock. 'I'll be finishing in a few minutes.'

'Says you,' he replied disbelievingly. 'Last night I came past at eleven and your light was still burning. That little ol' computer will blow a gasket.'

It was a harmless remark, and it was true to the last syllable, but Calla found herself rounding on the poor man in a blazing fury: 'Since when was it your business to check up on my movements, for God's sake! Is that what part of your salary's for, maybe?'

Too much bending over the drawing board, not enough sleep – you didn't need to be any kind of medical genius to make the diagnosis. But how else could she crack the problem?

Trying to plan something as ambitious as the new Charlesbury, she was discovering, demanded deep reserves of flair, inventiveness, concentration and self-confidence, quite apart from the run-of-the-mill professional skills she'd acquired over the years.

Each morning she started with a blank sheet and a vague but powerful dream of what she hoped to create. By lunchtime she had a rough outline, incorporating the essentials of the development – the houses, shops and leisure facilities, the factories and offices – linked by a revolutionary road network to service them in a way nobody had quite thought of before.

By the evening it had collapsed. The individual parts hadn't fitted. Then she worked desperately, not wishing to believe what her instinct told her, that she would have to begin all over again.

This blankness, she consoled herself, had been the curse of creative artists down the ages. Surely Michelangelo sometimes doubted whether he had the vision and the stamina to turn the Sistine Chapel ceiling into the masterpiece it later became. Didn't Tolstoy have teething problems with War and Peace? And Beethoven can't have had the Ninth Symphony complete in his head before he started putting the first notes on paper.

The difference was, she acknowledged with a growl of frustration, that every one of those artists had got the bloody job done. With little more than three months left, she'd begun to think she never would.

All the street lights were out as she turned her Porsche into the drive, emphasising the glow behind the curtained main room of the house.

'Please don't let him be waiting up for me,' she begged whichever all-hours deity might be on duty. 'I'm definitely not fit for the human race.'

As she pushed open the front door she heard low music and, above it, the murmur of voices. Two voices, at a guess. So much for deities, she thought. Remind me to cancel the subscription.

The first thing she saw in the room was Jason with a cigarette in his mouth, sitting on the floor and propped against a leather pouffe. The second thing she saw was Peta Abercrombie, also smoking a cigarette but sprawled the length of a sofa with one hand dangling onto the carpet. Their bodies were languid, but their eyes were bright.

'What in the name of glory's going on here?' Calla demanded.

Jason drew lazily on his cigarette: 'Precisely nothing, darling. You've met Peta?'

'The last time I met Peta I hoped it was the very last time,' she declared venomously. She could feel one of her rages coming on and she felt no inner resistance to it whatsoever.

'Charming,' Peta said, swinging her long legs from the sofa and sitting in a rather defensive posture.

'It's gone three in the morning, for God's sake!'

'Time,' Jason said languidly, 'has no meaning to me whatsoever. What does three in the morning mean? I suppose it means it's the time when dear Calla arrives home.'

'It means,' she exploded, 'that dear Calla's drained, exhausted, washed out, gutted. It means she's ready for her damn bed.'

'Which is upstairs,' he said. 'Where you probably left it. Only I don't remember. I don't think I was in it at the time.'

'Bastard!'

She reached for the nearest thing to hand, which happened to be a brimming glass ashtray, and hurled it at him. He held his hands in front of his face as it struck the ground by his feet and a chunk of glass leapt off and smashed against the wall.

'I think I'd better go,' Peta said.

'Stay where you are!' Calla yelled. 'You stay! Don't let me ruin the party. I'm the one who's going.'

Jason slowly rose from the floor and took an unsteady step towards her: 'You've got it wrong, Calla,' he told her. 'There's nothing going on here. We're just smoking together. Old friends having a smoke.'

He stepped back swiftly as he saw her reach for a porcelain bowl. Jason had seen Calla's tempers often enough, and thrilled to them even as he'd shrivelled in their heat. She seemed to vibrate with the passion, every sinew straining, every fleshy contour deliciously highlighted. But this one was the mega-temper.

'That's a Wedgwood,' he said.

It curved through the air like a frisbee, glanced off his shoulder and hit the floor with a brittle sound, smashing into a thousand small pieces.

'Well, really,' Peta commented, raising her eyes to the ceiling.

'Shut up, you bitch!'

Calla stood over her, and it was no contest. Absolutely no contest, whatever rules you were playing by. Peta's little snub nose seemed to twitch in recognition of the fact. She sat as upright as she could, flaunting her figure and her expensive gear. She was wearing Stella McCartney top-to-toe femininity. But Calla, in her working suit of plain grey over a white blouse trimmed in crimson, left her far behind in sheer class, beauty and animal sex appeal.

'Please,' Jason pleaded. 'Let's talk.'

'The time for talking finished long ago,' Calla fumed. 'This has been coming for many months, Jason. You've had your chance to talk.'

'And what about you?' he countered. 'Have you been ready to talk, for Christ's sake? How much have I seen of you these last months? What do you expect of a man?'

'A man!' she echoed with disdain.

Jesus, a warning sounded in her brain, but somewhere way out from the boiling centre of it. Jesus, don't destroy him, leave him something of self-respect. But she was in full cry, enjoying the violence of her emotion even as she writhed in internal anguish. All the frustrations of her life with Jason, all the frustrations of the drawing-board, were gathering within her and demanding to be released.

Peta sucked on her cigarette: 'He seems every bit of a man to me,' she said.

Poor blonde simpleton, she simply wasn't ready for it. Calla swung her hips, brought back her arm like a baseball pitcher and, mustering all her energy, swept her hand at Peta's cheek in a prodigious reverberating smack. It was the greatest smack she'd ever delivered in her whole life. She felt it tingling up her arm.

'Calla –' Jason pleaded.

'Listen, you worm!' she stormed. 'How many years of my life have I spent chained to you and your uselessness? There's not an ounce of drive in you, no vitality, no spunk!'

'That, apparently, isn't what Peta thinks.'

She swooped on a low table and seized a fragile bronze figure of a man on a horse.

145

'That's a Giacometti,' he said, holding out his hands in a gesture of despair.

'Giacometti spaghetti!' she laughed harshly, and flung it at a framed picture on the wall. The glass shattered, the picture fell and the frame crumpled as it hit the floor. A few pieces broke off the sculpture.

'And that was a Hockney,' Jason added.

What exhilarating *fun* it was to blow a gasket, especially when your heart was really in it. What a feeling of vitality it gave you. And how it cleared the mind and body of all the muck that had built up over a longer period of time than you liked to admit. Christ, this is good! she thought.

But every storm has to die down eventually – if only to allow pressure to build up again for a repeat performance of all that thunder and lightning. Calla drew breath. Jason sat on the sofa next to Peta, who was crying silently.

'You promised,' Calla said, 'to give up the cocaine.'

'And I meant it.'

'But you're too weak, is that what you're telling me? Whatever help and support you're given, you can't kick the habit.'

'Probably,' Jason replied quietly.

'This isn't cocaine,' Peta said defiantly, feeling more confident now Jason was sitting next to her. 'So he hasn't broken his promise.'

'Believe me, I do know that's not nicotine you're smoking, sweetie. I've learned almost to love that good oldfashioned killer these last few years. At least it doesn't damage the brain.'

Jason stretched his arm, offering her his joint

'Something new,' he explained. 'Doesn't smell at all.'

'Wonderful,' Calla replied. 'Some cheap and nasty substitute, I assume.'

'On the contrary, it's more expensive. *The* designer drug in fashionable circles at the moment. Extremely chic. 5-Meo-DMT.'

'You disgust me, Jason.'

'They call it a research chemical,' he went on, as if determined she should know everything about it. 'Gives a very intense high. Quite wonderful.'

'I won't ask what it costs.'

'A hundred quid a gram.'

'Shit!'

'But good value for money. The high doesn't last long, but it's incredibly intense.'

Calla turned away wearily. In this mood Jason could rationalise perfectly well, totally exhausting her, but he couldn't feel anything. She felt as if he was a complete stranger to her. She began to climb the stairs.

'You're going to bed?'

'No, Jason, I'm going full stop. I'm collecting a few things that I need and then I'm going for ever. You heard that, I hope. For ever.'

Upstairs she grabbed the largest bag she could find, and stuffed into it pens, inks, rulers and any other of her working tools she could lay her hands on. She snatched as many clothes, accessories, bottles and sprays as she could manage. She gave a last look at the room where she'd slept with Jason for so many years and, damn it, she did have to fight back the tears. But when she came back down the stairs and found Jason and Peta wrapped around each other like the Babes in the Wood it didn't take more than point one of a second to get gloriously mad all over again.

'You're each of you what the other deserves,' she spat at them. 'They call it corporal punishment.'

'Thank you,' Jason said.

'Cow!' Peta pouted.

'Don't even think about touching any of my stuff,' Calla snarled at the other woman.

'Oh, but I already am,' Peta said, stroking Jason's cheek.

Calla felt the anger rise in her like a whirlwind, spinning furiously and uncontainably. In the top of her bag there was a full bottle of red ink. She yanked off the top and hurled the contents at the model's beautifully embroidered top. The scarlet stain spattered across it like a Jackson Pollock painting.

'And you,' she bawled, pointing a finger in Jason's face, 'can have your money back whenever you want it. I don't need it. I can raise what I need from the bank. I've got a track record now.'

'Dear Calla –' Jason began.

'Just ring my solicitor. Whenever you like. I'll give him the go-ahead to make a deal. Just so you're out of my life!'

He shook his head: 'I can't do that, Calla. I haven't got a stake in your business any more.'

'What the hell are you talking about? Okay, I've expanded over the years, built up profits, but about half the practice must be yours.'

'No,' he replied, with a sheepish expression on his face. 'I sold my interest. I needed the money.'

'Sold it? When did you sell it? More important, *who* did you sell it to?'

Jason stared into her eyes.

'To my brother,' he said. 'To Patrick. A few months ago.'

'Holy shit!'

'He seemed to think you were a good investment.'

Words couldn't express the fire and brimstone of her fury. She wasn't sure that physical action would do the trick, either, but she found herself suddenly reaching for a violin which hung from a hook on the wall.

'Stradivarius,' Jason yelped, standing up for the first time.

'Of all the mean, stupid, immoral, gut-busting things you could ever have thought of doing!' she shouted. 'How could you pull a dirty stunt like that? How could you put me at the mercy of that cold, mean bastard you call your brother?'

'I needed the money.'

No, there was nothing which could express her fury, but she'd have a damn good try. She grasped the violin by the neck, took steady aim for a shelf stacked with Meissen porcelain and – with a loud and satisfying grunt – let fly.

• • •

Calla stayed angry. She had meant every word. The anger fuelled a tremendous surge of energy over the next few weeks as she pummelled her life into a new shape.

'Who needs men?' she demanded. 'Who needs their insufferable egos, their unclean habits and their crass insensitivity?'

She certainly didn't. All she needed were enough hours in the day to work and somewhere to rest her head at night – or what was left of it when the work had finished.

Her personal assistant was put on to house-hunting straight away. Adam knew London inside out. Okay, she admitted, so men did have a few uses. But she'd rather pay for what she needed and forget the rest of the tacky package they usually brought with them.

'Just make it somewhere close to work,' she said.

That first small office in Pimlico had been sold off long ago and Calla's practice was now in South Audley Street, just off Grosvenor Square in Mayfair.

'I hate to be hackneyed, but you really can't miss us,' Adam would tell clients on the phone. He wasn't kidding. Calla was in an intensely visual business and believed she should be seen.

Why did architects hide themselves away behind blinds and stuccoed facades as if they were practising some doubtful branch of alternative medicine? Selling was the name of the game and Calla used her shop-windows, as she called them, to show off the goods. Eye-catching glass displays of model buildings, beautifully lit, were part of her publicity campaign.

Inside, the emphasis was on light and simplicity. It was best for drawing plans and it was best for dreaming up ideas, Calla thought.

'Reminds me of my Godfrey's villa in Provence,' Adam would say.

In this pale oasis, Calla found that her anger concentrated the mind wonderfully. It sharpened her energy to a fine point. She homed in fiercely on the project, fuelled during the day by prodigious amounts of black coffee. Adam, worried for her health, secretly substituted decaffeinated – but not for long.

'I need the caffeine! It's the caffeine I crave when I want coffee!' she yelled in a style reminiscent of her older sister.

Adam gave her a reproachful look and put the real stuff on his lunchtime shopping list.

He found her a Georgian terrace in Bayswater. It was near enough to the office and had a huge light attic with roof windows she could turn into a studio. That was enough for now. She would do something with the other floors, she told herself with a defiant grin, when she'd won this damn competition.

'One day I'll be human and start accepting friends' invitations again,' she said to herself one Saturday morning as she settled to work at her easel. 'If I've got any friends by the time this is all over.'

She examined the previous night's drawings with a set face. Her tumult of dark hair was pushed back in a black bow. Her strong features were without make-up and didn't need it.

'The hell with it!' She flung her pencil against the wall and pushed her chair roughly back over the stripped pine floorboards. 'Why won't this bloody thing come *right*?'

She leant against the black metal pillar at the head of the spiral staircase which led up from the floor below. And she admitted something to herself for the very first time. It wasn't just the expense of energy which was wearing her down.

'I'm going to be broke at the end of this,' she told her room. 'Absolutely skint. I've given up everything else for Charlesbury. Half my staff are working on it full time. There's no possible way it can be worth the pain.'

The intercomm bell rang. She swore again. She couldn't afford interruptions. There was no Adam to fend visitors off here, alas.

Adam was invaluable to her. He was decorative, in the consumptive poet style. He looked after all the day-to-day admin of the business, dealing with appointments, client accounts and visitors. He was soothing. He cared for her. And, although not obviously camp, he was gay, which was a blessing.

All these things were useful to her. But best of all, he simply wrong-footed the arrogant and the rude. Clients and contractors who came to see Calla with the idea of easily riding roughshod over a woman, found themselves taken aback on two fronts.

First of all, there was Adam introducing himself as Miss Marchant's *secretary*. Few men knew quite how to handle a male secretary. Adam liked to watch their confusion.

'So funny,' he would say. 'The outrage of a straight confronted by a bendy-boy secretary. I love it!'

And then there was Calla herself. She was a match for most men in the business – eye-catching as a diamond and nearly as hard.

But one diamond can cut another. And Grant Locke had often said to his secretary, Dulcie: 'A rough diamond, that's what I am. Unpolished, but of incalculable value.'

And it was Grant Locke who was standing outside Calla's door speaking into the intercomm.

'Good morning, Miss Marchant! Are you receiving guests?'

'Guests have invitations, Grant. I don't recall sending one to your address.'

'But we know you don't bother with such formalities. Even with Dukes.'

'Ouch! I'm on the top floor.'

As she heard him clattering up the spiral staircase, she pressed the button again: 'Out of charity, mind,' she called. 'I'd hate to have you arrested on the streets as an undesirable.'

Undesirable Grant Locke wasn't. He was the sort of guy who looked sexiest when he was most comfortable. He wore soft black cords and a tan leather jacket which swung as he ran up the stairs (Locke kept fit – you never knew your luck with younger women after all). His greying hair was newly washed and his eyes had their habitual roguish twinkle.

They looked at each other across the sparsely furnished room. Calla was making no move. She liked Locke well enough, but he was still a rival. Let him show his hand first.

For there must be something behind this house call. Locke was a man with reasons. It was one of the things she liked about him.

'Drink?' he offered, crossing to a black glass cabinet. Since no offer was forthcoming from Calla, he thought he might as well do the job himself. That was in keeping, all right.

'Bloody Mary,' she replied, making it sound as much an oath as a request.

As he made the drinks, she covered the sheets on her easel.

'Secretive, aren't we?' said Locke.

'Can't be too careful with the company I keep.'

This was always the way whenever they met, Grant reflected. A verbal tennis match. This was a rival to be reckoned with. The prospect excited him.

Christ, she was a good-looker! And without the make-up, the strength which made her Calla Marchant and not just another striking woman was naked and revealed. What a bone structure!

He took in the details of her appearance. He'd never seen Calla off-duty before. She wore a scarlet cashmere sweater, wrap-over style, which clung slightly to her breasts. It was soft and casual to be sure, but it was tied tight around such a curved and supple waist. Yes, he thought, you know you're a knock-out, my lady.

Stretchy black leggings which seemed to go on forever were tucked into soft leather boots. What a pert arse she had! She didn't get that from sitting on an architect's stool all day. More likely there were regular work-outs at an expensive London health spa like the Chelsea Club. She knew, she knew.

And she was looking straight at him, those violet eyes piercing his reverie.

'You look rather hot,' she said pointedly. 'Do you need to sit down?'

She'd seen his appraising look and recognised it from a hundred meetings with men in the world of buildings. And did she mind? Like hell! It gave her a sense of power. It gave her a chance to grab the upper hand.

She cleared a handful of magazines off the black leather settee. Sitting at one end, she carefully rested one ankle on her other thigh, revealing her long, long legs.

'I suppose,' she smiled, 'those stairs do go on for ever and ever. Built for the young, no doubt.'

But Locke had recovered himself. Couldn't two play at that game?

'I'll stand for a while,' he said. 'It shows respect.'

Damn him, thought Calla. The man's playing body language with me.

He stood quite at ease, those playful eyes looking about her studio. His manner declared that he was completely at home here. That he was in charge of the situation: 'I like your place.'

He wasn't going to get away with this display of easy mastery, she determined. The bloody nerve! It might work with other women. She wasn't other women. It was *her* territory and she was going to call the shots. She shifted on the settee, aware that he was watching her as she rested on one elbow, her legs stretched the length of the sofa. She took a sip of her drink and met his stare with her stare.

'Thank you so much, Grant. In that case I may keep it on.'

Oh, she was a knowing bitch, he thought. He liked that in her. But he did feel a fool standing there while she eyed him as a cat might eye a mouse. He strolled around the room with an air of cool examination.

'A veritable retreat,' he suggested, 'from the turmoil of life.'

'You make me sound like a nun,' countered the most unlikely nun in ecclesiastical history, running the tip of her tongue round the glass. And then she remembered that she might so easily have become one.

'Much to be said for celibacy, is there?' he asked.

He saw her give a start and sit up. She was rattled. Good, he liked her rattled. He'd never understood what a girl of such spirit could see in Jason Andover. Oh, he had a foppish charm, no doubt about that. But no wonder she'd left him. Andover couldn't handle a woman like Calla. Grant Locke rather thought he could. He'd enjoy the tussle at any rate.

'Okay, get to the point, Grant.'

He was beginning to make her feel uncomfortable. The truth was, that in spite of the opiate of work, Calla was missing Jason. She knew she'd been right to walk out, but she missed the company, the jokes, the sex, even though they'd all been rather thin on the ground lately.

'It may surprise you to hear it,' she said,' but I've far more fascinating things to do this morning than talk to you. My nails, for instance.'

And now, to her own irritation, she found herself wondering vaguely what Locke would be like in bed. He had a brazen self-confidence, a way of saying to the world 'take me or leave me,' which Calla rather liked in a man. He could stand up to her. He'd be good to rage against.

There was nothing vague about Locke's speculations. He just knew she'd be a sensation in bed. Or out of it. Anywhere. In any damned place where the appetite took her. Her unpredictablility would be a bonus.

'Your talons, you surely mean.'

He walked behind her on the pretext of examining a poster of the Pompidou Centre. His ploy worked. She didn't like having him out of her sights. He watched those splendid legs uncurl as she stood to face him.

'Come on, Grant. What is it you want?'

Don't tempt me, he thought, grinning to himself. He tipped his glass to his lips and held the pose for a few seconds. All part of the game.

'I'm not known for beating about the bush, Calla.'

'Really?' she said. 'But I suppose they don't have them in Yorkshire. Icy winds across the bleak moors. Was life very, *very* hard, Grant?'

She laughed. Was that a blush creeping up his neck? He liked playing the tough northerner and it embarrassed him when someone called his bluff.

'It's Charlesbury.'

He was leaning against the black railing at the top of the spiral stair. He made a pretty pleasing picture, she thought. Perhaps she'd forgive his insolence.

'Forgotten the way, have we?' she teased. 'Need a sketch map?'

'It's what *you* need that I've come to talk about.'

She stood leaning against the pillar where the railings stopped. From his reference to nuns, from the look in his eyes, from the very fact that he was a man, she had a pretty good idea what he thought she needed. Men were such simple creatures. But that had nothing to do with Charlesbury. She was feeling mighty sensitive about the Charlesbury competition. Right now she didn't want to be told what she needed in that direction. No, sir. No, bloody Grant Locke. She arched her fine black eyebrows in an unspoken question.

'It's a big, fat, juicy plum,' he said. 'It'll make what's going on in Paris and the City of London look like Legoland.'

'So?'

'So we all want to win it, don't we? You included.'

She nodded warily. Feeling she wouldn't like what he was going to say, she went to the cabinet and fixed herself another drink.

'You're good, Calla . . . ' he began.

'Thanks.' The voice was deep and dangerous.

'Good, but not *that* good. You haven't got the muscle, the experience for this one. Maybe in a few years, but not now.'

He watched her closely. There was a flush about her neck and her cheekbones. It was a rising anger, but it was under the surface as yet. He wondered whether she was the type to start throwing things. He'd no objection. Some of the best sex he'd ever had with his first wife all those years ago was on the floor amid the broken china.

'Jesus,' she said. 'I don't believe it.'

She swirled her drink and tossed it back with a triumphant gesture.

'You're frightened, Grant. Is that it? Frightened of someone with an idea – a real idea instead of your cosy little reproductions of our architectural heritage?'

They stood facing each other. Locke had moved closer to her, but she stayed her ground, supporting herself against the pillar with the flat of her hand. God, he'd like to see the real animal in her unleashed, unfettered . . .

'I'm afraid you misunderstand me. You have to remember that the Duke likes my kind of building. I'm the flavour of the month as far as he's concerned. I've got nothing to be frightened of. You know full well that I've a decent chance of pulling it off.'

'You also know, if you're honest with yourself, that you haven't.'

'Balls!'

She didn't back away from his nearness, but stood her ground in a way which made Locke yearn to reach out and touch those proud, softly scarlet-clad breasts.

'Don't think you can put me off that easily.'

'I've no wish to, Calla. On the contrary I'd rather take you *on*. I'm suggesting a partnership – just for Charlesbury, of course. Teamwork. Two pulling as one.'

By now both were clinging to the black pole. He could feel the heat of her breath.

'You've got a bloody nerve,' she said.'

'Blessed with it from childhood. But just think seriously for a moment. The Duke wants a complete package. Never mind the bright ideas, he'll want evidence that the practice he chooses can deliver. Think detail design for the moment. Think project management. You're small. How many surveyors and inspectors can you put on the site?'

'Money buys them.'

'It buys bad ones as well as good. It can buy you incompetents and charlatans if you're not careful. I'm talking track record, Calla. I'm talking experience of individuals. You know I'm right.'

If she did know, she certainly wasn't admitting it. Either to him or to herself. She hadn't spent night after night hunched over a drawing-board only to throw in the towel. That's how it would feel. Anyway, the thought suddenly hit her, there was something strangely unbalanced about Locke's proposal.

'Since you're already the Duke's golden, blue-eyed boy,' she queried suspiciously, 'what's in it for you?'

If he makes a blatant sexist remark, she decided, I'll brain the bastard.

'Flair, Calla. I gain your flair.'

She shook her head. Was he genuine? The way he looked at her breasts when she moved, then let his glance fall to her legs, told her that he'd like to gain rather more than flair. But give him the benefit of the doubt.

'Thanks,' she said. 'But no.'

'Think about it, that's all I ask. You'll realise that I'm doing you a favour.'

Grant Locke didn't know he'd gone too far until he felt the remains of the Bloody Mary running down his face. Wow! The woman was an Amazon.

'You creep!' she yelled, her voice echoing round the rafters. That fine face was close up to his. Oh, the proud bitch, he thought. What skin she had. 'I'll do you a favour you don't expect, you little shit! Get out!'

He held her off with one hand on her shoulder.

'You don't have neighbours with normal hearing?'

'Fuck the neighbours! Out!'

Yes, she meant it, Locke decided. He nodded, took a step back and, blowing her a kiss, clattered down the steps.

13

Patrick Andover wasn't conceited enough to think he'd never made a mistake. What he *would* tell anyone who cared to ask was that he never made the same mistake twice. He had an excellent calculating brain. And because he wasn't deflected by such trivialities as wanting to do the decent thing or to make a good impression, he was able to concentrate a hundred per cent on the task in hand.

From an early age he'd regarded himself as the only sensible person in his family, next to his father. He couldn't quite understand why his mother existed. He would, of course, have missed her had she been snatched out of his life, but probably much as he would have missed the huge oak tree in the paddock had it been blown down by a gale in the night. It seemed to him that his mother did absolutely nothing of value. This wasn't a moral judgement in the first place. He simply looked at her dallying in the arts and asked himself Why? What did it profit her? Where was the pleasure in it?

In much the same way, he despised his older brother. Everyone liked Jason, said how pleasant he was, how amusing, what a good sportsman, a natural violinist and the rest of it. Some younger brothers would have felt dangerously envious and would have suffered for the rest of their lives, always moving in an oppressive shadow. Patrick, however, just couldn't comprehend why people seemed to feel this peculiar admiration. Sometimes, he couldn't help but notice, it was even close to veneration. It was a mystery.

For Patrick had the great advantage in life of being single-minded. To outsiders this attribute may appear only narrow-mindedness, but to those who possess it there's never any doubt of its power. Patrick quickly learned as a prime lesson in life that if you want something badly enough, you'll only be stopped from having it by someone who just as badly doesn't want you to have it. There aren't many of those determined individuals about, and if you're clever you'll defeat them anyway. Patrick started collecting scalps from an early age.

His hero was Robert, his father. It was obvious to both of them that an entrepreneurial gene had pass directly from the great Forsyth through Robert to Patrick. It bonded them. Robert, in fact, had far more imagination than his son, and he had a well-developed social awareness whereas Patrick had none at all. Robert had a gentle sense of the ridiculous, whereas Patrick understood a joke only when it was written on a wall six feet high.

They were, however, both happy to ignore these differences, which were simply little tricks of human nature. What mattered was that they were Forsyth's inheritors.

'That lad,' Robert observed to his wife, when Patrick was only twelve years old, 'is going to make my business dealings look like child's play. By the time he's finished, people will look back on this little empire of ours and regard it as a corner shop which became a Harrods.'

'Isn't it a little early to make predictions?' Sarah asked gently.

'Not when you've seen him in action as I have. He came into the study today and began to browse through the Andover Hotels balance sheet. Did you ever once see him so much as pick up one of those books in his bedroom? He doesn't even look at the pictures.

'When I made some comment about our healthy profit situation, do you know what he said? "If I were you, Daddy," he told me, "I'd re-schedule my borrowing into dollars while US interests rates stay low. I reckon the gain would just about offset your policy of more rapid asset depreciation". I mean he said that almost word for word.

'Not only that, but he's right! That's just what I've been planning to put to the board next week.'

Patrick had no loyalty to the family firm as such. After all, hadn't his father sold Forsyth's original business in order to branch out on his own? To stick with a product-line or a company that wasn't making the best return on investment possible was just sentimental. And that was the very worst word in Patrick Andover's vocabulary.

All through his schooldays he kept copious notes about share prices, financial dealings, commodities, who owned what. If the other boys laughed to see Andover junior swotting over the *Financial Times*, the joke was lost on him. He wasn't embarrassed because he simply didn't understand why they thought it was funny. Damn it, he knew that it wasn't.

Most of the family fortune due to him was tied up in a trust, but Robert advanced him £10,000 when he was only fourteen, and watched him double the stake within two years. He felt a fierce pride in his younger son who had a knack which even he lacked. It was a knack which derived from that dogged, blinkered determination.

'If I'd had his qualities,' he said, 'we'd be on a par with the Rupert Murdochs of this world.'

'On the whole,' replied Sarah, who was secretly appalled by her son's relentless drive, 'I'm rather glad that we're not.'

When Robert was killed in the power-boat accident, Patrick felt himself swell to twice his size. He went through a period of grief, of course, though he couldn't understand what the useless tears were doing running down his cheeks. They served no purpose. He knew his father had gone and that he missed him. Why this stupid snivelling? He felt ashamed of it, and cried alone and in private until the nuisance had passed.

He was at once the *de facto* head of the family. He had always known that he would assume this position when his father died, but he had imagined that his apotheosis would occur many years later. Now that the mantle was upon his shoulders, he felt that he would burst with the energy which flooded through his stocky frame. There was so much he could do.

At sixteen, there were still shackles upon his ambitions, and very frustrating he found them. But when he looked about him and saw his useless mother and his ineffectual brother, both stricken by Robert's loss, Jason seemingly unable to come to terms with his injury – when he saw all this, Patrick knew that he held the key to the future.

He couldn't wait for the future to happen!

• • •

His way with women was as direct as his way with finance. He didn't believe in sentiment, he did believe in realisable goals which were achieved by a sensible plan of action.

At the age of seventeen he decided that he should no longer be a virgin. The little he'd read on the subject, and the conversation of his fellows, taught him that a man was only a man when he'd been with a woman. He accepted this as he accepted the wisdom of the markets. It wasn't that he felt uneasy being a virgin. How would anyone else know? Patrick didn't believe in intuition. It was just that it had to happen sometime, and it really ought to be sooner rather than later.

He looked about him carefully for the best opportunity. 'Maximise the advantages,' was one of his mottoes, 'minimise the disadvantages.' He didn't want an inexperienced girl who might waste his time. Neither did he want the kiss-and-tell type, who'd gossip about him with her friends. It had to be easy and it had to be safe.

Laura Brand was the wife of one of his parents' friends. She was 35 years old, well-preserved and lively in a nervous kind of way, as if she was ashamed of her own vitality. Her husband, Dennis, was a stockbroker and about fifteen years her senior. Not much judgement, Patrick thought, after a few brief exchanges with him about the money markets. A country broker with a tidy income from handling the accounts of wealthy clients who didn't demand a constant shuffling of their portfolios. They would have been worried if he had suggested selling their favourite shares in favour of something less well known with a better yield. Too risky.

She had caught Patrick's eye more than once in the past, and the thought had even crossed his mind that her admiration for his fast growing frame was more than neighbourly. That had been a fleeting thought, though. What finally determined him was the sight of her at one of his parents' outdoor parties, flirting with Sam Masterman, the horse trainer. Late in the evening, strolling across the lawn and into the copse, he saw them emerging close together, and she had smiled uneasily at Patrick as they passed by.

He rang the bell at her house one hot afternoon at three. As he'd walked up the drive, his usual determination had been tinged with an unaccustomed nervousness. It was a sensation new to him, and he fought against it angrily. This thing has got to be done, he told himself. Why this useless trembling?

'Patrick?'

He shouldered his way inside and strode into the living room. There was a bottle of gin on the table, and a glass next to it with a slice of lemon floating. A women's magazine lay open on the arm of a chair.

'What is it, Patrick?'

She had no shoes on. She was wearing a mustard cotton dress which clung. He let his eyes rove slowly across her breasts. They rose and fell slowly. They were quite large and, he guessed, still firm. His gaze tracked gradually, unmistakably, down to her waist, held in by a narrow black belt, and then to the fullness of her thighs. Her ankles were, no doubt, less shapely than when she was young, but the bone structure was still good. His eyes ran along the length of her stockinged feet and then, with growing appreciation, all the way back again, up the legs, the torso, the breasts.

'Have you been drinking, Patrick?'

He shook his head: 'No.'

'You want . . .'

She didn't need to finish the sentence. It was quite obvious what Patrick Andover wanted. Moreover, the young man equally obviously thought he was going to get it.

'This is madness,' she said, flustered. 'Isobel comes home from school at four o'clock.'

His brow puckered with puzzlement: 'How long does this thing take?' he asked.

She laughed abruptly. There was a colour in her cheeks which hadn't been there a moment before. She reached for her glass and drained it in one quick movement.

'What kind of a woman,' she enquired, cocking her head to one side, 'do you think I am?'

He answered brusquely: 'I could ask Sam Masterman, I suppose. He'd tell me.'

Laura Brand bit her lip and leaned back against the wall. He could see that she was considering all the options. He hadn't meant that remark about Masterman as blackmail until the words were out of his mouth, and then he immediately meant it very much indeed.

He walked past her into the hall: 'Which way is it?' he demanded. 'You lead the way.'

Her calves were slender and firm. He followed her up the stairs. She unclasped her belt as she entered the bedroom, tossing it into a corner. She went to the window and pulled the curtains, so that the room was suffused in a warm glow.

He watched her lift her skirt to tug at the top of her tights. Then she sat on the edge of the bed to slide them down her legs.

'And you?' she asked.

He stood stupefied, but almost absent-mindedly began to loosen the buttons of his shirt as he watched her strip – the dress, unhooked, wriggling down her body; the tight bra springing off those ample breasts; finally the panties, which she raised her body to release, coming off to reveal a wild tangle of black pubic hair. This was his first woman.

Naked, he approached her, and she, still sitting, reached out her hands and ran them down the firmness of his muscled arms. Her fingers and thumbs found the outlines of his sinews. He was hard-packed, a man already in his body.

Her hands came across his chest, flattening themselves against the hairless strength of it, then descended slowly towards his navel.

'How do you want it?' she said.

Then he pushed her back, urgently, and fell on top of her, clamouring to possess her. She was straddled on the edge of the bed, at first instinctively flinching from his wild thrusts, but quickly opening to him, using her hands to guide him, to bring him into that moist channel.

He was a stallion, mad in his lust. He'd seen them out in the fields, heaving and threshing, and he was one of them now, his head thrown back, his eyes wide open and showing their whites, the sweat running down his chest into her sweat.

She was his mare, reeking of something animal he hadn't known but which drove him to frenzy, images of fornicating beasts coursing through his brain as he rose and fell upon her, heaving and threshing, her breasts proud beneath him with the nipples upraised and taut, her full mouth open, gasping, her eyes firm shut. Oh Christ, he thought, and thought nothing else but copulating animals and musty stables and the stench of the stables and straw and sweat and dung and urine. Oh Christ.

He felt the seeds gathering their force within him, a smarting, throbbing sweetness which became a thrilling ache and then an uncontainable pulsation as he continued to thrust and thrust, a rasping sound in his throat, until with a great shuddering convulsion he arched above her heaving body and poured his juice inside her.

But why, when he'd done, did she continue to buck beneath him, her fingers pressing into his buttocks, forcing him down? He was finished, but she struggled with him, wrestling, making little clicking noises in her throat until she suddenly subsided, breathing heavily.

He pulled himself away, sullen and withdrawn in his exhaustion. As he sat on the bed, his head in his hands, he was aware of her busying herself about him, pulling clothes on, plumping pillows. She padded to the door, then turned and came back to him.

Dropping to one knee, she opened his legs and reached for his prick, softer now but still swollen and coloured ruddy from the tussle. She put her palms gently on either side of it, so that it reared up again.

'Just remember,' she said with a little smile, 'this chap's got a long and happy life ahead of him. Don't work him too hard.'

• • •

But he didn't think in terms of happiness, whether in his sexual affairs or in any others. What Patrick Andover wanted was fulfilment, and that meant success, a goal achieved. Happiness was a gormless, negative state – angels with harps.

At the time his father died he already understood the ramifications of the Andover empire in the way that an army commander knows the territory he hopes to invade from poring over a detailed map. He could tell you much more than where the many subsidiary companies were and how many people they employed. That was child's play. He could telll you even more than which of these units were performing well, which needed a fresh injection of capital, which should be sold off before a downtown in business became apparent to prospective buyers.

In short, he knew not only the bone structure and the general health of the organisation, but its very chemistry, how the hormones were released into the blood stream. Ask Patrick Andover about the meat consumed in the Andover restaurants or the wine produced in the Alsace vineyards and he would reel off a dizzying catalogue of prices, suppliers, transportation routes and advantageous single-customer trade deals. His finger was on more pulses than anyone knew existed.

What he understood only vaguely, however, were the politics of the scene. He knew who ran each subsidiary, but he wasn't personally acquainted with more than half a dozen of them. That was a weakness he meant to put right before, as it must be, the crown was placed upon his head.

Waking from sedation in his hospital bed on the day of the tragedy, he'd done some quick calculations. Within two years he would reach legal adulthood. There was no way they could deny him a place on the board of the parent company: the tranche of shares owned by his mother and her sons was too large.

He'd give himself another year to seize the chairmanship of a couple of the main subsidiaries. Then, perhaps, two more to be in charge of the whole damn shooting match. That would make him twenty-one. Everyone would say he was ridiculously young – but noone would be able to stop him.

Of course they all knew what he was up to. Directors, managers, the most humble of staff, grew accustomed to regular visits from this stocky young man who prowled their territory with sharp eyes, every now and again asking an equally sharp question which they found themselves answering with great alacrity and a sense of foreboding, like schoolboys interrogated by a fierce and fearsome teacher. They could, technically, have had him thrown off the premises, but it was as clear as day that he was the coming man.

On his eighteenth birthday he presented himself in the chairman's office and carefully shut the door behind him. Leo Krantz was a worldly, intelligent man who'd just celebrated a birthday himself. Since it was his fiftieth, and since he'd spent half of these years as Robert Andover's right-hand man and business confidant, he felt comfortably in control of the situation.

'It's my birthday today,' Patrick Andover said, somewhat aggressively, Krantz thought, for an opening statement.

'Congratulations. You've come to tell me I forgot the card?'

'I've reached my majority, Leo.'

Krantz barely registered the fact that the young man scowled rather than smiled at his pleasantry. Patrick Andover never smiled. He was totally accustomed to the pompous way he expressed himself. What he did notice, with unpleasant surprise, was that Patrick had used his first name for the first time in his life. He'd known this headstrong, stubborn kid since he was mewling in his mother's arms. It had been Uncle Leo for years, and later a respectful, distancing Sir or plain Mr Krantz. This marked a sea-change.

'I want a directorship.'

Krantz laughed out loud.

'Hey, this is a bit sudden, Patrick.'

It wasn't sudden at all, of course. He'd seen it coming for years.

'We do have shareholders, you know.'

'You can cut that crap, Leo. Don't give me shareholders. Let's at least talk the real world.'

So they talked the real world, in which shareholders, even the institutions but especially the small investors, will rubber-stamp almost anything the directors want to do. Andover International had plenty of shareholders who enjoyed dining and drinking at places they felt they owned, but who wouldn't know a balance sheet from a toilet tissue. Getting Patrick Andover onto the board wouldn't really be at all difficult – and it wasn't. Within three months he was a third of the way towards his goal.

He was running the company long before he officially took it over. He was running it because everyone knew what was going to happen and they sure as hell didn't want to be remembered as having tried to stand in his way. Retribution obviously wouldn't be gentle. So they took up his suggestions, did things his way, even though he had only a couple of chairmanships and one place among a dozen round the boardroom table at AI house.

The one man who *was* prepared to stick his neck out was Leo Krantz. He had most to lose, after all, and Patrick saw himself falling behind his own schedule simply because this tiresome old man wouldn't budge.

'The kid has no soul,' Krantz would say privately, 'no imagination and no vision. He'll make money, but he'll kill the spirit of the company.'

Krantz had insight, but he was out of time. Patrick Andover was the sort of man who has trouble starting a business from scratch, owing to an absence of both vision and personal charm, but who's a veritable demon once he has money behind him and a team of bright thinkers to feed him alternatives to choose from. He had brilliant instinct. That was his strength.

Yes, Krantz had done well for the company, but progress would be slow rather than dynamic as long as the older man was at the helm. Therefore he had to go.

Patrick, frustrated beyond belief through having to wait to come into his kingdom, organised the coup with deadly efficiency. One morning Krantz was in charge of Andover International; by lunchtime he had resigned and was on his way to becoming an impotent honorary vice-president.

'What's the gist of all these bits of paper?' he asked when Patrick dropped the package onto his desk. It was half past nine. He'd just arrived in the office but Andover, as usual, had had a full two hours start on him.

'They show that you've been cheating the company, Leo,' the young man replied in a matter-of-fact voice. 'Persistently, over several years.'

'Baloney!'

'Of course, but they're invincible. There are people who'll swear to their validity, people in high places. You can try to argue consignments, prices, delivery dates, but mud sticks. I'd say you're finished.'

Krantz looked through a few of the papers, then hurled the whole pile on the floor.

'You're suggesting I've taken back-handers?'

'That's part of it. And, for good measure, that there are deals which haven't found their way into the books at all.'

'But you know this is a lie! You know I've given my life to this company. Since before you were born.'

Patrick shrugged: 'Let's not be sentimental, Leo. And let's not play games. We both know the reality. Shall we shake on it?'

He held out his hand and seemed mildly surprised that it wasn't taken.

'One day, you evil bastard,' Krantz said in a hoarse whisper, 'someone will shake you by the neck.' His face turning puce, he stalked from the room, wrenching his nameplate from the outside of the door. 'I hope it's terminal!'

At the age of twenty-two, just eighteen months behind schedule, Patrick Andover became chairman and managing director of Andover International.

• • •

Behind every successful businessman, he was sure, there was a hard-working slave of a woman. He wanted one of those, but his requirements were exacting. Patrick Andover's wife would have to be intelligent enough to understand the rudiments of his work, but not so intelligent that she wanted to give him advice about it. She would have to be attractive enough to bring reflected admiration to him, but not so attractive that she had men dancing around her like swarming bees. He couldn't countenance scandal. She would have to be good at the basics of shopping and cooking and child-rearing, but without putting them first and him second.

While he waited for this unusual woman to appear on the scene, he sowed his wild oats indiscriminately. Most women are sexually attracted to power, and Patrick had two kinds of it – he was a brutally successful captain of industry and he had an undeniable presence, emanating from his physical build and his single-minded drive. Women weren't hard to get, and he got them.

His first experience with Laura Brand had shown him what he wanted in a woman. He didn't care a jot about affection. He wasn't interested in a woman's personality, her little likes and dislikes. What he wanted, what he enjoyed so much that the thought of it would suddenly make him break out in a sweat at the unlikeliest times and places – in the middle of a business meeting, sitting in his car at traffic lights, once even during a funeral – what thrilled him was mastering a woman so that her body heaved and threshed beneath him, she wanting it so badly that she cried out for him not to stop. That pleading itself could bring him to orgasm. He loved that domination of a woman. He loved bringing them to humiliation.

But he was careful. Because he didn't care for the silly feminine things, the sentimentality and the romance, he wasn't tempted into liaisons which would be dangerous for his business. There were women enough who would satisfy his savage lust, without jeopardising lucrative financial deals. If he slept with the wife or daughter of one of his associates, he did it for a reason.

When his brightest marketing director was about to defect to an Andover rival, taking with him too much know-how than it was wise to lose, Patrick visited his wife on the pretext of discussing the matter. It was his well-won maxim that there was no woman who wouldn't. The trick was knowing how. In this case it took him three patient hours to discover her weakness – but he hadn't learnt the secret ten minutes before she was howling for it, demanding she be penetrated, urgently, 'now you shit, now now now', yelling obscenities as he held back, fighting for it until at last he yielded and allowed it to her, gave her a violent drubbing, and she subsided in a tearful flood of thanks and anger.

'Oh, you bastard,' was all she said.

'And your husband won't be leaving us?' he smiled, dressing swiftly. 'I'd hate him to know.'

He was twenty-seven when he met Mary Soper, and she was two years younger. They were fellow guests at a wedding reception in Harrogate. He didn't realise that she was the girl for him until they fell to talking about her family. Ah, *the* Sopers, the supermarket family!

It was a dull gathering and was destined to last for ever. They went for a stroll along the Stray, that green area which gives the Yorkshire town its grace. She was a sensible girl, he noted, and quite good-looking in rather a squared-off fashion. Well, she was bonny. She was bright, too, without being an intellectual. He thought she'd be capable.

Andover was, in short, struck by her. She didn't stir any lust in him, but that wasn't the point. He knew that the repose of the bedroom, the smell of a woman in his nostrils, his own rampant desires, would make for reasonable satisfaction in that direction. He didn't intend sex ever to be contained within marriage, anyway.

Over tea and Yorkshire fat rascals in Bettys, with a pianist lazily picking his way along the keys of a white piano, he prompted her to talk about her father and his chain of supermarkets. Andover had long been wanting to break into that field, but the price had never been right. He'd cast an eye at Sopers more than once: a family business concentrated in the north of England, with great potential for expansion.

They were married six months later, their own reception being at Claridge's. It was a lavish occasion even by this hotel's renowned standards. Two hundred guests mingled like a colony of ants across the black and white tiled floors, their number seeming to double by being reflected in the glorious Art Deco mirrors. Jason and Calla weren't invited.

'Not for this special occasion?' their mother pleaded.

'Especially not for this occasion, mother. He'll come stuffed full of drugs and he'll cause a scene.'

That night Patrick and his bride slept in a showpiece 1930s room at the hotel. The bathroom seemed to be made almost entirely of marble. Joan Collins had stayed there the week before.

'This is so romantic,' Mary said.

Patrick smiled affectionately upon her feminine idiocies. He was really very fond of his new wife. They made love in a gentle way that was unknown to him, and he found the difference interesting. But he woke in the middle of the night with a stupendous erection and had to take a cold shower to bring his throbbing member down to size.

His instinct, as usual, had been sound. She was a good wife to him, loyal, efficient and adoring. What did it matter that he had to go with other women to slake his lust? She was everything he wanted in a wife. She bore him two sons, Robert and Bruce, who were energetic, scarcely controllable and undeniably built in their father's image.

In business, too, everything went handsomely. Andover International acquired the Soper chain for a price which almost embarrassed him, and it kept expanding into other new and profitable fields. And Patrick Andover put his private money into schemes like property development which earned him large rewards. He had, people said, the Midas touch.

But it wasn't pure luck. He had learned to take the longer view. His instinct even told him when not to put complete trust in that infallible instinct. That was why, although he truly believed that Calla's business was destined to fail, he had written so many clauses into that document he'd persuaded her to sign all those years ago – clauses which allowed for the improbability of her success.

Now that success looked like being yet another feather in his cap.

14

It was a wonderwork in iron and glass and it was the biggest thing yet from the drawing board of Calla Marchant. Glinting in the sunshine of a Glasgow morning and freshly stripped of its scaffolding, the new concert hall was already pulling the crowds.

Among those who stopped to stare this bright July morning was Calla herself. 'Oh, I love it to pieces!' she said under her breath. 'And tonight it'll look even better.'

But there were several hours before the gala opening when the place would be thronging with musicians, visitors and VIPs. And just now Calla wanted to be alone with the light, clear dream she'd created.

Inside, away from the crowds, it floated like a canopy over her head. She turned and turned, her face lifted to the glass of the roof. The lightness rested on a delicate, deceptively strong network of iron.

Anyone who knew her would make the obvious connection straight away – in its combination of beauty and strength it was the very image of its creator. There truly was something of Calla in every building she made.

She was thinking other thoughts – that there was something of the ever-changing quality of the original sand in the glass here, something of the earthy rudeness of ore in the iron. And that she was the luckiest woman alive in being able to translate ideas of nature and beauty into a real hands-running-across-the-brickwork building.

A casual observer would have made another observation – that there was something still of the animal in the beautiful woman who stood, her dark hair set off by simple beige mini dress and long knitted coat, in the middle of the concert hall which had been her dream.

'It's just a building, you fool,' she said aloud, surprised by her own emotion. But she didn't believe that. Tonight it would be filled with music. The music would have the infinite space to soar which only glass can give and the people, dressed for a gala, would be reflected bright and beautiful in the glass against the dark evening sky.

'I was right,' she told herself, standing where the orchestra would play tonight and looking at the seats climbing to the back of the hall.

Sceptical critics had given her a hard time. She was young, practically unknown four years ago when she had won the contract. And she was English. Some Scots weren't keen on a sassenach interfering with their townscapes. Wasn't London 2012, the Olympic City, enough for them?

The design itself hadn't had the best of receptions, especially her use of an old coupling like glass and iron. 'More the stuff of Victorian railway stations than of a concert hall for the 21st century,' the *Glasgow Herald* had sourly remarked.

Calla had been convinced that she was right. Her own concern had been more for the acoustics of a place made of such hard materials. The baffling had been the key. She'd taken the best advice to make sure it would work. And it did.

Jason had loved the plan, she remembered. Calla's crystal palace, he called it. Things had been good between them then. So good that the early drafts had been ruined when he swept both them and Calla to the floor one heady Sunday morning.

'All work and no play makes Jason randy,' he'd said, making joyful love to her on the floor.

Calla bestowed a rueful smile upon the audience seats in her palace. All that was over now. Except for the hard work. She still had her buildings, and they were her life. She wondered, idly, what Peta had ever made other than a pout for the cameras.

She pushed the thought down and stood a while. Down the two sides were glass colonnades with bars for the interval. The coloured glass of the ceilings contrasted with the huge displays of white lilies along the walks. She liked that.

Charlesbury came into her mind. What a hell of a project that was. What did she need in order to catch the Duke's eye? Could she really let herself go, as she had with this beauty? Could she give Charlesbury a heart like this? Or must its heart be something more conventional ' maybe a market square or a park with water? She felt herself excited by the possibilities all over again.

So far away from London, in the midst of her own lovely achievement, she began to think more clearly about Charlesbury and to yearn for the prize. To hell with Grant Locke and his suggestion of partnership! She didn't need him, for anything. Anyone who saw her crystal palace must realise she was one of the best.

She certainly felt it at the gala opening that evening. And she looked it in a Katherine Hamnett dress of gold parachute silk, with a central panel running from below the bosom to the hem, flat and close to the suppleness of her body.

'This, Calla-lily,' enthused Bunny Simkins, filling his dinner jacket rather too well, 'is what they call a glittering occasion.'

He was her special guest. Any part of her success which wasn't a product of her own genius was undeniably due to him. Most beginners in the profession have to fight for every opportunity, fight for the breadth of experience they'll need in their future careers. But Bunny hadn't been a mere employer. He'd been her teacher and her friend.

Under Bunny's guidance she hadn't spent countless hours colouring up other people's drawings. She'd been sent out on site to brave hardened builders and surveyors who weren't at first prepared to accept the intrusion of a woman into their preserve. They hadn't got boots the right size for her, they'd say. The hard hats were too big. But they were no match for her charm and intelligence and very quickly caved in.

He'd taught her about materials, their properties and their stresses, but he also gave her invaluable insights into dealings with clients, the subtleties of conferences in oak-panelled rooms far away from any development land. Most invaluable of all, Bunny had taught her to trust her own sense of beauty.'

'It's quite superb,' he beamed now. 'Something afloat yet tied to earth.' He kissed her hot cheek. 'Supremely well done, my little pupil.'

The lights were reflected in Calla's eyes. Her shape was relected in the glass walls. It was *her* night.

It seemed her night, at least, until she found herself buttonholed by a pint-sized Glasgow dignitary, excitedly telling her about the city's cultural rebirth. He was impossible to interrupt. She tried it several times and gave up. He filled the slightest pause with a little 'Ahem' and went running on.

Listen McTavish, she thought despairingly, if I have to smile a minute longer my face will crack.

'And do you know, Miss Marchant, we had a very special visitor this afternoon? Ahem.' She didn't even attempt to look interested. Don't encourage the little bugger, she thought. 'Maybe you've heard of the Duke of Mercia? Ahem.'

'The *who*?!'

'Very interested in architecture. Came to look round. Ahem. On the way from his Highland estate.'

'And what did the Duke have to say?' she demanded, feeling like Sleeping Beauty waking after a hundred years. 'Tell me!'

But he suddenly turned away: 'Och, duty calls.'

I'll throttle this character, she thought. Please God, give me patience. 'Did he like it?'

'Must go. Here's the band.'

'Orchestra,' Calla couldn't help correcting him.

She slid onto her seat next to Bunny. Whatever the programme was, it passed Calla by. Try to concentrate thought she might, her head was full of Charlesbury and Harry Willoughby. He'd assured her that it would be a fair contest, and he'd come to see her concert hall, damn it. Was that a coincidence? Or, more likely, was he simply showing that maddening upper class veneer of polite pretence?

The evening whirled by in a kaleidoscope of noise, light and colour. Calla's face was alight as she and Bunny got into the cab to return to their hotel.

'If an old bumbler may say so, you look lovely tonight, Calla,' Bunny said, looking in admiration at the animated eyes and high colouring of his companion.

'I've been realising how much it all means to me, Bunny,' she said, gripping his arm. 'You can't know how much I want Charlesbury.'

Bunny smiled, but said nothing.

'I know it's hope against hope,' she told him, 'but I can do it.' A memory returned to her. 'And I can do it alone. I had a visit from the insufferable Grant Locke the other day, actually suggesting that we went into partnership for Charlesbury. Couldn't believe his nerve . . . '

Her old teacher looked out of the cab window at the spruced-up Glasgow streets. They saw the Stirling Library and the stock exchange, took a right off St Vincent Street and were soon passing the McLennan Galleries.

'You know, I think he's right, Calla-lily,' he said softly.

They travelled in silence for some minutes. She was clenching her fists, but trying not to show her anger. Her sudden hopes, the bright confidence she had felt in her palace of light and music – all this had evaporated in a moment. Who was he to tell her she was wrong? What right did he have?

But she knew the answers to those questions.

'Locke's right as far as that goes, Calla. The Duke is unlikely to risk his reputation on someone untried . . . '

'Untried?' Oh God, here came the explosion. She simply couldn't stop it. 'My concert hall hasn't fallen down, has it? The schools, the houses and the offices designed by Calla Marchant are all still standing, aren't they?'

He heard her out. He let her anger and frustration express itself in the way he well knew. Calla had never been the quietest of his employees.

'It's nothing to do with quality, my girl,' he said at last, 'and you well know it. You're still young and Harry Willoughby will want a track record, the sort of track record only a few architects have . . . '

She managed a little grin: 'Including yourself?'

'Including myself, maybe. I can admit to you, Calla, that it would absolutely set the seal on my career.' His eyes suddenly moistened, and his voice was unsteady. 'I'd give so much to win it.'

Then he collected himself: 'But it will probably go to a specialist community architect. Someone,' he said with a sigh, 'like Grant Locke.'

They travelled on to their hotel wrapped in their private thoughts.

That dark and brooding look of hers, he reflected, does make her an incredibly handsome woman.

He's a dear friend, she was thinking, and very wise – *But that doesn't mean he can't be absolutely, prodigiously, one hundred per cent wrong!*

● ● ●

It was Fern Willoughby's way with a man. She couldn't help it. Sooner or later in a meeting she had to speculate as to what sort of a lover he might be. And having made a guess, she usually decided to put it to the test.

'It does help pass the time,' she'd explain to intimate friends with a dreadful chuckle.

Now she was watching Langton Meredith out of those strangely pale green eyes, and wondering. He was certainly an unusual type of man. There was a whiteness about those unhaired hands, a sleekness about his clothes and a sheen about his hair.

She couldn't imagine him in the crumpled sheet mess of a lovers' bed. She couldn't imagine anything as direct and basic as good sex followed by a healthy orgasm. Not with this man.

Harry quite liked him, of course. But Harry, dear thing, didn't have her instinct. He was inclined to see the best in people. There was something about a stiff upper lip which affected the sense of smell, thought Fern. And there was certainly something in the air to sniff when Langton Meredith was about. Best Gieves and Hawke cologne on the surface, no doubt, but something less than wholesome in the man himself.

Quite what he was doing here in Eaton Square, she wasn't sure. But she was quite prepared to while away the time with small talk and large gins until he came out with whatever it was. She'd fix the drinks herself: he looked the stingy type.

'Perhaps you'd ring for ice, Mr Meredith?'

He pulled on the sash and wondered, in his turn, about the woman now pouring the gin into exquisitely thin Victorian glassware. He'd last seen her at Badminton, in her favourite surroundings, animated and competitive. Here in London, she seemed somehow a different woman – detached, even demure, in her white cotton blouse and on-the-knee white and black straight skirt.

Certainly she didn't look like the woman of the rumours – more ice cool than red hot. Hard to imagine her dispelling the chill of the marital bed, let alone scorching forbidden sheets with her lust.

He wasn't sure quite how to play this one. He knew what he wanted, no problem. He wanted Charlesbury and he wanted the Duchess's influence with the Duke. He'd done a good job on Willoughby himself, he thought, but who knew the power of a little pillow-talk between man and wife? If Fern Willoughby should be impressed by him as well, he reckoned he'd be home and dry.

That was why, hearing the Willoughbys were in town, he had arranged this interview with the Duchess. He intended to be his most charming self.

The trouble was that Fern was not the most easily charmed of women. When Meredith strode to the window and remarked 'Such a superb square', all she could hear were those hissing sounds, which made her think of snakes.

Would he never sit down? Or was he frightened of ruining the crease in his trousers?

'A new golden age of architecture may be about to dawn,' said Meredith pleasantly. At least, she thought, there was no hissing in *that* sentence. 'Thanks to the Duke's scheme.' *Hiss, hiss.*

'Come,' she said, making no attempt to disguise the languor in her voice, 'tell me about your plans.'

Cold as a tortoise, was her opinion. Would he scream in orgasm, though, as that creature was supposed to do, abandoning itself to an instinctive primeval urge? She doubted it. Langton Meredith looked sophisticated beyond sex.

A connoisseur of men, she rather suspected he got his kicks from something less wholesome. She hazarded a guess. A cruel streak, perhaps. Not overtly sexual at all. She thought he'd rather enjoy humiliating people. It wasn't something on *her* menu, but she thought it would be very much to Meredith's taste.

'A new town need not be without elegance,' he was saying in a pompous tone. 'You can build homes for the people and still look exclusive. A modern development needn't look like utility issue.'

Meredith was doing his share of watching, too, as he toyed with a scarcely touched glass. And he could see from the rather shapely unstockinged legs crossed away from him, from the wandering green eyes, that he hadn't yet done what he came for. The Duchess was a tougher nut to crack than the Duke.

He played his trump card. The idea had been only half-formed, but now it seemed the only way of making an impression on this woman. It would cost, back in the boardroom, but he was sure he could force it through.

Of course he could. He had the rest of the board eating out of his hand.

'We've been thinking that a really caring community, such as is absolutely *de rigeur* at Charlesbury, should find a place for charity. Since there's so much unspoiled countryside in the area, and because of your own interests....'

He allowed the idea to hang for a moment.

'You follow my drift?'

But she wasn't playing. She sipped her drink and lazily shook her head.

'Well, we thought immediately of Riding for the Disabled. How does the Mercia Special Equestrian Centre sound to you? Design, materials and labour given absolutely free, of course.'

Fern felt uncomfortably that she was being played. Does he think I'm one of my own ruddy horses? she thought. Does he think he can tug on the bit here, slacken the reins there, and I'm going to perform for him? Bloody cheek!

Yes, she knew she was being used to get at her husband. Divide and rule. What a nerve the tortoise had! He had guile, too. There was nothing to prove what he was up to. Nothing concrete she could tell Harry. Just something she could smell.

Fuck that for a lark! she decided. Blackmail was bad enough. Trying to put one over her husband was worse. She'd see what tortoises were made of.

If I'm right, she thought, he'll be crawling around Eaton Square in five minutes flat.

'A generous proposal, Mr Meredith.' Her voice deepened and her eyes blatantly travelled the length of his body, resting for a long moment at his crotch. 'Do you ride at all?'

The emphasis on the word ride was as heavy as it could be, and she wriggled on the settee until the white skirt was several inches further up her tanned thighs.

She saw him swallow hard and shake his head. She uncrossed her legs, letting them fall tantalisingly open for a second before standing up. She undid the top button of her crisp white blouse.

'So hot,' she said.

He stood paralysed in his corner as she approached.

'You're no expert in the saddle, then?' she breathed, standing close in front of him, feet parted and head thrown back, revealing a long, pale neck.

'Hardly.'

'I could give you lessons.' Her voice had become husky. 'On very reasonable terms.'

Meredith blinked and woke to action: 'I must be going,' he blurted out.

'Perhaps lessons one day, yes, perhaps so. Thank you so much for your time. And for the drink. Really quite splendid.'

With a final frightened glance at her, he almost ran from the room. Fern's long, low laugh followed him.

'They say tortoises move fast when they get hot,' she remarked to the empty room.

• • •

For all creative artists there's a low point during any project which is the moment of make or break. If it coincides with a combination of adverse biorhythms, a bout of flu, a family row, a run of bad luck and/or a visit from the creditors it can mean not only the end of the project but the end of a career.

'Is this the moment,' Calla yelled to the world at large, 'when I throw myself out of the bloody window?'

No heads turned. Not one pencil paused in its drawing. If this was indeed the end of the world as they all knew it, well, it sure as hell didn't feel much different from a thousand other moments working for CMP.

'I really don't think you should,' said the earnest voice of the temporary secretary, with the air of someone counselling a child. 'In any case . . . '

'*Please* don't tell me, Marigold, that we're on the first floor of the building. I have sound professional reasons for knowing this place. Would you like me to give you its complete dimensions, with a full break down of load-bearing ratios, the psychometrics of the air-conditioning, the dew points in the walls?

'And please don't tell me that your name isn't Marigold. I know that, too.'

It was true that not all the disasters artists are heir to had fallen upon Calla's shoulders. Her health was as sound as could be expected for anyone existing on a diet of black coffee and low-fat crisps. She didn't believe in luck, good or bad. The family row meant Jason, and she'd pushed that into the background quite satisfactorily. The bank wasn't yet baying for her blood, though God knows it might be one day soon: she pushed that thought into the background, too. As for the biorhythms, how could you tell what they were doing if you worked yourself into a frazzle right round the clock?

But she was having her difficulties, nonetheless. One of them was the deadline for Charlesbury, which was a little more than a month away. She was way behind schedule. Another was even more serious. For the first time in her professional life Calla was going through a crisis of confidence.

'I am trying to understand, Miss Marchant.'

A third – and right now the most disturbing of them all – was the oppressive incompetence of this infuriating woman who was so obviously doing her best to please. Why did Adam have to take a damn holiday? Why was he so absolutely irreplaceable? Why didn't the agency have intelligent all-rounders on their books?

'The telephone number doesn't look right, Miss Marchant.'

She had this afternoon, after great heart-searching, made one of the most difficult business decisions she'd ever had to take. Her stomach was in turmoil because of it. She had asked this secretary to do a simple thing . . .

'It starts with 00 33, Miss Marchant.'

'That's because it's a French number. You're ringing Paris. Remember?'

'But I thought you said I wouldn't need . . . '

'French. No, you won't. You won't need French because there are people there with excellent English. Probably even their secretaries have excellent English. So help me God, even *our* secretaries don't have English you can understand, spoken or written.'

'And I ask for . . . '

The poor girl peered from under her red curls, a picture of ignorance.

'Let me see the paper. It's all there, you see. Ask for this man and put him on to me. I could do this myself, but I was planning to design a building or two. Should we swap jobs, do you think?'

'Well, I'm not sure . . . '

'Please, *please*, get onto that phone!'

Calla had decided, as of half an hour ago, to accept the truth of what Bunny had told her. She needed experience at her elbow. Not because she couldn't do the job – she knew she *could*, even if things were going badly at present – but because other people might think she couldn't.

She had also looked a few months into the future. If she did get onto the shortlist in the Duke's competition she would have so much work to do on the detailed plans that the rest of her business might suffer. Her colleagues were already muttering about the time she spent away from the more routine work. They were missing her light, inventive touch. Far better if she could spread the load.

But who could she approach? Nobody at all, had been her first depressing thought. There was no way she would go crawling to Grant Locke, telling him that she'd changed her mind. That was pride, mostly, and justifiable pride. There was also the fact that, though she liked Locke, she didn't really trust him. He needed too much watching.

None of her big-name competitors would see any advantage of joining forces with CMP, and none of the smaller firms came up to Calla's high standards.

'I beg your pardon, Miss Marchant. But the pronunciation of this name . . . '

'Jeepers, creepers Marigold, are you telling me you haven't even started punching those little buttons?'

'I like to get things right, Miss Marchant,' she said with the patronising tone of the truly stupid.

With commendable patience she spoke the name, then ruined her saintly performance by scowling and giving the secretary's elbow a little push. She repeated it, enjoying the sound of it on her lips: 'Philippe Beauvoir.'

It had been a brilliant idea. A great track record, a large company, that Gallic appeal. And the thought of working side by side with Philippe had not, she admitted to herself, been any kind of deterrent.

Five minutes after she had first had the idea, and savoured it, she began to see the drawbacks. She didn't much like playing the hunter's role, whatever the circumstances. The complications of working with a man who made her pulse race might foul up the job entirely. And Philippe would probably have professional commitments for a couple of years ahead. It was crazy.

Still, she thought, nothing ventured . . .

'He's not there,' the secretary called across the room.

'Get him to call me. Urgently.'

'But I've just put the phone down, Miss Marchant.'

Now heads did turn to watch, and hands hovered over computer mice in the tracing of a drainage system and a service shaft. There were degrees in the rages of Calla Marchant and they knew, from experience, that this one was fast climbing the Richter scale.

'Pick the phone up again, Marigold.'

'It's Rona, Miss Marchant.'

'Pick up the phone, Rona. Dial the same number. Tell them who called. *Me*, I mean, not you. Say I very much want to talk to Philippe Beauvoir. Say it's important he calls me back very urgently. Then put the phone down again. Can you follow that?'

She had a wonderful colour when she was angry, and her skin glowed as if in a light fever. There wasn't a man in the office who didn't want to reach out and touch her. And there wasn't a man who would have dared. They watched her stalk from the room – it was the only way she could avoid throwing something at the girl – and they watched her just as keenly when she came back a few minutes later.

'You've done the deed?'

'I've done it, Miss Marchant. I hope he won't feel terribly harrassed, poor man.'

'Harrassed, Marigold? No, I'll rephrase that. Harrassed, Rona?'

'So soon after the great event, I mean.'

Calla inclined her head: 'And are we to be told what this grand event may be?'

'There I go again, Miss Marchant. I thought I explained the first time. Silly me! He's not there at the moment because he's away on his honeymoon.'

Nothing was thrown on this occasion. Calla felt something sharp tearing a great hole inside her. She felt empty, then angry, then foolish, and then angry again.

'Rona,' she said, with a great effort of self-control. 'I don't like it to seem that I'm blaming the messenger for the message, but I have news for you.'

'Miss Marchant?'

'Rona, you're fired!'

• • •

Daddykins,
   Your beloved daughter ecstatically finds herself worth dozens
of camels in the land of the Pharaohs and wonders
tremblingly which you'd rather have.

Oh shit, thought Grant Locke. What the hell's she doing there?

Daddykins had so far failed to come up with the goods so far as Malibu's future was concerned. The fact was that Grant Locke had been too busy drawing up plans – plans for Charlesbury and plans, not quite abandoned, for the seduction of Calla Marchant.

Young Malibu had sniffed freedom at the gates of her boarding school this July and, having sniffed and rejected rather more toxic substances inside the place, had left it for ever. Her father had last seen her about to board a plane for Cannes in the company of a schoolfriend who boasted dozens of relatives in the south of France. Sun, sea, sand and topless bathing were on the menu, along with the salad nicoise and bouillabaisse which were the local specialities.

Grant Locke's geographical know-how was up to the difference between Cannes and Cairo. This accounted for his perplexity. Perplexity, be damned. He was put out and, yes, he was somewhat worried. As Malibu would have been the first to point out, teenage daughters are supposed to make fathers worried.

Also ecstatically finds herself away from Nina's creepy auntie.
Lots of traffic in Egypt as well as oxen with all their jiggly bits
intact. Will see you soon if the mummy's curse doesn't get me.

'She'll know it if it does,' Locke said grimly, thinking of another mummy altogether. What in God's name was he going to do with this lively, dangerous, firecracker of a daughter?

By the time he got the postcard, of course, Malibu had left Cairo and was working her way along the Nile on a felucca – those oarless, engine-less boats which trust to the gods and a wind in the sails.

We shit straight into the sacred river,. she put on her next postcard. ('Her mother's daughter,' thought Locke.)
I would have made a first-class Cleopatra.

'And God help any Antonies,' murmured her father. Thank heavens there hadn't been any so far. One of the advantages of an English boarding school. But that affliction would doubtless come all too soon.

'Let's hope my daughter has better taste in men than her mother,' he said to himself. 'We could do with some class in the family.'

The problem with Malibu was that red lights meant nothing to her. She just didn't see them. It was green for go all the way. She was blind to any obstacles in her path. And rather like a baby who hadn't learned the danger of falling over, she possessed a strange ability to bounce back unharmed.

For now, Locke thought with a shudder. He admired single-mindedness, but he couldn't help thinking that Malibu would one day come a nasty cropper as irresistible force met immoveable object.

The first immoveable object proved to be the Egyptian police. She had made a dramatic reappearance in the capital. How did he know? It was the British embassy on the line.

'Tell me slowly,' he said. 'I want to write this down.'

It was simple. It was almost predictable. Half way up the dark, narrow passage along which the tourists crawl, doubled-up, to reach the very heart of the Great Pyramid at Giza, Malibu had caused a scene. Groped in that confined space by a lustful native, Locke's daughter had somehow found the room to take a hearty swing at him. She'd also sent several large American and German tourists flying and caused a massive disturbance in the final resting place of Rameses III.

'Frightful, Daddykins,' her excited voice had buzzed across continents along the embassy telephone wire. 'I spent a night in the cells – not very Cleopatra at all!'

Locke groaned: 'For Christ's sake do come back, Malibu. You're not fit to be allowed out.'

She didn't hear him, of course.

'I'm being thrown out of the country, so I'm going to come back . . . '

'Wonderful!'

' . . . via Morocco and Spain.'

The line went dead, leaving Locke with no option but to pour a huge scotch. He seemed to have been getting through a lot of it lately.

What *was* he going to do with her? Malibu had been a bundle of surprises from the beginning. Even her conception had been a surprise, he thought wryly. And whatever else he'd expected from his daughter, he hadn't envisaged a jail sentence and deportation by the time she was seventeen.

He knew he must find her a career, but it would have to be something a little different, where oddballs like his daughter would pass as one of the crowd. Most other father's could take the mother's advice. No chance here. He had no idea where Malibu's mother was. He'd never heard a word from her or about her since she walked out all those years ago.

'Wanted,' he dictated to the wall. 'Job for unreliable 17-year-old with a prison record.' Then he took another slug of scotch and added: 'Plus a hell of a lot of guts. They'll be lucky to have her.'

Her next postcard was from the Moroccan coast.

> *Daddykins. Have abdicated Egyptian throne in favour of being a mermaid Girl Friday for Australian telly crew doing underwater series called 'After Cousteau'. Am learning to dive. Have snorkel, will travel. Malibu.*

By this time, Locke was becoming blase about his daughter's travels. What blasted option did he have in any case but to let her get on with it? But when she came back, whenever that might be – *if* she came back – it would be time to take her future seriously.

Yes, he would find her a job and he'd insist that she persevere with it. For a time, at least. He'd make her promise on her honour.

'If she's still got it,' he muttered aloud as the postman came into view brandishing yet another pretty card.

● ● ●

The call came just as Calla was screwing one of her sketches into a tight paper ball and hurling it with venom at her favourite wastepaper basket by the far wall. She liked it best because it was large and just within range if she could muster sufficient rage to power her slender arm. This time the missile thwacked inside it without touching the rim.

'Bullseye!' she exclaimed with satisfaction as she put the telephone to her ear.

'Hello,' said a rather alarmed voice. 'This is Philippe Beauvoir.'

'Philippe!'

But what else were you supposed to say when you knew that the situation was preposterous from every point of view? Did you put the phone down? Or did you bluff it out? With Calla Marchant there was never any real question.

'You've had a good holiday, Philippe? Somewhere warm?'

'The Greek islands. Very remote.'

'Wonderful! So you've come back eager for work? I have a proposition you won't be able to resist.'

I sound, she thought, like some huckster selling double-glazing for a living.

'I've come back, of course, to piles of outstanding work, Calla. But what is it you wish to suggest?'

Calla was quite at home with the telephone, but she had to admit that it could be a pretty chilling device. Was this the man she'd felt so close to in Paris only a few months ago? He sounded strangely distant.

What you mean, she told herself bitterly, *is that he sounds horribly married.*

'Think of it as an opportunity, Philippe. You remember the Charlesbury scheme?'

'How could I forget? That passion of yours!'

'It was why I asked you show me round La Villette, remember? You told me there were similarities. You said there were lessons I could learn from that gorgeous development. Do you remember saying how much you would envy the winner of the Charlesbury competition? Do you remember telling me that your partnership had decided not to enter only because you thought the Duke was bound to choose an English architect?'

'Yes, I remember, Calla.'

'Then here's your chance! Come and join me here in London.' There was a silence at the other end. 'I mean, of course, only for the short time it takes to complete the initial plans.' The silence lengthened. 'I've already finished the basic design.'

'Calla,' he said at last, 'you know about my holiday?'

'Yes, I know, Philippe. I should have congratulated you before. Who is she?'

'Yvette. She is a very sweet girl.'

'Wonderful!' lied Calla blatantly. 'I'm very pleased for you Philippe. But,' she laughed, 'I *am* talking business, in case you doubted my motives.'

'Of course not for a moment. How could I? It's only that my life is rather in turmoil at present. In a pleasant way, naturally. When does this competition close?'

'September the first.'

This time the silence was preceded by a gasp and terminated, after what seemed an age, by a murmur of incredulity.

'You mean this year, Calla? *This* September the first? That allows just four weeks, I think.'

'Four weeks, two days and six hours five minutes. We're talking English time, don't forget. Every hour counts.'

'I like your humour, Calla, but this thing is impossible. Even if I could persuade my fellow partners that this was a good scheme for us, we haven't the time. Not possibly.'

'But you haven't seen my designs, Philippe,' she persisted brightly. 'I'm offering you what the Americans call a slice of the action for very little effort. What I get from it is your experience and your name. I wouldn't try to hide that from you. What you get is a back-door, last-minute entry into a competition which could pin another medal on your shirt-front.'

'And if we failed, would I not end up with something else down my shirt-front?'

'Nonsense, Philippe! Who hasn't lost in a competition before? In any case, you know that we'll produce something unsurpassable between us.'

'Do I?'

'Yes you do, dammit! And what am I asking? Four weeks of your time.'

'And if we are chosen for the short-list? Then we shall be occupied for a much longer time, creating models, making precise calculations, drawing up detailed blueprints.'

'For which you'll be largely reimbursed, because the Duke is putting money up for that stage of the competition. And anyway, Philippe, have you suddenly become some kind of time-and-money merchant?'

She almost added 'now that you're married', but managed to check herself. Of course any architect had to be conscious of time and money, but she knew there was a romantic side of Philippe to be played. She'd play it for all it was worth.

'Calla, I *am* excited by this project. I would like to be involved. It's just that I don't see how.'

'Every month of your life is planned and plotted, as if you were a cog in a machine?'

'No, no, clearly not. But even if I did manage to persuade my partners, I am absolutely tied up here until the middle of next week. Wednesday.'

'Still time enough,' she urged him. 'We could do it!'

'In three weeks?'

'Plus one day, five hours and fifty-five minutes. Are you telling me you've lost your zest for life, Philippe? And I thought the French had romance, caprice – passion!'

'You are teasing me, Calla.'

Yes, she was teasing him, cajoling him, charming him, twisting his arm, brow-beating him – doing any damn thing she could think of. All her doubts and frustration had fallen away from her during the course of this frantic duel. She was playing to win. She was playing for her future.

'Just three weeks of your life, Philippe. And for such a prize!'

He laughed. She heard him turn away from the telephone, then cover it with his hand as he spoke. She found herself clutching her handset with a grip which made her fingers ache.

'Listen, Calla,' he said at last. 'I have a meeting with my board this afternoon. I shall do what I can.'

'Oh, you wonderful man!'

No, on reflection, perhaps that wasn't the thing to say to someone with whom you wanted nothing more than a proper professional relationship. On the other hand, he was a pretty wonderful man, and she was feeling high as a kite.

'No promises.'

She could hear his smile.

'If you can't persuade them you won't deserve to design another single building in all your miserable life.'

'I shall do what I can,' he repeated.

Calla put down the phone, marched to the bin, took out the ball of paper, returned to her desk and hurled it all over again. It was another clean shot, clean as a whistle – and this time she wasn't angry at all!

15

The Bowerman Institute was situated in as angst-free a location as it was possible to find. In that beautiful Welsh border country the only problems you had were the ones you brought with you. From all the windows there were views of the Black Mountains, with oak, chestnuts and ash in full summer leaf. The grounds stretched away, all lawns, lakes and flowerbeds, as far as the eye could see. Sheep grazed placidly beyond a distant rustic fence.

'The only rule we have here,' Desmond Fesh was saying, 'is a pretty tough one. You have to see me three times a week and at least go through the motions of a proper consultation.'

Fesh was the organisation's senior psychiatrist, a man who'd long since escaped the exhaustion and low pay of a consultancy in the National Health Service. Here he was highly regarded and handsomely rewarded, and he was never in a hurry.

'Ridiculous to put so much power into one set of hands, I know, but if you don't turn up, or if I don't like your attitude when you do, then it's goodbye and thanks for the memory. And thanks for the cheque, of course.'

'Which isn't exactly a small one,' Jason remarked.

'Bloody huge, if you ask me.'

They were sprawled at either end of a large leather sofa in Fesh's room. The William Morris pomegranate wallpaper, the delicate water-colours in their pine frames, the swags of curtains in a rich cream colour, the huge windows which allowed the bright August light to swamp the interior, all seemed designed to increase the atmosphere of repose. Fesh's dry cynicism seemed oddly at variance with it.

'The only excuse for it,' he said, 'is that we get results.'

'Guaranteed?'

Fesh guffawed: 'My arse!' he said. 'With you lot?'

He slid a sleek silver box from his pocket and, having first offered it to his new client, prised out a filter-tipped cigarette with a bony finger. He lit it and blew a cloud of grey smoke happily into the air above his head.

'Addiction. We've all got it. Or it's got *us*. But some of us, boyo – as they're supposed to say around here, but rarely do – are in a tighter grip than others.'

'Thank you.'

'Don't mention it. If you do have reason to thank me, you'll be in a minority.'

Jason frowned: 'This isn't exactly reassuring. What about this success rate you're supposed to have.'

'Do have. We're very successful. Twenty-five per cent of our inmates' – he stressed the word satirically – 'go away completely cured. For the kinds of case we get in here, that's bloody remarkable. Most of them don't give themselves a chance.'

'In what way?'

Fesh pointed his cigarette towards Jason and thrust it out like an accusing finger.

'Naughty boys who don't take advice,' he said. 'Who, for instance, insist on coming accompanied.'

'Peta needs it as much as I do,' Jason replied sullenly. Who was this jerk calling a boy? 'And we'll give each other moral support.'

This time Fesh gave a belly laugh: 'As the bishop said to the actress! Ha!' He sucked on his cigarette and peered through the smoke with narrowed eyes. 'What will actually happen is that one of you will drag the other down. That's the reality of it. Because you're both looking for ways to give up this spartan regime and get back to the good old life, that exciting life with coke taking charge of your brain.'

'I'm sure you know best,' Jason said sarcastically.

'Bloody well ought to, old thing. I've seen enough of it. Wasted lives is one thing, but all those wasted cheques! Seems all wrong to me.'

He noticed that Jason's eyes had roved more than once among the watercolours.

'Wouldn't mind your advice on what to buy,' he said. 'You *are* the Jason Andover who writes for the arty magazines? Don't suppose you'll find much of interest here.'

Jason ignored the comment: 'What do I have to do to get out of here cured?' he demanded. 'What's the big secret?'

'Wanting to.'

'I want to, damn it.'

'Really wanting to. Wanting to so much that you're prepared to face the truth about yourself. That's the sticking point usually.' He waved away the smoke that was drifting between them. 'Do you know why you need the coke? Correction, the ice. Bloody expensive, that.'

He saw that Jason was struggling for a reply: 'No, no, don't sweat over an answer now. This is just a casual, friendly chat for starters. But think about it. I'm not talking about the good feeling it gives you. It would give me one, too, I don't doubt, but I'm quite satisfied by my ciggies.'

'So may I ask,' Jason ventured, 'why you need cigarettes?'

'Bloody impertinent, but you may. And I reply that I've never bothered to ask myself the question. I'm not bothered, you see. I've read the cancer statistics and for some reason they don't frighten me. They should, but they don't.

'If you're not frightened by what coke or ice can do to you, fine. Save your money. I don't need it. There are plenty of other mugs out there.'

● ● ●

After the initial craving came the heaviness in the limbs, the constant fatigue. He dragged himself around the grounds like an old man. His heart seemed to pound with a dull slowness inside his chest, and he was aware of the throbbing whenever he stood still.

Why were these trees and the mountains which showed above them not things of beauty? Jason knew that they must be, he had a memory of their beauty, but he was unable to feel anything. They were only shapes. He gazed upon them with a great sourness of spirit.

He was unapproachable. Other people seemed unreal to him, and he ignored them, even when they spoke. What did they matter? What did their thoughts and opinions matter? What did anything matter?

Then the dreams began. The first came in a long and agonised night of sweat and threshing. It repeated itself over and over and wouldn't go away. He tore at his sheets and muttered and raged like a madman.

He was being dragged along through liquid, with a roaring sound in his ears and an ache in his stomach. It was the sea! He was deep in the sea, and being pulled by something, but he couldn't get his hands free. The noise was an engine. He saw it descending, floating past him, with its propellors still whirring, the engine of a boat. And then he saw something caught up in the engine, something red and mangled and his eyes turned away from it in horror and saw only a giant fish, pulling him through the water.

The underwater darkness cleared to a bright green, with sunlight playing through it and he saw a female form sitting by a kind of monument, smiling and beckoning with her finger. But as he tried to approach she gave a flick of her skirt, like a fish, and spun away, still smiling and beckoning. He could not reach her, however hard he struggled. He was held back by the tow of the water. He was screaming but his voice could not be heard for the movement of the water and the continuous whine of the engine.

He found himself on the floor in a drenching sweat, the sheets wrapped round his legs, torn. It was three in the morning. His forehead suddenly felt terribly cold. He sat on the bed, hugging himself, not daring to return to bed and to sleep.

• • •

Desmond Fesh flicked open the file marked 'Andover, Jason' and made a few deft squiggles on the topmost sheet of paper.

'End of round one,' he said. 'Opponent unscathed.'

'Opponent feeling absolutely ghastly,' Jason replied. 'Give me a fifteen-rounder with Lennox Lewis any day.'

'At least you've still a little humour left. Enjoy it while you can. The worst is yet to come.'

'You're a great encouragement,' Jason said bitterly.

'I'm a bloody realist, matey, that's what I am. You've told me nothing yet. Wait until you do.'

'As far as I'm concerned,' Jason told him, 'I've waded through more trivia about my early years than anyone in his right mind would want to know. Or perhaps that doesn't apply.'

'Bullseye, old chum! All psychiatrists are mad. I am a particularly good psychiatrist. Therefore I am madder than most. You may be glad of that.'

'How come?'

'It takes a nutter to understand one, that's how. There'll be moments when you'll think you're going off your head, and that's when you must remember to come to me in a hurry. What you don't do is take a taxi to the River Wye and throw yourself in. Is that a deal?'

'No promises.'

• • •

Soon the dreams began to invade his waking hours. He staggered along the gravel paths and across the lawns like a drunkard, totally disorientated. He was more alive in his nightmares than in what everyone else took for the real world. He somehow avoided benches and trees, but he wasn't seeing them. He was seeing faces he half recognised, hearing sounds that were indistinct but which filled him with terror. He would sit staring at the landscape, overcome by self-loathing.

'I can't stand much more of this,' Peta said, hunched beside him on a wooden bench. 'Do you remember when we used to get a kick out of life?'

'How many years ago was that?'

'This isn't life, Jason. It's a fucking slow death. I want to go home.'

'I'm not coming,' he said doggedly. He almost added 'not yet'. He wasn't sure he could take much more either, but he was hanging on. Desperately hanging on.

'How's your trick cyclist?' she asked.

'Fesh is okay.' No he's not, he thought. He's an arrogant bastard. But Jason didn't want to admit any of this to Peta. He was hanging on. 'We just talk.'

'Oh we talk, Miss Langport and I. Zeeta Langport. Real buddy buddies. I tell her anything she wants to hear. There was a good story about me and the oddjob man at school. Behind the bicycle sheds.' She laughed. 'I was very proud of that one.'

'You mean you're making stuff up?'

'Of course I am, Jason. Isn't that the idea? It's a delicious game. You invent rivetting yarns and they try to find out how close to the truth they are. It's the only thing that's keeping me going. It's incredibly tedious here.'

'And the dreams? Are you having dreams?'

'Ooh, no Jason – you lucky beggar! How come you're having all these lovely fantasies and I just feel zapped out and bored? Are you paying extra or something?'

He stood up, with difficulty, and shuffled away from her. Meeting people, even the lovely Peta, was almost impossible now. He stared into their faces and their eyes were like split cinema screens. He watched ghastly dramas being played out there. When they spoke he heard other conversations trying to break through.

Underneath everything there was a scraping sound, which sometimes rose to a kind of screech. He felt he knew what it was, but he couldn't find the name. It was there behind the drone of that engine, behind the suck and burble of the sea. It accompanied him like a private ghost which nobody else could hear. They would see him cock an ear to the wind.

'Poor guy's off his head,' they'd think.

Then one morning, when the air was very still, he heard it very clearly and knew exactly what it was. Those scrapings were the rasp of a bow on violin strings.

• • •

'Tell me about the music,' Fesh said, crossing his legs to reveal a pair of patterned socks. 'What's your first memory of it.'

'The piano. My mother playing it.'

'Ah.'

Oh God, Jason thought, his brain still working well enough to understand the satisfaction in Fesh's murmur. It's the mother thing. Oedipus next?

'And can you remember the first time you heard it? Where were you? Next to the piano, perhaps?'

'Under it.' No, this wouldn't do. Peta made up stories. He was trying to play the game. He was serious. He was going to beat his addiction. 'I can't remember.'

'You don't want to remember, maybe.'

How had he come to be here? How had the addiction started? He really couldn't remember, not right now. His head was muzzy. But it was nothing to do with his mother, that he was sure of.

'Spare me this routine, please,' he said brusquely.

'We don't like it, eh boyo? Hitting home a little, is it?'

'It's very wide of the mark, actually.'

'Is it, *actually*? Forgive me if I insist on being in charge here. I'm the brainbuster, remember. You're the patient. Didn't we agree on that at the outset?'

They returned to the piano and his mother. They talked about his mother's artistic interests and how they had been passed on to her older son. He tried as hard as he could to trawl up a few distant memories. He felt that he wasn't doing well enough.

'Whose life is this?' he demanded at one point. 'Aren't I allowed to know something about how it was?'

'Don't be disingenuous, Jason. I don't need to tell you that people erect barriers against distressing memories.'

You couldn't win with a psychiatrist. If what you told them supported their theories, fine. They accepted it. If what you told them threatened their theories you must be covering up, lying. Jason began to feel more rebellious. Perhaps Peta was right. He didn't want to be hooked on ice or coke, but that felt one hell of a lot better than being turned into a zombie and interrogated by a survivor of the Third Reich.

'How good were you with the violin?' Fesh asked, checking his watch. The session was nearly over. He'd begun to sound a little bored.

Jason sat forward and spoke deliberately: 'I was shit hot.'

'Really? Just *how* shit hot?'

But why should he tell him? It was impossible to explain all that, especially in the few minutes left before he was discharged for another forty-eight hours.

'I used to charm the birds off the trees,' he said sullenly.

'Hm,' Fesh responded. 'Haven't got it with you, I suppose?' He closed the file with a loud clap. 'I'll get hold of one for you. I'd like to hear you play.'

• • •

He had never known how vital it was to his life until the accident took his genius away.

In that golden youth of his, where there was so much love, vitality and glamour, it was easy to believe that happiness was somehow indivisible – that all the parts of it were equal. He loved playing the violin just as he enjoyed hitting a cricket ball to the boundary, running his fingers over a bronze statuette or bracing himself against the seat of a careering power-boat. It was a charmed existence.

Jason had felt sorry for anyone who didn't thrill to the variety of life as he did. Patrick, for instance. He'd never understood his younger brother. The poor little fellow seemed to have been born with essential parts of his nature missing. So many of the things Jason relished, Patrick didn't respond to at all. And when the younger boy did share an interest, he seemed to have an all-or-nothing attitude to it, as a kind of gross over-adjustment.

At first his accomplishment with the violin had been nothing but another technical achievement to feel satisfied about. He took to it naturally, and therefore undervalued it. Later, effortlessly progressing, he enjoyed leading the orchestra. He loved the applause, and milked it for all he was worth. Playing solo to a large audience was extremely gratifying.

But if you'd asked him, he would have said he could give it up tomorrow. There were so many other things to do.

'You don't take life seriously,' Patrick once accused him, in the direct manner he'd grown accustomed to. Jason was then nineteen and his brother fifteen, but really Patrick should have been born first. 'You're aimless.'

'What sort of aim do you think I need?'

'It doesn't matter what it is, Jason, but you have to have it. In my case it's making a success of the business. Turning investments around to make a profit. I know that means nothing to you, but it's what puts fire in my belly. There's nothing you really want to achieve, is there?'

No, there wasn't. Jason didn't see life as a challenge. It was simply there to be enjoyed. Of course there was an immediate challenge in playing a piece of music well, hitting the shot just right and the rest of it. But there was no ambition tied to it. That's where they differed.

'Don't you ever ask yourself,' Patrick went on, 'what the point of your existence is?'

'Thanks, little brother.'

He suddenly felt something heavy smash against his cheek so that he toppled to one knee.

'Bloody hell!' he said.

'Don't ever call me that again,' Patrick bellowed, his face red and his fists waving in the air. 'Okay?'

It was fathers and their teenage sons who were supposed to have these battles of the will, Jason thought, already seeing the humorous side of it. Patrick seemed to be picking him off first. This was the first rung on his unstoppable climb up the ladder.

'Okay,' he agreed, making sure that he didn't laugh. The kid was wild.

That incident not only brought their differences into sharp focus, it also established their relationship to one another ever afterwards. In his own mind, Patrick saw himself as the serious, responsible one. Jason was some kind of parasite. He was no use to anyone.

And Jason? He adopted a satirical view of his brother's behaviour. Privately he laughed at Patrick's boorish ebullience, but he didn't do a thing to check it. If Patrick wanted to win battles of his own making, let him! Jason wasn't even concerned about getting knocked over every now and again.

What he couldn't possibly have explained to Patrick was the importance that his violin playing had begun to have for him. He just wouldn't have understood. What would have made sense to Patrick was an ambition to be the greatest musician of the century, with the financial rewards to match. You could measure that. But pure pleasure? For Patrick that was like the fierce satisfaction of an orgasm. There was no harm in it – in fact you needed it urgently and frequently – but you wouldn't base a life on it. Patrick needed sexual conquests very badly, but no woman would ever stand in the way of his career.

Jason, who was so much more sensitive than his brother, found a pleasure in his music which was as keen as an orgasm but which was much more profound. It was somehow an expression of his very being. He had begun to explore his own thoughts and feelings by coaxing those wonderful, elaborate sounds from his violin. This discovery crept up on him very stealthily, and he still hadn't come to terms with it at the time he swam among the wreckage of the *Andover Ace* and ruined his talent by saving his brother's life.

'It's a blessing in disguise,' Patrick told him bluntly, while they were still recovering from the trauma. 'You were wasting your time fiddling away with that orchestra.'

'Absolutely.'

His tongue was somewhere in his cheek, but Patrick couldn't see that. Patrick assumed that his brother had yielded control of the family's destiny to him. And Jason, because his only weapon was this subtle irony, found that he had, in fact, given up that control with scarcely a murmur. He didn't care enough about it.

'Far better,' he told Calla in their early days, 'that the business is in the hands of someone who's fanatical about it. I'd bankrupt us within a month.'

That was why, as the tragedy of his wasted talent began to take hold of him, he made no effort to put himself right. Patrick was the one who looked after the material world, who got things done, who rolled up his sleeves and achieved things. It was Jason's lot to reflect, to observe, to cast a whimsical eye on things. That became his habit, then his philosophy. He gradually began to abandon the control of his ultimate responsibility – himself.

It was inevitable that, when Patrick approached him about his investment in Calla's business, he should put up no fight whatsoever.

'I've drawn up the document,' Patrick said, waving it under his nose. 'It's simply a matter of playing the grown-up, Jason.'

'Calla should be asked.'

'I've already cleared it with her. She's signed it. See for yourself. Do you want me to spell out what it says?'

'Only if you think I'd understand it. No – you know that I wouldn't. You're the financial genius. Hand me the pen.'

• • •

Desmond Fesh plucked the strings pizzicato-style, then thrust the instrument towards Jason.

'I don't think so, thanks very much.'

'It won't bite.'

Yes it will, Jason thought. He was frightened of it. He couldn't put out his hands towards it. Those ghostly scraping sounds had begun to dominate his waking and sleeping hours.

'Not a very good one, I dare say. It belonged to the daughter of our chef. Excuse the presumption, old cock, but you'll have noticed we don't call him the cook. Bit infra dig in such a classy establishment. Borrow it for as long as you like.'

'I've forgotten how.'

'Balls! Do you think if I had a bit of a lay-off I'd forget how to provoke my patients?'

'Doubtless not.'

'Ah! A touch of sarcasm! How long since you played?'

Jason shook his head. The tiredness, the state of absolute apathy, had intensified every day, and now he felt sick in his stomach, too.

'A year?' Fesh watched the head shake again, heavily. 'Two years? Five?'

'Damn you!' Jason shouted. 'I don't want to talk about it!'

'Excellent. Now I really think we're getting somewhere.'

● ● ●

It was hottest day of a hot summer. Jason lay, shirtless, under a tree, his hand picking slowly at yellowing blades of grass. Peta, her little snub nose a shade of red, sprawled in a cotton dress which had slipped off one shoulder, revealing the soft swelling of her breast. Her hair was loose and she hadn't worn make-up for days.

'I'm going back,' she said.

'When?'

'Now. Right now.'

'You don't seem to be moving.'

'I'm going once my brain and my body come back into contact. That hasn't happened much since I entered this godforsaken place.'

Jason breathed deeply and reached out with his hand until it covered hers: 'Please stay, Peta. I need you here.'

'And what do I need?'

He spoke slowly. Even opening his lips was an effort: 'Not me, evidently.'

Somewhere he remembered that Calla hadn't seemed to need him recently, either.

A four-seater light aircraft buzzed in the sky, passing from left to right. It was bright red and the sun winked off its windows. This constituted an event at the Bowerman Institute, and they followed its progress as if they were hypnotised. Nothing ever happened inside, unless one of the patients threw a wobbly. Outside, there were only trees, mountains, sheep and the sounds of distant cars.

'Why don't you come with me? It would be like before. That was good.'

'If it was good, why did we come here?'

'One more kick,' she said lazily. 'Try anything once. But it's not any fun. It's never been the slightest fun.'

'It's not supposed to be fun, Peta.'

'Then why do we do it?'

He watched as she laboriously raised herself to her knees.

'Help me up,' she said. He shook his head. 'Damn you,' she said and, panting, pushed herself up with extended arms. She leaned against a tree, trembling.

'Don't go.'

'You're stupid, Jason,' she told him, a little smile puckering her lips. 'You know what you are? You're a fucking moron.'

'Thank you.'

'Come with me, eh? Come with your Peta and she'll do all the things she did before, only even better. She'll do them in lots of different ways and much more often. Eh?'

He covered his head with his arms. Through the gap he watched her walk away, unsteadily.

'I'll be waiting,' she called.

She continued to the house and went inside. Jason sat staring at the building for a very long time. Eventually a car drew up outside, and then the door opened and she came out carrying a suitcase. She got in the car and it drove off.

Jason reached forward and took hold of the violin which was propped against the tree. When his fingers tugged at the strings they made the noise that had been in his head for days and wouldn't go away.

16

Philippe Beauvoir looked out of the plane window at the French coastline below. Back there were Paris and his new wife Yvette. On the other side of the iron grey strip of water lay the biggest architectural prize of the decade. And Calla Marchant.

'Monsieur. Votre boisson.' The Air France stewardess brought him the champagne which goes with all that airline's first class seats. And he watched the fizzing bubbles and thought of the last time he saw Calla Marchant. It was months ago. Before his marriage.

He smiled at the thought. Yvette was so sweet. He had never felt such a desire to protect a woman before, to bend over her, wrap her up in him and keep her from harm. She was his jeune fille, his light, his sweetness. Discovering her had been like finding a precious, untouched part of himself.

The smile faded slightly as the plane lost itself once again in cloud. There were so many different sorts of women, at least to a Frenchman's eye. And Philippe, though no playboy, knew he could have loved very differently.

See the stewardness in her neat high heels, her just-so make-up and her scraped-back hair. What might she be like with loosened locks, bare legs and champagne to drink instead of to serve?

Ah, he liked to let his mind play around women, those fascinating creatures of emotion and drama, facade and frippery. No imagination was needed with Calla Marchant. Every fibre of her being spoke the true woman. Philippe had been aware of that from the beginning. Calla was no more likely to crave protection than she was to wear a uniform and do other people's bidding.

'Elle est comme feu,' he murmured.

She was like fire – ever-changing, dangerous and yet compelling. There had been a time when he had felt drawn by the heat and the shapes he thought he could see in the flames. But that was months ago.

He sipped the champagne and wondered how on earth this had come about. Why was he sitting here, rushing to the muggy uncertainty of a British summer, to the unruly sprawl which was London at the whim of a woman who had simply caused his heart to beat a little faster months ago?

He had reluctantly left his young wife and the bed made warm by her soft, yielding body that morning and yet he now found himself excited, almost against his will, by the prospect of the next few weeks.

'Imbecile,' he said, half-aloud. All that was self-deception. He knew, of course he knew, exactly how it had come about. As Calla cajoled him on the phone, each phrase had re-painted the violet eyes, the curve of her neck, the passion she showed every time he took her to a new building.

When he had put the phone down, he could almost reach out and touch the painted canvas, almost feel it turn to flesh. That was how it had come about and he knew it. But Calla must not know it. He owed that, at least, to Yvette.

Charlesbury after all was a hell of a project, with prizes to match. They would make a fine team, he and Calla, a handsome pair of winners. How good she would look at an award ceremony – every bit as good as the chichest Frenchwoman. Again, he had to call the wandering thoughts to order before they began to explore that magnificent, forbidden territory. He was a married man and Calla Marchant was strictly out of bounds.

They would be working too hard for that kind of thing, anyway. Time was so short, the task so huge. The weeks would pass quickly and then he would once again be alongside his Yvette, where he belonged. That was right, he thought. And once the plane landed and his feet touched solid ground, no doubt he would feel it was right, too.

He ordered more Champagne. And thinking she gave him a special smile, he looked appreciatively at the stewardess and gave her a lazy wink in reply.

And Calla Marchant? She was giving a few sedate BMWs driving lessons on the M25. She had a flight to meet at Heathrow and was cutting it fine, in habitual style. It was a Sunday and the red Porsche was able to speed along without delays towards Heathrow.

She couldn't help grinning as yet another indignant looking young man in his GTi was left in her scarlet wake. They loved to try it on when they saw a woman at the wheel of a powerful car. They took it as some sort of challenge to their manhood, which could only be answered by a right foot pressed down to the floor.

But Calla liked a challenge, whether it was making male drivers look very small in her rear window or turning a broken-down old church into designer flats complete with stained glass and chapel-shaped kitchens. That one had won an award, she remembered.

She'd caught the market when it was at its height and single people with lots of spare money roamed the east of London looking for flats within reach of the City – the City with its markets for making their money and its wine bars for spending it.

In the early days, she remembered, she'd had support for her dreams. She remembered how she and Jason had wandered derelict sites, imagining what might be built there. When she had begun to see her own designs become real buildings on those sites she had turned to him for praise – and seen only a vacuous stare.

But she cut off these thoughts. Even now, she couldn't bring herself to destroy the last thread of feeling for Jason. The wound was too fresh and too deep for that. The early years were still sweet in her memory, in spite of his weakness, his betrayal. Even in spite of that insipid streak of blonde nothingness he had taken to his bed.

There was no time for men now. The only man she wanted to impress was the Duke of Mercia. It would take some doing, she knew. The planning sheets she had got through were testimony to her sleepless nights, her working weekends, her utter determination.

'Half a Brazilian rain forest here,' Adam had remarked as he had waded into her office one Monday morning, when she had started at 6am. 'Perhaps you should plant a few forests at Charlesbury? Uh-oh! Don't throw that ink. I've got your Lagerfeld jacket here, just back from the cleaners.'

Adam was a gem, even if he could be as bitchy as the Barracuda and less than inclined to take Charlesbury as seriously as he ought. She had spared the ink and the jacket.

Calla leant forward to turn up the stereo, without taking her eyes off the road. It was Paul Weller and Wild Blue Yonder.

'Ha! No time for men? Like hell!' she said with a wry smile. 'And here you are breaking speed limits to pick up a high quality masculine sample from the airport.'

She flashed an ambitious Renault 21 out of the way and added: 'A second-hand sample. Used, married, shop-soiled. Snatched from his honeymoon. And, gawd damn it, knee-trembling material for all that.'

She could still feel that hand under her elbow leading her to the hotel on a sunny spring afternoon in Paris. 'Good job this is strictly professional,' she thought, taking the turning off the motorway for the airport.

In the moments before he came through Customs and into the arrivals lounge, she wondered how to greet him. A handshake was ridiculous, surely, between people whose eyes had rested almost as closely as two hands. The French kissed naturally upon meeting, after all.

'Relax, woman!' she said under her breath. 'It's professional, remember.'

She knew she was a liar as soon as she saw him, framed for a few seconds in the customs doorway, looking this way and that for her face. She throbbed as she recognised the greying hairs among the dark, the casual way his jacket was thrown over one shoulder, the very reality of having Philippe just a few feet away.

Calla had an advantage over him of a precious few seconds. She used them to pull herself together. She was a woman of strong physical responses and she knew it. She could recognise the animal in herself, and her instinct was to go for what she wanted. But she checked it.

Whatever happened, she mustn't scare him off. Her whole ambition rested on making a success of the partnership. Other lusts would have to be suppressed. 'So let's collect the married man,' she murmured, waving to catch his attention.

His embrace was friendly and polite – a Gallic kiss on both cheeks, the hand which had once taken her elbow as if by right now resting lightly on her arm for a moment, that was all.

All passion spent, was Calla's thought as she felt the lightness of his touch. Working together would be easy enough if he kept this up. No danger of distraction under the duvet at any rate. She saw no hint of a struggle to keep down an unruly passion. All to the good, of course. Of course.

Calla was wrong. Philippe had even considered going through the red channel though he had nothing to declare, just to give himself time to fight the mounting sense of excitement. As he emerged, he was momentarily unable to visualise Calla, though she'd been in his mind most of the flight. For a few seconds he couldn't remember what she looked like.

Then she was there and he was brushing those beautiful high cheekbones with his lips, still feeling that his senses were left behind him, up in the clouds.

But it was real, as real as his wedding ring, and he was relieved to see that Calla was greeting him with calm pleasure. There was no dangerous amour beating beneath the surface here, after all. That imagined passion had been the influence of a spring day, of Paris and of those glassy pyramids with their plays on light and water. That's what he was thinking. With relief.

And – *merde!* – with a tinge of disappointment.

There would, though, be other passions in the crowded days and weeks ahead. There were dreams to realise, buildings to make, people's lives to shape.

'This is madness, Calla, is it not?' he said as the gleaming red Porsche headed south west for Charlesbury. They had decided to inspect the site even before Philippe had checked into his hotel – there was no time to waste. 'Whoever heard of a whole new community designed in three weeks? I think it's quite impossible, and that we're a little crazy to try it.'

'Yes, crazy,' laughed Calla. 'But isn't everything that's great a little crazy, too?'

Like a certain lady, he almost said. But (he made a sudden vow to himself and the absent Yvette) flirting was out on this trip. Even with a woman apparently poured into her jeans and watered with a lagoon blue shirt of washed silk.

They strolled round Charlesbury and walked the ground where the new community would be built. From the far bank of the river, they looked across at Willoughby Hall, aloof from the town itself and yet about to take charge of its destiny.

'Very autocratic,' said Philippe. 'And yet, so English. Our French aristocracy never imagined they had any responsibility towards the peasants. Their chateaux are fortified against the outside world, like a castle. Your English stately homes aren't like that at all.'

He surprised her by insisting that they visit the churchyard at Charlsbury to discover what local heroes the place had bred.

'A pattern for the living may be suggested by the dead,' he murmured.

She laughed: 'That sounds rather philosophical.'

'But of course. There's no philosophy in your architecture?'

Calla looked at her watch. 'There's no *time* for philosophy, Philippe.'

As they walked towards the car, he shook his head and grinned: 'Perhaps I do have something to teach you, after all.'

• • •

'Maria!' Calla bawled, holding the sandwich a few inches from her mouth. 'You're murdering me!'

They were in the cafe round the corner from CMP's offices in Mayfair. This malodorous greasy spoon joint was a sure candidate for a *Bad Food Guide* if anyone volunteered to write one. Five stars for everything dreadful. But it was also an inviting oasis in a concrete desert when Calla found herself working round the clock.

For the past week they hadn't had time even to *look* at the clock. Ignoring telephones, headaches, tummy rumbles, the rest of the CMP staff, they huddled over separate drawing boards under glaring anglepoise lamps, every so often barking out a question, confirming a measurement, asking how the other was progressing. It never seemed fast enough.

'Oh my gawd,' commiserated the podgy Maria in faultless Cockney delivered in a Greek Cypriot accent. 'It's the salt again, ain't it?'

'It's the salt, Maria. Have you bought up a concession?'

She had dreaded their first morning. Philippe had gone through her drawings, measurements and estimates, his lips moving, his head nodding or, sometimes, shaking. She couldn't look at him directly for fear of seeing anger in his eyes. How had she dared to ask him?

'I get you another.'

But he hadn't ranted and raved. He hadn't scowled. He had sat for ten minutes in silence and then swivelled in his chair to face her.

He liked it. That's what he said. The task was still impossible, but what she had done was good.

So why the long silence? What was missing? Uh-huh, she knew what was missing. It was that philosophical stuff again, wasn't it? Yes it was. It was something Philippe kept returning to, gently reminding her. Now, in the cafe, safely away from the tyranny of on-screen design and drawing board dreams, he was determined to get his way.

'I think you're a gifted architect, Calla. But you need an idea.'

'Thanks,' she said in an offended tone.

'Your sandwich,' stated Maria, delivering it with a clatter. Wasn't there a single clean plate in this dive, for God's sake? 'No salt.'

'Thanks,' she said again.

'A grand idea. An idea of the whole. The new Charlesbury won't be its library, its schools or its market place, Calla – enchanting though you have made some of those buildings. No, Charlesbury will be *your* idea.'

Philippe was a surprise. She had expected a little French chic, the occasional daring leap of the imagination, the help of an eye experienced in new town development. Perhaps he would re-draw her swimming pool, dream up a breath-taking design for the railway station or suggest an island church in the very centre, rather like Notre Dame. But all this abstract talk she had definitely not expected.

'We have to write the philosophy of our scheme,' he urged.

'To write it?' she exploded. 'When we haven't even got time for the basics? You must be crazy.'

'Ah, you English pragmatists,' he said with a sigh. 'You like to pretend that a clever idea never enters your heads. Fancy notions? Not us! Leave them to that strange race across the Channel.

'But with our French schemes, Calla, we like to create an intellectual background. We include a little essay with our plans. We introduce history, mythology, spirituality.'

'Oh my Gawd!' she exclaimed, mimicking Maria.

'Bricks and mortar need a philosophy,' he said, ignoring her put-down, 'just as a regiment, a political system, an order of nuns, need a philosophy. Everything has a philosophy.'

'Everything?'

She frowned. She was truly excited by a great deal of modern French architecture, but this sounded too damned clever by half.

'Look,' he said playfully, whisking her plate from under her nose. 'Shall I explain the philosophy of a cheese and tomato sandwich?'

She laughed: 'You couldn't.'

'You're daring me?'

'The loser pays for the coffee,' she said, feeling suddenly relaxed and very happy.

He lifted the topmost slice of bread and prodded the bottom one with his index finger.

'Basic design,' he explained. 'Like the roof and the floor. Can't get away from that. Okay?'

'Okay.'

'Now the size of it. This one's for a lady. A man's happy to tackle a fullblown club sandwich and shrug his shoulders if bits of the filling drop out. A lady's more careful. So there's a designer at work here. Maria's already an architect, yes?'

'Maybe.'

'What can you tell me about the bread?'

'That it's brown, you mean?'

'Exactly. The colour of health.'

'Please, Philippe,' she grinned, 'don't try to persuade me that one morsel of food in this place is healthy.'

'True. This brown bread isn't really very healthy at all. It's rather stale. But you chose brown, not white, because you're a modern young lady who thinks of her health. And of her figure.'

'Mm.'

'So there is a theory of health and nutrition here. It's built into the sandwich.' He put it back on the plate. 'Now we come to aesthetics.' ,

'Oh, spare me!'

'The colours, Calla. The red and the yellow. Don't they look good together? Imagine that cheese was red. Do you think anyone would then make a cheese and tomato sandwich?'

While he waited for her to reply, he leant forward and took a bite of it.

'Hey,' protested Calla. 'That's mine, you pig!'

'Sorry,' he smiled, 'but I needed to check the flavour. You'll agree with me that these ingredients taste very different from one another? They make a contrast?

'Maria's not such a bad architect, you know. She realises that we like variety and excitement. You can get a plain cheese sandwich, but they don't sell very well. Did you realise how much went into this humble creation?'

'Don't tell her,' warned Calla, 'or she'll be charging double.'

'But something is missing from this sandwich. Something which was present in the first one.'

'Bloody salt!' Calla giggled.

'Precisely. Maria is lavish with salt. And why?'

'An unsteady hand?'

'No, no. Look at her. She's solid as a rock. Listen: where Maria comes from they throw salt on their food by the handful. Why is that? Probably from some race memory of food going bad in the days before refrigeration. It's a tradition, Calla. She brings that tradition with her to everything she cooks. It's a vital part of her cheese and tomato sandwich.

'So you see, if I were to write a little philosophical treatise on Maria's sandwich . . . '

'Stop!' Calla pleaded with a chuckle. 'Enough, Philippe. I surrender. I'll pay for all our coffees for a week if only you'll spare me any more of this.'

'And you'll allow me to write our Charlesbury philosophy for the competition?'

'Anything, anything!'

They left in high spirits and found themselves bowling along towards the car arm in arm. Why on earth had the task seemed so difficult? she wondered. Suddenly everything seemed possible.

● ● ●

As Philippe ran a practised eye over the plans, Adam ran one over Philippe.

'Love the trousers,' he said. 'Are they Cerruti?'

'Couldn't say,' Philippe replied tersely with the ghost of a smile. He was working like fury, faster than he'd ever worked in his life. This interrogation he didn't need. He'd summed Adam up very quickly. If Calla was still having problems with that old boyfriend of hers, she'd have to look a lot further than her personal assistant for what every girl needs. 'They were a present from my wife.'

What sort of new bride concentrates on getting her man *into* trousers? Calla couldn't help wondering.

'Perhaps I shouldn't remind you,' Adam added, 'but the deadline for this competition is six o'clock this evening.'

'Merde!' Philippe muttered under his breath.

'And it's now five past four.'

'For God's sake, Adam,' Calla said sharply, 'are you trying to wind us up or something?'

The tension had been unbearable all day. They had been driving themselves for weeks, but now everything depended upon the last few hours. They snatched at the blueprints, cursed violently when anything fell on the floor, ran everywhere at the double. Calla was aware of twenty things which needed to be done and any one of them would take at least half an hour.

'Relief road plan,' Philippe called, waving his arm.

'I do beg your pardon?' queried Adam, pouting. 'I'm sure I'm not accustomed . . . '

'Give him the plan, for Christ's sake!' roared Calla.

'Tut, *tut*,' said Adam, obeying.

'Go home, Adam,' she told him. 'If you can't stand the strain.'

'*Me* not stand it?' he protested. 'Well!'

'Yes, go home,' threw in Philippe, looking up from his drawings. The two of them had never got, on for some reason. Philippe seemed to resent Adam's feyness. Adam regarded Philippe as an interloper. Now there was the whiff of murder in the air.

'Please, Philippe,' Calla said. 'Don't make things worse.'

'You think they could be worse, uh? We have less than two hours to finish, and look what has to be done.' He waved an arm in a circling movement which took in piles of print-outs but also a few bundles of work-in-progress. 'I give up the comfort of my home for this great mess?'

'Blast your home comforts!' Calla yelled, feeling tears coming to her eyes. 'Do you think I have home comforts? We've got a job to finish and all you can do is whinge.'

'Perhaps I will go,' Adam said. 'Goodnight.'

But he stopped in the doorway and came back inside: 'Suppose I collect up everything that's finished,' he suggested.

'Then make some more coffee,' ordered Calla.

They continued working in the same edgy, irritable way until half past five. Then Calla threw her pen across the room and began frantically to gather up sheets of paper from the printer tray and add them to Adam's pile.

'Jesus, look at the time!' she cried. 'Let's get out of here.'

'Nearly finished,' said Philippe.

She pushed him aside impatiently, pulled his sheet off the drawing board and rolled it up: 'Forget it,' she said. 'We're not going to win or lose because of a few extra lines on a blueprint.'

'Roll on Monday,' Adam said as Calla and Philippe ran out of the building, 'and normality. I'll lock up.'

They sped through Mayfair, Calla throwing the Porsche through the busy late Friday traffic with a finesse which brought admiration, a screeching of brakes and a sounding of horns in equal measures. As they swept into the seething cauldron of tight nerves and hot tempers which is Hyde Park Corner, Philippe closed his eyes and said a silent prayer.

'Chicken,' she laughed.

Through Grosvenor Crescent and Belgrave Square and the dashboard clock said 5.53. There was a snarl-up in the square, and Calla leaned out of the window to shout something at the cars in front.

'Are we going to make it?' Philippe asked nervously.

'You may have to run.'

A small gap opened up, and Calla shot forward, swerved onto the pavement for a few yards, then gunned the car forward and into Belgrave Place. They swept round the corner and screeched to a halt in a spattering of loose chippings outside the Duke's offices in Eaton Square. It was 5.58.

'I could have finished that coffee,' Calla said.

Philippe, cradling the plans in his arms, ran up the steps and rang the bell. She watched as the door opened and he went inside. A few minutes later and he was out, climbing into the car with his thumb raised.

'And now let's celebrate,' he said. 'Let's get changed and find somewhere for the best meal we've ever had in our lives.'

'Not a bad idea,' she replied.

Some understatement, she was thinking. *I'm agonisingly, gut-clenchingly ravenous!*

● ● ●

It had to be Bibendum, that hymn to art deco and gastronomy on the Fulham Road.

'You mean you've lost the booking?' Calla exclaimed in an outraged tone as the ornamental young man looked through the table list.

'No mention of Marchant, madam,' he said – which wasn't surprising since there was no booking at all.

'I rang on Wednesday,' she insisted. 'I specifically mentioned your baby octopus in squid ink!'

She was a beautiful liar, thought Philippe. He interrupted with a smile: 'But I'm sure you can find us a table.'

Quite how he did it Calla couldn't fathom, but his air of self-confidence and knowingness managed to imply the £20 note which would be passed over discreetly upon arrival at the table. Philippe was used to getting his way, in restaurants as in other aspects of life.

'What an intriguing place,' he said as they were seated. 'I love that stained glass!' The two Bristol-blue windows depicted a Frenchman, first on a bicycle and then smoking a cigar.

'Monsieur Bibendum himself in the windows,' she told him. 'Glorious, isn't it? It's an old art deco Michelin garage, actually. Decor by Terence Conran, no less.'

'The man who founded Habitat?'

'Exactly. It's his restaurant.'

'So everything,' Philippe grinned, 'is cooked in one of those chicken bricks, yes?'

'Or a wok, perhaps!' Calla laughed, tossing her head back. She felt an almost girlish sense of fun. It was one hell of a relief to be able to indulge in mere pleasantries without feeling that valuable working time was being wasted. She was so relaxed she was floating.

Philippe laughed too. They were in one of those merry moods when everything is liable to seem hilarious.

'No salt in your cheese and tomato sandwich?' he asked playfully. 'The food should be good in a Michelin – even in a Michelin garage.'

Calla leaned forward, eyeing him from one side of the candle: 'I don't want to shock a Frenchman, but right now I'm more interested in quantity than quality. I could eat until I look like a Michelin Tyre Man.'

'I approve of appetite,' smiled Philippe, as he poured golden coloured Chablis into two tall glasses.

'Appetite? Christ, I could eat *you*!'

Enormous prawns appeared, spitting on an iron skillet. 'Smell that Pernod!' said Philippe sniffing them. 'It reminds me of La Maree in the rue Daru in Paris! Such *fruits de mer*! I must take you there.' And then he paused, rather awkwardly, thinking he had perhaps gone rather further than a newly married man ought.

But Calla seemed to have eyes only for the prawns. Abandoning the niceties, she seized one, lifting it to her mouth. Cracking its thin shell, she pulled it off with her white teeth, very white indeed against the pink of the prawn flesh.

Philippe watched her keenly. She did have an appetite, but not just for food. There was an appetite for life in Calla which took your breath away.

He hadn't really noticed it these last few days. He'd been working close beside the woman he had briefly yearned for that spring day in Paris but, slaving over the drawing board, he had hardly registered the woman in her. She'd been a colleague, with a shared passion and a reservoir of energy. She hadn't been the female animal she now so clearly was.

Philippe's method with a prawn was rather gentler. It seemed almost to yield its transparent coating to his firm fingers. He then put the flesh, whole and moist with the liquor, straight into his mouth.

'It's good,' he said, savouring the delicacy of its flavour. His eyes rested on Calla's lips, shiny with the juice of the fish. As he gazed, her quick tongue darted out in a lick. Their eyes met.

It was as if the meal was suspended in time, cut off from mundane hours and minutes. They exchanged few words, but were blissfully unaware of the long silences. They gazed boldly and without shame into one another's eyes.

The skillet was removed almost without being noticed. Under the table, Philippe's knee came to rest against hers, and Calla did not move it away.

They ate hungrily and with enjoyment, their eyes occasionally fastening upon each other with an equal relish. Calla watched as Philippe ate the long shoots of buttered asparagus.

'How is it?'

Her voice brought him out of his reverie. He said nothing in reply, but held out a dripping shoot on his fork and let her take it in her mouth. She sucked it in, her eyes smiling at him all the while.

He reached out for his glass. What he really wanted, he thought, was to fill himself to the brim with Calla. Wine was a poor substitute for the real, womanly, heady thing.

'To Charlesbury!' he said, raising the wine. 'And to us.'

Calla ran her fingers along the stem of her glass:'To our partnership,' she said, and their eyes met again.

They both knew at that moment. There was no question. From a bubble outside time, they were ferociously plunged into a world of urgency where every minute counted.

'Let's not bother with coffee,' suggested Philippe. And Calla felt his knee push gently between hers under the table. Poor Yvette.

'Let's not.'

He helped her into her coat, taking in the curves which strained against the tight black dress. God, it was a shame to cover such a form in a coat.

All evening he had been the model of attentiveness, but now there was something almost abrupt in his manner as he piloted her from the restaurant, his hand in the small of her back.

Calla recognised the breathless urgency of his lust. God, she could almost taste and smell it. Her vibrating senses smarted and stung. Raising the tight skirt a couple of inches, she slipped behind the wheel and, lightly revving the engine, swept them into Brompton Road and towards Knightsbridge.

He watched the shiftings of those sheer-clad legs as she changed gear and braked. She handled the car like a woman who knew exactly what she wanted. That masterful, swift touch on the gear lever was almost unbearable to watch. The smooth speed and the silence were electrifying.

At a set of lights she turned to look at him, her eyes calm and wide.

Her lips were parted in an expression which wasn't quite a smile. Philippe could read that expression. He'd seen it on the faces of women before. He had to fight back the urge to reach across and touch her, to take her there and then.

For the first time in weeks they had no need to watch the clock, but a fresh urgency now drove them on through the lighted streets to Bayswater and to Calla's front door.

The damned key didn't want to fit the lock. She wrestled with it, beyond measure. When at last the door swung open, there was no need for words. They took the stairs two at a time.

In the bedroom they shed their clothes swiftly and silently. His hands were everywhere, touching, clutching, arousing each inch of her without lingering anywhere. She abandoned herself to a panting urgency which willed him on and on until he had every part of her.

He pulled her to the floor and parted her legs with his. He pushed inside her expertly, his way eased by the moistness of her hot and throbbing channel. She took him gratefully, gripping his shaft, knowing that the agonising wait for the thing itself could not be long.

Nothing else in the world seemed so desperate as this. All her buildings could fall, if only this craving which tingled and tightened inside her could be satisfied. Her eyes held his for a moment, then closed as all her very being concentrated on the sensation his fullness created inside her.

Over and over they rolled, locked into each other, their hands grasping at every centimetre of flesh in greedy embrace. Then he flexed and forced her legs wide open with his and she cried out.

He fell and rose upon her, fell and rose, each time rocking back onto the probing finger which squirmed in the secret recesses of his arse. With each thrust he felt her tighten around him, meeting his dark curls with hers. They came in a tumult.

Wave after wave left Calla throbbing and breathless. All the tension of the past two months seemed to have left her body – blessed release, exhausted happiness.

Philippe lay drunk on self-knowledge. Through the months of denial, even through the very hour of his wedding, he had denied the truth to himself. Whatever his soul wanted, whatever his emotional ties to Yvette, this was what his body, his animal self, had wanted. And he lay drunk on Calla Marchant.

For both of them it was like breathing after long suffocation. They stumbled into bed and fell asleep without a word.

It was still dark when a strange sensation crept into Calla's almost unconscious brain. She lay in that no-man's land between sleep and wakefulness, her physical senses stirred, but scarcely able to think.

What could she feel? She realised, but only gradually, that she was not dreaming. Philippe's tongue was stroking to and fro across her clitoris, sending sweetly pricking sensations to her sleepy brain. She felt his warm breath between her legs massaging her into consciousness.

One helluva way to wake up, she thought. He was kneeling in the darkness, his thumbs ever so gently holding the folds of her flesh apart – licking, licking. God, let this never end, she prayed.

Philippe had been woken by his own desire ' not the evening's savage lust which would not be refused, but a persistent longing. He yearned towards the beauty he could only just make out in the dark – the tousled mane and steadily breathing form of bed-warm Calla. He paused, wondering when those still-closed eyes would open.

'Don't stop,' she whispered, tongued almost unbearably into re-arousal.

Now that pink tormentor travelled up her body, across her pelvic bones, over the hollow of her belly to her nipples. They were hard. He licked gently round each one in turn.

'Philippe,' she murmured as she reached for him.

It was tender exploration in the dark, exploration guided only by silhouette. Sitting, lying, kneeling, she found every contour of his muscled frame.

She lingered over the soft flesh behind his ears, the shape of his shoulder blades, even the soles of his feet. Then she found the warm and yielding sac which held his seed. Her tongue ran around it, feeling the gaps between the two balls. As she lifted her head, her cheek brushed against his upright member and she greedily inhaled his smell.

Calla knelt astride his thighs as they rocked each other, his cock rubbing her clitoris to a frenzy. He held her steady, controlling the movement, and as she began to tremble and pant he slipped deeply inside her.

● ● ●

She awoke, with bright sunlight against the curtains, to two discoveries – that Philippe was not in the bed beside her and that her watch said it was after mid-day. A clatter from downstairs told her he hadn't gone further than the kitchen.

'Food,' she murmured dreamily into the pillow. 'Sex and food. Trust a bloody Frenchman.'

'Oeufs fumes,' announced Philippe as he walked in bearing a tray and wearing Calla's white towelling robe. 'Or scrambled eggs to you. A cook you will never make, cherie. What a terrible fridge! Nothing but eggs, milk and Sancerre. We shall have to eat out again tonight.'

'Inviting yourself?'

'Mais oui. To save you the embarrassment.'

They lingered in bed all afternoon, laughing, dozing and caressing. During the brief interludes they talked desultorily about architecture, Charlesbury and the pressures of the last few weeks. And they drank the Sancerre.

'The trouble is, cherie, that being in bed with you causes certain symptoms,' murmured Philippe as they lay close. Calla laughed softly. She could feel his erection hard against her stomach.

Gently, she kissed his neck, then licked his stomach. She felt him tense as her exploring tongue travelled along the prominent blue vein of his prick. It darted in and out of the wet cleft and prodded softly inside the foreskin. Closing her lips around his shaft, she moved rhythmically over it, up and down, up and down, suck and release, until, salty and sudden, he came in her mouth.

A minute or two later, Philippe half-opened his eyes to see Calla smiling wickedly at him.

'Symptoms relieved?' she asked.

Hours later, Philippe dragged himself out of the bed, took a shower and drove off to collect his suitcases from the hotel where he'd been staying. He was supposed to have flown home today, but tomorrow morning would have to do. He and Calla needed another night of each other to finish what they had started.

She rang Le Gavroche to book a table, expertly negotiating a receptionist who at first protested that there were no vacancies. Then, her flesh deliciously toned by the vigorous exercise, she stepped into the shower.

'Yvette may find her husband rather shagged out,' she reflected with a grin as she dried herself off.

He returned to find Calla getting ready in the bedroom. When he kissed her he found that her animal smell wasfor the moment gone. She was scented, with her hair freshly washed. Her dress lay ready on the bed. It was the sort that calls for minimal underwear, and that was what Calla was arranging in front of the cheval mirror just now.

He sat behind her on a chair, admiring. A ruched ivory silk camisole top, rather than a bra, gave a hint of restraint to her breasts. She was knickerless. She pulled on lacy topped stockings and slipped her feet into Italian leather high heeled shoes.

Calla regarded herself critically and bent down to straighten a stocking. The sight of that black hair parting to reveal her pink womanhood was too much for a man to bear. Too much, anyway, for Philippe.

Hastily unzipping his trousers, he pulled her by the waist so that she fell back on top of him. Holding her breasts from behind he flexed his thighs, pushing into her with short quick thrusts. She grunted and gasped, coming with an ecstatic shiver at the very moment he felt himself gushing inside her.

They were caught up in a heady madness of desire, intensified by the knowledge that it couldn't last. They ate out again, made wildly hungry by their exertions, then returned to make love again, lavishly, throughout the night.

The next morning she drove him to the airport.

17

The Christmas lights were switched on earlier every year, Bunny Simkins thought as he came out of the underground station at Oxford Circus. It was the middle of November, yet the darkness of a cold winter's evening was turned almost into day by the electric glitter, illuminating the great swags of decorations across Oxford Street and, even more expensively, down the entire length of Regent Street to the south.

He liked the atmosphere. He was one of life's optimists, and he enjoyed the spirit of peace and goodwill which seemed to transform even the gloomiest mortal at this time of the year. People were shaking charity boxes by a huge Christmas tree, and he paused to drop a pound coin inside.

'Happy Christmas!'

'And to you!'

Above his head Father Christmas was urging his reindeers through the sky. Simkins turned into Great Marlborough Street, fishing in his pocket for directions to a pub he'd never heard of. He was, as ever, rather early. He hated that feeling of panic which came when he was lost and running out of time, especially when, as in this case, he was meeting someone he didn't know.

'The Old Rooster', when he at last found it down an alley off a side street, seemed a pretty low kind of place. It was nothing more than a characterless drinking shop, even more mean inside than out.

'O'Rourke,' the man had said on the phone. 'You don't know me, but there's something you ought to know, Mr Simkins. Meet you in the lounge bar at seven. Don't worry, I'll recognise you, all right.'

He ordered a pint and pulled a rolled-up copy of the *Evening Standard* from his coat pocket. There was a juke box, playing something he didn't recognise and wouldn't expect to, very loudly, and there were three fruit machines standing side by side, each surrounded by knots of young people who said nothing, staring at the revolving cylinders with a kind of reverence as they chewed gum like cows with cud.

Time passed. He was on his second pint, and had checked his watch a dozen times, when he felt a tap on his shoulder and turned to face a gaunt man of about forty wearing a threadbare suit and scuffed shoes.

'Mr Simkins, is it? Got a message for you, sir. The gentleman you're waiting for has been unfortunately delayed.'

'Something the matter?'

'No, Mr Simkins, everything's all right. But if you'll come this way you can wait for him in comfort.'

They left the bar, turned the corner at the end of a narrow passage and entered a small room with a simple leather sofa against one wall and no other furniture at all. There were blinds at the windows, and the lighting was very dim.

'If you'd like to wait here, sir.'

'It's rather warm,' Simkins said. 'I think I was happier in the bar, if you don't mind.'

'*I* don't mind, Mr Simkins, but I was specifically asked to have you wait here for the gentleman in question. He won't be long.'

'If you say so,' sighed Simkins, who was the most easy-going of men. But it was damn hot in the room. He began to feel rather woozy, as if he had drunk much more than a couple of pints. He took his coat off, and then his jacket. He undid the buttons of his waistcoat and loosened his tie. He'd give O'Rourke a little while longer and then call it a day. The whole thing seemed stranger by the minute.

He was tucked comfortably into the corner of the sofa, half asleep, when the door was flung open and he was aware of people running up to him and shaking him.

'Eh, what?' he exclaimed in alarm.

Before he could gather his wits, he felt himself being manhandled. His waistcoat came off, his shirt was torn open and – he couldn't understand what was happening – his trousers were loosened and tugged down to his knees. He tried to flail his arms, but they were held fast.

'Help!' he shouted weakly. 'What's happening to me?'

His attackers next yanked at his underpants. He couldn't do a thing to prevent it. Down they came. His shoes were wrenched from his feet. He lost his socks. Then his tormentors left as suddenly as they had come, pushing him down and running from the room. He heard their footsteps receding down the corridor, followed by a shout.

Sweating profusely, he was just about to replace his clothing when he realised that he wasn't alone. In the murky light he saw, to his horror, that two young men stood in front of him, completely naked.

'What is this?' he whispered hoarsely.

They didn't hurt him. One of them sidled close and put a hand inside Simkins' shirt. The other grabbed one of Simkins' hands and pressed it against hard, warm flesh. There was a vivid flash of light, and then another. The two young men wrestled with him, adroitly turning him, manipulating him, fondling him, and there were more flashes of light.

Dear God, he thought, this is a nightmare. Why are they doing this to me?

Then at last the young men ran off and the door closed behind them.

Simkins dressed himself, his legs strangely unsteady, and staggered out into the corridor. At the end of it he saw a group of men, huddled in conversation. One of them he recognised.

'We've met,' he said. 'Do you remember?'

'Listen, Mr Simkins,' Martin Kingsley said, 'I honestly didn't know what I was here for. We all had separate tip offs, that's all. That's how the media works.'

Drawing closer, Simkins realised that one of the men was carrying a camera with a flash attachment.

'I don't understand,' he said. 'What's all this about?'

'Well, I'm genuinely very sorry, Mr Simkins,' Kingsley said, 'but you've been expertly stitched up, haven't you?'

● ● ●

Bunny Simkins hadn't realised there was anything wrong with him until the evening of his twenty-fifth birthday.

'A charmed existence,' is the way even he himself used to talk about his life. The family was well-to-do. Daddy was a City analyst, mummy a warm, strong personality who organised their social life with great aplomb. They lived in a large mock-Tudor house set among trees in Leatherhead. Bunny was their only child, and had been cherished since the day he was born.

'A pleasant, well-mannered boy,' was what school reports used to say, adding that he was moderately successful at the academic things.

No, that wasn't quite it. Bunny Simkins was certainly an obedient boy, the sort a teacher could rely on not to lead a rebellion. He was certainly placid – but not at all in a negative way. The fact was that Bunny Simkins was extremely happy with the world and his own place in it. He glowed with optimism. He was really quite a bright lad, but because there was nothing driving him, because he had no complaints about the divine order of things, he didn't really bother.

Later, as he came to realise that he lacked great energy but really ought to make an effort if he was going to get anywhere, he forced himself to work harder. It wasn't difficult to force Bunny Simkins, who was such an easy-going young man. He passed his exams and, having been inspired by one of his father's friends, won a place at a school of architecture.

Since the school was within easy reach of Surrey, he remained living at home. Life continued to be charmed as far as Bunny Simkins was concerned. In the evenings he read and listened to music; at the weekends he went to the theatre with friends or drove out into the country. He had a dashing little MG which he handled with tremendous flair without ever being reckless.

For his twenty-fifth birthday his parents threw a party in the garden. It had been a scorching August day, and the air was still sultry throughout the evening. Everyone had brought swimming gear, and they were in and out of the pool between bites and drinks.

Bunny's mother was in her element, organising the refreshments and talking to everyone for just the right amount of time. 'I do like Bunny's friends,' she told her husband. 'They're such a civilised bunch.' She meant that they all came from the right social class. The young men were all training to be something responsible, with good money to match, while the young ladies were demure and feminine, but above all practical. They'd make someone a good wife.

She watched her beloved son sporting in the pool with a few of his pals. A large rubber ball was flying through the air and coming down with a hearty splash. She saw Bunny's head dip below the water so that only the topmost hair showed on the surface.

What his mother didn't see was the hand of one of the nice young men, Jeremy, sliding itself up and down Bunny's thigh as they struggled for the ball. At first Bunny thought the movement accidental, but it continued after the ball had gone. And he realised, as he shook his eyes clear of the water and the fingers continued to brush ever higher, that he enjoyed the feeling it gave him. He felt his penis swelling inside his trunks and, just for a second, he lowered himself in the water so that Jeremy's questing hand should touch against it.

Then he kicked away, violently, and struck out for the far end of the pool. His brain was in turmoil. He didn't want to believe what had just happened. He loathed himself for it.

He got through the rest of the party in a daze. He heard Jeremy joshing everyone, as he tended to do, but he couldn't look him in the eye. Of course it meant nothing to Jeremy. Everyone suspected that he was a bit of a . . . you know. Queers, they called them. Poofters. That's what they said about Jeremy. *Was it true about himself?*

During the next couple of years Bunny passed through the dark night of the soul. It took him that long to face up the reality of his own sexual make-up. He first asked himself about women. He went through a period of working himself up into a liking for Marianne or Jennifer, asking them out to the cinema or home for tea. They were nice girls, some of them good-looking even, but he knew that it was a farce. If one of them took his hand in hers it felt heavy as lead.

He knew, in short, that he had never been properly aroused by a woman.

Then he began to ponder his feelings for the men he knew. Wasn't there something excessive about the warmth he felt for some of them? There was that gentle romantic glow he felt in their company, that satisfaction when, in a quite proper and manly way, they made physical contact – patting a shoulder, perhaps, or taking an elbow.

When he had admitted this much, he was ready for the next self-confession: that he liked in particular the litheness and pertness of certain men rather younger than himself. There was something about a graceful youth in his mid to late teens which did excite him. He honestly hadn't registered the fact before, and the realisation of it made his skin crawl. Until very recently, he knew, it had been illegal to do those things. But, far worse, it was unclean. He felt physically sick.

For a time he went about his business in a strange vaccuum. He was working for a firm of architects, now, and beginning his climb up the ladder. The wonder was that he didn't fall off. He dealt with his colleagues and with clients, he drew up plans, he visited sites, but part of his brain was elsewhere. He was fighting a battle within himself.

The turning point came one evening as he was walking down a dimly-lit street towards Waterloo station. There had been a minor celebration after work. It was quite late, and he had had rather a lot to drink. He was suddenly aware of being in step with a lad of about seventeen. Where he had come from he couldn't guess.

'Going far?'

'To the station,' Bunny replied.

'I've got somewhere you could take a rest. Wouldn't cost you very much.'

'Really?'

'And I think you might enjoy it.'

He had never been propositioned before. He eyed the youth up and down, and the idea excited him. For a second he imagined that slender form stripped of its clothing and pressing up against him. He thought of a hand caressing his thigh.

'There's plenty of trains,' the young man said.

The idea excited him, but he somehow couldn't face the reality of it – the exertion, the messiness, the sheer awkwardness of dealing with it all. That was why he shook his head and hurried on, losing his pursuer only as he climbed the station steps and thankfully mingled with the throng in the busy concourse.

After that, Bunny Simkins came to terms with his condition. He accepted his homosexual leanings because he knew that he wouldn't act on them. He had a low sex drive. That and his guilt would prevent him ever taking part in an act which he feared as much as he desired.

It was a pact he made with himself. He would tolerate his own leanings on the condition that he never succumbed to them. He would go through life in the knowledge that he would never do that deed which would bring with it shame and the possibility of punishment.

When the law changed and it was no longer a crime for men to make love to other men, Bunny had no thought of 'coming out of the closet'. There was nothing to admit to. In those more knowing times the odd eyebrow was raised because of the posse of bright young men he kept about him, but nobody would think of a scandal befalling Bunny Simkins.

'He likes to encourage the younger generation,' some would say, not allowing themselves to think the unthinkable.

'A bit of a romantic,' the wiser ones decided. 'Rather fond of the boys, in an innocent sort of way. But nothing whatsoever to worry about.'

And there wasn't. Not in the slightest. Bunny Simkins was a lovable innocent.

● ● ●

Jake Broughton tossed a copy of *Private Eye* onto the boardroom table and gave Langton Meredith a challenging gaze.

'I hardly need ask whether you've seen this,' he stated.

Meredith took the magazine and made a pretence of reading the paragraph for the first time: 'Most interesting,' he lisped. 'This must refer to Bunny Simkins, I presume.'

'I'll bet you damn well presume it, Meredith.'

Here we go again, thought Brent Lorimer. The meeting hasn't even started and it's been taken out of my hands. What the hell is this about? He reached out his hand and Meredith passed him the *Eye* – not the kind of scurrilous rag he'd normally pay the slightest attention to. He searched through the ragged-edged text for some time before finding the cryptic heading MUCKY MERV'S BLUE PRINTS:

> *Pathetic efforts by the Street of Shame to clean up its act before it gets clobbered by Government legislation has landed porno paparazzo 'Mucky Merv' Ryder in more trouble with his neurotic bosses.*
>
> *Following his widely-leaked mauling by tame editor Roger 'Gettem' Down for taking pictures of the royal princes in a state of nature during their Caribbean yachting holiday, Ryder is now having to explain how he came to snap intimate scenes of playfulness between two naked youths and a certain architect with a national reputation.*

*Mucky Merv is privately threatening to flog his set of exceedingly
blue prints to the highest bidder if his hitherto tacky newsheet
persists in parading itself as holier than the Christian Herald.*
(Which might not be difficult – See p. 7 *Ed.*)
*But he's finding it hard to argue that exposing the predilection
of a hare-brained architect for the flesh of young boys can possibly
be regarded as in the national interest.*

'Why should this refer to Bunny Simkins?' Lorimer demanded.

Meredith raised an eyebrow: 'Hare-brained?' he asked, thoughtfully.
'And a certain taste . . . '

'It's Bunny,' Broughton told him. 'The buzz is all round the circuit. Of
course I don't believe it for a moment.'

'Oh, surely,' Meredith said with a scornful laugh. 'You're not so naive,
Jake.'

'Not so naive as to think this happened by accident, no. The newspaper
has its photographs, sure. But do you think Bunny would really be
involved in a scene like that?'

'The camera cannot lie.'

'I didn't realise,' said Stew McClear, peering at the article, 'that Bunny
Simkins was of that persuasion.'

'Ha!'

Langton Meredith couldn't prevent a little of his jubilation from
showing. He'd been gratified to discover that several of his Fleet Street
contacts had fallen for the bait and hugely pleased that one of them was
a photographer. Of course, he knew they wouldn't use the story: since
neither of the lads was under the legal age, there couldn't be any police
involvement. That wasn't necessary at all. His ploy was to get a whiff of
scandal in the air and to make sure that the scent reached the delicate
nostrils of the Duke of Mercia. He'd have managed that without a word
in print, but this little piece in the *Eye* was icing on the cake. He had a
sweet tooth for that kind of thing.

'The whole thing stinks,' Broughton said. 'I only hope that we're not
involved in any way.'

Lorimer sat back in alarm: 'Us? How could that be?'

'I mean I hope none of us had anything whatsoever to do with fitting
Bunny up, as I think the underworld has it. I'm afraid I wouldn't put
money on it. Not a penny.'

Meredith turned a cold eye on Broughton: 'Since you're staring so
hard at me, Jake, I think you'd better explain exactly what you're getting
at. I hope you haven't got the damn nerve . . . '

'Gentlemen,' pleaded Lorimer. 'Enough. This business leaves a bad taste in the mouth as it is. It's a tremendously bad advertisement for the profession.'

'Stuff the profession,' Broughton broke in. 'If we're involved and the truth comes to light it'll be the end of Broughton, Hughes, Lorimer.'

Meredith smiled: 'Comfort your nervous self, Jake, with the thought that it means the end of Simkins' bid to design Charlesbury. He hasn't a snowball's chance in hell now.'

'That matters rather more to you than to me, I'd say.'

'Oh certainly, much more. That's because I have a vision for the future of this company, Jake. I don't want it to stand still. And that means we have to fight for our survival in the market place.'

'By fair means or foul?'

'Through the chair, gentlemen, through the chair,' sang Lorimer, attempting to assert his dwindling authority. Picking up the offending magazine by one corner, he held it over a wastepaper basket as if it was something offensive the cat had brought in.

'If I may . . . ' smiled Meredith coldly, claiming it. He reached out a long arm.

'For research purposes,' he added, returning Broughton's baleful stare.

● ● ●

'If you'll forgive me saying so,' Adam remarked, taking off his overcoat and carefully fitting it onto a padded hanger, 'none of this would have happened if he'd been open and honest.'

'Come through into my office,' Calla said. 'And no, I don't think I will forgive you.'

'It's so bloody sordid.'

Calla screwed up her face in an expression which he knew very well. It meant, roughly translated, What you are telling me is irrelevant to the matter in hand and rather tiresome.

'Do please shut the door,' she said. 'We don't want the whole world knowing.'

He fell into an armchair: 'There we go again,' he said with a wry grin. 'Not in front of the children. Heterosexuals of the world unite. You have nothing to lose but your hang-ups.'

'Do I need a lecture at this moment, Adam?'

She didn't. She had been surprised at how emotionally she'd reacted to the news of Bunny's disgrace. That's how everyone saw it. He'd been caught out doing something disgusting. Calla didn't pretend to know what had happened. All she knew was a feeling of grief that so dear a friend should have been held up to ridicule and contempt. It might not yet be general knowledge, but it had certainly gone the rounds of the architectural profession within days.

She had heard about it on the telephone while working at the office. First she felt angry that anyone should do this to Bunny. Then she realised that the tears welling up her in eyes were caused as much by her affection for her old mentor as by her rage. She had to go to the ladies' room, lock herself in a cubicle and allow the hot tears to run down her face. After she'd calmed down she pleaded with Adam to use all his contacts in the gay community to discover the truth.

'I've found out what I can,' Adam now told her, 'and it isn't much. I'm no great shakes at playing what you might appropriately call the private dick.'

'Jesus!' She shook her head: 'Spare me.'

'It's obvious that he fell into someone's trap.'

'Whose?'

He shrugged: 'Someone who knows how to cover his tracks. Simkins was lured to the pub by a man supposedly called O'Rourke, though that's obviously a fake name. Several journalists turned up, following a tip-off, and a press photographer took the pretty pictures. All in a day's work for them, I suppose. They won't think twice about it.'

'It's sick,' Calla said. 'What about the boys?'

'They're not boys,' Adam said. 'They're a couple of nasty young men who'll do anything for money. They don't ask questions about where it comes from. Ditto the landlord of the pub.

'And Bunny was innocent?'

He laughed bitterly: 'Now there's a loaded word. What do you mean by *innocent*?'

'I mean, pretty obviously, that he wasn't doing anything – that the pictures were false.'

'And if he *had* been doing something he'd have been guilty? Is that what you think?'

'Adam' she said. 'Is it a good idea that you and I should talk about these things? I'd hate to ruin the perfect working relationship.'

'Who needs enemies when he's got friends who find his preferences loathsome?'

'Listen,' she said, beginning to get heated, 'it's not me, for Crissakes, who hired people to ruin someone's reputation.'

'But it's what you get, although I'm not allowed to say so, when you try to turn something natural into a perversion. If people accepted it there wouldn't be anything to take photographs of. Who'd care?'

Calla kept control of herself. Recent memories of her own rampant sexuality made her disinclined to condemn the tastes of others. She'd never felt strongly about homosexuality in any case, so why should she fight Adam about it? It was his problem.

'I do respect your preferences,' she said. 'I respect Bunny's. I worked for him for years, and I love the man. Do I have to say anything more?'

'Okay, I'm sorry.'

'Don't be sorry, Adam. Be vigilant. I want to know who played this dirty trick on Bunny Simkins. Please find out for me. I *need* to know.'

She pummelled the desk top with a fist so that her poor personal assistant flinched.

'Remind me that I said this,' she demanded, her cheeks flushed, her eyes intensely bright: 'Don't ever let me forget it. I'm making this solemn vow – that when I find out who did it, I'll crucify him!'

18

As Neri Corinthian approached her front door, Tom Cruise came out of it.

'Hi!' he said. 'Great party!'

'It is?'

'It *was*,' he smiled, raising those delicious eyebrows. He pecked her on the cheek as he passed. 'Keep snapping,' he called cheerfully as he disappeared, signalling his chauffeur to bring the limo alongside.

'Party?' Neri mused. Well, of course there was a damn party going on. You could hear it two streets away. It was just that she didn't quite remember ordering one. What day was it, for heaven's sake? What night of what day? She swung her suitcase into the lobby and slid the camera bag from her shoulder.

'Adeline!' she bawled.

There were people everywhere, there was music, there was food and drink. And there was an indefinable, but immediately familiar, atmosphere which promised fun and laughter, brilliant talk, challenge, risk, sex and sheer competitive drive. This, in other words, was a genuine New York society party. But that didn't answer her question.

'It's a sincere pleasure to see you, momma.'

Barney emerged from the ruck and held out a hand in greeting. Before she knew what she was doing she'd shaken it. Her own baby son, for Crissakes! She ought to be throwing her arms around him in a smothering, mothering hug – though maybe, she half-conceded to herself, the handshake was more fitting in his case, after all. Really she couldn't fathom when he was being satirical, if he ever was. She clipped him playfully round the ear in any case.

'You got nothing more endearing to say than that?' she rebuked him. 'Most ten-year-olds would fall on their long-lost parent with tears of affection.'

Over his shoulder she saw Oprah Winfrey pushing her way through the party towards her, rather successfully. People tended to give way.

'Eleven,' Barney said with great tolerance. 'You forgot the birthday.'

'Jeez!' she scowled. 'But no I didn't,' she yelled above the din. 'I sent you a huge card and some electronic toy. A space-walker, was it? I just couldn't be here, that's all.'

'We got by,' was all Barney said in reply.

Okay, the plan *was* to have been back for the kid's spree. It was just that she got a call as she was finishing her assignment in Sydney, and she somehow found herself agreeing to hop across to Papua New Guinea for a couple of weeks. That's how life was. What the hell could you do about it?

'Lovely party,' glowed Oprah Winfrey, kissing Neri firmly on both cheeks. 'Been looking for you all over. It's such a crush. Must go now. Keep clicking!'

'My view is,' Barney stated, 'that we should talk.'

'Do I need my solicitor along?' she asked him with a cackle, slipping her coat off. 'Look, crumbum, this is a pretty bad time, right? I get back to my home after weeks away and I find it's been taken over by some celebrities' convention. Can't you see I'm in a state of shock?'

'Oh, Miss Corinthian,' sighed the indispensable Adeline, lines of exhaustion etched into her face. She was carrying a tray of canapes in one hand, a floorcloth in the other. 'You're back.'

'It rather feels like it, Adeline. In fact, twice over. What the hell's going on round here? And please don't tell me it's a party, or I'll scream. Not that anyone would hear.'

'But it's the Wednesday before Christmas, Miss Corinthian.'

'This is some minority religious festival I wasn't taught about at school?'

'You asked that I should organise it, Miss Corinthian. Months ago. We sat down with the diary. You said I should ask everyone you'd photographed this past year, plus the usual old friends and acquaintances. You did say that, Miss Corinthian. I could fetch out the diary in evidence.'

'Calm down, Adeline, this isn't the third degree. Bejaysus, the world's going mad. Barney, will you please take that tray from Adeline and do something useful with it. Take it over to the corner there – Dustin Hoffman has that hungry look about him. I recognise it all too well.'

'I'm sorry, Miss Corinthian,' Adeline said. 'But it does seem to be going rather well.' Her face suddenly creased and she buried it in the cloth, shaking with tears. 'Honest it does.'

'Heaven help me,' Neri muttered. 'Did I ask a difficult question?'

She threw her coat over one arm, took the suitcase in one hand and the camera bag in the other. 'Go for a liedown, Adeline,' she said, starting to fight her way through the throng. 'On second thoughts, no. You'll never find the space. Go take a walk, eh?' She trod on someone's toe, heavily. 'Oops' she said. 'My apologies, Bill.'

'Can I help in any way?' her victim asked, reaching for the luggage.

If you had to stoop to using bagboys, she thought, it might as well be one of the Clintons. They struggled through the crowd and reached the door of her bedroom.

'I'll be saying farewell,' he smiled. His lips brushed her cheek with graceful gallantry. 'Wonderful party!'

'Thanks.' Well, it was a decent compliment: the man had been to a few. 'See you soon.'

'The wanderer returns!' came a shriek, and Betsy Clutmayer bounded into view. 'I've no end of messages.'

'Get lost,' Neri told her with a smouldering venom to which her secretary was thoroughly accustomed. 'Preferably until some time next year.'

She dragged the suitcase and bag into the room and sat heavily on the bed. Then she took several deep breaths.

'Most of the calls can wait,' Betsy said.

'This is the one haven of peace in the entire house, Betsy. Possibly in the entire universe. Please don't defile it.'

'Except one.'

'You just defiled it. What's the one?'

'Abel Krostow. He said the pictures didn't arrive, and he's jumping. In fact, he's almost out of his mind. I told him I wasn't used to that kind of language.'

'Ha!'

'One's own employer doesn't count, Miss Corinthian. I accept that as part of the terms of service. Shall I get him for you?'

'While I fix myself a drink,' she said.

There was a tide of partying people lapping against her door, and only the urgent need for an uplift gave her the courage to prevail. Why did all her needs always have to be urgent? She avoided eye contact so as not to be sidetracked on her way to the all-important glass.

'Say, Neri,' came a confident woman's voice behind her, 'you look like someone with a pretty important goal in life.'

'Which is to find a martini before I drop from liquor deprivation.'

Joan Rivers laughed: 'You're in luck. Nicole Kidman just thrust this into my hand even though I protested I was on my way out. Cheers! And thanks for a great party.'

'Cheers,' murmured Neri, elbowing her way back through the yawping, chattering, gesticulating festivities. Was this place really her home? She didn't recognise any of it.

'So you want the good news first?' Betsy asked.

'Why not?'

'The pictures have arrived.'

Neri kicked off her shoes and made herself comfortable on the bed. She took a healthy sip of her martini, then held out her hand for the phone.

'Thank you, Betsy,' she said, 'you can leave me to the bad news. Just bring me a plate of anything whatsoever as long as it's rich and heavy. And a couple more drinks to chase it down with. Hello?'

Abel Krostow was in one of his avuncular moods. That meant a request wasn't far away. He loved the pictures from Papua New Guinea. If they didn't win a national award – *another* national award – he was a pink-arsed penguin. She didn't ask whether such a breed existed. She drank her martini and let him talk. It was what he was good at.

'No,' she said at last.

While he was talking some more, Barney came into the room and carefully shut the door behind him. He noticed the untidyness of her dressing table and began to put it right.

'Look, Mr Krostow,' she said, 'it's been a long haul. When were you last in New Guinea? Have you any idea how long it takes to get a decent shot of a bird of paradise in the wild? What? They *ought* to be marvellous, the agonies they caused me.

'If I could nutshell this response, Mr Krostow, what I'm saying is I have a need to reacquaint myself with my own native environment. I feel like a displaced person. I'm likely to get lost just driving downtown. My own son shakes me by the hand like a stranger.'

Barney paused in the act of blowing dust from a shelf and adopted an offended expression.

'Call me after Christmas, Mr Krostow, okay? Yes, that's a deal. No promises, but I might just be feeling human again by then. I have a folk memory of the condition. And a happy Christmas to you, too.'

There was a knock on the door and Betsy came in with a tray and a gale of noise from the party. On one plate there was ravioli stuffed with spinach in a dark walnut sauce. On another there were mashed broad beans with olive oil and wild fennel. She'd brought mushroom vol-au-vents, oozing with juice, and a small dish of marinated courgettes. And there were two fresh glasses of martini.

'Did I ever say a bad word about you?' Neri asked, tucking in. 'If so, cancel it.'

A hand waved through the doorway.

'I didn't see what I just saw on that plate!' Jane Fonda laughed, retreating. 'Thanks for a lovely party.'

'How come I missed it?' Neri growled.

Barney followed Betsy to the door and, as carefully as before, shut it after her: 'We need to talk,' he said.

Mntrrgnplrwttr,' Neri protested, her mouth full.

'It would seem,' he said, 'from the case studies I've been reading, that I'm at a crucial age as regards maternal bonding.'

The phone rang. Someone else could answer it. There were extensions all over the place. She reached over and turned off the bell. The plates and glasses slid across the tray with a clatter, and only Barney's rapid intervention prevented a disaster. But why bother? Disasters were inevitable. They stalked her. Here was another one.

'Maternal *what?*'

'If we miss the opportunity to cement our relationship as mother and son I may end up psychologically malformed. I've already seen the signs in a few of the guys I know. It's real spooky.'

She chewed on a chicken drumstick: 'You're feeling deprived? That's what you're telling me?'

'Personally, momma, I can handle it. That must be my inner strength. I've kept the damage at bay. But Popeye Pringle has his own shrink already, and Hal Abercrombie is really off the rails. Do you know, he took his dad's credit card and ran up a thousand dollars?'

'Now I'm beginning to listen. How did he pull off a stunt like that?'

'He's big for his age, I guess.'

'So I'm cutting your rations,' she told him. 'Vegetables are out. Listen, do you think I enjoy living out of a suitcase? And don't answer that question, please. I don't. I like travel, but I like being at home, too.

'And I very much like,' she added, feeling schmaltzy, 'being with my Barneykins.'

There was a knock on the door and Betsy came in and hovered.

'And what's more,' she persisted, 'haven't I tried six times in the last nine months to fix for us to fly to London to see your long-lost aunt? Am I not right, Betsy?'

'Four times, Miss Corinthian.'

'Four. Six. What's the difference? I've tried hard, but something always crops up. What is it, Betsy?'

'A transAtlantic phone call. Guy named Pannick, can it be? Insists on speaking to you. Says it's personal. I've tried telling him you're engaged on important matters of a work nature, but the sound effects don't help. Especially when Woody Allen keeps making funny voices into the mouthpiece.'

'Oh,' she remembered, 'he kissed my cheek when he left, and said it was for you.'

'Perhaps,' Barney conceded, 'we should leave our talk for another time.' He collected the empty plates and carried the tray to the door. 'I'll try not to crack up,' he pledged manfully over his shoulder.

'Okay,' Neri sighed wearily. 'Put him through, Betsy. What's one more phone call, anyway? And do shut the door behind you. I'm sure there's noone out there I'd possibly want to see.'

She plumped the pillows and settled back into them with a glass of martini. Life really wasn't so bad, she thought. All in all, this was how she'd choose to live it.

'Speak to me, Darl baby,' she attacked the telephone. 'Is this about to be a waste of my precious time?'

Time was a nonsense, she thought, closing her eyes and curling her body into the foetal position. It must have been in another age that she'd been chased around a Rio bedroom by this hairy little architect.

'Well of course I remember,' she giggled. 'There are some things a woman doesn't forget . . . No, as it so happens, I haven't enjoyed such a jolly romp since, but are you sure nobody can be eavesdropping on the line? This conversation may breach the telegraph laws on the grounds of immorality . . . Yes, Darl, I have thought about a trip to London, but not for the purposes you have in mind . . . I mean I have other, personal reasons for wanting to visit. Isn't a woman allowed her secrets? . . . Because I'm too busy, that's why. And too well paid. I need a good excuse to come to England – a good financial excuse. Work . . . If I did have work in London would I find a little time to look you up? Sure. That could be arranged. So what's next? You find me work? . . . You have got to be kidding, Darl Pannick. I don't believe you have those contacts . . . No, I'm not wagering anything on it . . . And certainly not *that*! . . . Okay, okay, see what you can do. I'll wait to hear from you . . . And you, too, bad boy. Ciao!'

She put down her drink, stretched lazily on the bed, then swung her legs to the floor and stood up. What in God's name was the time? She opened the door. The music was still playing (a mellow Ella Fitzgerald) and the last guests stood quietly talking among the detritus of the party – dirty glasses, paper plates, forgotten articles of clothing. Adeline, her eyes still puffy, was in the process of clearing up.

'Everything all right?' Neri asked.

'Perfect, Miss Corinthian. Barney got off to bed in good time. There were no fights. Nobody got badly drunk. No one was sick on the floor.'

'And you call that a party?'

'Oh – and John Updike said to say goodbye.'

● ● ●

Peta put a hand out to steady herself on the fireplace, missed it and stood transfixed, swaying prettily. She looked a dream and felt as if she were in one. A long white, sparkly sheath dress, split from ankle to thigh, revealed a shape which looked both ethereal and girlish.

'My, look over there,' said Ella Lepard, standing in a gaggle of guests and motioning towards Peta with her cheroot-holder. 'Has something fallen off the Christmas tree?'

The fact was that if someone had tried to put Peta on a Christmas tree, she wouldn't have murmured. Standing there, sparkling and spangling, she almost thought she *was* a Christmas tree fairy. She wasn't quite sure where she was, but everything looked very nice, in spite of the haze. There were lots of pretty decorations, full glasses and beautiful people. But there was no one quite so beautiful as Peta.

'Beautiful Peta!' she squeaked, though no one heard her above the party noises. Ella Lepard swam across her blurred vision, all red-painted nails and rock-hard hair. 'And there's the wicked stepmother,' the abandoned model mumbled incoherently.

She'd been brought here by some young man – an assistant editor of a magazine, who'd left her standing all alone just as soon as she'd begun to get, well, a little confused. The Gucci mirror and the rolled banknote weren't in evidence tonight, but no one doubted that Peta, who now looked thin enough to break, had had a pretty hefty snort of something.

Technically, they were wrong. Peta's snorting days were over. She was into hallucinogens now. The pictures were better. It's just that she wished she could stop going hot and cold. And that someone would turn down the volume of the party. Like all LSD trippers, she was finding normal sound deafening.

The Barracuda had more of an expert eye than most when it came to drugs. She'd been there, so to speak. And she wasn't going back. But she still took a morbid interest in those who couldn't make the return trip.

'That young girl,' she pontificated, 'has had too much of everything. Too much spoiling, too much LSD. And I don't mean pounds sterling.'

The sophisticated young man with her laughed and obediently stubbed out her finished cheroot.

'This place is full of lost causes,' he said. 'But it's quite a party, isn't it?'

His voice was a strange combination of carelessness and keenness, the voice of a creature who earns by pleasing. Ella liked him now, but he knew full well that at any moment she might stop his allowance and pass him on to a friend. Or she might simply turn him out with nothing but his Armani wardrobe and his proud reputation of being her Italian stallion. Life was precarious.

It *was* quite a party – full of diverse groups of people invited by the new magazine *Interior Worlds*, celebrating its first birthday party with an eve of Christmas party. *IW* was one of the new breed of 90s magazines which catered for aspiration, for dreams and dollars. Expert marketing had angled it at the class which buys and sells taste. And tonight journalists rubbed shoulders with designers, architects and models.

The huge room at Brown's Hotel, that model of expensive English understatement, was heavy with scent, booze, the smell of Ella Lepard's cheroots and the stink of bitchery.

'By herself,' remarked the one-time Barracuda of Fleet Street, unable to avert her eyes from pretty, helpless Peta. 'I wonder where the luscious Jason can have gone.'

'As luscious as me?' smirked her olive-skinned escort. He was no more than 26, a tuxedo-clad Italian with a sort of dancing courtesy which reminded Ella of a gigolo. He wouldn't last much longer, she thought. She couldn't stand the hair oil on the pillows.

'*Just* as luscious, Julio.' She pronounced his name with a hard J just to annoy him. 'And a million times brighter and more entertaining.'

She watched him struggling to maintain his smile. God, he was oily. He almost shone with it, right down to the mirror-like surface of his shoes. She could almost see her age reflected in him. Yes, he would have to go.

Perhaps she really needed someone her own age. But then what about the sex? Stallion was certainly the word. At her time of life she preferred a partner who'd allow her to lie back and enjoy it. Julio might lack imagination, but by hell he had stamina.

'Well! If it isn't Ella Lepard! And no blood on the carpet!'

It was Sir Alfred Birtle, La Lepard's former editor on the *Daily News*, now official doyen of Fleet Street and champion party-goer. The two were old rivals and old lovers.

'You rogue, Alfy. You know I'm the sweetest thing since sugar.'

One sight of him was enough to make Ella realise that she'd be hanging on to Julio after all. At least until the New Year. *This* was a man of her own age, she thought, as she negotiated his stomach to give him a kiss on the cheek.

'But sugar's not had too good a press recently, eh? How's the magazine world. How's *Chic*? When are you coming back into the real world of newspapers?'

Birtle ignored Julio utterly. Ella's little weakness for young men was well-known. Distasteful, no doubt, but at least she paid them and never brought them to dinner parties where their total ignorance of anything before 1979 would be tiresome and embarrassing.

As Birtle and the Barracuda chatted, someone else was moving steadily towards Ella through the throng. Grant Locke had a problem on his mind, and the problem's name was Malibu – thanks to her mother. Thanks to her stupid, scatter-brained, irresistible mother. It hadn't shown an ounce of foresight to call this particular daughter after a drink, he thought. The last thing you could do with Malibu was order her.

'Need a sparky 17-year-old in the *Chic* offices, Ella?'

Malibu had disgraced herself. Again. After only six weeks into the job, she'd managed to have herself thrown out of an independent television production company. Six weeks! God knew, he'd been disposed to be tolerant of his wayward daughter when she finally returned from her tour of the world and its overcrowded jails. After all, she was back home – with a prison record, true, but all in one piece. He'd been surprised by his own delight when she turned up unannounced at his offices. Regardless of his colleagues, he'd hugged her and twirled her round to check she was quite unharmed.

And now this. A good start as a junior camera assistant at Shoots could have led to anything. But Malibu had thrown it away in a fit of pique.

'Move your tatty arse,' the leading lady had growled as she swept from the set during a break in filming and nearly fell over Malibu, crouching to steady a camera leg.

It hadn't been kind, especially from someone supposed to be playing Florence Nightingale. In fact, it had been bloody rude. Malibu's revenge was swift and direct.

'So what's so great about *your* arse?' she demanded. 'No, don't tell me, I'll ask around the set. Most of the men have had access to it.'

The actress had rounded on the teenager, slapping her across the face. But she made the mistake of turning away. That was never a sensible tactic with Malibu, who took a flying leap after her, grabbed her costume at the waist, pulled off skirt, petticoat and drawers, and left the arse in question blatantly open to public opinion.

It was, not surprisingly, the end of Malibu's career at Shoots. She was sacked on the spot, she was out of a job and she didn't seem very worried about not having one.

'Don't tell me you're releasing your young and lethal cocktail on a waiting world?' Ella asked, looking aghast. She held out a cheroot for her gigolo to light, moving her head all the time so that he had to jump about awkwardly with the lighted match.

Locke smiled wearily. He wasn't really much of a party man. He'd rather be at home cracking the *Times* crossword puzzle and listening to trad jazz. And in spite of the invitation, he had little time for arty mags like *Interior Worlds*.

But a father's love is boundless and, when Malibu was the daughter in question, it had to be. She'd expressed an interest in magazines that very morning and Locke had immediately thought of Ella Lepard, whose country retreat he'd just finished redesigning and who was bound to be at tonight's party. He could be straight with Ella. They'd got on well during work on the house ' their combination of blunt and sharp resulted in plain dealing and a mutual respect.

Not only that, but Locke looked likely to get the contract to put a new face on the magazine offices, largely thanks to a good word from Ella to the American moneymen. He'd hooked the invitation out of the wastepaper basket, adamantly refusing every piece of cajoling by Malibu to bring her along. She might be only 17, but she was dangerous. He could see her asking a waiter to dance or drinking herself sick.

'Oh, come on, Ella. *Chic* is full of youngsters just like my Malibu.'

'So maybe I've got enough.'

'This one's unique.'

'Spare me,' she said, blowing smoke. 'She wouldn't prefer to dally with Julio would she? I'm looking for a home for him shortly, you know. Not necessarily a kind home....'

Locke laughed. That was what he liked about Ella. Under that tan there was a toughness and realism which reminded him of the people of his native county. There was something a little like Yorkshire grit in Ella Lepard, and he liked her for it.

'She's dangerous, mind,' he admitted.'

'So am I. And I eat 17-year-olds for breakfast.'

'I thought that was only well-hung boys,' Locke riposted, and it was Ella's turn to laugh. He told her the story of Malibu's night in the Cairo cells. That was the clincher.

'Send her along for a chat. We'll see if she's able to tackle the *Chic* gropers. That's the main qualification.'

Locke nodded, his mission accomplished. His attention was taken by a large woman in black silk baggy trousers and a voluminous top making her way through the crowd. Her shock of blonde hair was fiercely back-combed and the only colour on her whitened face was a gash of plum lipstick.

'Bunty,' Ella reported. 'Swiss. Bent as the spring inside a cuckoo clock. Cold as an Alp. The editor of *Interior Worlds* and therefore our esteemed hostess.'

'I rather think that should be host,' interrupted Birtle, who had returned bearing fresh martinis. 'Is she the one tipped to be deputy MD of Design Mags Inc. in the New Year?'

'The very same Bunty. It's good to have another woman at the top.'

'As, no doubt, Bunty herself often remarks.'

'Wicked, Alfy, wicked!'

By the fireplace, Peta was still swaying dreamily, but her eyes were fixed on the doorway. She had that startling and hard-edged clarity with which an LSD tripper sees either reality or fantasy when the drug's influence is at its height. With that clarity of vision she now watched the entrance of Calla Marchant.

She could see every curve from her cheekbones to her ankle bones.

She could see the arch of her eyebrow, the softness of her mouth. And she could see that Calla was alone.

Peta wasn't the only one looking. From all parts of the room, eyes were drawn to the doorway.

'Just her Gorgeousness all alone,' shrugged Ella. 'Bloody good she looks on it, too, damn her.'

It was dead simple – a black velvet dress, short and shoulder-strapped. The male temperature rose by several degrees as she moved. The slightest smile played on her moist and parted lips. Calla could feel that familiar crackle of excitement around her and, quite frankly, she loved it.

'Just look at Bunty!' Birtle said. 'Talk about mentally undressing!'

Calla's appearance had stopped Bunty in her purposeful track just as it had stopped every man in the room except the waiters. And even the waiters walked with a lighter step. The truth was that the memories of Philippe were still fresh in Calla's mind and body. She felt alive, vital, and therefore she looked it. She was energised by her sexuality.

'Bitch!' Peta suddenly cried in a high voice which cut through the noise of the party.

The Barracuda, a purposeful smile on her face, hurried across to where Calla was rapidly being surrounded by admiring men. She could smell blood.

'As the poor girl said, Calla darling, where's the poor boy? Have you any idea? How's he getting on with his little problem? The last news we had wasn't good, heaven knows.'

Calla responded icily: 'You're the expert on drug recovery, as I recall.'

'Oh, quite,' Ella replied, unruffled. 'And I have the contacts too. According to my informants – or should I call them inmates? – poor Jason's chances aren't very good.'

Calla felt heated by anger, concern, and, dammit, a little guilt. Why the hell had she come tonight? She'd turned down plenty of invitations in her time, and she was damn sure she could live without the publicity and good offices of *Interior Worlds*. And why hadn't she known the answers to those questions? After all, she'd lived with the man for a dozen years. He'd inspired her, helped her, loved her. Didn't she care at all?

'I say,' Peta shrieked, 'that you're a callous bitch!'

Now all eyes moved from Calla's vibrant beauty to the watercolour version standing by the fireplace. Peta, rocking backwards and forwards, her eyes fixed on Calla, dropped her glass on the marble with a smash.

'Jason's back inside,' she mumbled. 'You don't care.'

Calla strode forward to confront her.

'*I* care,' Peta stuttered – and passed out in a spangled heap at her feet.

'You have to hand it to the Marchant woman,' La Lepard remarked audibly. 'That's what I call a drop-dead entrance.'

• • •

The Duke of Mercia turned in his saddle to look back along the snowy road towards Willoughby Hall. Where was It wasn't long before the off and still she was nowhere to be seen. He was puzzled. There were few things she liked as much as the first meet of the hunting season, few places she'd rather be than on a horse flying over a fence to God-knew-what lay beyond. She had said she'd be there before him.

'Not like her to miss the stirrup cup, either,' he murmured to himself as he took a swig from the silver mug of sherry. It went down like fire. In the car park of the Willoughby Arms, where the hunt always met, the Duke was served first by the lad going round with the tray.

Inside the hostelry, the faded sporting paintings in the snug recorded notable gatherings of the past. There were foxes' heads on the walls. Out here the breath of around 60 horses and riders hung thick in the winter air. The mounts, though not of the nervous showjumper type, were restless. Vague memories of last season's sport stirred within them, and they flared their nostrils to the keen chill and shifted restlessly.

It was a typically English scene, eccentric, dictated by rules and all faintly ridiculous – and even more ridiculous now that you couldn't actually hunt in the old way at all. The countryside lobby was up in arms against a government which had banned the sport unless you played silly games to get round the law. That was why, in a distinctly non-English way, a prominent feature of the gathering was a huge eagle owl perched menacingly on the arms of a sturdy falconer. You could hunt foxes with birds of prey, after all, and it didn't matter how many hounds trotted along in their wake. Already about twenty English hunts had recruited raptors to keep the police off their backs.

Before them today lay miles of country, spattered with a light dusting of snow, much of it through the Duke's estate and farm land. There were fences, hedges and streams to negotiate, rough land and smooth, trees and open fields.

Willy Watts, a lean, lined horseman with grey hair and a ramrod back, stood whip in hand, his hounds about his feet. They were the finest pack in the south-west. They stood sniffing the air, sleek and eager. They would soon be off to draw the first cover for the hunt.

'Where the hell's Fern?'

It was the Hon Marion Mason-Fox, on a sturdy black cob. Bombproof, thought Willoughby as he looked at the beast. It would have to be.

Marion's tally-ho was like John Peel's – it would awaken the dead, let alone frighten a horse.

It was Marion's second time out this season. Her own hunt, where she was joint mistress, had been out the week before. No eagle owls for her. After all, you were allowed to give the hounds exercise by innocently following a scent, so that was her solution. Only of course they *would* find a bloody fox by accident, and they might just kill it, and nobody would say a damn thing about it. Typical British compromise. They'd pursued three of them without the slightest success, so she was hoping for rather better sport as a guest of the Charlesbury Hunt today.

She was also a guest at Willoughby Hall, and the Duke was far too polite to give her an icy reply. He let her remark go. But Marion wasn't the sensitive type. She blundered on regardless, somehow managing to call the pub boy over for a second stirrup cup as she did so.

'She was only calling in at the Vicarage to say hello to the new chap, wasn't she?'

'Was she? I didn't realise. Then that's probably why she's late.'

'Why a bloody vicar should be put before a day's sport, I can't imagine.'

'He's a curate, Marion, not a vicar.'

'Even worse. She'll be leaving her calling card with the churchwarden next.'

Marion didn't see her friend's momentary distress. He shifted slightly to pay some attention to the length of his stirrup straps and managed to be quite composed by the time he looked up.

'I don't believe it!' cried Marion. 'It's old Buffy!' She walked her horse through the throng to a white-whiskered man in an ancient pink coat astride a rather whiskery horse of similar age. 'Buffy, you old bastard! How are you?'

'Topping, my dear. Absolutely topping.'

Willoughby breathed a sigh of relief. Thank God she'd gone. He wished he could come to terms with his damnable jealousy, but he couldn't. Old Buffy was the former master of the Charlesbury, who had handed over the reins to his son, young Buffy, with great reluctance, four seasons ago. He could be relied upon to keep Marion occupied.

He scanned the gathering again. There were lovely young women aplenty – foxhunting is full of fresh English prettiness with the bloom of youth and the open air on its cheeks. And, dammit, the air was fresh today, he thought. But he couldn't see the face he wanted to see. There were some good enough female figures in well-cut black coats, but none of them belonged to his wife.

He sighed. It would quite take the edge off the day's sport for him if she didn't come. Riding was one of the few things they still did together.

It was his chance to be close to the woman he still yearned for despite the obvious waning of her ardour for him.

'Passed her Grace on the way, Harry.'

It was young Buffy, whose real name was Richard Barrington. He was a handsome, regular featured young man with thick well-brushed black hair. Young Buffy was one of the reasons there were so very many pretty young things in the Charlesbury. He was good-humoured, single and moneyed. He was, as Fern had once remarked, rather less intelligent than his uncle's big toe.

But he was fearless over the fences and undoubtedly a good sight on horseback. The women of the hunt knew how to judge what a man had in his wallet by what he wore on his back. And Barrington was very well turned out indeed. His scarlet coat was by Bernard Weatherill, the Savile Row livery tailor to the Queen, and his boots were the best from Swaine, Adeney, Brigg and Sons of Piccadilly.

'She was going into the churchyard. Gathering mistletoe, I suppose, eh? Festive season upon us and all that.'

The Duke nodded. Fern was the last person to need mistletoe, he thought. If she wanted a kiss she'd scarcely look around for a bit of greenery to stand under first.

'She'll be along later. Join us in the field, I expect. Decent turnout today, Barrington.'

Young Buffy nodded. 'The old man doesn't know how some of 'em got into the hunt. Says in his day as master they were all gentlemen and now the field's full of pop stars and estate agents – not to speak of ruddy great condors or whatever that thing is over there clapping its wings.'

The Duke laughed. 'We're not elitist, I hope. As long as the celebrities and eagle owls don't frighten the horses.'

'All to do with market forces, Pa, I told him. Dash it, not everyone can afford £80 a week for a hunter's livery, not to mention our £500 subscription – especially when it's not the real thing any more. Old Tilda in the rectory dower house has had to pass this season. Can't afford the sub.'

Willoughby made a mental note to make sure Matilda Sherring had a subscription as a Christmas present. She was a countrywoman, well into her sixties, who'd hunted all her life.

'There goes Watts with his hounds,' the young man observed. 'I'd better muster the field.'

He was off, gladdening the hearts of several young horsewomen with a cheery word as he pushed through the packed car park. He sat his mount well, a thought which brought a flush to the female cheeks that chilly morning.

Willoughby looked down the road again. Even against the white snow, there was no sign of Fern and her mare. A shadow clouded his features. He knew the marriage had somehow failed his wife. Where had he gone wrong? She gave her loyalty more out of sense of duty than passion, he knew that.

As for her physical faithfulness, Willoughby was no fool. He didn't know how often she had other men, but he knew she didn't find him enough, and it hurt. It hurt again this morning that she wasn't there with him. The morning's sport would be nothing for him without his Duchess.

Wishing he'd stayed at home in the library with his plans of Charlesbury and his newspapers, the Duke of Mercia turned his horse to follow the horn. As they rushed through the gate into the fields, he looked once more over his shoulder and saw nothing but a snowy road disappearing into the distance between naked trees.

'The sport's in this direction, Willoughby, not back there!'

It was Old Buffy, charging by him, keen to get to the front of the field and be in for the kill of a fox. Or an estate agent. He didn't mind which.

Fern Willoughby heard the horn too: 'Oh, Christ! Sorry, Nigel! Blasphemy and all that.'

She was scrambling back into riding trousers, watched by a bemused and slightly knocked-out young man. He was sprawled semi-clothed on the floor of the church vestry. Around him, on pegs, hung choirboys' cassocks and spare vestments.

Fern, frantically pushing her hair under her riding hat, paused to look at him.

'You will be all right, now, won't you?' She bent down and patted him on a damp hot cheek. 'You'll have to find a wife, you know. Can't have you seducing your parishioners. Not over Christmas at any rate. Come on! Get dressed! You must have some pensioners or young mothers to visit. I'm off! See you!'

She left him, still dazed and shaking his head, but on his feet and attempting to get his legs into his trousers. Fern ran down the yew-lined church path, regardless of the snow and spangled frost, to the lychgate where Salome, her grey mare, was tethered.

'Blast! I'll be late and Harry will wonder where the hell I am.'

She flung a leg across the animal and set off at a pace for the Willoughby Arms. She was still wet between the legs from her lover, but the incident was all but forgotten. Her thoughts now were concentrated on the hunt.

The curate was a beefy young man, all smiles and boyish clumsiness. He had surprised himself by the deep urgings Fern had awoken inside him once she'd had him at her mercy in the vestry. He'd never had a woman before and had never felt quite so swept along by anything since his famous 50-yard dash at public school which had won him a tassled cap and a place in the rugby first fifteen.

The pubic hair had been a surprise to him, in spite of furtive adolescent glances in magazines. Such appetite in a woman had been even more of a surprise to him, particularly in a woman who had called in for coffee at the vicarage and then suggested visiting the church to discuss flower arrangements.

But his own desires, his own lack of shame, were the greatest revelations of all. What a perceptive woman! She was quite right. He must find a wife.

As the curate gently bathed away his sin in a basin of warm water, wondering all the time at the godlike power of the now flaccid organ in his hand, Fern rode on. It was just the sort of day she liked to be on a horse. No one would have taken Fern for a horsewoman if she'd been seen in her own drawing room, but out here, astride the animal she loved, it was impossible to imagine her as anything else.

'Dammit!' She was cross with herself. She'd disappointed Harry and missed the stirrup cup for the sake of a romp with an inexperienced boy. Halfway along the road she pulled Salome sharply to the left and through a gate.

'No point in going to the meet, old girl. Let's go across country and join them at Buffy's Brook, eh? We can pretend we've been there hours.'

Off the tarmac road they could go faster. In spite of the snow, which wiped out the familiar contours of the fields, Fern was confident she knew her way.

The Duchess was what they call a hard woman to hounds. Years of hunting with the four-day a week Exmoor when she was a girl in the West country had made a bold and skilled huntswoman of her. There wasn't a jump in the Charlesbury country she wouldn't take.

She looked at her watch. By now the hounds would be drawing Willoughby's Gorse, hoping for a fox which would run due north across to the Brook. She guided Salome to the point where a drystone wall was easily jumpable.

Only a field and a fence lay between her and the brook. She heard the hunt's horn and urged the mare on faster, taking the fence without a pause for thought. As soon as Salome's front hooves lifted clear she realised her mistake.

'Oh, you bloody fool,' she told herself. 'You bloody careless, reckless fool!'

That was all she had time to think. She saw, with a sharp intake of breath, that the icy ground on the far side fell away sharply, far too sharply – that the level land she'd aimed for was much further along the fence.

She felt her head thrown back and then everything went black.

• • •

It was Willoughby who made out the riderless grey mare against the snowy field. His heart was thumping wildly. What could have happened to his wife, to his lovely Fern?

He hallooed to the rest of the field to halt before the fence. He could see that Salome was limping. Somewhere on this side of the fence lay his wife. He was sure of that. He dismounted and walked along the deep rut, dusted by pure snow, guessing what he would find at the steepest point.

She looked so frail lying there, her hat thrown off and her fair hair flung out on the snow.

'I'll go for help!' cried Barrington, already off towards the nearest farm cottage.

Harry Willoughby knelt beside his Duchess. How long had she been there? She was lying awkwardly, but he dare not touch her. Her gloved hand was still warm, but her eyes were shut.

He felt a sudden and violent pulsation of love. Please God, let her be all right. She was everything to him.

'Not good,' said Old Buffy quietly, kneeling by the side of him. 'Sorry, old man.'

They could both tell from her crooked position that something was broken. Willoughby took his scarlet coat off and tucked it gently around her. Still she did not stir. He felt the tears welling up in his eyes.

19

The Grosvenor House Hotel in Park Lane is the place they hold most of the really large London functions. It has a vast banqueting hall and a staff which knows how to make you feel an individual even if you're in a crowd of hundreds. It was the obvious place for Harry Willoughby to choose for the announcement of his short list in the Charlesbury competition.

He could, of course, have written to the competitors individually and held a small press conference anywhere in town. That wouldn't have suited his purpose at all. Over the past few years he'd come to realise that he'd touched a public nerve over the state of the British architecture. Maybe most of the architects thought he was an upstart and a ruddy nuisance, but the man and woman in the street seemed to think he'd got it right. Something had gone wrong with the buildings of England, and he was helping to bring about changes for the benefit of future generations. He intended to promote his views with all the energy, and cash, at his disposal.

So here he was on a bitterly cold January morning, being driven across from his house in Eaton Square almost beside himself with excitement. For the first time in weeks he allowed the awful thing that had happened to Fern to slip to the back of his mind. This was his moment. He'd watched the Booker prize ceremonies on television, with a room full of authors and other literary types, all of them on tenterhooks as the time for the announcement drew closer. That's where he'd got the idea. But he knew he could do better. The Booker judges drew up their own short list, which meant that there were only half a dozen writers in the running on the big day. Harry Willoughby thought that was far too narrow a field. Far better to keep the whole lot of them guessing!

As many as 140 of them had entered. He'd opened each package with trembling fingers, wondering whether this would be the one which embodied his glorious dream. Few had got very close, of course. He'd been disappointed by the overall standard. So many of the architects had simply played safe. He almost preferred the few who had bravely ignored his own preferences and gone for something outlandishly modern. They hadn't a chance, but he rather admired their spunk.

His car turned into the hotel forecourt just before noon. The place was already busy. He'd decided that every architectural practice which had entered should have a representative at the lunch. Add a considerable number of journalists and a bevy of distinguished guests from the world of architecture and about two hundred people would be sitting down to lunch. He ducked out of the car, shook a few important hands and was soon sipping dry white wine as he mingled with his guests. The hubbub of so many excitable people engaged in dozens of separate conversations was almost deafening, and his keen senses detected an undercurrent of near-hysteria.

'A splendid occasion,' smiled Langton Meredith, extending his hand.

The blasted trouble was that you couldn't make any movement, any expression which seemed to give anything away. You mustn't be too friendly or too curt, to have a significant look in your eye or a distant one. The Duke was accustomed to conducting himself impeccably, but he'd never felt himself walking a social tightrope as precariously as he did at this moment.

'Wonderful, isn't it?' he replied lamely. Must do better than this, he thought, moving on.

Meredith had never felt so strung-up in his life. It wasn't only the competition itself but his reputation with his colleagues at Broughton, Hughes, Lorimer. Jake Broughton was after his neck, that much was obvious. If he lost today he'd have a hell of a battle in the boardroom.

He stood by the board with the placings for lunch. It had been arranged alphabetically, which at least made it easy to discover that he was on table 17. He hated the usual game of hide-and-seek, which had you poring over the plan for ages and then made you feel you'd been seated with the most boring people only because you were thought to be boring yourself. Here it was simply the luck of your birthright.

Having sorted out his own position, he found his eyes moving down the plan looking for another name. There it was: Bunny Simkins was actually on the guest list! A little shot of fear ran through him. Suppose that his plan hadn't worked. Suppose Simkins was chosen rather than himself. That would be the greatest humiliation of all. Surely, he thought, trying to calm himself, the name was on the list only because he'd entered the competition in the first place. Simkins couldn't be expected actually to turn up. Everyone knew the story – Meredith had made sure of that.

He was wrong. Even as Meredith turned from the board he saw Bunny Simkins entering the room. A murmur spread like a forest fire. All eyes were focused on this elder statesman of the profession as he ambled forward, wearing his usual crumpled suit and sporting a typically garish orange tie as if nothing whatsoever had happened at all.

But something had. Normally there would have been no shortage of people taking him by the hand, slapping him on the back and asking him how life was treating him. Bunny was a hail-fellow-well-met. Everyone liked old Bunny. Today they all stood back, nervous and wary.

One or two of the braver men lifted a hand in feeble greeting, but they all felt themselves on show. Let someone else be the first to make a move.

He would have made his way towards the drinks table all alone, with that large gathering opening up to either side of him, except that the only woman in the room – a ravishing woman in a crimson dress which clung to her curves – now darted forward and threw her arms around his neck.

'Bunny!' Calla rejoiced. 'I'm so glad you're here!'

She was glad for two reasons – because she always loved to see him and because it was a two-fingered salute to the dirty, narrow minds which condemned him. She'd run up to him quite spontaneously, but even as she'd done it she'd known that she was raising two fingers of her own. She could hardly believe the treachery of his friends and colleagues.

'Don't like to miss a free nosh,' he smiled. 'What's on the menu?'

'Beef Wellington. I hope it's hot enough to thaw this lot out. You've noticed the chill in the air?'

'Ah, it's what we must expect,' he replied philosophically.

Yes, she thought, you knew it would be like this, and yet you came all the same. She never ceased to be surprised by Bunny, by the strength which underlay that easy-going exterior. He'd obviously been badly hurt by what had happened, but he hadn't let it sour his outlook on the world. The same evening she'd heard the story she had driven to his home with the idea of consoling him. In the event, it had been a case of Bunny consoling her. He had dampened down her anger.

'I hardly slept last night,' she confided in him now, telling him, as always, things she would never have admitted to anyone else. 'I know it's stupid, but I see this competition as make or break.'

'It will make the winner for sure, but I hardly see you as a broken woman, Calla-lily – whatever happens. You're not the breaking type.'

'Don't be too sure.'

'In any case, I've put money on you.'

'You're joking!'

'In the office sweep. All very unofficial, of course. A bit of fun. But we amateur punters like to choose a horse we fancy, no matter what the form book says.'

'That,' she laughed, 'is a back-handed compliment.'

'As for me, I've the luxury of being the only man in the room without butterflies in his stomach.'

She longed for it all to be over. This was just like being back in school for the exams. She experienced again that helpless, frustrating feeling of being judged yet not being able to express herself properly. In school there was never enough time to finish the paper. If you did finish it, you were always aware of what else you might have said. They weren't judging the real you, with all your knowledge, all your ideas.

That's how she felt now. Of course she'd submitted those detailed plans which she and Philippe had sweated over. It was all fair and above board. But how could lines on paper really do justice to the dreams in her head? How could she rely on the Duke's appreciation of what she was trying to do?

Then she thought of Philippe's 'philosophy'. He'd waxed rather poetical, she thought at the time. All that history and fable. Quite mad! But perhaps there might be something in it, after all? She thought of a particular cheese and tomato sandwich and found herself grinning all over her face.

'The smile of confidence?' asked Grant Locke, joining them. Whereas every other man in the room wore a dark suit with trappings to match, Locke was in a comfortable brown corduroy jacket over a checked shirt. It was rather surprising that he'd bothered with a tie. He raised a glass in Bunny's direction. He'd never thought the man anything but an old bumbler, well past any prime he'd ever had, but he enjoyed being seen to mix with the outcast and downfallen. Being the odd one out suited him. 'Or have I missed a good joke?'

'I'm sure it happens to you all the time, Grant,' Calla teased him. 'You need a sense of humour to understand them.'

'Ee, lass,' he said in a stage-northern accent, 'life's too grim for laffs where I come from.' He gave her a quizzical look: 'Beginning to regret that we didn't team up?'

'Not a bit,' she replied spiritedly. Not one tiniest little fraction of a bit, she thought, recalling the passionate consequences of teaming up with someone else. 'Are you?'

'It might have been fun,' he said.

Locke found that he cared more about this competition than he would have thought possible. He'd always taken success in his stride. His failures had been few enough to ignore. But now he felt that his very competence was being weighed in the balance. He started as a front-runner, that was the trouble. Everyone knew that he'd made his career out of small-scale community architecture. Everyone knew that the Duke held that kind of development in high esteem. If he didn't win the competition it couldn't because of his overall philosophy – it must be because he wasn't imaginative enough in the detail of his plan or couldn't be trusted to handle a project of this size.

'At least I've had my wish today,' he told her. 'Your seat's next to mine!'

The food and wine were very good, the Duke had seen to that. He'd planned everything meticulously, because this was one of the great moments of his life. After so much worry about Fern, it was a huge relief to throw himself into his pet project and to have nothing else on his mind at all. He'd allowed himself that indulgence, and he knew she understood. He tucked into his meal with relish.

Few of his guests had the same appetite. Calla had Grant Locke on her left and Langton Meredith directly opposite her, and she noticed that both picked at their food. If she had to choose a word to describe the mood it would have been neurotic. The architects spoke to one another, but in little bursts, as if their minds were somewhere else. As, of course, they were.

She could see the dishevelled bunches of Bunny's hair several tables away and, a little closer, the bald dome of Darl Pannick. He caught her eye and made a gallant little gesture which indicated how pleased he was to see her. She winked at him, and immediately wondered whether she had gone too far. *Steady on, girl*, she rebuked herself. *Don't let the nerves lead you astray or you may do something really disgraceful!*

Pannick was in a bad mood, and the sight of Calla simply lightened it for a moment. He felt he was a performing animal in some run-down, second-rate circus. Why in God's name was he taking part in this meretricious show? He loathed everything architectural the Duke stood for. He'd entered in a spirit of anger, and he felt even more angry now that the thing was nearly over – over as far as he was concerned, at any rate. The short-listed practices would have to go through all this again, presumably, and good luck to them. He hated the whole backward-looking charade. Why build classical buildings in the twenty-first century? He couldn't understand it.

'We are witnessing,' he said to the architect sitting next to him, 'the death throes of our own profession as anything more than tired purveyors of second-hand dreams.'

'Oh, I say,' chortled his neighbour, spearing a potato. 'Steady on, old fellow!'

Whoever won, Pannick knew, would be feted by the popular press as some sort of saviour of the British way of life. For every serious article which had something intelligent to say, there'd be a couple of dozen which churned out the usual rubbish about traditional values. He didn't have much faith in the press. No, that wasn't correct: he didn't have any faith in it whatsoever.

Even the Duke seemed to have his doubts, because he'd made an exception to his alphabetical placings by having a separate table set for the press. But perhaps that was something to do with reporters needing to rush away to meet their deadlines. At least the food was the same.

'Best grub we've been served up since that Richard Branson do at the Hilton,' said the journalist to Martin Kingsley's left.

'Except for the poncy wine,' replied the photographer to his right with a sneer. 'I've given up trying to get a decent pint of lager at thrashes like this.'

By the time the port was served, Kingsley was feeling nicely mellow. True, he still felt a shade uneasy whenever he looked across at Bunny Simkins, and he made sure that their eyes never met. That had been a disagreeable episode. Whoever had left that tip-off message for him had set Kingsley up every bit as much as Simkins. He and his colleagues were the unwitting witnesses who would corroborate the rumours rushing around London like a keen winter wind through the canyons of its sky-scrapers. Of course, he had more than a shrewd guess as to who it must have been. He'd even rung Meredith about it, only to be met with strenuous denials. Whatever had given him that idea? A mere coincidence that they'd spoken about Simkins' sexual tastes only a few months before.

That, though, had been the one blemish in what had otherwise been a very satisfactory long-term assignment. Kingsley had never before known the journalistic pleasures of specialising – of getting to know everything about a certain field and all the people in it. At the start he thought he'd been given a bum job, but now he was really sorry that it was coming to an end. Oh, he'd no doubt be sent on follow-up stories as the months went by, but he'd miss these day-to-day contacts with architects and their rivalries. Maybe, he thought, he'd try for a job on the *Architectural Review*. Did they pay well?

He was jolted back to reality by a hammering on the top table and a simultaneous poke in his ribs. All the reporters were reaching for their notebooks, and he bent down to take his own from the floor under his chair. The MC, having wielded his gavel to miraculous effect, gave a brief and completely unnecessary introduction to His Grace, the Duke of Mercia. The applause almost took the roof off as 140 palpitating architects gave vent to their excitement and terror.

'Most of these hands,' murmured Grant Locke close to Calla's ear, 'will very soon be wanting to strangle him.'

The Duke took his time adjusting the microphone and shooting his cuffs. There was a little of the showman in him. He enjoyed creating an almost eery silence where seconds before there had been the sound of two hundred people feasting.

'Ladies and gentlemen . . . '

At least he'd remembered her this time, Calla thought. But no: a couple of the dignitaries at the top table had brought their wives with them, so there was no guarantee that she was in his mind at all. She found herself playing with crumbs on the tablecloth as the Duke ploughed through the tiresome preliminaries. Curse her cheek in paying him that visit at Eaton Square! She'd made a bloody fool of herself, she was sure. If only, she thought, she could quietly, invisibly, get up from the table and go home!

When she raised her eyes and looked around her, she almost laughed. She was good at reading body language in all its various dialects, and everyone in this room was saying exactly the same thing. She took in the unnatural tension of limbs, the stiff necks, the tightened fingers. Yes, they were all, to a man, speaking the same language. They were all, in short, shit-scared.

'And so,' the Duke continued, at last reaching the part of his speech that mattered, 'I came to draw up my short-list.' This comment brought on a universal shuffling of bottoms on seats. 'I had no preconceived notion as to how many plans would appear on this list, but as I had no wish to raise false expectations and involve your practices in unnecessary expense. I was hoping to make it a short one. I'm pleased to say that I have managed to achieve this.'

Now the tension was unbearable. The shorter the list, the smaller the individual chances of being on it, and Calla noticed the anxiety on the whitened faces around her. Several of the architects had suddenly developed nervous tics.

'In fact, I have chosen just three.'

He had to pause because of the volume of expelled air from 140 pairs of lungs. As far as most of the architects were concerned, that was it. End of contest. Put a dozen on the short-list and a great many of them would have an outside chance. But three? Forget it. They let their disappointment gush out of them in shuddering sighs and they shifted noisily on their chairs.

'A few words in commiseration to those practices which almost made the list, but not quite . . . ' the Duke rolled on. Calla, ceasing to listen, found herself feeling heavy and intensely miserable, almost as if she'd gone down with a bout of the flu. She had to fight back the tears in her eyes. The folly of it all overwhelmed her. She'd thought she could beat the system, whereas everyone knew a woman had never made it to the top in this profession. She'd thought her relative youth would be an asset, whereas everyone knew you needed experience. Although she sat among all of two hundred people, she nevertheless felt terribly lonely.

'Cunning bugger's dragging it out,' Grant Locke whispered into her ear.

' . . . and I have been relieved to discover how much good design there still is in this country. Moreover . . . '

242

'He was probably a torturer in a previous life,' Locke muttered. 'With the Spanish Inquisition.'

Calla smiled. God, she needed some moral support right now. She put her hand on his and squeezed it.

'But it's time,' the Duke said, 'and I daresay rather past the decent time as far as you're concerned . . . '

'Bring on the dancing girls,' Locke suggested.

' . . . for me to announce the results of the first stage of my competition. I shall give the names in no particular order. All of these three designs have great merit, and I look forward to discussing the finer points with the practices concerned in the near future. It's my intention that the final plans should be submitted by the first day of August this year.'

He paused to take a luxurious sip of water, all the while swivelling to enjoy the spectacle of so many people hanging on his every word.

'Congratulations, first,' he announced, 'to the Grant Locke Partnership.'

As a tumult of applause broke out all around him, Locke simply smiled and raised a hand, rather like the more modest kind of footballer celebrating a goal. Then he stood and gave a slight bow towards the Duke. There were fixed smiles on the faces of most of the men who were so desperately clapping – false smiles which spoke of dashed hopes – but Calla saw a contemptuous scowl on the face of Darl Pannick and something like a sneer on the thin lips of Langton Meredith.

You blind fool, she accused herself. You could have been sharing this triumph. But your pride wouldn't let you, would it? You had this great, fanatical belief in yourself and now you've seen it crumble to dust.

She held out a hand to Locke as he sat down, but he brushed it aside and kissed her warmly on the cheek. He wasn't the type, she knew, to say 'I told you so'. But, sure as hell, he must be thinking it.

The Duke, having described Locke, his track record and his plans for Charlesbury in suitably glowing terms, now took up his glass again and gave them a repeat performance. No, it wasn't for them: he gave it for *himself*. He was immensely happy. He had found his mission in life and was revelling in the power to carry it to a glorious conclusion.

'The second practice I have selected,' he beamed, 'is almost a household name. I mean, of course, Broughton, Hughes, Lorimer.'

Langton Meredith, whatever else he felt, was careful to show nothing more than a quiet, almost shy pleasure. His bow towards the Duke was rather more demonstrative than Locke's had been, but he certainly didn't raise his arms in an unseemly manner. Not even one of them. He meant his audience to think that this triumph was only his due.

At the press table Martin Kingsley was feeling pretty happy. He had a centre-page spread to write for the following morning, but most of the work had already been done. He'd written the background and ordered the photographs. There'd be breakouts on the three winners, but that would take no time at all – he'd interviewed at least thirty of the top architects over the past few months and he could hack the copy into shape in no time.

All was going according to plan, he mused, as he took a shorthand note of the Duke's praise of Broughton, Hughes, Lorimer. It would take the choosing of an absolute outsider to make him break sweat today. That wasn't going to happen. He knew Locke's work inside out, and he'd had more dealings with Langton Meredith than with any of the other competitors. Evil bastard, he thought.

The light was reflected from the bald pate of Bunny Simkins. Wouldn't it be a kick in the teeth for Meredith if he was chosen after all! But that, of course, was nonsense, a mere dream. Kingsley was a realist. He liked to think of himself as a bit of a cynic.

Calla was also wishing that the Duke would surprise them all by choosing Bunny. Go on, Harry Willoughby, she silently urged him. Prove that you're above all that pettiness.

'And so to my third choice,' said the Duke, again taking up his glass. He swirled the water thoughtfully. The silence gathered.

'Perhaps at this stage I may make a few remarks about the presentation of your plans . . . '

'Can I go home please, sir?' whispered Locke. 'I've had my fun.'

The atmosphere was almost hostile now. Each of the competing architects had retreated into his own private thoughts. Those thoughts were agony: he was teasing them, torturing them. They were all hunched and tensed. They were mastered by a stifling fear.

'I'm sure,' the Duke went on, 'that you all pondered deeply on the challenges of Charlesbury. You surely set this development within the broader context of the geography, history and culture of our islands . . . '

'Ee oop, squire,' murmured Locke in a heavy accent. 'Tha's using reet big words.'

' . . . but I regret to say that few of your submissions reflected those concerns. That's why I was particularly pleased by my third choice, which not only tackled the problems and the opportunities in an exciting manner, but which gave verbal expression to their underlying philosophy.

'My congratulations to the Marchant-Beauvoir Partnership.'

Before the applause began there was a silence which was long enough to register the shock. It was plain from the way that puzzled glances were exchanged throughout the room that most of them hadn't a clue who it was that had won. Beauvoir? It rang a bell, perhaps, from Philippe's French triumphs, but it didn't seem to fit here. And Marchant?

Calla rose slowly to her feet, prompted by Locke's guiding hand under her elbow. 'Take a bow, genius,' she heard him say. She was more shocked than any of them. This couldn't be real, could it? Just for a second she had the temptation to wilt, to play the little girl, to blush and squirm as if she was unworthy of the honour. No, it was for the merest fraction of a second. Then she was Calla Marchant again, telling herself to think wild and to think big. Telling herself those plans were damn good. Telling herself she was set to be *the* architect of the Millennium. Yes, take a bow, genius! She stood up straight, inclining her head towards Harry Willoughby in a decorous acknowledgement.

'Shit!' Martin Kingsley thought. 'How did I miss that one?'

It seemed to Calla as if the boisterous clapping would never stop. There were, in fact, two reasons for the length and the violence of the architects' acclaim – the outlet of so much pent-up tension and the sheer, breathtaking, undeniable sexual appeal of the lovely creature who stood proudly before them. The applause meant, in a bowdlerised translation: 'Don't ever sit down. Stand there glorying in your triumph and let us feast our eyes upon you for ever.'

The next hour was spent in a joyful daze. She was whisked away with Locke and Meredith to meet the press, then joined the Duke and the top-table dignitaries for a private celebration. She smiled, shook hands, smiled again, hardly knowing what she was doing. Surely this was the happiest moment of her life.

Afterwards she remembered very little of it in detail. Only three things stuck in her mind. One of them was Bunny's warm and generous embrace no sooner than she sat down in the banquetting hall, the applause still in her ears. She'd had to fight back the tears then. The second was an overheard remark by Langton Meredith as the three winners prepared to meet the Duke.

'Thank God that's all over,' Locke had said agreeably, with the air of a man who has better things to do with his time.

'On the contrary,' Meredith had replied without the hint of a smile. 'This is where the real cut-and-thrust begins.'

The third thing she couldn't make sense of at all. She knew that, as soon as the celebrations were over, she must get to a telephone as fast as her legs would take her and tell Philippe the incredible news. He'd be so delighted. She wouldn't be surprised if, in his typically extravagant Gallic way, he didn't instantly decide to take the next flight to Heathrow.

So why was it, amid all the turmoil of the celebrations, the drinks, the handshakes, the flashes of the newspaper cameras – why was it that the only person she longed to be able to tell, but couldn't, was Jason?

20

Malibu. Sweetness and light. Fizz. Gaiety. Twinkling lights along a promenade. A girl with bare toes dancing on the beach.

She wasn't real, even to herself. Especially to herself. She was an iridescent bubble floating in a clear blue sky. She was a free spirit. She was air.

'Come down to earth,' everyone seemed to urge her. 'Be like us – put lead in your shoes.'

But she couldn't. It wasn't in her nature. She rarely touched the ground, and then with a light skip which sent her soaring again. She inhabited a rarified atmosphere, the strata of the balloonist, the glider, the swooping free-fall parachutist.

Laughter and play. The ripple of water on a lake. Sunbeams breaking through a canopy of young spring leaves. She wasn't real.

• • •

'Where is that damn girl?' cried Ella Lepard for the third time in an hour. 'How can she lose herself in an office this size?'

'I'm working out,' called Malibu from behind a filing cabinet. 'While there's a spare minute.'

She stood up. Five feet two, trim as only an energetic 17-year-old can be, a frizz of black locks over an oval face lit up by dancing eyes – eyes of a lustrous blue seeming in some lights to darken almost to purple.

'There *are* no spare minutes, sweetheart,' barked the Barracuda, sucking in the smoke of a cheroot. 'And if you lie on that floor too often I won't answer for your moral well-being. This place breeds perverts like a cat has fleas.'

A slender imp in black. Tight wrap-over cotton top, leggings tucked into leather pixie boots. Huge multi-coloured earrings, with bright ethnic beads to match.

'Junior craves forgiveness,' she grinned, cocking her head to one side and folding her arms across her chest in a gesture which defied the Barracuda to be angry.

'Just give me three good reasons why I should keep you on.'

'But I gave you three brilliant reasons this morning!'

'Which, like yesterday's three, my pet, were highly imaginative. But not convincing.'

'Umbracious!'

Wasn't this good going? Arrived: January 2nd. First bawling-out:

January 4th. First threat of termination of trial employment: January 5th. First scene of absolute chaos undeniably caused by oneself: January 8th (after the weekend). Second threat of termination of trial employment: January 8th. First strategic absence through toothache: January 9th. Third threat etc: January 10th.

Today was January 11th.

'What do you mean, "umbracious"? Do you know the meaning of *half* the words you use?'

'Naturally not. I'm young and unformed. But I have a love of language. It's what cuts me out for magazine work.'

The Barracuda held a card in her crimson talons: 'Unless you want to end the day *mal*formed,' she barked, 'bring me a set of pics from that agency by four o'clock. You take a tube, not a pumpkin pulled by a team of white mice, okay?'

'Splendiferous,' Malibu replied, skipping to the door. She put her head round it after her body had gone. 'Fairy godmother!' she added, as an afterthought.

Malibu. A dash of rum. Completely nutty. A refreshment.

● ● ●

If you're deserted by your mother while still in your cradle, aren't you entitled to feel deprived? That was never the way Malibu looked at it.

To begin with, didn't she have the darlingest Daddykins around? Grant Locke was the kind of father who made adoration seem entirely natural. He was besotted with his daughter, and there was nothing he wouldn't do for her. He was always around when she needed him, and he tolerated her worst excesses – as a young child and, later, as a teenager – with a shrug of his shoulders and a wry smile. He was immensely proud of her.

He was an amusing companion, too. Life with her father was full of fun. He knew how to make her laugh even when she thought she was in the worst mood anyone had ever been in since the universe existed. For one thing, he exaggerated almost as much as she did.

And then there was the romantic aspect of the desertion. This, of course, was something that struck her only gradually, but it surely gave her a tragic air. No, she didn't *feel* tragic, except in those glorious moments of self-pity which all young girls indulge from time to time. But other people must think her lot a pretty wretched one – poor, abandoned waif, fighting an uphill battle against the slings and arrows of life.

Secretly, she preferred the wonderful image she had of her long-lost mother much more than she could possibly have loved the real flesh-and-blood woman. She knew a few things about her: that she was beautiful, that she was impulsive and that she wouldn't leave her father's memory alone.

Not that Grant Locke talked much about her. There was a single photograph in the house, and that was blurred, creased and faded. Apparently there'd been more, but he'd burnt them in a fit of temper or grief after she had left. But it was significant that he had never thrown away the one surviving picture.

Malibu knew that her father still harboured deep longings for her mother. She was sure of it. After all, why had he never married? There'd been plenty of other women, God knew, and not all of them were silly bits of fluff. (Malibu thought most of them were.) It must be that he still pined.

If all these years hadn't been enough to wipe out the memories, Malibu's mother must be a pretty remarkable person. And if she was remarkable, it stood to reason that Malibu herself must inherit most of her exceptional qualities. Plus, of course, a few more that had come from her father. Therefore, logic insisted, Malibu must be a fantastically gifted person.

It was a form of conceit, and it came in large doses, but Malibu wasn't the sort to brag and pose. She knew the kind of woman her mother had been – lively, noisy, prone to extravagant outbursts of temper – and she fashioned herself somewhat along the same lines. She thought of herself as dynamic and characterful, and she wasn't far wrong. Actually, she lacked her mother's fiery temper unless really provoked, but dynamic and characterful she certainly was. And her father seemed to encourage her.

'You've picked up all your worst traits from your mother,' he'd scowl – but she knew that he was pleased in his heart of hearts. She had a licence to be intemperate.

It was only as she neared adulthood that she began to imagine her mother as a fully-rounded human being. What was she really like? She couldn't actually be a human tornado all the time, as her father's comments suggested. Noone was quite like that. What did she like to do when she wasn't roaring with rage or laughter? What had happened to her during all these years?

More to the point: where was she?

For Malibu had increasingly begun to have fantasies of meeting her mother. In her dreams she would be trying on a fantastic new dress at Chloé in Sloane Street when her eyes would meet those of an older woman who was fishing among the fabrics across the room. They would both know immediately, and her mother would gaze upon her with moist-eyed pride.

The dreams came in different varieties, but that was always where they stopped. She didn't dare to guess the rest. She didn't even know what she wanted to happen next. It was the recognition which was important.

Now she began to probe her father for more hints about her mother's personality. She asked about events and dates. She wanted to know what kind of perfume her mother had used, which colours she'd liked to wear. Locke hadn't that sort of memory, and he only grunted his replies. He didn't want that part of his life stirred up again.

'She's gone,' he'd say flatly. 'Completely and utterly. We don't know where. We don't know a damn thing about her. Let's leave it that way. We've got our own lives to live.'

But she couldn't. Her mother's presence was always hovering behind her. When she acted in her usual over-the-top way she imagined her mother smiling her approval. It encouraged her even more forcefully than her father's indulgent spoiling ever managed to do. She was performing for her absent parent.

'Grow up,' Locke was apt to growl.

But she wouldn't. Her mother was for ever young, and that's how Malibu would always be. Light and airy. Extravagant. A sparkling cocktail.

● ● ●

'Where is that damn girl?' Ella Lepard cried yet again.

This time there was no answering chirpiness from behind the filing cabinet. This time Malibu was elsewhere.

'I'll give her another hour,' the Barracuda fumed, 'and then she's fired. Terminally.'

This time she rather thought she meant it, however much the infant's charm had touched her wizened heart.

Malibu wasn't there, owing to unforeseen circumstances. Most circumstances were of that nature for Malibu. For other people life was a succession of repetitions – and very dull, too. For Malibu every second was as fresh as dew upon the grass at dawn.

'If you'd just wait a minute,' the girl at the agency desk had intoned, picking up a telephone.

Sure she'd wait. What a magical place the reception of Carter's Press Agency was! It was a huge cavern of art. Behind that door it might be the most boring place this side of the Florida swamps, but the walls here were decked out with the most fabulous pictures you ever saw. Some of them were blown up so large they had more grain than a bowl of meusli. Others were shot with such contrast that your eyes almost ached as they moved across them.

'Who took these?' she asked in wonderment, but the girl at the desk had glazed eyes and was muttering 'yep, yep, yep' into the telephone.

The agency's freelances had taken them, that much was pretty obvious. As she spiralled around the room, rotating from one stunning photograph to another, it struck her that she had never truly looked at anything before. All this vibrant visual imagination, concentrated in the one place, almost made her pass out with excitement. So *this* was what a camera could achieve.

'Stupefactious!'

She felt that she couldn't wait to get out of the building and rush home for the 10-megapixel digital camera with vibration reduction, face priority focusing plus wide angle and zoom lenses that her father had bought her for Christmas. (It had cost him simply hundreds, but of course she was worth it.) She, too, could be an artist like these people, creating a new world with the click of a shutter. Never mind the technique, she felt the urge flex inside her like an uncoiling spring.

People were coming and going, but she had eyes only for these wonderful shots of the dynamic, exciting world around her. Many were action pictures – sport and war. There were character studies, too, of famous people. Sure, she'd seen them on television (actors, rockstars, politicians) but they had never seemed as real as they did here. She raised a finger towards Madonna and fully expected to encounter warm flesh.

'Pics for *Chic*!' called a voice.

'We prefer,' said the girl behind the desk, haughtily, 'that people don't touch the prints on the walls. If you don't mind.'

'And nuts to you!' grinned Malibu ferociously, taking the package.

She put out the tip of her tongue, crossed her eyes and wiggled her eyebrows. It was her favourite facial distortion and it always worked a treat. It was unanswerable. If only she had a pen in her hand she'd ink a moustache on the Russian leader for good measure, she thought. As a farewell message to the girl at the desk, who reddened and glowered and couldn't for the enraged life of her think of anything to say. But no she wouldn't. That would be a form of sacrilege. Malibu had suddenly discovered a new religion.

Why should she go just yet? What were a few minutes more when you had this very moment made one of the great discoveries of your life? She sauntered about the reception area, wondering that so much could be expressed in only two dimensions and, very often, in simple black and white. Only it wasn't simple at all. Malibu had discovered a mystery, and it thrilled her.

'Pulchritudinous!' she breathed – and stepped straight back into the path of a man who was bustling past with a camera (large, old-fashioned, non-digital) slung over his shoulder. They tumbled into an undignified heap. Bits of his camera skidded across the floor, but Malibu was more concerned about the pain in her knee.

'Ouch'! she exclaimed.

'Are you all right, Mr Kazinsky?' enquired the girl behind the desk, standing up. 'Should I fetch anyone?'

'Blast!' he said, sitting up to retrieve the scattered parts of his camera and staring intensely at the lens.

Malibu studied him at close quarters. He was a thickset man in his late fifties, with grey hair, a reddened nose which suggested a drinking habit and a pair of keen, dark eyes which seemed younger than the rest of his body. He had no dress sense. His grey suit was a couple of years out of date, and it had obviously been crumpled even before the collision.

'I'm all right,' he added gruffly, returning Malibu's stare. 'No thanks to you.'

'You charged right at me,' she protested. 'Like a white rhino in the bush. And you've hurt my knee.'

'If this lens is damaged,' he added, 'I'll expect you to pay for it.'

'Hoity toity,' she replied, standing stiffly and rubbing her knee.

'I could get the police,' the girl at the desk threw in helpfully. 'She's been making a nuisance of herself.'

The photographer made no reply, but cradled the camera against his body and barged through the door into the offices beyond. It slammed to behind him.

'Is he someone I should know?' Malibu asked.

'Oh no,' said the girl with heavy sarcasm. 'He's only Rudi Kazinsky. He's only just about the most famous photographer on our books. No one you should know.'

'That's interesting,' Malibu commented thoughtfully. 'Thank you.'

She thought perhaps it was time she made herself scarce. Even Malibu could take a hint. But she didn't go far. She waited outside the agency's front door, and she didn't feel the cold for a second. Those brilliant images on the walls inside were running round and round in her head.

It was dark by the time Rudi Kazinsky emerged. She accosted him with great expertise, standing squarely in front of him so that he couldn't do anything but stop.

'I've decided to give you another chance to apologise,' she said.

'You what?'

'For cracking my knee. You could have ruined a promising career at the Royal Ballet.'

'You're a dancer.'

'No, but I might have been. You didn't know that when you crashed into me in your crazy blind haste.'

Kazinsky looked at her more closely: 'What do you want?' he asked her. 'Are you propositioning me, for God's sake?' But he could see that she wasn't.

'Tut, tut!' she replied. 'Where's your car? I'll keep you company.'

In luck, she thought. He *has* come by car. They walked in step along the busy street, saying nothing. Occasionally the pavement was so busy that she had to drop behind him, but she quickly sprang back to his side. She gave him searching sideways glances, trying to judge his mood.

'Will you teach me?' she asked.

'What exactly do you want to learn?'

'Only everything. How you take brilliant pictures. How you catch all those moods. How you *see* it all.' They stopped by his car, an ancient white Rover. 'Then I'd forgive you for your atrocious manners.'

'You think I'm going to say Yes, just like that?'

'The alternative's saying No, just like that. And then you'd never know what you'd missed.'

He shook his head in amazement, opened the door of his car, climbed in and leant over to release the catch on her side.

'Here's a compromise,' he said. 'You can see my studio. Will that do?'

'For starters,' she replied with a grin.

They made their introductions as they drove with agonising slowness through the London rush-hour. He began to mellow, unable to resist her happy liveliness. After a few minutes they passed the *Chic* building, and Malibu suddenly remembered why she'd been at the agency in the first place.

'Help!' she cried, opening her door. 'I'll catch you at the end of the block!'

She ran across the road to a symphony of car horns, all the while fishing in her pocket for a pen. At the door she rested the packet of photographs on her knee and scrawled on the outside: *'For Ella Lepard. I resign. Malibu Locke.'* She posted it, then sprinted along the pavement, darted among the crawling vehicles and clambered back inside the Rover. She wasn't even out of breath.

'They should name a hurricane after you,' Kazinsky said.

For some time they drove in silence, but it wasn't an awkward silence. It already felt like the silence of old friends who don't need to talk. Kazinsky couldn't understand it. For sure it wasn't sexual chemistry. She was only a kid, and his tastes didn't stray that way. He was a happily divorced man who was glad to have had no involvements for years. His work was his life. No, but it was a kind of intimacy, for all that. They were on the same wavelength.

'My knee's all right now, thank you,' she said out of the blue, teasing him, and he laughed out loud.

'And luckily,' he replied, 'so is my camera. Shall we forgive each other?'

She held out a hand and, risking a crash, he reached out to shake it with his. It was a deal.

'Quits,' she said.

Rudi Kazinsky was a name which registered only vaguely with the general public but which was whispered in almost reverential tones within the profession itself. The man had been everywhere, had done everything and was still turning in pictures his rivals envied so much it made them sick.

He'd come to England with his Polish emigre parents after the second world war. It was a typical second generation story. His family had had nothing, but Rudi had worked his butt off to make something of his own life. He'd stumbled into photography by accident, but had become a master of it within the space of no more than a couple of years.

His first experience with newspapers was in fields of war. He was completely fearless, and he sent back pictures which somehow came to symbolise those conflicts even if most of the people who saw the photographs hadn't any idea who had taken them.

Kazinsky got out before the warping took place. There's a time for all war photographers when they seem to stand some little distance from themselves and watch the camera being focused on a dying child or a burning house with a family inside. Then they ask themselves what the hell they're doing making a career out of other people's agonies.

There's a smart answer, of course. It goes like this: the readers of the newspaper or magazine you're working for need to know what's going on out here. You've got a responsibility to bring the facts home to them. Maybe your pictures can change the policy of this or that government and bring the killing to an end.

The dumb guys believe this useful doctrine. It enables them to look themselves in the shaving mirror between battles before picking up the camera and starting all over again. But there's a price to pay, and it's a terrible one. Callousness. In the end it's a case of the greater the agony, the greater the picture. You come to thrive on it.

Kazinsky escaped before that drug took hold of him. He declared that part of his life over and done with, and he turned his hand to whatever kind of photography left him with a clean feeling when the job was finished. What drove his rivals to despair was that he was so damn good at every part of the business he turned his hand to. He was the best landscape man around, but he also took the best portraits. And if you wanted social comment, Kazinsky was the man to send – whether it was to probe the sleaze of the inner-city slums or the shimmer and glitter of a debs' ball.

'You need an assistant,' Malibu told him as he flicked on the studio light to reveal a scene of undeniable chaos. 'This is awful.'

'I know where everything is,' he said. 'Ask me for anything at all and I'll find it within half an hour.'

'Brilliantine!' she replied scornfully. 'Time is money, that's what my father always says.'

Kazinsky had met Grant Locke once or twice and was familiar with his work. It was one reason he'd let himself be coerced into taking this slip of a girl to his studio. He knew where to dispatch her if she became impossible.

'I've got someone to type my letters,' he said. 'The answerphone deals with the callers. I don't need anyone to make my life complicated. You'd wear me out.'

He began to show her what little there was to see. She examined the darkroom and wrinkled her nose at the smell of the developing fluid. She tugged out the drawers of large filing cabinets, flipping through prints and contact sheets. She picked up cameras and felt their satisfying weight in her hand.

'Do you ever turn work down?' she asked innocently.

'When I'm busy. I pick and choose.'

'So there'd be plenty for me to do as your trainee. I could take on the grotty stuff. Babies gurgling their heads off while rolling about on shawls. That kind of doomy thing.'

'What kind of a photographer do you think I am, for God's sake?'

'I could hold the tripod steady while you concentrate on stampeding elephants.'

Kazinsky opened a cupboard and took out a glass and a bottle of scotch. Should he offer her one? No, she was too young. He felt some responsibility for her. Was she a little crazy? She was certainly a strange mixture of the tough and the incredibly fragile.

'And I'd work for a month for nothing,' she added, folding her arms across her chest in a characteristic pose.

What energy she had – far more than he could muster. In the face of such determination, what could he do? There was, after all, something appealing in the idea of training an apprentice. Perhaps it *was* time to pass on his knowledge. In short, he knew when he was defeated.

'I'll speak to your father in the morning,' he said, swirling the amber fluid in his glass.

He had no chance to drink it. She leapt onto his lap and planted a large kiss upon his forehead.

'Frabjous!' she cried.

Malibu. Tangy. Effervescent. A tonic.

21

'I believe I've an undeniable claim for a pay rise,' Adam remarked a few days after the triumphant event at the Grosvenor House Hotel. 'To begin with, I've never had to deal with so many telephone calls and so many visitors . . . '

'You must have been underworked before,' Calla grinned, scribbling yet another reply to a card of congratulations and dropping in onto the pile.

' . . . and furthermore, as the personal assistant . . . '

'I thought you liked to call yourself my secretary.'

'Not when I'm negotiating a pay rise. As the personal assistant to a celebrity I expect to get more than a counterpart who's involved with someone much more ordinary.'

She leant forward and tweaked one of his ears. She'd never done that before, but it hardly surprised him. She hadn't come down from Cloud Nine for a single second since she'd won her place on the Duke's shortlist.

'That, Adam,' she beamed, 'is a load of crap. Thanks to my sorry obsession with Charlesbury, I'm worse off than I have been for years. I should be *cutting* your salary, not raising it.'

'Forget I spoke,' he said wryly.

It had been a marvellous few days. Wasn't this what she'd been working towards for the past ten years and more? She'd gone around with a feeling of power coursing through her veins, as if she could simply wave her arm and a gorgeous building of her own would spring up in the middle of London, bringing cries of admiration from everyone who passed. It was a high to beat all highs.

There had been the interviews with the press. The lower echelons of Fleet Street had made great play of her looks, her figure and her relative youth. There had been some dreadful headlines – 'Duke's Delight', 'The Mistress Builder' (a hint of something doubtful in that one, she thought), 'Charlesbury Charmer' and the like. Awful. But, as Adam said, it was all publicity. However briefly, she was a celebrity.

The serious newspapers hadn't quite known what to make of her, or even how to deal with the competition in general. There'd been plenty of copy, but the architectural correspondents were a bit sniffy about the Duke. He wasn't in the least progressive, and they liked it best when there was something new in the air. That was what journalism was all about. Charlesbury was new in one sense, but they suspected that it would be oldfashioned in design. Therefore they were guarded in what they wrote.

'Let the buggers sweat on it,' Grant Locke had said, pouring her a glass of champagne. 'I understand Harry Willougby's keeping the plans close to his chest for another month. For an old reactionary he's a bloody smart publicity merchant.'

'And what if the press tear our ideas apart?' she asked.

'Stuff 'em!' He raised his glass: 'To our critics. Stuff 'em all!'

For the moment there were no dangerous critics. When the telephone rang it was someone she knew wanting to say how pleased everyone was at the news. Her mail was full of the same sort of thing.

'Mind you,' she said to Adam, adding another note to the pile, 'I could do with some new offers of business. Congratulations don't pay the rent.'

Or, he was tempted to say, my salary.

'I've had a call,' he said, 'from someone who says he wants to see you urgently. I tried telling him that there's a queue forming, but he wouldn't be put off.'

'Someone I know?'

'He didn't bother with niceties of that kind. His name's Patrick Andover. He runs Andover International. He practically ordered me to fix a meeting.'

'Yes, he would. Ignore him.'

'I'm afraid I told him that I'd ring him back. He was strangely persuasive.'

'Okay, ring him back.'

'To say what?'

'Anything you like. I leave that to you, Adam. But I don't want to see the man. *Finito*.'

It was the first sour note since that glorious afternoon when she'd floated about the hotel, drawn to the bubbling acclaim like a moth to the flame of a candle. She remembered Harry Willougby's exquisite good manners as he drew her to one side for private congratulations. She remembered the excited telephone conversation with Philippe, the dinner with a highly emotional Bunny Simkins. The bad memories and the threats she had managed to smother.

'He's an influential man.'

'Not with me,' she insisted, more in bravado than because she believed it. 'Earn your substantial salary, Adam, by getting rid of him.'

'It's as good as done.'

In her heart, however, she knew that getting rid of Patrick Andover was impossible. She was merely putting off the inevitable.

● ● ●

It had been a quiet year for Andover, and he didn't like that. He wasn't designed for peace. Just as a racehorse is bred for speed and a carthorse for strength, so Patrick Andover had been fashioned for the relentless pursuit of the only just attainable. He had to strive, or he shrivelled like a punctured balloon.

Running Andover International had long since ceased to give him all the buzz he needed. Once he'd got it into the shape it needed, once he'd done the necessary hiring and firing, the long-overdue buying and selling, it was easy to keep the business forging ahead. It was no achievement as far as he was concerned. Another man would have been proud of the way he had turned the company round within three years, but that was already history for Andover. What mattered was what came next.

The truth was that being chairman of a company which answered to shareholders didn't suit his temperament. Sure, most shareholders were mere cannon-fodder, easily manipulated, but everything had to be too far out in the open for his comfort. It wasn't that all his concerns were dishonest, but he knew that anyone with a talent for reading balance-sheets could probe the very soul of his enterprise – just as he'd done himself as the up-and-coming young man. That made him uncomfortable. He didn't like to be looking over his shoulder all the time for fear of a dawn raid by some corporate rival making smart assumptions about the price-earnings ratio.

So he began to turn increasingly to his own private affairs – in both senses of the word. He knew his own appetites. When he felt restless, his need for a woman increased with a savagery which always surprised him. While somehow keeping his brain functioning separately for his essential business operations, he would seize upon every available woman for days and nights at a time. None of them were safe.

The old Patrick Andover adage was proved correct time and again: if you want something badly enough, only someone who needs to resist just as strongly will prevent you having it. Not many women had that kind of resistance. He would solicit them at the most unlikely times, in the most improbable situations.

He would pass a note across the boardroom table to a curvaceous marketing executive, tightly buttoned into a suit which suggested power-dressing, even while she was in the middle of a detailed financial presentation. That lunchtime, while his colleagues took refreshments in the canteen a floor below, he would straddle her bucking body on that same boardroom table before brusquely zipping his trousers and hurrying downstairs for lunch.

In this mood, Andover wasn't discriminating. He wanted the smell of a woman, the heat of her body, the sound of her cries in orgasm, and he didn't care where she came from or where she was going. It was the pleasure of the moment, but over and over again. He had prodigious energy.

Over the past year he'd noticed that this violent randiness had begun to grow more frequent. He thought he knew why. His grip of Andover International was sufficiently strong for him to manipulate its affairs without great effort, and since his family's shareholding was large he was damn sure the company was going to keep increasing its profits ahead of market expectations. But that wasn't where he got his business kicks. The truth was that he was happier to be involved in smaller, more obscure deals where his fine judgement (which appeared to other people as a gambling instinct) could bring instant personal rewards against all the odds. That was what he needed. He loved these challenges, even if the rewards were sometimes peanuts when compared with the profits Andover International regularly clocked up. It was like beginning again.

That was why he'd decided to play the Calla Marchant card. It had been somewhere at the bottom of the pack for years. He knew it was there, of course, and he knew pretty well how it might be used, but the timing hadn't been right.

Now it suddenly seemed to be a court card, and in trumps, to boot.

'Balls!' he said to Adam when his phone call was returned. 'Who do you think you're talking to, bumboy?'

'I beg your pardon.'

'And don't come all coy with me. I know the clubs you use. I know who your best friends are.'

'How –' Adam began, before thinking better of it.

'I know everything about Calla Marchant Practice and who works for it. And you may have reason to know *me* before very long, so let's not play hard to get. I want to meet Miss Marchant at the place I mentioned and the time I mentioned. It'll be worse for her if she refuses. You tell her that. Understand?'

'Yes, sir.'

'That's better already,' Andover said.

• • •

They lunched at Lindsay House in Romilly Street. The choice didn't surprise Calla one bit. 'Practical, but classy,' she told herself, taking in the silk curtains and the chandeliers. There was an English menu, which Patrick Andover, in his no-nonsense way, would like. There was the style of a private house. Ditto. And there was privacy. They sat in what was little more than an alcove where no one but a waiter would pass.

'Let's take the congratulations as read,' he suggested, running an index finger swiftly down the menu.

'By all means,' she replied. The last thing she wanted to have to cope with was artificial graciousness from Patrick Andover. 'You don't want anything sticking in your throat at mealtimes.'

He didn't seem to have changed at all. She was drawn once again, as she had been all those years ago in his city office, to the mesmeric stare of those hard blue eyes. She felt that power once again – and disliked the man every bit as much as before. He was taut, driving, aggressive. His jaw seemed ready to take the whole world on.

'Quite simply,' he said, as soon as the ordering was done, 'I'm in a healthy position, vis-a-vis CMP.'

'Do I get the chance,' she asked, stunned by his complete lack of any preamble, 'to ask how the hell you had the nerve to buy your brother's share in my company? Without so much as telling me!'

He frowned, as if something offended him: 'That's not the right question.'

'Really? You even dictate the questions people ask?'

He sat back while the waiter poured wine into his glass. He sniffed it, filtered it over his palate with little sucking noises and, rather grudgingly, nodded his approval.

'No, the first question is why you signed that agreement without even reading it. I know the answer, of course. You were angry.'

'You're damn right I was angry.'

'And it clouded your judgement. It was a stupid document to sign.'

Calla felt herself at a disadvantage. To start with, this was his meeting. She'd been practically forced to attend it, knowing he was a man whose threats weren't idle. Even so, she might have held her own quite happily in a series of witty exchanges. She had quite enough spunk for that. As it was, his shameless directness threw her off balance. He didn't believe in sublety.

'You admit as much?'

'Of course. Why shouldn't I? It's to my credit, not yours. You forgot any business sense you had, which probably wasn't much, because your emotions got the better of you. I made a series of sensible provisions which allowed for success as much as failure – even though I genuinely thought your company wouldn't survive. That's why I have money and you have none.'

'What the hell do you know about my financial circumstances?'

He smiled: 'This is quite like old times! I shall reply as I replied then. I *do* know. I know that you've taken out a fresh bank loan within the past month. Merely to tide you over, of course.'

'Damn you!'

'And you're getting excited again, which isn't wise. Especially as we're going to talk business.'

She pushed her whitebait hors d'oeuvres to one side. She didn't feel hungry. In fact, she felt like pushing his face into his brown windsor soup and stalking from the restaurant. But she couldn't.

'Of course,' he said, 'my poor brother Jason was no smarter than you – though for another reason entirely. He signed that document as readily as you did. Have you ever read it?'

She shook her head and watched his hand go into a jacket pocket. It came out with a thin sheaf of papers which he thrust at her.

'A copy, naturally, so there's no use in eating it.' He laughed aloud over his attempt at a joke. He had no genuine sense of humour, she thought. He lacked any sense of the ridiculous. Life was challenge. You triumphed or you went to the wall. That was all. 'Read it. Go on. It's very clearly set out. Tell me what it says.'

God rot you, Patrick Andover, she thought. Buying me a lunch doesn't give you the right to lecture me like a primary school teacher with the reception class.

'I'm sure you'd rather tell *me*,' she said.

Their main course arrived. Glancing at the pages, she could see at once what a blind fool she'd been. He'd flown a kite all those years ago, and she'd simply puffed her cheeks and sent it spiralling up into the merciless blue sky. Had she really been so naive? Yes, it was here in black and white. She'd check it when she got home, but she knew this was the real thing.

'In many respects,' Andover told her, 'it was entirely reasonable. Jason's interest did need protecting. But it was cushioned to a quite remarkable degree. And that option of selling the interest was a stroke of genius, if I may say so.'

She forced a piece of asparagus quiche between her lips. If she ate much of it, she thought, she'd throw up. For a moment she lost the will to fight him. It was only a moment.

'We met on unequal terms all those years ago,' she said defiantly. 'I'd learned practically nothing about running an architect's business. Today, if I may presume to remind you, I run a highly successful practice. You do read the papers?'

'Why do you think I wanted to meet you?'

That, she reflected for the umpteenth time, was something she couldn't answer. She only knew that whatever resulted from this lunch appointment must be to Patrick Andover's benefit. That also meant, presumably, that it must be to her detriment.

'If you haven't worked out a likely scenario or two,' he persisted, 'it proves that you still haven't learned enough. Do read that document a little more closely. Paragraph seven, for instance.'

She read. She couldn't believe what she read.

'I signed *this*?' was all she could mutter, feeling utterly devastated.

'With a flourish as I recall.'

'It gives you the right to buy into my partnership, you bastard.'

Andover glanced towards the waiter, a little smile on his thin lips.

'Tut, tut,' he said. 'A lady doesn't use that kind of language in a place like this.'

She felt the rage mounting. She couldn't see what Andover saw and relished, like so many men before him: the intensity of those violet eyes, the tautness of that wonderful skin, the sheer voluptuous ferocity of her expression. She did see her own fingers clutching the white linen table cloth. And she felt a tidal wave of anger seething and frothing inside her, all the while knowing that somehow she had to control it.

'So?' she asked, scarcely able to breathe.

'Let's begin,' Andover smiled, 'by making you an offer. You may know that I'm quite a substantial land-holder these days. Of course I did my buying at the best time, price-wise. I shall also develop it at the best time. Within the next couple of years, I imagine.'

He took his time finishing the last potato on his plate, first forking it into the gravy, then chewing it slowly as he gazed at his beautiful companion with eyes that had no innocence in them at all.

'There'll be a wide range of buildings at the various sites,' he went on eventually. 'Plenty of houses, some factories, maybe a leisure complex or two. I'll need architects.'

No, she wanted to say. Count me out. Don't let me ever have to work with you at close quarters. She hated and feared his raw animal dynamism – a dynamism which she recognised all too readily in herself.

'Or perhaps just one architect,' Andover said. 'One architect who could make a lot of money from hitching herself to my star.'

'And what's the price?' she demanded.

'Ah!' He signalled to the waiter, who seemed to collect their plates and present them with the menu in a single movement. 'You're learning.'

'Just coffee for me,' Calla ordered, pleased to be able to make at least one decision which couldn't be contradicted. 'Black. And as strong as you can make it.'

And hemlock for this shit across the table, she wanted to add.

'You won't mind if I have a pudding?' Andover enquired politely. He was in no hurry, that's what it meant. Nobody could possibly need anything else after what he'd just eaten. How the hell did he keep his body in that razor-sharp condition? She'd already noticed that he didn't have a spare ounce of flesh on his athletic frame.

'My price,' he said when his apricot tart had been delivered, 'is really very generous. Don't forget what I *could* be demanding. Clause seven is quite specific. So, for that matter, is clause three. No, please don't bother to read it just yet.

'All I ask, at this stage, is for a commitment. What I want is your assurance that, if you win the Charlesbury competition, you'll move heaven and earth to get me in on the development. There are some wonderful pickings to be had there. And I mean pickings. I don't want the maggot-ridden windfalls.'

He tucked into his tart with a gusto which would have suggested to an onlooker that he had nothing else whatsoever on his mind. Calla watched the head bent over the dish, the hair immaculately styled to give the casual look. Everything about Patrick Andover was calculated, and he rarely got the calculations wrong.

'I'm just an architect,' she said, 'not the Duke of Mercia. He'll choose the developer.'

'Let's not be childish, Miss Marchant. Please. I'm well aware of the way the game's played. You don't need to tell me what's probable and what's only possible. But credit me with knowing rather more than you about the day-to-day realities of business at the top level. The realities of influence, for one thing.'

'Which I don't have.'

He waved a hand dismissively.

'If you believe that, you don't deserve to get the Charlesbury contract. The world's full of people who don't know how to use the influence they have. They're the idiots who fail.

'If you win this competition you'll have influence. Plenty of it. That won't mean you rule the world, but it'll certainly have a large bearing on what happens at Charlesbury. Just believe me on that score.'

He took a small tube from his pocket and dropped a sweetener into his coffee.

'What you're suggesting,' Calla told him, 'has the whiff of corruption about it.'

'Does it?' he replied agressively, spreading himself across the table. 'Does it really? Simply recommending a company which will do a damn good job for the Willoughby Estate? Your idea of morality must differ a good deal from mine.'

'I daresay it does.'

'Balls!' he exploded. 'Calla Marchant playing her Virgin Mary role. We're talking about a simple business deal which noone can begin to question. Why shouldn't you favour one developer over another? Is there some law against it?'

'It might not look good,' she protested.

'Which is precisely why I'm not proposing to activate clause seven. If I were a CMP partner someone might raise a question of ethics, as I think they're called. The RIBA probably. Those stuffy middle-class institutions like to put on airs. Mealy-mouthed bastards, the lot of them.'

'Then why,' she asked, 'doesn't your financial involvement in my practice have the same effect? Aren't the same ethics involved?'

He shook his head slowly, an expression of contemptuous amazement on his face: 'You know,' he said, 'people like you make me ashamed of calling myself a rational human being. The difference, Miss Marchant, is that nobody's going to know that I've got a stake in your firm. It doesn't show up. Do I need to write this in letters a foot high? As long as you say nothing and I say nothing, nobody on earth is going to know. Is that clear enough?'

It was. They sat in silence for a few minutes as she considered her response. He wasn't, in truth, asking for anything specific. If she decided not to use her influence on his behalf there was no way he could prove she hadn't tried. And he was offering her new business, too. This imbalance gradually dawned on her.

'And what if I refuse?' she asked.

'Ah! At last, a sensible question!' He beckoned to the waiter to pour more coffee. 'If you refuse I'll have to think seriously about activating clause three.'

Now she picked up the document again and tried to make sense of it while the blood pounded in her head and her palms sweated.

'To paraphrase,' Andover said lightly, 'I can take out my stake in CMP at six months' notice. That stake includes interest accrued over the years at the agreed rate. I won't hazard a guess at the exact sum, but we can safely assume that it's far more than you can afford.'

'Bastard!' she breathed.

'A prudent businessman,' he countered mockingly. 'Do you play chess? A good player never makes a move without knowing its implications. Every move, even of a humble pawn, has an effect on the potential of several pieces all around it. The good player can sense all this potential even if he hasn't worked out every detail in his mind. That's how I proceed.'

'I can raise the cash easily enough,' she said boldly. 'I've got a reputation now.'

He laughed: 'You could try,' he said, 'in which case I might activate clause seven after all, just for spite. But I think you'll find that, since you're already in debt, the banks will be extremely wary of advancing that kind of money. They're not gamblers, you know. You may well lose the Charlesbury competition, and then you'll become one of Warhol's people – those who've been famous for fifteen minutes.'

Her first thought was to blurt out that she was a damn good architect, that she'd design brilliant buildings even if she didn't win the competition. But she checked herself. He was right. Sure, she'd still be the same architect she was now, with all her talents and possibilities, but she'd have to work her butt off to get herself financially back in a sound position. She'd taken a gamble herself, and Patrick Andover was using her weakness for all he was worth.

'I need time,' she told him. 'To think about it. This is all too sudden.'

He smiled: 'Naturally,' he said. 'We've no need to rush things, have we?' He looked at his watch. 'Except that I've a board meeting in half an hour, if you'll excuse me.'

Excuse you? she thought. *The second you're out of my sight I shall start to breathe clean air again.*

'But as a precaution,' he added, rising from his chair, 'I've had this little thing drawn up.'

He passed her a single sheet of paper.

'It's formal notice that I wish to take my money out of your business six months from today. You'll have to prepare a complete set of accounts in the meantime so that our solicitors can sit down and agree the figures.'

'Bastard!' she said again.

'Naturally,' Andover added, slipping into his suede overcoat, 'I shan't go ahead with this if you agree to be cooperative. I'll very happily tear up that piece of paper before your very eyes if we can come to an accommodation on the other matter we spoke of.

'Do we understand one another?'

22

It wasn't like Fern Willoughby to cry. But then, it wasn't like Fern Willoughby to be helpless. And just now she was – as helpless as a baby. In a heap on a shiny linoleum floor, she sobbed.

Through the tears, she could see the help button, way out of reach, half way up the wall. The high hospital bed was just behind her, but there was no way she could pull herself on to it.

'Christ, what a mess,' she mumbled through the salt streams which were meeting the corners of her mouth. 'What a bloody awful mess. I've had horses shot in better condition than this.'

She couldn't bring herself to yell for help. It was more her style to wait until a nurse came on her normal round and then to pretend she had only just fallen out of the bed. She'd be in trouble if they knew she'd tried to stand up.

The tears subsided and she waited on the cold floor, tugging a blanket down to keep herself warm. She'd wait as long as it took. Her surroundings were bleak, the comfortless cleanliness which belongs to a state hospital.

It was all rather new to Fern, whose apparent fragility hid an iron constitution which had never needed hospital treatment. Apart from the one quirk of nature which had left her childless, she was a robust specimen.

Oh, she'd visited friends in hospital, to be sure. But her friends had money and fashionable ailments. They gave birth, had nose jobs and treatment for M.E. in the Humana Hospital Wellington. The beds there were covered in designer fabrics to match the wallpaper. Meals were chosen from a wide menu. The channel on the colour television was changed by bedside remote control and there was full room service. You paid thousands of pounds to feel like a million dollars while you were ill.

Stoke Mandeville Hospital in Buckinghamshire, which specialised in cases like hers, was very different. Funding went on serious medicine, not on the latest from the interior design catalogue. It was the best, but it was far removed from Fern Willoughby's accustomed surroundings.

'What a fool!'

Fern had lost count of how many times she'd said it, how many times she had re-lived that final jump to disaster. If she'd thought, if she'd been in less of hurry and had taken it further along. If she hadn't been late to meet Harry because she'd followed her fancy with that ridiculous young curate . . .

'Fool!'

She remembered little. She knew that Harry had found her and had been by her bedside almost 48 hours later when she'd regained consciousness in that first, local hospital. It had been dark and she'd been aware of the warmth of his two hands clasping hers before she had made out his shadow.

She had been unable to speak at first. All she had done was move her fingers in his. She hadn't known it, but this was the sign the Duke had been waiting for, and his own cheeks were wet with tears as the sign came.

'If she moves anything,' the surgeon had told him, 'her toes, her fingers, *anything*, we'll know she's not totally paralysed.'

And in the silence she had come to and moved her fingers. 'Thank God I haven't lost you,' was all she could remember Willoughby saying before her wandering mind swam away into its own unconsciousness.

Later, she had come round properly. Bewildered, she had tried to sit up and found that only her neck muscles obeyed her instructions. Below that there was nothing. No pain, no response, no sense of belonging to Fern Willoughby at all.

'Tell me!' she had pleaded with the surgeon.

'We don't know yet, I'm afraid.' It was the same answer every visit.

'Tell me!' she had pleaded with Harry.

'They think your back is broken, sweet.'

'My back?' She had hardly been able to take the information in. How could she live with a broken back? How could she ride? How could she be Fern?

Harry had explained the mobility tests they would do, the X-rays which were being taken to assess her chances of ever walking again. She could move her head and her arms, but her back was broken further down.

'I might as well be dead.'

'Not as far as I'm concerned,' her husband had whispered hoarsely, and she had never said it again.

Two days passed, which Fern spent gazing at the ceiling or craning her neck at the sound of passing footsteps. But her mind was far from empty. Her thoughts were filled with a pageant. Everything that her life had been now passed before her. Her schooldays, her youth in the west country – she remembered all of it as never before.

She recalled the excitement of horse shows without number, of hours spent in the saddle on her favourite moors. Tears rolled from her eyes, wetting the pillow on either side of her head. It was almost too painful to think of those days, knowing she would never ride a horse again.

There were other things to remember too. There were her acting days, there was Harry and there were all those men. The men were a blur to her, a blur of sensation which left her feeling oddly empty, like a meal presented in a recipe book instead of on a table. What had it been, that appetite which had driven her into so many different arms? Just now she had hardly any appetite for anything except news of her own pitiful condition.

Then she would hear Harry's voice at the foot of the bed and painfully raise her head in an attempt to catch a view of his. He would bring her flowers – not a showy and expensive arrangement but, showing a thoughtfulness that was pure Harry, simple freesias, so that she should enjoy the lovely scent of flowers she was unable to sit up and look at.

'We've a journey to make, old thing,' he said on one occasion.

He couldn't sit on the bed for fear of jarring her back, but he pulled up a chair as close to her head as he could. As he smoothed the fair hair from her forehead he explained that she was being moved to Stoke Mandeville for specialist treatment.

'Will I ever come out?' she heard herself ask with a self-pity she immediately despised.

'Of course.'

'Yes, I will Harry. And very soon!'

The journey to Buckinghamshire was unbelievably long. So as not to further damage her spine, the ambulance was driven at fifteen miles an hour all the way.

She had a room of her own, but that was the full extent of her luxury. Fern's specialist was a brisk Scot, who didn't approve of the aristocracy and its titles. His briskness extended to his bedside manner. He made no secret of the fact that she'd be lucky ever to walk again.

'And believe me, Fern, with this kind of injury, you make some of your own luck.'

'What do you mean?'

'I mean that even if we can stick the bits together, you'll have to make it work. If you know what work is.'

Her reply to his sarcasm, even as she lay staring at another hospital ceiling, took him aback and improved his opinion of her no end.

'Listen, doctor, have you ever got up at dawn, sweated to groom a horse and ridden it until you were saddle-sore? I've done that all my life. I've sat up with colicky horses. I've delivered foals. I've trained hunters and jumpers. And that's hard work, believe me.

'I might not be Mother Teresa of Calcutta, but I'm not Milly Molly Mandy either, so spare me your prepared speech on lords and ladies, will you?'

He did, but it was all that Roland McIvrey would spare her. He described to her in detail exactly what had happened to her broken back and exactly how the surgeons would attempt to repair her damaged nervous system.

And then? There was quite simply no certainty about what would happen then. She had been pushed past the physiotherapy rooms on her way to surgery two or three days earlier and seen the weakened limbs being exercised inch by painful inch. And she knew those were the lucky ones. In other rooms, therapists lifted the limbs and worked the muscles of those who weren't able to do it for themselves.

And now here she was after surgery, still unable to move and still none the wiser. And still, thanks to her ridiculously indomitable spirit, helpless on this damn floor.

'I'm here until supper,' she said aloud to herself.

Then the door opened. McIvrey stared for a second, before calling for help to lift her onto the bed.

'You're a bloody fool, Fern.'

'Thanks.'

'I was coming to tell you the X-rays suggest we could have a go at physiotherapy. And what do I find? You think you can be bloody Olga Korbut!'

'Actually I'd be quite content just to be Long John Silver at the moment, Mr McIvrey.'

He couldn't help but laugh: 'Anyhow, if you haven't damaged yourself, we'll see if you can start this afternoon.'

When he was gone, she found herself terrified. This, she knew, was the moment of truth. Dreaming about it and wondering when it might happen had been one way of keeping hope alive. She had imagined herself surprising them all with her agility. Now that seemed the ravings of a delirium. She was so weak! Suppose that she collapsed. Merely trying meant facing the risk of failure.

Harry. Suddenly she wanted him here very badly. She had taken for granted his daily visits, hardly realising how much they meant to her. The memories of all the other men had dried up now: she could hardly remember their names let alone recall what the appeal had been. She turned her face on the pillow, gazing towards the window, wondering with each arrival in the car park whether it might be her husband.

'In sickness and in health,' she thought.

Later that afternoon, McIvrey and a woman therapist made a joint visit. Fern found her legs swung gently over the side of the bed and her back supported by firm hands as the Scotsman took her under her elbows and pulled her upright.

'Courage!'

He held her firm. The feeling was strange. She felt unbelievably heavy. Her feet seemed quite useless. It was like trying to balance a great weight on two balloons.

'Now don't be frightened.' McIvrey's voice was uncharacteristically gentle. 'In a few seconds I'll take my hands away, but they'll be there if you fall, never worry.'

His hands released her gently. She felt as though she were toppling forward, her heavy body rolling from her flabby feet. In fact she just crumpled into her doctor's waiting arms.

Tears rolled from her eyes again as she looked into his: 'I'll never walk. will I?'

McIvrey's tone was dryly professional again: 'Technically, you could. It depends on luck, and on your determination. You'll never win Badminton again, dearie, let me tell you that. You can sell the horses.

'But there's still a chance you'll be able to walk with that husband of yours round the ancestral acres. Now, let's try again, eh?'

Damn him and his casual comment about her horses, she thought. The tears came again, but now they were tears of anger. She'd show the brute! Her spirit had been roused, and she instantly felt a little charge of energy pulse through her, like sap flowing through the cells of a tree.

He held her under the elbows again. As he let go, the door opened and Harry Willoughby stood, white faced, before her. Fern peered at her husband over the doctor's shoulder and, her eyes fixed keenly on his face, stood unsupported for more than a minute before reaching out for McIvrey's arm.

'Aye,' he said. 'With time and hard work, you'll yet be able to take your Duke for a walk.'

● ● ●

Langton Meredith ran up the steps to King's Reach flats, that fashionable Thames-side block which protrudes over the river, giving a 280 degree view of London from its glass sides.

His new shoes made a sharp noise on the marble. He was in a hurry. He paused impatiently for the automatic door to accept his plastic key-card and let him in.

'Evening, sir,' said the security man out of habit.

But of course there was no point. There wasn't even a nod of acknowledgement. No one ever got a friendly greeting out of Meredith unless there was something in it for him. Other residents would pass the time of day or ask after the children, but not Meredith.

'Mr Snotty Arse,' the security man added very quietly.

You only heard from him if there was a complaint or if he needed help to carry one of his fancy paintings up to the flat. He'd tip then, and generously too, but you never got to set foot over his threshold.

The window cleaners, who had a good view of all the flats, reported that the bedroom paintings were rather rum. Not page three tits and bums, or anything like that, but not quite your Constables either. They couldn't make head nor tail of them.

Low lights came on as Meredith unlocked his door on the sixth floor. Everything was on a time switch for his return. The flat had a magnificent view of the capital. He could see the Houses of Parliament, honey coloured in the floodlighting, and the whole stretch up to the clear white dome of St Paul's. It was one of the best city prospects in the world.

Not that Meredith had much time for it, tonight or any other night. It was merely an impressive part of an impressive apartment for those important little parties which won contracts and influenced people. That alone was its value as far as he was concerned.

He pressed a button and blinds instantly obscured the whole magical picture. He fixed himself a vodka – neat from the freezer – and dropped elegantly into a black leather armchair, smartly contrasted with the white tile floor. With one immaculately creased trouser leg across the other, he sipped slowly and stared into the uncluttered space of his flat.

'And next,' he murmured, hissing in his characteristic way over the last word, 'a little thinking music, perhaps.'

Soon the hypnotic strains of an Indian sitar were winding round the white walls and the black furniture. Meredith, still gazing into the distance, began to look satisfied with himself. This was his getting-in-the-mood routine.

He nodded slowly, put down his drink and reached for the cordless phone on the all-glass coffee table. Carefully (Meredith could never be said to punch numbers) he pressed the buttons. No need to look in his contacts book. Anything which was useful to Meredith he carried in his head.

'Luke? Langton Meredith. Sorry to bother you.'

Luke Hanley was one of the most admired and loathed journalists in London. The two adjectives always seemed to go together in his trade. You didn't expect ever to be *liked*. He specialised in Sunday stitch-ups. Hanley would go to ground on a single story for weeks. His very absence from the bars and bolt-holes of Fleet Street was enough to give rival news editors the heebie jeebies.

When Hanley disappeared you could be sure his eventual return would be announced in enormous headlines over revelations of some belting scandal. What he wrote was always outrageous, it was always death to somebody's reputation and it was always watertight – an expert stitch-up in other words. Lawyers might threaten, but in the long run there was never any comeback on a Hanley story except resignation in the case of a public figure or a quiet divorce within a few months if the scandal was domestic.

'Luke, you owe me one, I think. Tell me what you know about Harry Willoughby's favourite architect.'

There was a faint noise at the other end of the line.

'Don't switch the tape on, Luke, there's a good chap. Off the record, eh? Do you have anything on Grant Locke?'

Hanley's voice was slow and cautious, the voice of a man used to checking his facts: 'Nothing known, Meredith. He's professionally clean. You won't find *him* mixed up with any doubtful contractors or cutting any corners to make a fast buck.' He paused meaningfully. 'If that's what you wanted to hear.'

'Not exactly.' Meredith didn't care for Hanley's tone of voice and he didn't care to be kept at arm's length with a surname when he was being friendly. But he was thick-skinned. 'What about his personal life? The daughter? His lovelife?'

'Clean. You can't pillory a man for an early fling, and I wouldn't want to. Or for bringing up his daughter afterwards. That seems damn heroic to me, but I've never had any.

'As for his more recent sex life, as long as he keeps off rare sheep and royalty I couldn't care less. He's hardly headlines, Meredith.'

'Ah.'

'What's on your mind? You sound disappointed.'

'Another time.'

'If you hear of anything, you know we pay good money.'

'Me, too,' Meredith replied, putting the phone down.

He poured more vodka over ice and watched it crack. For his next call he'd need a really stiff drink. It took courage, but he was after dirt, any dirt, that might be clinging to his rivals for the prestigious Charlesbury project.

Again he rang from memory.

'The one and only Langton Meredith!' boomed Ella Lepard into his ear. 'Is this a call to twist my arm? It would take more than your cuff-linked and gold-Rolexed wrists, Langton.'

'I don't understand.'

'Didn't they tell you the *Chic* office design job's gone to someone else?'

'Of course I know that Locke got it, Ella. And no doubt he'll do a decent-enough job for you, if somewhat low-key. I simply wondered if you'd like dinner. I've an idea for a piece on architecture in the nineties which would be ideal for *Chic* readers.'

'Sounds a perfect yawn, darling. You'd have stood more chance if you'd asked me directly for my body. Ring my features editor with your idea. She's a polite girl. In fact, that's her problem.'

'I actually thought it might give your magazine a little intellectual weight, Ella,' Meredith said, unable to keep the acid out of his voice. 'No doubt you'd rather run a piece on Calla Marchant's wardrobe as your contribution to the great British architectural debate.'

'I like your second idea better than your first, darling, though to be truthful I'd rather see Ms Marchant locked in a wardrobe than let loose in London. She once robbed me of a perfectly luscious toyboy. Years ago, but it still rankles.'

'Who on earth was that?' Meredith asked, keeping the conversational flow going. He reckoned she must be on at least her fourth gin of the evening by now and maybe about to get a little indiscreet.

'A lovely youth called Jason Andover. A crying shame. He'd have had no chance to get into drugs if he'd taken me up on my offer. I'd have kept him fully occupied.'

Meredith's fine white nostrils twitched, sensing something which might be useful. It was certainly worth dinner, he thought. With a little careful drawing out over the restaurant table the deadly Barracuda might just supply him with the venom he needed.

'Come on, Ella, let's do dinner. Shall we say Orso's?'

'Only if you promise to be on your worst behaviour.'

'Done!'

He smiled, put the phone down and fixed himself another drink. He took it into the bedroom, where he smoothed his hair with a pair of silver-backed brushes.

'Yes,' he murmured to himself. 'This is where the real cut-and-thrust begins.'

He might almost, he thought with a mirthless grin, be talking about his art collection here on the bedroom walls, steel-framed pictures of women tightly clad in animal skins. What a furtive pleasure they gave him. Each one was in a posture suggestive of humiliation – nothing glaringly obvious, just a tastefully manacled wrist, a roped ankle, long tresses of hair fastened to something which couldn't be seen.

Picking up his extension telephone, he began to dial again.

• • •

Jason gazed at the mountains and trees of the Welsh border country and wondered whether he would be seeing them again. He'd left Desmond Fesh's consulting room with the psychiatrist's cynical last words ringing in his ears.

'The bed's always here,' he'd said with his usual ruthless realism. 'Waiting for you like a faithful bloodhound. Whether it's this Monday, next month or next year. As long as you've got the readies for it, our capacity to milk you of them knows no bounds.'

Words both comforting and chilling. Not many people could manage to express both, but that was Fesh, worn to scepticism by trying to keep the tide of drug dependency at bay. Worn by seeing so many addicts go home for a weekend's leave and never come back, never contact him again, until it was almost too late. Worn by all those he wrongly believed were as near cured as addicts can get.

There were successes, of course. In a difficult job, Fesh was known for his successes. But he still wouldn't wager a single copper on which of his patients at the Bowerman Institute would stay clean of the powders, the pills or the syringes which had brought them to his couch.

He'd certainly seen cases as hopeful as young Andover's go to the bad. Some of these wealthy young men ought to have the probation officers their less fortunate contemporaries were allotted for attacking old ladies, destroying phone boxes, doing whatever it was the lower orders did when they went off the rails these days.

Once away from the rural simplicity of the Bowerman, the silver-spoon brigade were back in the jungle of parties, launches and balls where the predator is the pretty young girl or the decorative young man next to you, who has white powder in his pocket and an emptiness in his heart.

'Lead us not into temptation?' Fesh had scoffed at Jason. 'You lot rush back to meet it, showing a clean pair of upmarket heels.

'Sorry to sound like a fire-and-brimstone preacher, but unless you've changed – really changed inside – you'll be rolling up your fifty quid notes and sniffing again in no time. Because the world never changes. Too bloody right, it doesn't! It's what we bank on in our trade. Quite literally.'

Jason honestly had no idea whether he'd be adding to Fesh's bank balance again. Certainly a life wrapped in cotton wool, away from all temptation, didn't appeal to him one bit. Yes, he wanted to beat his addiction. Yes, he wanted to be his own man again again and not the creature of the dirty chain which begins with Bolivian drugs barons and ends in needles, humiliation and death.

But he wanted victory on his own terms – not to play safe and avoid the fight. He wanted to take it on, in the absurd battleground of the London party scene, and prove to himself he didn't need the drugs.

The taxi arrived at the institute ten minutes late, as everything was late in this sleepy Welsh countryside. Even the sheep went on eating hours after it was dark, so what hope was there for an efficient cab service?

He bundled his bags inside the car. There was no violin. He'd returned that to the Bowerman cook, whose daughter it had belonged to. It wasn't much of an instrument, really. It took a player of skill to get a decent tone out of it. 'Kept with the pans I shouldn't wonder,' Jason had thought when he first raised a shaking bow to its strings.

Very different from his Stradivarius, precious fiddle, he thought, as he sat in the taxi. He winced to remember how the instrument had been splintered by something even more precious. It had been Calla, at once splendid and wilful, who had done that. Dear, fiery, lost Calla.

'The station is it, sir?' the driver asked, eyeing Jason and trying to fathom whether he was an addict or one of the doctors.

Jason nodded and turned his eyes to the hills once more. He recalled how in the depths of his withdrawal, when he was haunted by dreams and out of touch with reality, he had been unable to appreciate their beauty. He could enjoy it now. They were solid, rounded, undeniably of the real world.

'Wonder if I'm destined to see those hills again?' he murmured, in a voice curious and calm.

'Don't worry, we see 'em from the far side, sir,' said the helpful cabbie. 'Just ten minutes or so before we get to the station. Lovely view from there.'

• • •

Oh, Jason. Where are you? Help!

That was the first message on his answer phone when he got back. Peta. Of course she never used the thing properly, giving date and time. Her disembodied voice came as a shock – it was like hearing a ghost.

The machine went quiet, then crackled to life again: *This is Ribbetts Auctioneers. We've a fine art sale this Friday, Mr Andover, and wonder if you'd like a preview. Any time after ten. Thank you.*

Christ, he thought, that was long before Christmas. Where has that part of my life gone?

Hey, man, it's Donovan. Look, we're fixing this motherfucker of a party at Sal's Christmas Eve. You bring the substance, we supply the bodies, okay? Fail not our feast!

Jason, please. It's Peta. I need you, I mean really need you or I don't know what I'm going to do. Will you please ring me the moment you hear this? PLEASE!

Sorry to trouble you, Mr Andover, but I'm Bill Brunt's secretary at New Design and he's asked me to ask you about the article on Corbusier and his lasting influence into the nineties. I'm afraid the first deadline's passed, and Bill says we must have the copy by December 22nd at the latest. Would you mind ringing to confirm? Thank you.

Another customer lost, he thought. Just one more among the many who'd been unable to tolerate his increasing unreliability over the months and years. Especially the past few months when his brain had seemed to go into hibernation. He suddenly felt a gentle prick of conscience about the people he'd let down. This surprised him. Nothing had troubled him in this way for ages. Was it a good sign?

Jason, I'm moving out of my place for a while. I need to be with someone who'll brush away the insects that crawl over my skin.

Peta was too far gone, he thought. There was no way he could help her. She'd have finished him off, too, and he wasn't finished yet. Was he?

He listened to the aural garbage of yesterday's urgency. December passed into January. There were some more deadlines he'd missed, some more invitations, a few cryptic calls from people whose names he didn't even recognise. And where was Calla's voice? he demanded to know, with a flush of self-pity. Why didn't she call to ask how he was?

Hello, you don't know me, but I'm an artist and I need to sell my work. Someone said you'd know where I could find a market . . .

This is the Amadeus Record Club, Mr Andover. Our register shows you have a box set of Stravinsky which should have been returned or paid for . . .

Jesus, Jason, I'm dying. I'm REALLY dying. You remember that night at your place when we saw the graves opening? It's like that, only it's twice as bad as that. I'm pleading with you Jason to come and rescue me....

Barrington Gallery here, Mr Andover. We've a reception this coming Friday the 19th and you're most welcome to attend. A range of emerging English artists . . .

Hello Jason . . .

Here the tape ran out, cutting off a woman's voice. His heart leapt when he thought, for a second, that it was the voice he most wanted to hear, and he urgently pressed the buttons to replay it. But no – he was fantasising.

Hello Jason it repeated parrot-fashion.

'Goodbye Peta,' he replied wearily.

• • •

God, it didn't seem real. The faces were familiar enough, the greetings friendly, but it seemed to Jason as if he were taking part in an illusion. Any minute now the scene before him would dissolve like something from *Alice in Wonderland* and he would be back in the familiar surroundings of the Bowerman Institute.

There were plenty of pictures on the walls, but if the Barrington Gallery really thought they were painted by 'emerging' artists either they or he needed a crash course in aesthetics. All he could see was The New Jokiness, and the triviality made him cringe. The actors in this strange scene occasionally came up and exchanged a few platitudes with him. He heard the odd barbed remark about absent stars of the arts and social scene. But very little touched him. Was he imagining everything? He sipped the champagne: that was real enough.

'Bloody hell, it's Jason Andover! Looking pale and interesting. Where have you been all my life? Isn't this quite the bloodiest preview you ever came to? Can't think what's happened to the art world. I went to an opening last week in Stepney, for God's sake! Stepney! I mean, the cabbie had to look at a map!'

He slowly focused on Hilary Catford, estranged wife of Fowler Catford. The one-time nightclub king had long ago fallen out of love with his brash wife, but he'd amassed such a formidable collection of modern art that he couldn't bear the cost of divorcing her. She, meanwhile, had picked up just enough about paintings from her husband to pass herself off as a discerning art-lover. She wasn't.

'Hilary, how nice,' Jason lied.

'Isn't it! Seen anything of Peta lately?'

'Not for a while.'

He knew exactly what he thought of Hilary Catford. She was one of that teeming breed of hangers-on in the art world, one of those untalented ticks who get proudly bloated by parasiting themselves on the few genuinely creative people in that busy scene. She loved to see and be seen. It was what she lived for. She'd go, as the gossips said of her, to the opening of an envelope.

'What happened Jason? Did you drop her? Poor love looked ghastly last time I saw her – fit to model for one of those Victorian paintings of anorexic women with the vapours. Did you know she collapsed at a Christmas party at Browns? Had to be carried out feet first. I thought, if that's how Jason Andover breaks hearts, thank God I fought him off! Eh?'

She poked an elbow in the direction of his ribs, then took herself off across the room, laughing loudly and slopping champagne from the glass.

'What the hell am I doing here?' he said out loud, almost deafened by the babble and the clink of glasses, his eyes offended by every picture he saw, even the champagne leaving a dull taste on his palate.

But he knew full well what he was doing there. He was testing himself against the world he knew. He was trying to discover whether he could survive in it without turning to drugs. That was why he'd come. That was why he was trying to prevent himself dashing down the stairs and out into the street. It had to be a fair test.

He stood in front of a very odd looking picture of an old-fashioned red phone box in which a sheep was dialling a number. It was entitled When I'm Calling Ewe.

'Bleeding awful,' said a man's voice over his shoulder. 'They used to say kids could paint better than your average modern artist. I'd say for sure their jokes are better.'

'Hello, Kipper,' Jason nodded, recognising his fellow critic's voice without having to turn. 'What's new?'

'On which front? Artistically, nothing. Professionally, less than nothing. Scandal-wise, not much. You've heard about Peta?'

'Tell me.'

'Shacked up with that Fleet Street diary man Richard Mepton-Keeler. He's hoping to reform her, but he hasn't got a chance. The last thing I heard about her was a scene at Crazy Larry's....'

Jason decided that he couldn't take any more. He had to get out. Fast. He felt it as a panic, with a quickened pulse, perspiration, shallow breathing. He already knew quite enough about himself, what he could cope with and what he should do about it. There wasn't a single reason why he should stay in this artistic turkey shed for a second longer.

'Was it something I said,' Kipper asked in the direction of his retreating form, 'or the way I said it?'

Once down the stairs and into the open air he felt more in control of himself. But he had already made up his mind. He knew what he needed, and he needed it as he'd never needed it before.

He turned up his collar against the wind and began to walk. He kept walking until he reached the Soho area, then approached an unmarked door and knocked solidly over and over again until someone called out and he heard footsteps approaching.

23

'Same place, same flight, but complete with wife,' Calla murmured to herself as she followed the airport signs to international arrivals.

Heads turned as she strode through the hall, knitted jade mini-dress nearly meeting thigh high leather boots, a few inches of tempting creamy leggings between. She left a trail of Vivian Westwood scent behind her. In a sea of tedious business suiting and faded denim, she was luminously lovely.

Quite what she should do with the wife, Calla wasn't sure. Wives were foreign territory to her, strange colourless accessories that powerful men would occasionally dust down and bring out before changing for something with more glitter. They were creatures who sublimated their own identity in husbands and children, who had dull routine sex when they'd rather be knitting.

Oh, she knew she was exaggerating. There must be some wives who had mulitiple orgasms more frequently than they washed up. But she couldn't quite believe that this time Philippe would walk to the arrivals barrier with Yvette. She remembered so vividly the last time she had waited there – and she was suddenly almost pole-axed by a memory of how it felt to have him inside her.

The colour rose to her cheeks. Theirs, to be sure, had been an animal passion with little of the soul about it. They'd been two hungry people whose appetites had suddenly converged after long weeks of working on a shared project, that was all.

'That was all,' she said under her breath, remembering that unbelievable weekend. 'And the fact that we were both bloody good at it!'

Now he was coming back, her partner in the Charlesbury project, coming back to decide what they should do next, how they could triumph over the other finalists. There'd be more long, hard days, leaning together over the drawing board, shoulder to shoulder before the screen.

'And he'll be sleeping with his wife at the end of those long hard days.'

She was aware that her cheeks must be flushed. 'Christ,' she thought, 'you might as well have a label saying Impure Thoughts hanging over your head. Calm down for heaven's sake. Try to think of something decent, girl. Think of the nuns, of your bank manager . . . '

Then she saw him, walking towards the barrier, just as she had seen him last time. She felt an immediate pang in the womb. It was the leap, the involuntary spasm which no woman can deny, which leaves her in no doubt that she craves a man. Long before he saw her, she was aware of her own gathering moistness, bringing her longing right home to her.

None of the men looking at her animated beauty and proud body would have dreamt of her state of arousal.

Nor would Philippe, she determined, though he had the sort of sexual palate that could smell and taste desire a mile off. And he knew her vintage and flavours intimately.

'Some men are like pop-bottles, Calla Marchant,' she lectured herself. 'Once you've drained them, they're returnable. Beauvoir was just fizz, bubbles, a dalliance francaise.'

Suddenly she realised that she was looking at Yvette, her arm loosely through her husband's as they walked along. Calla's face immediately felt cooler. She nodded, murmuring: 'A proper mademoiselle! Married to make a respectable man out of him, I shouldn't wonder...'

A creamy pale face with widespread dark eyes and a wide mouth. No make-up. Shiny chestnut hair in a perfect swing bob. Clothes as simple and effective as the hair. A blonde cashmere sweater over a narrow chocolate skirt. Slim ankles. Bare brown legs. Heeled shoes.

'The classic look,' Calla thought dismissively. 'All she needs are the pearls.'

The woman coming towards her, who would at any moment be introduced to her by Philippe, was no head-turner. She wasn't the sort of woman who caused a sharp intake of breath as she walked by. But she was the sort of woman whom a connoisseur of such things might notice and appreciate. She was a cool classic, to be admired as she strolled by pavement cafes or stretched across a street market stall to feel the fruit and vegetables.

Cool had never been a word to apply to Calla. She liked the blood to rush, the heart to pound. So much quiet good taste made it hard for her to breathe. No wonder Philippe had needed some bad behaviour. Did he still, she wondered? Did she?

Then the moment of recognition: she felt Philippe's quick kiss on her cheek and she smiled at Yvette's smile, all the while remembering how his tongue on her clitoris had licked her to delicious awakening that morning.

Philippe protectively slipped an arm around his wife's waist as he met Calla's glance. It was himself he was protecting, for all that, and Calla knew it. He didn't quite trust his feelings.

Her eyes held his and when his glance fell, it travelled all the way down the long neck, full bosom and enticing legs he had enjoyed so lustily a few months before. She had the fleeting impression she could have him again: he could be hers for the asking, in spite of his apparent coolness. Whatever desire she felt was coursing through his veins too. A snap of her fingers, a sway of her hips and she could have him back.

How she revelled in the knowledge of her power! But did she want him? She toyed pleasurably with the idea. Oh, the sex had been bloody good, there was no doubt about it. But Calla got a high, too, from just running the show with men, deciding who to favour and who to spurn. She liked holding the cards. And she'd never expected to hold them with Philippe. Suddenly she felt good, desired and strong. There was no feeling quite like it.

Calla hadn't bothered with a car park. Her red Porsche, pulling up just four minutes before the flight was due in, had been left on the unloading only yellow lines outside. As they walked towards it, Yvette took her in. She registered every voluptuous curve. She noticed the proud and lovely face, the clothes which flaunted confidence, the raw sexual energy this woman put out and men picked up.

Dangerous, was her silent verdict.

'I'm so glad I have come,' was what she said to Calla, in carefully correct English as she got into the car. And Calla heard both meanings and knew that Yvette was more than a mademoiselle with a good taste in jumpers. She idly wondered if she knew, or if she guessed, of her husband's infidelity.

'Straight to work this afternoon, Calla?' Philippe's voice was casual. 'I shall take a taxi to your office from the hotel and we will begin revising our sketches?'

'Yes, but let's not make the whole trip work!' Calla let the words hang in the air, feeling Philippe tensing up beside her in fear of what she might say. 'I mean that, while you and Yvette are here, you must see some of our exciting buildings here in London.'

In her rear-view mirror she could see Yvette's pale face watching her husband in the passenger seat. She pulled on to the M25 and moved smoothly through the gears to speed. She felt Philippe's awareness of that gap between the top of her boots and the bottom of her dress, widened now she was seated and moving her legs as she drove.

It was like that mad drive back to her house their first night after the restaurant. Her every touch on the gear lever had sent him into a frenzy of want.

The vibes were still there, thought Calla. And how! In the back seat Yvette watched, and the married man kept his eyes firmly away from the driver's erogenous zones. Difficult in the case of Calla, as that meant her whole body.

They were staying at the Berkeley hotel in Knightsbridge. Philippe stooped to help Yvette out of the car. He cast a glance back into the Porsche, keeping his eyes firmly on Calla's face, in spite of her slight wriggle in the seat.

'About two o'clock?'

Calla nodded, smiled at Yvette and drove away. There was mischief in her eyes. And she laughed even as she shook her head: 'It's his brains I'm after!'

• • •

'Phil!'

There were two things about Adam's greeting which annoyed Philippe Beauvoir. The first was being called Phil. The second was Adam himself.

'All on your own? I thought Madame Beauvoir was coming too?'

'Why don't you go and collect my Balenciaga dress from the cleaner's, Adam?' Calla suggested pointedly. She could read the irritation on Philippe's face. She wasn't prepared to lose an ounce of his goodwill just because Adam felt like camping it up this afternoon. This relationship was going to run smoothly, however hard she had to work at it.

Adam went, shooting a meaningful look at his boss. 'If you're thinking of coffee, we're out of milk,' was his waspish parting shot. He made sure to disappear before he could be sent for some.

'So, we will take it black,' smiled Philippe at Calla. 'And while we drink, you will show me your ideas, your detailed projections, yes?'

At last he was looking at her without pretending not to see her, Calla thought with satisfaction as they unrolled the plans on the large coffee table. And he was looking at her with distinct pleasure.

Bending over plans for everything from the drains to the shopping arcades, the two slipped straight back into their easy old manners. His passion for Charlesbury was unmistakeable, she thought. He remembered everything in great detail – everything about the project and many other things besides, no doubt. She felt a surge of optimism.

'You have strong opponents, Calla,' he said, 'but they will have to be on good form.'

'You mean *we* have strong opponents,' she said, laughing.

'Calla, I hope you will always think of me as a friend, someone you can ask for any advice you need. But just now, I have so many demanding projects . . . '

Like your wife? Calla thought, but didn't say. Shit! Was she understanding this? If he was thinking of letting her down, why had he bothered coming all this way to tell her so? Why inflict his drab wife on her if he'd intended to back out all along?

'There is to be a new gallery in Paris. I am submitting preliminary plans now. There is talk of a new bourse – a brand new stock exchange –

and I cannot afford to be missing from the list of finalists. You see my problem?'

Oh, she saw his problem. But she saw her own far more vividly. She had confidence in her abilities, no doubt of that, but she knew that Philippe had flair, too, that his name carried clout. They had made the final as a partnership. How would it look to the Duke if her colleague dropped out at this stage?

It would look something close to a fraud, that's what – as if she had used the Philippe connection purely to reach the final stage. She'd stand accused of double-dealing. Perhaps she'd be disqualified. That mustn't happen. She needed him on board. Badly. And she'd do anything to get him.

'You see, Calla, this is the time for detailed plans, for making sure that the Charlesbury philosophy we drafted works as a real town. Its sinews need to stretch, its heart needs to pump, its blood to flow.

'And I can't spare the time, Calla.'

She stood up, walked purposefully to the window and swung round to look at him.

'You realise what you're turning down, Philippe? Do you? This is the architectural project of the decade, probably of the 21st century. Will anyone live in your stock exchange? Will anyone be inspired by your display case for paintings? Charlesbury is an incredible concept, Philippe, you know that.

'It's architecture for people. It's the architecture which will fill the pages of newspapers on both sides of the Channel. Your bourse might make a second section picture caption in a quality Sunday, but Charlesbury will be everywhere.'

She had come alive. Her violet eyes were bright, and colour suffused her cheeks. This was Calla Marchant when her emotions were roused, Philippe thought, aware of the stirrings in himself of an old feeling, too.

'I'm a married man, you know, Calla,' he said quietly, as much to remind himself as her.

'You were a married man before,' she snapped back. 'It didn't stop you drawing pretty pictures then. So what's new?'

'You know what's new.'

His tone silenced Calla for a moment. It was the moment Adam chose to walk in, clutching Calla's cleaning and a pint of milk.

'I think,' he drawled into the tangible silence, 'that Madame Beauvoir is outside paying a cabbie. Très chic, too, I might add. And laden with parcels.'

As Yvette walked in, smiling her cool smile, Adam rushed forward to make her a coffee. He approved of Madame Beauvoir's existence. Calla didn't, but even she would think twice about seducing a man whose wife had come to pay a social call.

'I desired to see where you work,' she said. 'As our visit is so short, I thought I would call in after the shopping.'

'So short?' echoed Calla. 'I'd hoped you could be here for a few days, at least. Is the Berkeley not very comfortable?'

'I think we cannot stay very long.'

'But I'm your tour guide,' Calla protested, as light-heartedly as she was able. 'You *must* see some of our new buildings, Yvette. It's all planned. And Philippe and I need time to think before we make any decisions about Charlesbury.'

She saw the brown eyes look slowly and meaningfully at Philippe. It was obvious that some deep discussions had been held in Paris before they set off, and Calla sensed a battle of wills in the making. Well, they'd see who would win.

'You'll think over what we said, Philippe?'

'I will. And you?'

She nodded and allowed Yvette to bear her husband off to the hotel. Round one to the Frenchwoman, maybe, but there'd be several more rounds yet.

Yvette paused at the door: 'You must come to dinner at our comfortable hotel, Calla. You have a husband?'

Only yours, thought Adam, as he watched Calla smile rather distantly and make an excuse about work.

• • •

The next day Yvette made the mistake of yawning.

'Please forgive me,' she said prettily.

Born into an aristocratic French family, she had little interest in new buildings and absolutely none in her husband's passion for architecture. If asked, she'd say she supposed she liked buildings which were fine and regular, classical and unfussed by imagination.

London was horribly cold in that special February way: raw, grey and intimidating. And Calla seemed to have chosen the strangest destinations for their architectural tour. William Whitfield's headquarters for the Department of Health at Whitehall *might* be a masterpiece, but Yvette simply couldn't see it. That Gherkin, as they called it – it looked as though some vital part of the structure had melted and tipped the whole thing over. And as for Richard Rogers' conversion of the Billingsgate fish market into a bank's headquarters – well, converted or otherwise, what interest was a fish market to *her*?

So Yvette yawned, obviously and often. She'd finally agreed to two days of this, and already she was regretting it. Philippe suggested in concerned tones that she take a cab to Tate Modern – or even to the old Tate itself or the National Gallery. But that wasn't in Yvette's plans at all. Yvette was sightseeing too, but she was looking for something else.

As the two architects absorbed their surroundings, discussed nuances and disagreed over details, Yvette was watching. She watched their growing intimacy in the face of her obvious lack of interest. She watched their shared enthusiasm and noticed their apparent ease with each other's personal space. Seized by a sudden enthusiasm, Philippe would take Calla's elbow, or touch her wrist, pointing out his find excitedly.

And Yvette had to admit that the woman had something – had everything, in fact. It was a shade too obvious for her taste, but men liked the more obvious. Yvette knew that. Yvette could see that. Now she understood why Philippe had said so little about his business partner after he'd returned from England before.

As for Calla, she had obviously forgotten Yvette's existence altogether. She drank in everything Philippe had to say, whether she agreed with it or not. The two shared an ardour for buildings which was almost tangible.

As the morning wore on, Yvette became convinced that the two had been lovers. She shuddered to think that it might have been after her marriage. Philippe had, she remembered, been somehow different after his English trip. Strangely high at first and then rather low, like an explorer who has seen a new world and is disappointed to find the old one unchanged.

Like a true Frenchwoman, Yvette had suspected sex was at the bottom of it, although she'd been inclined to give her newly-married husband the benefit of the doubt. *Cherchez la femme*, indeed! Looking at Calla now, as she threw her head back and let her long white neck ripple with laughter, she felt all too sure that she had found her.

But Yvette was nothing if not practical. She had to endure their intimacy throughout the long day, yet when she and Philippe eventually parted from Calla at the entrance to their hotel, she was smiling to herself. That was because of the valuable card she had up her sleeve. Well, perhaps not her sleeve, exactly. Oh, it was an ace of trumps! She had hugged it to herself for a week, a whole week of suspense, but she was in no doubt that now was the time to play it.

She liked the Berkeley. It was a modern building, but without any pretence to architectural daring, and it had a clubby atmosphere which she found quite charming. It was so English. And she was well looked after there, with a head porter who was himself the very best example of an English gentleman.

They took the lift to their room on the top floor. Philippe was in a particularly attentive mood, as if to make up for paying court to another woman all day. Good: let him try. Wasn't it the least he could do? She played up to it shamelessly, sending him all the way back to reception for a bottle of Dior perfume she'd spotted the day before.

It was time to dress for dinner. She slipped gracefully out of her skirt and sweater, and stood waiting for him in a simple silk petticoat. She looked in every way the kind of woman that men long to protect.

'Philippe,' she called softly as he entered the room. 'I have some news.'

'My love?'

She gazed upon him with eyes that were moist and tender with love: 'I'm pregnant,' she said.

• • •

The Glasgow shuttle flight wasn't the stuff of passion, thought Calla as she took the Kit-Kat and coffee offered by the steward. Its seduction possibilities were distinctly limited.

There was hardly room to cross long legs, let alone flaunt them for Philippe's benefit. As for meaningful glances betraying hidden yearning, they were out when you were elbow-in-rib with the object of your lust. Such a pity when she had the man entirely to herself.

'The Orient Express it's not,' she smiled at him. 'But it's quick.'

'If not painless,' said Philippe, wincing as he tried, unsuccessfully, to uncross his own legs.

For most of the hour-long journey he was silent. He made no attempt to recreate the intimacy of the day before. Calla would have given anything to have read his thoughts. Was he absolutely decided? Was there still hope he might play a full part in the designs for Charlesbury?

She'd decided to use every weapon in her power to make sure he stayed in with her. And if that meant sexual weaponry, she told herself, so be it. She wasn't above flirtation and suggestion. Or even more, she resolved. Not when she was poised to win the biggest prize of her life.

And she might even enjoy it, she thought rogueishly. After all, she'd sucked the very juices of the experience that previous time. Ha! She snapped a finger off her Kit-Kat and bit it with her white even teeth. What an appetite the man had revealed that weekend!

And now? Well, she'd immediately rekindled his desire, she knew it. Yesterday, going round the new building in Whitehall, she'd felt the warmth of his breath upon her despite the watchful presence of his wife. He had often been far closer than he needed to be, his fingers deftly finding her.

All this had been as she expected. Calla knew full well what effect she had on men, and Philippe was every bit a man, there wasn't the slightest doubt about that. She would have been much more surprised if he'd managed to resist her, whatever the circumstances. Was that arrogance? No, it was reality. She'd seen upright, happily-married men straining to contain their lust for her.

So why had he gone off the boil? Had Yvette given him a dressing down? Or was their own lovemaking so fulfilling that even he had no more capacity for ecstasy? Dammit, what more could she do? Take her clothes off and dance with a python?

She stole a glance at him. He was looking through the window, lost in thought.

Philippe was wondering how to tell Calla what decision he'd come to. The news of Yvette's pregnancy had finally made up his mind. He would volunteer to be an unofficial consultant for the Charlesbury project, but that would be as far as he would go. There would be no more London trips, no detailed drawings, no designs, no decisions.

It wasn't that he didn't want to work with her, Christ knew. She was the most exciting thing he'd come across since that distant day when he'd first had a woman. Just being near her intoxicated him, and even more when she was in a building she loved. That ferocious enthusiasm was an added aphrodisiac.

There were times when he was in bed with Yvette and all he could think of was Calla's hot silky skin, the rich depth of her pubic hair, the moist den where his own sex belonged.

And there were times when Yvette's placidity, her stillness beneath him, her unsweaty whimperings, made him long for Calla's bucking body – her athletic, demanding, generously giving body. He suffered maddening visions of how she would arch her back, howl, scratch at his buttocks as she ruthlessly seized and prolonged the moment of orgasm. That display of animal instinct and release was alien to his lovely, proper wife.

But it was that wife who was expecting his baby. And after all, he did love Yvette even if she scarcely understood, let alone answered, that primeval sexual urge of his. Fatherhood appealed to him as it does to so many Frenchmen as tangible proof of virility. He imagined himself the father of a big, convivial family. What was an architectural project compared to that, after all? Yvette would need him in the months to come. His place was by her side.

The plane had begun its descent to Glasgow. He turned his face from the window: 'Calla, there's something I must tell you.'

'You don't like Kit-Kat?'

'No, I don't like Kit-Kat. And Yvette is having a baby.'

There was a pause.

'Congratulations, Philippe.' She tried to sound pleased, but she knew full well what it meant. 'When's the happy event?'

'Seven months from now.'

There was no jealousy in Calla's reaction. Becoming a mother herself had never occured to her. And, although she'd envy any woman a spell in Philippe's bed, she didn't want him for a husband either. It was lust, not love, he inspired in her.

'It means,' Philippe was speaking gently, 'that I must pull out of Charlesbury.'

'Oh?'

'Yvette will need me.'

She's giving birth, not having a kitchen extension, thought Calla. *Who needs an architect around for that?*

'Of course,' she said. Of course that scheming little paragon of a tasteful wife had known the trick to pull. That cool, clever mademoiselle!

So that was why Yvette had changed her mind about coming to Glasgow, entrusting her husband to a woman she must have suspected of tempting him to distraction. She felt sure of him now, sure that he wasn't going to have anything more to do with Charlesbury. Having coolly played her trump card, she was now triumphantly swanning round the Bond Street shops. No doubt, thought Calla bitterly, she was looking for cashmere maternity wear.

'I'd be honoured, Calla, if you'd use me as an unofficial consultant. Anything you'd like a second opinion on, you only have to ask.'

'Thank you, Philippe.'

Somehow, she didn't know how, Calla kept up a chatter about buildings and babies in the taxi to the concert hall. What was the point of any of this? she was asking herself. Why show Philippe her lovely creation if he was letting her down?

Philippe, on the other hand, allowed himself to relax. She was taking it well, after all. Now it was out in the open, he could enjoy the day in lovely company.

And how lovely it was, he thought, taking in for the first time that day the clingy high-cut Jean Muir satin leggings (what would she do now that the business was closing down?) and the brightly patterned satin jacket with its broad shoulders and softly nipped-in waist. Calla Marchant was good to look at, and good to be seen with, even if he was a father to be.

After the cab had drawn to a halt outside the concert hall, he sat motionless for lengthening seconds, simply staring at the creation before him.

'Your foreign friend not getting out, hen?' queried the cabbie as Calla paid him.

Philippe had lapsed into French for a few moments. Most appreciative French, Calla realised. He got out of the cab clumsily, his eyes still fixed on the glass-and-iron display before him. The man loved buildings. Erecting them was like a physical lust to him. He envied other men their creations of stone and brick just as he envied them their women.

'Magnifique!'

This feast of light had been created by a woman. By the beauty standing by him, in fact. He was in a turmoil of longing – longing to possess both the building and its creator. As he opened the door for her, Calla felt his hand in the small of her back. She remembered that evening leaving Bibendum, and her heart jumped.

They stood in the middle of the hall, just where she had stood all those months before on the morning of the gala opening, looking out at the auditorium. The light shot, dived and glowed off a thousand panes of glass. Philippe nodded, immensely moved, taking it all in.

'So beautiful!' he breathed. 'I wish she were mine!'

As he spoke, Calla felt his fingers on the nape of her neck, stroking. She stiffened. He was hardly aware of what he was doing of course. He was so entranced by the building that all his pretences had disappeared for the moment. He was no longer struggling to seem indifferent to her. Was this her chance to make him change his mind? Might she keep him interested in the Charlesbury project after all? She knew instinctively how to use her sex.

But as she stood frozen under his touch, the sound of violin music escaped from the rehearsal room – a soloist was practising for tonight's performance, no doubt. The music, though distant, was mournfully lovely. It was familiar, too. She had heard the melody many times in an untidy but much loved flat where art magazines and sheet music had littered the table and spilled onto the floor. It went straight to her heart and found Jason there.

Even as Philippe's fingers made small circling movements on her flesh, she realised that it was Jason she wanted. Just as it was Jason she had wanted to tell when she reached the Charlesbury finals.

'Come and see it from the stage,' she said, moving away.

She realised in an instant that something vital to herself hadn't changed at all. She had simply suppressed it. She'd been made unhappy, and there had been other things to throw her energies into. But it was still there.

What was the point of it being still there? a little voice demanded of her. Nothing's ever going to come of it. Forget it! Enjoy yourself! Use every trick in the book to win the Charlesbury competition!

But that was the moment she knew she wasn't going to use her sexuality on Philippe Beauvoir, after all. Whatever the consequences. She had no regrets for the past: Philippe had been a good time, no doubt about that. But as her feelings overwhelmed her on a tide of violin music, she knew that to revive the relationship would be to deny something which couldn't any longer be denied.

'You make lovely things,' Philippe murmured into her ear. 'I'm sorry I can't make them with you at Charlesbury.'

● ● ●

Adam manoevred Calla's Porsche out of the tight space behind her offices. He'd rather surprised his boss by volunteering to run Philippe back to the Berkeley. And she'd certainly surprised him by accepting, especially as it might be the last time she'd ever see the man. He was taking his charming wife back to Paris early the following morning.

'Say goodbye to Yvette for me,' Calla had said rather stiffly, letting Philippe kiss her on the cheek.

Adam thought he understood how she felt. He usually did: there was a strange but strong bond between them. Adam knew how much Charlesbury meant to her, and he sensed that something had gone badly wrong.

He seemed in no hurry to get to Knightsbridge, apparently enjoying his ride in the showy car. He didn't often get a chance to drive it. He stopped at a set of red lights and gave his passenger a sidelong glance.

'Hate to be inquisitive, Phil, but you're leaving us for good?'

'Yes.' Philippe's reply was curt, as if to say that it was none of Adam's business.

The lights changed and the Porsche purred comfortably along a succession of side streets. Philippe had no idea of where they were, but he suspected vaguely that they weren't taking the most direct route.

'Seems a shame. I'd have said yours was the winning partnership.'

'Would you?'

'Professional partnership, of course. Glamorous English ambition and Parisian *je ne sais quoi*. Forgive the accent, Phil, won't you?'

'It's a question of time,' said Philippe, ignoring the banter. 'I'm too busy.'

'Great pity,' Adam lamented. 'Very high-profile project, you know. A duke, money, ancestral land – no end of publicity in all the right places.'

'I'm quite well aware of all that, thank you very much,' Philippe replied scornfully. 'And I don't need publicity.'

'Quite!' They swung into a leafy square which Philippe could have sworn they'd passed through several minutes before. 'Particularly on one subject, I assume.'

'What are you talking about?'

'Your marriage, probably.'

They travelled in silence for some time. Philippe thought he must know what Adam was talking about, but he didn't dare to mention it directly in case he was wrong. Was he really being blackmailed? He turned to examine Adam's profile as they crawled slowly along another anonymous back street. Yes, he rather thought he was.

'You'd do anything to have me working on Charlesbury?'

'Please don't misunderstand me, Phil. Personally I'd be very happy never to set eyes on you again. I don't actually approve of you very much. Not at all, in fact. But Calla needs you here.'

'This is preposterous!' Philippe said with a hard laugh.

'Probably. But we're both men of the world, I think.'

'That depends–' Philippe began, but thought better of it.

'There's a mobile phone in the glove compartment, Phil. It would be so easy to ring Calla and tell her you've changed your mind. Either that, or I shall have to tell Madame Yvette all about Calla.'

'What about Calla?'

'Oh everything!' They glided under the trees, and this time Philippe was damn sure it was the same square yet again. 'You wouldn't want your wife to know about your little amour, would you? She doesn't deserve it, in my humble opinion. In fact, that's not all she doesn't deserve.'

Philippe shook his head with an expression which looked very much like admiration: 'You're a loyal little bastard, aren't you?'

'I try, Phil, I try. And, anyway, consider that I'm doing you a favour. It won't exactly break your heart, will it? I'll suffer much more than you will. Shall I stop the car or can you manage on the move?'

Philippe, still shaking his head, found the telphone, scrolled down to the address book and put in the call. The Porsche gathered speed. For the first time, he noticed, they seemed to be on a main road.

'Calla?' he said. 'I've changed my mind. Count me in. I'll ring from Paris.'

24

'Believe me, Darl baby,' Neri Corinthian bawled into the telephone, 'I just love being back in the mother country.'

It was true, goddamit. She had a suite on the twentieth floor of the Park Lane Hilton and right now the low February sun was painting the tree trunks gold and glinting fiercely on the windows of cars scurrying along the London thoroughfares.

'I am *not* ungrateful, honey. It's a wonderful assignment. But how am I supposed to show my gratitude? No – on second thoughts, don't tell me.'

She swung open the refrigerator with a booted foot and took out, one at a time, a bottle of gin and another of tonic.

'Listen, I haven't even yet contacted my sister, do you read me? My darling kid sister I haven't laid eyes on for, shit, seventeen years! I've been too up-to-here busy to see even my wonderful, sainted sister, so how the hell do you think I could have made room for little you?'

She cradled the receiver under her chin as she got to work on the bottles, tipping a generous portion of gin into a glass, then watching the tonic fizz and settle. Jesus, it was a low calorie tonic! Crazy, she thought – a pathetic pretence for weight-and-fitness freaks. She simply couldn't understand those boring people who always took half measures, who lived their lives at half throttle.

'Bejayzus, you'll have me weeping puddles,' she laughed hoarsely. 'If I invite you over you'll do things the hotel management wouldn't like. The sound-proofing's not so good here, sweetheart. I just heard a man shaving next door. How would it cope with you hoofing it about the room like some entrant in the Grand National?'

But that night in Rio had been damn good, she remembered with a huge grin. She hadn't sprinted about naked like that since she was a tiny child on the beach. And it hadn't been so much fun afterwards on the beach, either.

'Okay, okay raunchy man,' she conceded at last. 'In return for all you've done in finding me work in England I'll allow you to buy me dinner. No, you won't have to wait another month. Hey, what do you mean *another* month? I've only been here a couple of weeks, for Chrissakes. Just let me see my sister. She doesn't even know I'm in the country. Don't you know what blood ties mean?'

The things men said to women in the intimacy of a telephone conversation! If she hadn't got past the blushing stage about twenty years before, she'd certainly glow bright red now, right the way down to her toes.

'Hell, Darl baby,' she said, 'that's improper. No question, you've got the sexiest tongue I ever heard.'

• • •

The two men sauntered into Bunny Simkins' office without more than a nod towards his secretary on the way through. They flashed their cards at him and hovered about his desk as if they were about to pick it up and hurl it from the window.

'Jenkins,' said one.

'And Graff,' said the other.

This, he supposed, is just how he would have imagined CID men to have looked. Smooth. Confident. Well-groomed.

'What can I do for you, gentlemen?'

And that was exactly what he would have imagined himself replying. It was an innocent remark, but it seemed a bit *too* innocent, as if he was hiding the fact that he really knew why they had come. Didn't he know? He suddenly felt very frightened. His stomach turned to jelly.

'We've got some photographs,' Jenkins said. 'Why don't you take a look.'

He pulled several prints from a large envelope and scattered them about the desk.

'For God's sake,' Simkins said, 'shut the door.'

'Embarrassed, are we?' Graff asked with a smirk. 'I think *I* would be, too. Very embarrassed.'

Jenkins shut the door: 'This is you flaunting yourself for the camera, I take it? The face seems remarkably similar, though I can't speak for the other parts.'

They both laughed harshly. Simkins felt anger mingling with his fear.

'It was a trick,' he told them.

'Oh, and very cleverly done,' Graff crooned in tones of congratulation. 'Down with your trousers and a boy's hand on your prick in five seconds. Bet the Magic Circle couldn't improve on that.'

'Not that kind of a trick. I was set up.'

'They all say that, don't they, Graff?'

'They do, Jenkins, they do.'

The phone rang: 'No calls, Maggie,' Simkins heard himself practically shouting into the receiver. 'Please,' he added as an afterthought. Why was he allowing himself to be terrorised by these men? He was innocent. There was nothing they could do to him.

Jenkins put his face close to Simkins' face: 'You may have heard,' he said, 'that coppers come in pairs. One's the nice guy, the other's the bastard. You've heard that, have you?'

'I don't know.'

'Course you know. Tell me you've heard that, Mr Simkins, or I shan't be inclined to believe anything you say.'

'All right. Yes, I have.'

'Well, we're different. Aren't we Graff?'

'Yes, we're different Mr Simkins,' Graff said. 'Neither of us likes playing the nice guy. That's funny, isn't it?'

'What the hell do you want?' Simkins blurted out.

But he knew they'd already got most of what they wanted. They had him frightened out of his wits. When the story had broken in *Private Eye* all those weeks ago he'd been shocked and ashamed, but he'd been determined to carry on. A visit from the police put the whole thing in a different light – a dingy, unwholesome light.

'We don't think there's any point,' Jenkins said, 'in asking you detailed questions about what's happening here.' He stabbed a finger at the most explicit of the photographs. 'We can see for ourselves.'

'And by great good luck for themselves,' Graff said, ' the young men involved have their backs to the camera. Lovely backs, aren't they? Don't they turn you on?'

'I've no idea who they are,' Simkins said. 'Or why they did that.'

'Can't imagine,' Jenkins said. 'And I don't suppose you'd tell us their names however much we tried to persuade you.'

'I don't know them, for God's sake!'

'Don't lose your temper, Mr Simkins,' Graff advised him. 'Your secretary might start to ask you awkward questions. As far as we're concerned you're a mucky old pervert who mustn't be allowed to carry on corrupting the youth of this city. You've got to be stopped.'

Simkins felt tears coming to his eyes: 'I've done nothing,' he protested. 'Why won't you believe me?'

'Not our policy, Mr Simkins,' Jenkins said regretfully. 'We've heard too many tall tales in our time, haven't we, Graff?'

'Far too many, Jenkins. Just one more and I think someone will end up in the police cells for interrogation. And that can be pretty tough.'

'Especially when both the cops are bastards,' said Graff.

Simkins put his head in his hands. 'What do you want me to do?' he asked quietly.

He was innocent, but he wasn't naive. They had enough to make his life a misery. They might even have enough, if they lined up a few false witnesses, to persuade a jury. How old had those youths been? He wanted to howl with grief and rage.

'It's what we don't want you to do, Mr Simkins,' Jenkins said. 'We don't want you going anywhere near young boys in circumstances which might tempt the dirty beast in you.'

'We want you to keep that disgusting thing to yourself,' Graff said, collecting up the photographs. 'And we'll be keeping a close eye on you to make sure that you do.'

'Am I on a file?' Simkins asked. 'Police records?'

'Is he on a file, Graff?'

'I'm afraid he is, Jenkins. Only a suspects file, of course.'

'So that's not so bad, Mr Simkins, is it? We pride ourselves on holding a man innocent until proven guilty. You're only under suspicion.'

They both retreated to the door.

'I trust we won't be seeing so much of you in the future, Mr Simkins,' Jenkins said with a chuckle, opening it.

'Not in the flesh,' smirked Graff, following his colleague from the room.

After they had gone, Bunny Simkins sat in silence for several minutes. He felt unclean. He felt as if his whole life had been held up to public gaze and been found to be soiled and foul smelling. He wanted to shrivel up and disappear from the face of the earth.

But why? Why was he being persecuted? What did it mean? He had to know. He reached into a drawer, fumbled for his contacts book and, with misted eyes, riffled the pages in search of Martin Kingsley's telephone number.

● ● ●

'Tell me if I've got this right,' Malibu said, jumping onto a high stool. 'You used Fuji Neopan.'

'Correct,' Kazinsky nodded, realising that the movement had stopped in his studio for the first time in an hour. Perhaps he should chain her to the stool. 'But what specification?'

'It was 400 film, but you uprated it one stop to ISO 800 because of the low light. 'How am I going?'

'You're cooking on gas. What else?'

'It's an ancient rusting car in the undergrowth, right? A Rover even older than yours. You wanted to highlight the contrast between all that greenery and the shabby paint work – so you used a red filter.'

'Bravissimo,' Kazinsky smiled, reaching for his glass of scotch. 'Which meant what?'

She aimed a long finger at her temple as if about to shoot herself and thought long and hard.

'Which meant,' she said eventually, 'you'd got even more of a light problem. The filter shuts out a lot of the light.'

'A couple of stops' worth,' he agreed.

'Therefore,' she said, leaping from the stool in triumph, 'you selected a slow shutter speed! Have I passed my test?'

'With crisp and flying colours, girlie. Though you might have mentioned the tripod. At those slow speeds an old alky like me tends to get camera shake.'

He watched her on the move again, skipping about the studio like a young lamb. She was exasperating, exhausting, extreme in every way, but she was also completely captivating. There were no slow speeds as far as Malibu was concerned. And the shutters never came down.

True, there'd been times during the past few weeks when he would gladly have strangled her. Such as the time when she'd burst into the darkroom while he was developing an especially arty black and white picture.

'I've a good mind to pack you off to Kodak,' he'd yelled, 'with the label Completely Undeveloped! The way you behave, nobody will ever take you on.'

'Never mind, Rudi,' she'd sighed instantly with the most mischievous grin. 'One day my Prints will come.'

What could you do with a girl like that? How could you throw her out on the street? And, to be fair, she had worked bloody hard. More than that, she'd become almost obsessive about the business. You couldn't tell what she'd do or say from one moment to the next, but you did know that she'd be in the studio every spare minute she wasn't accompanying you out on location. Some nights he had to push her out of the door so that he could lock up and go home.

For Malibu this had been the most exciting time of her life since being locked in a Cairo jail. Rudi Kazinsky's easy-going attitude reminded her of her father's. It was so different from the kind of authority most people wanted to impose upon her that she found that she wasn't in a perpetual state of rebellion. That freed her to concentrate on the job in hand – and she discovered that she loved it.

This was new to her, actually caring about what she was doing. The film scene had had its glamour, but there really wasn't much of it when you saw everything close up. And day-to-day life in a magazine office was a hell of a lot less glossy than the product which came out of it. She didn't like being part of a large team.

There was something much more personal about photography, and it was more immediate, too. You decided what picture you wanted and then you used your imagination and your technical skill to get it. Once you'd clicked the shutter you didn't have to wait for a month until the magazine came out or maybe a couple of years for a film to appear on television. You hurried back to the studio and developed it yourself. It was the nearest thing to magic, she thought, that a paid job could offer. If it *was* paid.

'You've noticed the date, Rudi?' she asked, hopping onto the stool again.

He was signing a pile of letters which had been left on his desk by the part-time secretary.

'I'm about to miss a deadline?'

'It'll be damnation and ruination to you if you do,' she asserted. 'My month's up. My dear Daddykins is no longer paying.'

'Ah.' He signed a few more letters, his face expressionless. 'A month already is it?'

God, how much she suddenly found she cared! She actually wanted a job of work! She knew she'd do something utterly drastic if he refused, something like (she could see it now) running through the city streets naked, painted vividly in woad like an ancient Briton, crying aloud the injustices of the world....

'In that case,' Kazinsky said, 'if we can agree a suitably meagre salary, I'd better take you on.'

She swooped upon him. Even the scotch on his breath, which she normally hated, had the sweetness of nectar.

'And here's a job you can do,' he laughed, fighting her off, 'all by your little self. Look, I've written a letter saying we'll cover it. Can I trust you? You'll have to use a real camera, mind – not one of your horrible digital abominations.'

She cartwheeled around the studio until he had to cover his eyes for fear of feeling dizzy.

'Trust me?' she demanded with attempted indignation. 'I'm a professional!'

● ● ●

'I assure you, Miss Marchant,' Humphrey Tenison said with a deferential smile, 'that this is simply good professional practice. There's nothing at all unusual about it.'

'Perhaps not for you, but it's highly unusual for me. And not at all pleasant. What have I done to deserve the third degree?'

'I hope that's not how it appears,' frowned her bank manager, sitting back in his chair as if to suggest how relaxed he was about the whole affair. He was one of those men who try too hard. There was an executive toy on his desk – silver balls that were supposed to swing up and down for ever once you'd set them in motion – but Humphrey Tenison was the last person you could imagine ever using a toy. There were photographs of his wife and grown-up family, and the effect was almost comical. Nothing quite fitted.

'It's not long since I took out a small loan,' Calla persisted. 'That was agreed without any difficulty.'

'By one of my under-managers.'

'That's right. Are you suggesting the man was incompetent? Is he some kind of un-person now, relegated to the vaults?'

'No, no, not at all, Miss Marchant. I'm sure he judged your case carefully as well as sympathetically. It's merely that I would be grateful to understand your present situation myself – with a view to helping as much as possible, naturally.'

Calla remained perplexed. She had never needed many dealings with banks, but she'd grown up in an age when financial institutions were falling over themselves to lend, not penny-pinching and stuffily moralistic. Were times changing for some reason?

'My situation, Mr Tenison, is that I run a very successful architectural practice. I have recently been short-listed for the Duke of Mercia's Charlesbury project. If I win that competition I shall have enough business to last me for years.'

'If,' Tenison said with a patronising smile. 'You're gambling everything on that one throw of the dice, perhaps?'

She felt the beginnings of anger stirring inside her: 'I'm not aware of any gambling. What do you mean by that?'

'I mean that you've had to take out a loan with us. Smallish, but not inconsiderable....'

'To tide me over.'

'Yes, yes, of course. I'm not trying to alarm you, Miss Marchant. But I do wonder whether you've fully considered the financial implications of *not* winning that competition. How would you be placed then?'

She stiffened: 'I have been concentrating on Charlesbury, yes,' she said. 'My other work has diminished during the last few months. But I have a reputation. I can soon pick it up again.'

'With the requirement of another loan first, do you think?' He looked through the papers on the desk in front of him. 'From my under-manager's notes, I see that you asked for the option of another loan before the end of the year.'

'That's right. By the end of the year I shall know where I stand over Charlesbury. All I'm asking for is the financial backing to tide me over that period. Is that unreasonable?'

'Not unreasonable, no,' he replied. 'But I shouldn't wish to encourage a tendency towards...shall we say, adventurousness, which you may come to regret.'

Calla couldn't reply. She was so angry that she thought she might say something not at all appropriate to the placid surroundings of a banker's eyrie. Who the hell did he think he was to lecture her like a kid?

Or was he right? Had she really charged into an adventure without proper consideration of the consequences?

'Let's just say, Miss Marchant, that I should be extremely reluctant to commit my bank to a longer-term investment in your practice without rather more detailed evidence of your future prospects. The amount you have asked for is reasonable, but I hope you have no thoughts of needing very much more.'

'No, I don't.'

'In which case,' Tenison said, 'I'm very happy. I do hope you haven't misconstrued my interest. You seem somewhat ill at ease, if I may say so.'

Calla, ignoring the remark, rose from her chair to go. Before leaving, however, she couldn't resist approaching the desk and setting those stupid silver balls in motion. She was glad to see him thrown out of his stride.

'Have a nice day,' she said sourly.

Once she had gone, Tenison picked up the telephone and gave his secretary a number to dial.

'It's Humphrey Tenison,' he said when she had put him through. 'Just to report that everything's all right, Mr Andover.'

'She got the message?'

'Yes, she certainly got the message. I'd say that Miss Marchant left here a very worried young woman indeed.'

● ● ●

Arriving at Ryall Park, Malibu had sauntered up the gravel drive feeling a million pounds. She would certainly have skipped towards the nineteenth century mansion but for the weight of the expensive cameras slung round her neck.

'Malibu Locke,' she'd announced herself to the lady at the table with the press badges scattered all over it. 'Representing Rudi Kazinsky.'

She'd certainly noticed how the blankness of expression which greeted the first name had given way to bright-eyed interest over the second.

'You're with *him*?'

Don't look so gob-struck surprised, she felt like snarling in reply. I'm a professional, aren't I? Look at my gear – you don't pick that up in Woolworths.

'He's with *me*,' she said instead.

She had taken the train to leafy Surrey, thinking it was about time Daddykins stumped up with a car. Something sporty, of course. Then she really would buckle down to those boring driving lessons he'd been talking about. As if she could be expected to take them seriously when there was no souped-up little number to leap into immediately afterwards, roaring away in a cloud of dust!

Ryall Park was an extravagant Gothick pile built by a man who had made his fortune from South American guano. An independent character, he'd insisted on a number of outlandish features which could never be described as tasteful but which now, all this time later, gave the place a queer distinction. The turrets and the fake drawbridge were particularly admired. It had to be preserved as a monument, despite the fact that no individual in his right mind – not even the guano king's descendant, Lord Mennith of Ryall, a middle-ranking banker – was prepared to spend the money on it.

The solution was a typical late-twentieth century one. The National Trust would buy the house and its extensive grounds and allow Lord and Lady Mennith to live in one wing for the remainder of their days. The change of ownership had been accomplished about two years before, and now the Trust was showing off its thorough and historically sensitive refurbishment of the place.

'This wallpaper,' Lord Mennith was explaining to the journalists and photographers who had flocked to the place in large numbers, knowing a cushy job when they saw one, 'is a William Morris.'

'Or, rather,' smiled the expert from the National Trust, a stout, tweedy woman in her middle years, '*after* William Morris. It's a design by one of his disciples.'

'Quite so,' agreed Lord Mennith enthusiastically. He'd only been brought up in the house and lived there all his fifty-two years. He hadn't known a thing about it until a few months ago.

Flash bulbs exploded as the army of photographers went into action, Malibu among them. She was enjoying herself immensely. How she pitied the poor journalists who were having to scribble everything down! All she had to do was get herself in the right place and press her finger on a button.

Rudi Kazinsky received dozens of invitations in the post every week, and most of them were to events totally irrelevant to his own work. This one was a case in point, but he thought Malibu deserved a break. More than that, she needed to find out what it was like to cover a picture assignment by herself. Maybe she'd do really well and come up with something he might want to keep on his files for some future use. If so, that would be a lucky bonus. He was quite prepared for her to fail dismally – though he certainly hadn't told her so.

And if she ruined his good name? she'd asked him with a little grin, knowing her own lamentable habit of getting into trouble. He'd only shrugged. He could handle that, his gesture seemed to say. Kazinsky didn't need anyone's good favour. He'd made his reputation long ago, and it was unassailable.

'Could we have these tables cleared out the way?'

It was the wild woman photographer with the American accent. God, she was like a force of nature. She only had to speak and everyone turned to watch her. The vividness of her crimson trouser suit, contrasting with the blackness of her riotously tumbling hair and her knee-length boots, seemed an echo of her vibrant personality. Malibu had noticed from the start that she was somehow separate from all the others. She didn't seem interested in the same shots. While they were all clustered in one spot, following the cue given by Lord Mennith or the National Trust expert, she was striding off to some other part of the room – or even *out* of the room – in search of her own pictures. She seemed totally oblivious of everyone else. Malibu thought that was rather fine.

'Sorry to break up a cosy party,' she said in a voice growing louder with every syllable, 'but is there a chance of some action here?'

'Well, I'm not really sure,' Mennith replied defensively. 'They would be rather difficult to move, don't you think?'

'You don't have flunkeys about the place these days?'

The problem was that the tables this determined woman wanted moved were heavily laden with food – the buffet lunch which the press party had begun to eye with sharpening pangs of hunger.

'Hardly,' smiled Mennith

'Don't you think,' smiled the National Trust expert, 'we could leave things as they are?'

'Baloney!' exploded the lone photographer, looking as if she was prepared to lift the tables herself and throw them out of the window onto the lawn. 'Aren't we here to do a job?'

Malibu heard a whisper running among the photographers all around her: 'It's Neri Corinthian....yes, *the* Neri Corinthian.'

'And who *is* she?' she whispered back with the innocence of youth.

The stupefied faces told her it was something she shouldn't have needed to ask. But what the hell? As if there weren't plenty of things she could tell them! Malibu didn't know what embarrassment was.

'Come right here,' Neri commanded, 'and take a look at what I can see.' She waited until Lord Mennith and the National Trust woman had obeyed. 'You see this shot – the oak pannelling, the bay window and the drapes, the view out past that fountain to the trees in the distance?'

They shrugged their shoulders.

'Damn it, take a look into the blasted camera? It's a great shot, ruined by those plates of ham and the bowls of fruit. I want them *out.*'

She swung round on her fellow professionals: 'Well, guys. Am I nuts or is there a picture?'

There was a picture. Of course there was. Whether it justified over-turning Lord Mennith's luncheon arrangements was a moot point, but they could all see what she was driving at.

'Lost our frigging tongues, have we?' Neri cackled in disbelief. 'What can the lord of the manor do to the peasantry these days, for Chrissakes?'

This particular lord was totally perplexed. He simply didn't know which way to jump.

'It's a scrumptious view!'

Malibu had peered through Neri's viewfinder, but she would have made her own characteristic contribution to the debate in any case. She was totally bowled over by the older woman's pzazz. So this was what it meant to have a good time at work! You called the shots. You dominated the scene.

'I'd like to take the picture, too. Pleeeease!'

It was her infectious enthusiasm which won the day. The other photographers began to mutter that, yes, it was indeed a bloody clever composition, artfully combining the interior and exterior. And before anyone realised it was happening, Lord Mennith had made deft signals and members of his staff were moving the food and rearranging the tables.

Neri smiled at Malibu: 'Thanks, little sprog,' she said. 'We've got to keep these grandees on their toes.'

She was here as part of a much larger project. The Royal Institute of British Architects had decided to commission a sumptuous photographic dossier of the nation's buildings ancient and modern, and Darl Pannick had acted as midwife. No problem: the RIBA were paying good money and Neri Corinthian was the best. It had been easy to arrange.

It was typical of the woman that she'd thrown herself into her work the moment she arrived in England. Of course the real purpose of coming was to see her sister, but Neri reasoned (if that wasn't too strong a word) that she'd probably be staying here for a good three months, so what was the hurry? She felt the same about Darl Pannick. That had been a great experience in Rio, and they might just recreate it – but not yet.

When she was tipped off about the Ryall Park press day it seemed too good an opportunity to miss. As long, natch, as she could shoot the pictures on her own terms.

'Do you mind,' Malibu asked, 'if I watch how you do it?'

Neri guffawed: 'Be my guest, sprog. Then you can tell *me*. It's pure instinct.'

Malibu knew that it wasn't, not most of it. She trailed in Neri's wake as her new heroine ransacked the house and grounds for good shots. They got on famously, the two of them. Neri made outlandish statements which had Malibu rippling with pleasure. Malibu flitted and hovered like a flimsy butterfly, delighting the ebullient Neri who rejoiced to discover a kindred spirit – free, lively and unpredictable.

'In this dining room,' Lord Mennith was intoning gravely, 'my great grandfather entertained Victorian notables such as Gladstone, Robert Browning and Isambard Kingdom Brunel . . . '

'By playing the ukele in his pyjamas,' Malibu whispered.

'While smoking a cabbage stump,' Neri threw in, 'and riding an ostrich.'

They were bad for each other, really. They encouraged the worst in each other. They both fell about laughing, until everyone else was affected and nobody could take the noble lord seriously again. The National Trust lady wasn't at all pleased.

'Perhaps it's time for lunch,' Lord Mennith suggested.

But Malibu surprised herself. Much as she enjoyed the fun, the jokes, the larks, she discovered that she was drawn time and again to the techniques of photography which Neri Corinthian was employing. She'd watched Rudi Kazinsky closely over the weeks, but all photographers are individuals with their own methods. She found it fascinating to see how Neri solved problems of light and composition and texture.

'You been doing this long, sprog?' Neri asked, as they fitted lenses for a shot across a valley.

'Ages!' Malibu said. 'Over a month.'

Neri laughed: 'Well, you're doing okay, kid. You've got the makings.'

Malibu couldn't remember ever feeling as proud in all her life.

When it was all over the two became separated in the melee of farewells and the handing out of press packs. Malibu shrugged and set off down the drive, but she had only gone a hundred yards when a hired Ford estate car skidded to a halt on the gravel.

'How'd you get here?' Neri asked.

'Walked.'

'*Walked*, for God's sake?'

'From the station, anyway. I'm going back to London.'

'Jump in, sprog. I need the ballast.'

So they had the journey together, too – a journey made longer by the fact that Neri was driving from memory and that Malibu had spent too long away at her boarding school to know the south east of England any better than the northern territory of Australia. It didn't seem to matter.

'I know Rudi Kazinsky,' Neri said, when she heard who Malibu worked for. 'I must look him up.'

Neri seemed to know everybody. For once in her short life Malibu had found someone who talked even more insistently and more vivaciously than she did, and she sat back and enjoyed story after story. What she wouldn't give to travel the world as this woman had done! She reaffirmed the vow she'd made every day for the last month, that she was definitely going to become a photographer.

Become one? Oh, wonder: she *was* one!

They eventually hit the London traffic just as the rush hour was building up. Neri swerved in and out of the lanes of traffic New York-style, which would have worked, they agreed, if she'd known where she wanted to go. As it was, they occasionally recognised a name on a sign which seemed familiar, but it invariably led them in what even they realised was the wrong direction.

'Bayswater,' Neri recited. 'Hey – *Bayswater!*'

'You know it.'

'That's where my kid sister lives,' Neri enthused. 'Here, hold the wheel.'

As Malibu struggled to keep them on the road, Neri hunted in her bag and eventually fished out an address book.

'Yep! Got it. Pull over and we'll ask the broad with the umbrella.'

'I can't drive.'

'This was your big chance to learn, sproglet,' Neri bellowed, taking the wheel. 'You blew it.'

They asked directions several times and seemed to go round the same circuit over and over again before pulling up outside a handsome Georgian terrace.

'Do you recognise it?' Malibu asked.

'You joking? I don't expect to recognise my own *sister*. It's seventeen goddam years since I set eyes on her. You're witnessing something akin to Columbus meeting the New World.'

'I feel privileged,' Malibu giggled, not for a moment questioning whether she ought to be involved in such a momentous event. After all, it could be a lot of fun.

Neri pressed the button and waited. There was no good reason why Calla should be home at this time. She was a working woman and a successful one. Neri knew what that meant. In her case it meant she was seldom in her own country, let alone her own home.

'Hello,' came a faint voice on the intercom.

'Is this Calla Marchant?'

Upstairs, in her working area, Calla was at the computer putting the finishing touches to a blueprint, and she spoke almost absent-mindedly.

'Speaking. Who's that?'

There was a brief pause, and then a loud, almost raucous voice burst into the room: 'Hi, little sis! Think big and think wild!'

25

A hundred miles away, in the darkened bedroom of her Oxfordshire manor house, Sarah Andover lay dying. She felt peeved, rather than anguished or terrified. A month before she had been unaware of anything but the slightest inconsistencies in her bodily functions, yet now she had a matter of weeks left to live. She was peeved that the cancer had left her so little time to prepare, and she was peeved that it should have struck her so young. Why should older friends of hers seem in the first flush of their so-called Third Age, with many fruitful years still to come?

There was a knock on the door and Carrie, her maid, stepped inside. Sarah looked at her silhouette against the light from the passageway. No, surely she herself was the silhouette, she thought – something blank, one-dimensional and about to be extinguished.

'Master Patrick's here, ma'am.'

The words echoed in the room. How Victorian they sounded! Sarah realised that time had, indeed, stood still these past years. Her money had bought her whatever she wanted, and one thing she'd wanted had been these age-old certainties. She had created, or maintained, a life in which servants catered for her every need while she enjoyed those finer things she had always appreciated, spiritual things like music and painting.

And what good were they now? she asked herself. What solace did they give? None at all. She was almost ready to die.

'Send him in,' she ordered, her voice still strong enough to be heard across the room. 'Jason's not here yet?'

'Not yet, ma'am. Would you like a light?'

'Just the lamp by the bed here, Carrie, if you please. My eyes can't take more.'

'Very good, ma'am.' She switched on the lamp, bobbed her head and retreated from the room.

She was too young to die, Sarah thought, but she had nevertheless lived so very long. Memories had flooded into her brain these last few days – memories of people, of events, of feelings. Had all of that happened to her? And to what end? Alas, she had no faith. It seemed to her that all of this experience was being wrapped up in a tight parcel in order to be delivered to a distant address where nobody lived.

Or it was like a rubber ball which was about to bounce away from everyone and disappear down a deep, dark well.

Or it was a tangle of fluff, with colourful but useless bits of this and that stuck to it, which was about to be sucked into the gaping, black nozzle of a relentless vacuum cleaner.

'Mother?'

How long had he been standing there? Perhaps it was several years, her fanciful mind imagined. Since Patrick hadn't really changed since he was a careering, powerful, dominating eight-year-old, time was immaterial.

'Always the same,' she said, noting the puzzlement on his face. 'I never did understand you, Patrick.'

But he didn't understand his mother, either. All he knew was that she'd summoned him here to arrange family business before she died. He'd arrived expecting a sensible discussion, and he felt confused by her attitude. Perhaps her mind was wandering, he thought.

'How are you, mother?'

She bared her teeth in a tired smile: 'You were never any good at small talk, Patrick. It was always an ordeal for you, wasn't it?'

'I could never see the point of it, mother. I still can't.'

'But your father could manage it, however much of the driving businessman he was. He knew how to talk to people. That's funny, isn't it?'

'Is it?'

Patrick felt himself growing restless. He didn't need this vacuous nattering. On the other hand, he knew that it had to be endured if business matters were to go according to plan. What irritated him especially was the scarcely veiled criticism. Other people spoke of him in the same breath as his father, and he was proud of that, but his mother had always given him the impression that he fell far short of the ideal. As far as she was concerned, he had the worst attributes of Robert and lacked the best.

'I wish we had known each other better, Patrick.'

'It's rather late for that, mother.' No, that was too blunt. He felt taken off guard. This wasn't a situation he was used to. 'But I think so, too.'

'You do?'

'Of course. I know you've always favoured Jason.'

Christ, he thought, that was another wrong thing to say. Why did it come out like that? It was true, but why did he need to say it? It wasn't as if it mattered to him. He despised Jason and thought his mother a weak and useless woman. All right, he despised his mother, too.

Sarah closed her eyes: 'You see,' she said, 'Jason and I always understood each other without needing to speak. We did speak, of course, but we didn't need to. Whereas you and I never really spoke, although we desperately needed to.

'That's funny, too, don't you think?'

Not at all funny, he thought. He had never felt this desperation. As far as he was concerned, the less contact he had with his mother, the better.

These last few years he had visited her dutifully once a month, chiefly prompted by his wife, but he had never enjoyed a single minute in her company. She was an irrelevance.

He could hear a clock ticking. The weeks would soon pass, he comforted himself. There'd be very little more of this agony, and then she would have gone, leaving behind a dull memory, considerable savings and a very large block of shares in Andover International.

'Come closer,' she said. 'Sit on the chair, Patrick.'

He obeyed. It wouldn't hurt to do every damn thing she wanted for the short time that remained, to agree to every last thing she said. That's what he would try to do. He sat on the chair, but upright, unyielding.

'Of course,' the voice came more quietly now, 'it's too late for that. And I blame myself for it, Patrick, as much as you. I'm not saying this to hurt.'

'It doesn't hurt, mother.'

It didn't. Nothing had ever hurt Patrick. He was inviolable. You could make him angry, but you couldn't find any softness which might be damaged.

'What I would like, before I go, is to see you and Jason reconciled. You're brothers. You should behave like brothers.'

'Which means what, exactly?'

'Do I need to tell you how brothers should behave to one another, Patrick?' she asked. 'Yes,' she reflected in a weary voice, 'I suppose I do. Perhaps it's too late for that as well.'

There was a silence between them for a long time. Patrick, hearing her slow breathing, thought that she had fallen asleep.

'Mother . . . ' he said softly.

'Yes?'

'I'm concerned about the handling of the family finances after you've gone. That's what I thought we would talk about. I thought that was why you'd asked to see me.' She said nothing. 'Isn't that right?'

The clock seemed to get louder, but that was only because he was waiting for his mother to speak. He found himself counting the seconds as they ticked. Why did there have to be this fuss? he thought angrily. Let them sort out the money together and then, if she was going to die, let her die quickly. She opened her eyes.

'Did anything but money ever matter to you, Patrick?'

To think that I'm the son of this woman, he groaned inwardly. To think I was brought into the world by a woman with so little grasp of reality. How in God's name had his father put up with her fragility, all that 'fineness', her tiresome immersion in the world of the arts?

'It's necessary, mother,' he said firmly, 'for someone to look after the basic, essential things like business and finance. Who else could have done it after father died? Would you really trust Jason with a penny?'

'He's not a child.'

Patrick remembered the same remark being made by Calla all those years ago. His reply would have been the same now, but for the need to watch his tongue.

'Perhaps it's best that we don't talk about Jason,' he suggested.

'That's your usual way with something uncomfortable,' she said in a flat voice. 'Don't mention it. Pretend that it doesn't exist. You've never spoken a useful word to me in all your life.'

'I don't think that's fair, mother.'

Sarah lay still, trying to calm herself. Her heart was beating rapidly because of the anger she felt. And the anger derived in part from frustration. She knew that there was truth in what her younger son was saying, and she knew that she owed it to the memory of her late husband to use his money wisely. Even on her death bed she found it impossible to have the last word. Robert must have his will.

'Tell me then,' she said slowly. 'What do you propose?'

'I propose?'

She raised a stick-like arm as if to strike him with it: 'Don't play the innocent with me, Patrick!' she all but screamed. 'Don't pretend that you haven't worked everything out to the last decimal point. I know you.'

That was the one thing she did know about him. What he was feeling at any time she hadn't a clue, but she never had any doubt that his brain was calculating every second of the day.

'Well, I've given it some thought, mother, of course I have. But it's difficult for me to explain what I think is best for the family. It can't help but sound as if I'm motivated by self-interest.'

'Surely not,' spoke those lips in the gloom. The words were uttered quietly, but it was impossible to avoid their sarcasm. They stung him to the quick.

'If you leave money to Jason,' he said with a sudden boldness, 'it will be thrown away. I don't have to tell you what he does with it. That money will be utterly wasted instead of helping to build up the Andover estate for the long-term future of our family.'

'Your sons,' Sarah said.

'Your grandchildren, mother. All that will be left of the Andovers. You don't suppose that Jason is ever going to make a contribution in that field. Or any, come to that.'

'In the arts, perhaps,' Sarah said, giving wan voice to an old hope of hers.

'He's impractical in everything,' Patrick insisted. 'I don't know what paintings he's got left, but I do know he's never bought with an eye on the market. He's irresponsible. I realise this is painful to you, mother, but it would be an act of folly to leave more than a token amount of cash in Jason's hands. I'm sure father would have seen it that way.'

That's right, she thought, wheel the big cannon onto the field of battle. What Robert would have wanted. Let me sink into death as ineffectual as I have been all my life. Hand it all to Patrick: he'll look after it as his father would have done.

'He's my son, too,' she said with as much defiance as she could muster. She was feeling very weak.

'I'm not suggesting he has nothing,' Patrick protested, as if he'd been grossly misunderstood. 'I'm not being hard, mother, but practical. It's what is best for everyone, Jason included. He's not safe with large amounts of money in his pockets. He has expensive habits, and they're dangerous.'

Poor Jason, Sarah thought. Once she'd gone there would be nobody left to speak up for him. Nobody to understand him. He'd inherited from her an appreciation of the finer things of life, but she felt that she'd left him with a curse which far outweighed it – an inability to cope with the Patricks of the world. Why did Life divide its spoils so unevenly, so unfairly? No wonder a dying woman felt peeved and almost ready to go.

'I've brought something with me, mother,' Patrick said, leaning close for the first time. She looked and saw only a dark shadow in his hand. 'It's a document which you ought to discuss with your solicitor. He'll make everything clear to you.'

'He knows about it?'

'In broad terms, yes. I thought it best to outline my proposals to him, knowing that it's not really your strong point.' He put the papers on table by the bed. 'I hope you agree it's for the best, mother, but I've asked him to see you tomorrow.'

Sarah lay still in the silence. There were times when she didn't even hear the clock. That was of this world, and there were moments when she sank into a numb limbo which was half way towards the next, wherever that was. Probably, she thought, it was mere oblivion.

'Good. It should be sorted out.'

'I hoped you'd see it that way, mother. You can rest assured that my proposals assure the future of the family's investments.'

Sarah felt her body shuddering: 'Tell me what it means,' she said. 'What are you going to do with my money?'

He paused. How could you explain sound financial practice to such an innocent? It was like defending meat-eating to St Francis of Assissi.

'In short, mother, Jason will have regular payments from a small but sufficient trust fund which I will help to manage. A substantial part of the estate goes to a trust fund for your grandchildren, assuring our family's financial future. The rest comes to me to manage for the immediate enhancement of our position.'

'Thank you, Patrick.'

'You approve, mother?'

'I'm sure it's what your father would have wished.'

He breathed deeply. It might have been more difficult, all things considered. Who knew what the prospect of death might have done to her reasoning? But he'd counted on the influence of his late father. He could almost feel Robert's hand on his shoulder, congratulating him. Almost, but that would be a sentimental thing to feel, so he didn't.

'It's for the best, mother.'

They heard voices outside the door. Carrie knocked and put her head round it: 'Master Jason's arrived, ma'am.'

'Bring him to me,' Sarah said. She had a gentle smile on her face. 'Patrick is leaving.'

'Perhaps I should stay,' suggested Patrick.

'No!' She tried to raise herself in the bed. 'Go now, Patrick.'

He rose, thought about forming a suitable farewell speech, but finally almost stumbled from the room in his awkward haste to leave. He passed Jason in the passage, the first time the brothers had met in months.

'I'll wait for you,' Patrick said. 'We have to talk.'

It took Jason a few seconds to adjust to the darkness of the room. He saw his mother only as a shape, her face a black shadow on the pillow. He bent low over her and kissed her forehead. She grasped his hands and held them tightly to her.

'My boy,' she said.

'You're in pain, mother?'

'No. Very little. Not now.'

He sat on the bed, withdrawing one of his hands to feel her forehead. It was cool. She wouldn't, he thought, die in an agony of pain and sweat but would gradually withdraw. Decorously, as she had lived.

'I'm sorry to have been so often away,' he said. 'There was something I had to do.'

'And was it useful?' she queried, her eyes searching his in the semi-darkness.

They could talk. And, although Jason had never explained the worst of his drug addiction to her, they had shared enough for her to understand. He never felt judged by his mother.

'Yes,' he said. 'I've learned things.'

It was as she had told Patrick. Because they could talk, they often didn't need to. Now she lay in the bed in a state of great calm, while Jason stroked her forehead and thought his thoughts.

He was thinking of his mother's life, and feeling an old guilt over failing to champion her cause over the years. He had, after all, shared the same passions. They were the same kind of person. He remembered how, as children, he and Patrick had always assumed that their father's will would triumph over their mother's. There had been no fight involved: it had just happened that way. Why hadn't he resisted that? Presumably because he was too busy with his young man's energetic activities, his music, his cricket, his parties. He regretted it now.

'What will you do?' she asked him simply.

He was rather taken aback: 'When you've gone, you mean?' She nodded, slowly. Yes, that was what she meant. 'I'm not a child, mother,' he said.

She laughed, and because she hadn't the strength to control it, she shook and cackled until the fit subsided.

'No,' she said at last. 'You're not a child, Jason. But you're not a man like Patrick, are you?'

'No, I'm not.'

'Thank God!'

She said it vehemently, and he felt the pressure of her fingers on his again. Because she didn't release her grip, he knew there was something she wanted to say to him. And because it took her a long time to find the words, he knew it must be something that mattered a great deal to her.

'Jason.' She spoke in little more than a whisper. 'I want you to tell me something. Will you promise?'

'Promise?'

'To tell me the truth. It's very important.'

'Of course, mother.' He moved closer and put an arm behind her head, holding her. 'What is it?'

'A long time ago,' she said, still finding it difficult. 'When Daddy died.'

'Yes, mother.'

'I want to know what happened, Jason. I've never really known. I couldn't ask at the time, and then it was too late. Please tell me.'

'What can I tell you? There was the accident . . . '

'Of course, yes.' She spoke in faint little snatches, somehow finding renewed bursts of energy. 'But you know, Jason, I was watching the race through binoculars. You were a long way off, but I could see you in the glasses.'

'And?' he breathed.

'Something happened, didn't it – after that other boat exploded, but just before the crash? I had the *Ace* in the binoculars. You and Patrick seemed to be struggling together. Fighting?'

Jason closed his eyes. It was all there before him again – his father's cry of alarm, the manic look in Patrick's eyes, his own desperate attempt to force his brother to release the throttle. Then he saw himself in the water with his father's body. He opened his eyes, but the vision wouldn't go away.

'What happened, Jason?'

'It was so confused, mother. And it was so long ago.'

'Tell me!'

It would have been so easy to tell, to reveal that the very male aggressiveness of the Andovers, that craving for domination passed down from Robert to Patrick, had destroyed the head of the family in one fit of madness. But Jason wasn't even tempted. To have told the truth about his brother would have felt somehow unclean, dishonourable. He loathed everything Patrick stood for, but that was no excuse for the telling of tales, however terrible.

More than that, he knew that his mother wanted not to believe what she had seen. She had dared to ask because she needed to know, but the knowledge would be more than she could bear.

'It was incredibly choppy out there that day,' he said slowly, taking care with every word. 'When the Italian boat capsized it was utter chaos. A great spout of water shot into the air. You saw that?'

'Yes. Go on.'

'I think father must have tried to swerve to one side, though it was impossible for him to see clearly through the spray. All I remember is that I was suddenly thrown across the *Ace* with tremendous force. I careered into Patrick and we might both have gone into the water if it wasn't for his strength. He managed to hold on and push me upright again. Seconds later we hit the wreckage of the other boat.'

Sarah sighed: 'That's exactly how it was?'

'Just like that, mother. Don't torment yourself about it.'

They sat close together for some minutes, saying nothing. Jason remembered happy days in this old house, loud, boyish games out in the grounds. Sarah, her favourite son's hands in hers, felt for a blessed moment that the world was not spinning away from her.

'Do you know,' she asked at last in a clear and level voice, 'what Patrick wants me to do?'

Jason smiled: 'I think I could guess,' he said.

'He wants me to leave everything to him and his sons. Practically everything. A mere token amount, as he calls it, to you.'

'For sound financial reasons, I'm sure,' Jason said. 'The money means much more to him, mother. It's his natural environment, like water for a fish.'

'He says it's what your father would have wanted.'

'Isn't it?'

'Yes, Jason, it probably is.' She was gazing at the shadowed ceiling with a dreamy expression on her face. 'I can see him now, can't you? I imagine your father pacing the room to explain the arrangements he's decided on – you know that restless wagging of his hands as he makes one suggestion after another. Dear Daddy! So imaginative at the same time as he's absolutely, almost ruthlessly practical. So unlike Patrick in that respect.'

'And what's he saying, mother?'

'Ah, it's all rather above my head, Jason,' she smiled. 'But I'm afraid that it's as we expected. Patrick knows best what to do with the money.'

They fell to silence again. Jason found that he didn't really care about what he'd always ironically thought of as 'the family fortune'. He hadn't come here thinking about it, and he appreciated the logic of Patrick's argument as much as his mother did.

Outside, in the darkness of early evening, a male pheasant made its rusty squawk. There was a light pattering of rain on the window panes. Jason hadn't felt such an intimacy with his mother since he was a child – perhaps in this very room when he had snuggled against her, warm and secure, after waking from a frightening dream.

'I shan't even insist that you spend it wisely,' Sarah said.

'Mother?'

'Your half share.'

He brought his face closer to hers. No, there was no delirium. What he saw was an expression of utter determination.

'All my life,' Sarah said quietly, 'I have been compliant. All my life I have accepted that other people's opinions should come before my own. I was trained that way. I was a nice girl, a good girl, and then I became a nice woman, too, and a good wife. People were proud of me.

'It was all too easy, you see. I let them take away the responsibility for my life. They set the rules. All I had to do was obey them and they'd give me lovely rewards. Like a performing parrot content with cashew nuts. Of course I was happy. I thought I was happy.

'But I've been lying here for days and nights, Jason, thinking about my life, and one question has kept returning to me, like a horrible, insistent echo. *Was* it mine? What, really, have I had to do with it? What control have I had over it? I gave that up before I even had it.'

Jason ran a finger down her cheek: 'Mother,' he whispered, tears in his eyes.

'Yes,' she said. 'Mother. Wife.' She reached out a frail hand and stroked his hair. 'They were good roles to play, but where was Sarah? Who was Sarah?

'Sarah loved music, but music was sentimental. Sarah loved art, but she made a huge mistake. She loved beauty rather than the money paintings could make. Sarah always loved things which didn't really matter. She didn't have anything to offer to the world except obedience. She never existed in her own right.

'Do you know, Jason – I think Sarah was a ghost.'

There was nothing he could say. He wrapped her in his arms and rocked her gently, his lips caressing her brow.

'But here I am,' she said, 'still alive, if only just. And at the very end I'm *not* a ghost.'

'You're real to me,' Jason murmured.

'I'm real to myself, that's what matters. I shall make the decisions about myself and what is mine. I know where I want that money to go. If it wasn't for my grandchildren I'd leave every penny to you, Jason.'

'That might not be wise,' he smiled.

'Perhaps that would be a good reason for doing it,' she countered.

'And the family's destiny?'

'Ha! I believe the real Sarah cares as little for that as you do. My mistake was to mix up my love for your father with his personal ambitions. They were his own affair. Let them remain so. I shall be seeing my solicitor tomorrow, thanks to Patrick. And I don't think Patrick will be very pleased by what happens.'

'Mother?'

'Patrick has plenty of money. He has his own shares in Andover International and he's always fixing some deal or other. He doesn't need any more. He won't get anything from me. Not a penny.'

'Are you sure that's quite fair?' Jason asked softly.

'Dear gentle, honest, predictable Jason! Is it fair? Has any of this been fair, I ask you? I don't care about being fair on anyone else's terms. Not any more. I've got a bundle of shares worth a lot of money and I've decided where it's going. Half to my grandsons and half to you.'

Jason frowned: 'I think you're right to suspect that Patrick won't be very pleased.'

'I sincerely hope not,' Sarah replied. 'I just pray I live long enough to witness his rage.'

The release of so many pent-up thoughts and feelings had wearied her. She sank back into the pillows and closed her eyes, one hand still in his. She was breathing deeply and comfortably and he stayed with her until she was soundly asleep.

Poor mother, he thought. Even her one last declaration of independence was only a reaction to what other people wanted. It was an act of defiance rather than a spontaneous expression of her own individuality. Yes, she wanted Jason to enjoy her money rather as she would have done, but he couldn't help thinking that her desire to thwart Patrick was an even more powerful motive. He looked down at her tired face, serene in sleep, and wished that the true Sarah could set out on her life all over again, being only Sarah. What might the fresh and eager young woman not achieve! Then he thought of his own tarnished life, and wondered whether new beginnings were possible.

He had left his mother to Carrie's care and was on his way to the front door when Patrick hailed him from the drawing room.

'You're still here?' Jason asked, stepping inside.

'Didn't I say I'd wait?' his brother replied aggressively. He rose from his armchair and came forward. 'What's been happening?'

'I don't understand.'

'Did she tell you what's been decided? I talked family finance with her.'

'Mother did mention it,' Jason replied, 'but the money side really isn't important to me.'

'No, it isn't, is it?' Patrick snarled at him, prodding with a finger which didn't quite meet Jason's chest. 'And you're mighty proud of that, aren't you? You've always looked down on father and me for the fact that we could make money work. While all you've done is spend it on stuff I'd be ashamed even to recognise.'

'That's a fair comment,' Jason said.

'Of course it's a bloody fair comment! You're a disgrace to the family, and you deserve all you get. Or don't get.'

'Have you been drinking?' Jason asked. He knew the simple answer, because he could see a glass and a bottle of scotch two-thirds consumed. But he was wondering whether his brother had started with a full bottle. His manner was oppressively bullying.

'Don't start moralising with me,' Patrick commanded, and this time his jabbing finger did make contact. 'I just want to know what she told you.'

Jason retreated and sat on the arm of a chair: 'Confidentiality, little brother,' he said, feeling strangely calm. 'You've heard of that concept?'

'Tell me, damn you!'

'You'll find out soon enough. Mother's seeing her solicitor tomorrow.'

'And you know what she's telling him?'

'I've a fairly good idea, yes. And I understand that you've already made a detailed presentation. I think that's the word you use, isn't it?'

Patrick seemed to interpret this remark in a way which pleased him, because he backed off and poured himself another scotch.

'It's for the best,' he said. 'You wouldn't know what to do with money if you had it.'

Jason strolled to the french windows and pulled back the heavy curtains. The light spilled onto the patio his father had built many years before. Further out there were dark shapes which were the trees and the outbuildings he knew so well.

'There is one piece of business I'd like to do with you, Patrick,' he said.

'What's that?'

'I'd like to buy back my share in Calla Marchant Practice.'

There was a long silence during which Jason could feel the violence of his brother's emotions. There was anger, malice, outrage in the air. He felt, for a moment, physically afraid. Patrick strode across the room, put a hand on his shoulder and swung him round.

'You can't afford it!'

'Perhaps I can,' Jason replied as calmly as he knew how.

'How? Where's the money coming from?'

'If I have it,' Jason asked, 'will you sell?'

'Like fuck I will!'

Patrick seized him by the lapels of his jacket and shook him hard. He seemed to have superhuman strength. Jason tried to resist but felt himself jolted against the wall.

'I'll go in and ask her what happened,' Patrick snarled in his ear.

'Not a very bright idea,' Jason managed, despite the pain he felt. 'Do you think?'

They stood struggling for some seconds, Jason trying to release the grip of those powerful fingers, his brother rocking him backwards and forwards against the wall. Then Patrick let go and, all in the same movement, brought a fist crashing against his jaw. He crumpled.

'Bastard!' he heard Patrick shout.

The front door slammed. An engine was sparked to life. A car, accelerating fast, swept past and out along the drive towards the main road.

27

Now the time had come, she didn't want to go. Now the time had come, even Roland McIvrey seemed like a close friend to Fern Willoughby. The spartan room at Stoke Mandeville where she had lain looking at the ceiling for so many weeks seemed safe and unthreatening. She wanted to stay.

'Are you sure I'm ready to go home, Mr McIvrey?'

She stood at the window, resting one hand on the sill for support. It was no great view. The tarmac car park was nothing like the rolling acres of Willoughby Hall. But it was the car park Harry had driven into almost every day since she had arrived months ago. And just now it seemed his Duchess had no desire for the Capability Brown landscaped gardens of her country home.

'You're telling me you'd rather stay here? Grown accustomed to our cuisine, have you?'

Roland McIvrey's voice was its usual sarcastic self, but his eyes were fixed very keenly on his patient. Spinal injuries meant long-term care and over several months you got to know people. Sometimes you even, whatever fellow professionals in other fields might feel, became their friend.

And McIvrey had grown to like and admire Fern Willoughby. She'd had the silver spoon taken out of her mouth rather roughly that day her back had been broken while hunting. It wasn't, if truth be told, the sort of accident McIvrey had much sympathy for: hunting was scarcely an essential pursuit, after all. But, God, she had guts! He'd fully expected a whingeing, complaining county type on his hands, prepared to settle into the most sophisticated wheelchair money could buy – and into a life of being waited on hand and foot. That type didn't take kindly to orders. They didn't like hospital routine. Nobody had told them when to get up since boarding school, and six am was rather too soon after their usual bedtime.

As for the indignity of physiotherapy, the sheer repetitive sweat of forcing a broken body to gain strength bit by painful bit, he'd rather expected Fern to lose her temper with both him and the exercises.

Instead, he found he had a fighter on his hands, a fighter who was prepared to give as good as she got. And, with McIvrey, that meant being tough. Some of his medicine was nasty. She had hauled herself round the physio room long after he'd told her to go back to her room. She'd worked so hard in the treatment pool he'd been frightened she would pass out in the water. When both those places were shut, he'd found her stretching and bending in her own room, striving for the agonisingly slow responses from her legs which told her, however painfully, that she was getting better.

And he'd watched her with her husband. There was something not quite right about that relationship, he'd guessed. A case of a very stiff upper lip indeed on the Duke's part. And maybe something a little wayward on hers? He wasn't sure, but whatever the stumbling block was, he sensed that it wasn't the whole story. He sensed it because he'd sat by Fern Willoughby's bed at night and heard her say her husband's name again and again during the quieter periods when she wasn't reliving the horror of her last ride.

And he'd seen her face as she stood up for the first time – stood up, surely, because her husband was in the doorway. Roland McIvrey wasn't given to sentiment. What sober Scot is? But he hoped the Willoughby marriage wasn't quite a hospital case yet.

So why didn't his star patient want to go back home?

'What's all this about Fern?'

'I just don't know if I'm ready.'

'Who's the doctor round here? I know you're ready. If you think we can keep you tucked up in a comfortable bed just because you're not sure, you're wrong. Right now, there's some idiot on a motor-bike doing somersaults over three lanes of merciless traffic about to break his back on the tarmac. If he's lucky. And when he comes down, he's going to want your bed, Fern. Care to argue with him?'

The Duchess turned from the window and slowly made her way to the bed. Her pale face showed the strain of the last few months, but the green eyes were as startling as ever. And, McIvrey realised, they were wet.

What the hell could it be?

'Don't tell me his Grace is a wife-beater?' he joked.

The change of tone worked. Fern half-laughed through her tears: 'It's the bloody horses.'

'Horses?'

'I don't want to see them. I can't bear it. What can I do with them, now? I'm not a rider any longer, am I?' She paused, looking at McIvrey, her face calm again. 'So what am I?'

The surgeon ran his hands through his wiry, thinning hair. This was a facer, to be sure. He was no psychologist. Fern had done so well physically, succeeding where many would have given up, that he had rather taken her mental strength for granted.

He remembered with a wince the time he'd told her she would never hunt again. Perhaps that had been rather brutal. He had caught a look of black despair in her eyes. It had been true, though. Oh, some gentle hacking across the countryside would be harmless and probably good exercise. But competitive jumping and hunting was right out. The Duke could save a chunk of estate funds on the stables, no doubt about that.

Fern was now quite composed. She didn't repeat her question. But it hung, unanswered, in the disinfected hospital air: What am I?

'You're Fern Willoughby. Isn't that enough?' In desperation, McIvrey risked a sentimental addition: 'I'm sure it's enough for your husband.'

Fern stared blankly at him: 'I've been bloody awful to my husband.'

'Fern, everyone with a life-changing injury begins to see himself differently. Or herself. Look, you're more than your horses. You're more than the way you've behaved in the past, however that might have been. You put in a hell of a lot of effort to get better. In a few months, you'll realise why you did it. You'll know it was worthwhile.'

A car pulled up under the window. It was Willoughby's, come to take Fern home.

'Where's your case?'

'Oh, God. I'm not packed.'

'Stay put. I'll do it. I'm the fastest packer you ever saw. I want to make sure you're really going, young woman.'

McIvrey's way with a suitcase was simple. He put it on the floor and simply dropped the contents of the drawers into it. La Perla lingerie followed Ralph Lauren sweaters into a hopeless jumble. Books were heaped on top.

Fern had never seen anything like it. She sat on the edge of the bed and laughed: 'You'd never get a job at Willoughby Hall!'

Harry Willoughy paused in the doorway, pleased to see his wife so happy. He kissed her lightly and shook hands with McIvrey.

'Ready for the off?'

'Yes. Mr McIvrey insists on kicking me out. And to make sure I go, he's doing my packing.'

The Duke raised an eyebrow as McIvrey finally slammed the suitcase lid and carried it, frills and straps spilling over the sides, out to the car.

Rather more tenderly, McIvrey helped the Duchess into the passenger seat.

'Off with you! Take care!' Then the surgeon found himself being sentimental again. 'Of each other,' he added for his own ears only.

● ● ●

It was strange to be out of hospital, alone with her husband on a journey which was far more than a return home. It was the start of a new life. And Fern rather dreaded it.

But Willoughby was quite simply elated to have her back. His joy was obvious. As he drove along, he would shift in his seat to sneak proud glances at her. And once (Fern could scarcely believe it of her undemonstrative husband) he gently rested his hand on her thigh.

As mile after mile brought her nearer and nearer to Willoughby Hall, she tried to take her mind off her doubtful future by asking her husband for all the gossip on their friends and taking the chance to exercise her wicked tongue.

'How's Marion? Still broad of beam and short of tact? Has she driven you quite mad with concerned telephone calls? And how about young Buffy? Has he worked out quite why there's a queue of local maidens wanting to join the hunt? Or does he still thinking wedding tackle is something rugby players do?'

The Duke let her run on, mimicking local characters and asking for more news than she ever paused to receive. What a joy it was to have his Fern back! She was lightsome and frivolous, as she had been when they first married, before things started going wrong.

He resolved that they shouldn't go wrong again. He'd been giving some thought to how Fern might react to her changed lifestyle. McIvrey had sorted out the physical damage, but it would be up to him to cope with the rest.

How he wanted to look after her! If only he could be sure she would let him. What if she simply ran away? He was worried how she might react to the stables at Willoughby Hall. Horses were so much a part of the place, what with the hunt and Fern's eventing as well. If she were frightened of horses now, he wouldn't give a second thought to getting rid of the lot. If not, if she still wanted to be near them and to work with them, well, he had an idea . . .

His Charlesbury project had been a blessing during the long months that Fern had been in hospital. His visits to her had been almost daily, but it had been a relief to be able to think about something else. Now she was home, he was glad there was still some time before the judging. He wanted to spend it with his wife.

'Seamus has been quite in mourning for you,' he said, watching to see how she reacted to the mention of her groom.

'I wouldn't have thought it possible, but he looks more unkempt than ever. Whole coalmines under his finger nails and not a word for anyone except the horses.'

'I don't think I want to see the horses, Harry.' Fern was suddenly serious and quiet. 'Not yet.'

'Then you shan't, my darling. You'll do only what you want to do.'

'Whatever that might possibly be.'

Harry looked at her and he understood. She wasn't frightened of the horses but of the gap they left.

They swept into the long drive. The April sunshine highlighted the fresh spring green of the lawns and the trees. The white stone of the house gleamed in it. Fern took a deep breath. She was here, at her new life.

'Take my arm.'

As Harry helped her out of the car, a strange notion came into her head – that she was leaning on the one thing she could trust. It was a comforting notion. She walked up the great steps without glancing once at the stable block where she had spent so much of her time since her marriage.

That night Willoughby was restless, worried for his wife, who was sleeping in her room next door. He dozed fitfully, kept starting awake. Finally he got out of bed, walked quietly to the adjoining door and listened for her breathing. Hearing no sound, he crept in. By the light of the moon he could see that her bed was empty. It was two o'clock.

There was only one place she could be. Willoughby pulled on some clothes and made his way out of the house to the stable block.

Fern, with characteristic disregard for pomposity, kept her certificates and the press cuttings which charted her successful equestrian career in the tack room. She rarely looked at them herself, though Seamus read and re-read every word, pointing out the smallest inaccuracies in the coverage. But tonight, in only a silken dressing gown, Fern was sitting on the rough bench, reading them all.

It was a desperate search for herself among the cuttings and the commendations gathered in a life of equestrianism. She saw pictures of herself as a girl, astride a pony with a rosette in its bridle. She ran through articles in *Horse and Hound* from later days and she read, most recently of all, glowing reports in the national press.

Carefully and slowly, oblivious to the cold, she piled them neatly in date order and put them away in a drawer. She looked around at the tack, kept immaculate by the unkempt Seamus, hanging in line on the walls. Was this Fern? And the cuttings? Were they her?

'If so, it's goodbye Fern, because there's no more hunting, no more press cuttings.'

The cold room with its distinctive smell of leather and saddle soap held other memories for Fern too. She'd never found them painful before, but now she had to force herself to think about her infidelities. More than once she had romped in this very tack room while her own husband and stable staff were safely off the scene.

'Unbridled lust,' she said with a grim smile. All those romps, here and everywhere else, the other women's husbands, the visitors to

Willoughby Hall, everyone from the picture restorer from Sotheby's to the absurdly inexperienced curate – were they the real Fern? If it wasn't the horses and it wasn't the sex, what was left? She sat on the wooden bench, holding her head in her hands, and could think of nothing.

She hadn't seen or heard Harry Willoughby come in. She knew nothing until he stood before her and gathered her aching head to his chest, stroking her fair hair.

'It's all right,' he whispered, wrapping a warm coat round her huddled shoulders. 'Let's go inside.'

Walking at Fern's hesitant pace, they made their way across the darkened courtyard into the house, the Duke with his arm round his wife all the way.

'Christ, I'm sorry, Harry. I don't know what came over me. I just felt so confused and empty. I thought maybe I could sort things out if I went to the tack room . . . '

He silently squeezed her hand and led her through the darkened corridor and up the grand staircase. Helping her into the warmth of her bedroom, he settled her under the blankets. She gazed back at him, a bemused smile on her face.

'God, Harry, what have I done to deserve you?'

'Can't think, but I'm afraid you're stuck with me.'

'Now's your chance, you know. I can't run away and I'm probably going mad. You could lock me in the attic like Mrs Rochester and hire a governess to fall in love with.'

'No, I'm afraid not.'

'Servant problem? Shortage of governesses?'

'No lock on the attic.'

Fern laughed as he straightened her bedclothes and stooped to kiss her forehead. She was surprised to find she half wished he would stay with her in her room.

Over the last few years, she'd been the one to take the lead in sex matters. Not that Willoughby didn't want her – he wanted her badly, but he was too gentlemanly, too restrained, to force himself on her when he knew he was less than welcome. Fern, who had lost all sexual desire for him, nevertheless had enough affection to behave warmly every now and then, allowing him to stay if he lingered in her room.

Tonight, Willoughby was careful not to take her in his arms: 'I'll be next door if you get frightened, my darling,' was all he said. 'Just call.'

He didn't trust himself. He was frightened of this overwhelming desire he had to be with her every breathing moment. She was surely in too delicate a state, emotionally and physically. So he stroked her hair and kissed her forehead and left.

Fern slept soundly until a noise on the gravel outside made her glance at her bedside clock. It was almost 11 o'clock. She lay motionless for a time, thinking over her strange visit to the tack room the night before. She felt strangely calm and rested. She wondered where Harry might be and what he was doing.

Then she heard his voice under the window outside: 'It's a superb piece of work! Eventually of course we'll put it in the coach house, but first we'll let Fern take a look.'

'Shame we can't put a bloody great bow on it, eh?' came the instantly recognisable tones of the Hon Marion Mason-Fox.

Dear Harry, Fern thought, turning over on her side, might have spared me an early visit from the blessed Marion.

She longed to pull the blankets over her ears and pretend she hadn't heard her friend's hearty voice. But there was no point in trying to keep Marion at bay. She'd think nothing of whipping the blankets off a sick bed and ordering the patient out for exercise.

'The restoration seems impeccable.' It was Harry's voice again, in tones of admiration.

'Bloody good. Old Evans is a real craftsman you know. Deaf as an earless owl, at least when I try to talk to him, but a real craftsman.'

'Fern will love it. She has an eye for beautiful work.'

'And if she really takes to it, you'll get her a competition job?'

'The best I can find.'

Fern could stand it no longer. What the hell were they talking about? She sat up and slowly swung herself out of bed to peer from the window to the drive below.

'A carriage! Good grief! He's got me a barouche!'

The eighteenth century four-wheeled carriage gleamed in its black and green livery, with the Mercia coat of arms on the door. It was a lovely thing, from an age when morning exercise meant a horse-drawn drive round a London park or a Bath crescent.

Fern's back wouldn't allow her to fling up the sash window and shout her delight at her husband. Instead she waved madly, then retreated behind the curtains to get dressed.

There was a time when getting dressed in the mornings while in the country meant only one thing to Fern: riding clothes. Now she was rather at a loss to know what she should put on. Not that she had long to think about it. A sharp knock, followed by a door flung open wide, announced Marion.

'Come on! You must come and see, Fern dear. How are you? Have you seen what Harry's got you? Why aren't you dressed? It's past eleven o'clock. You can't lounge around just because you've been ill. It's a perfect beauty! Do you recognise it? No? I'm not surprised. Evans has done an incredible job on it. Now, here we are! Put this wool frock on and come downstairs for heaven's sake! I'll leave you to it. Nothing worse than fuss when you've been ill!'

The Duchess had scarcely said a word before Marion had dragged the simple magenta dress out of the wardrobe and left the room almost as noisily as she had come in. Fern stood laughing for a moment before trekking off for a shower. No wonder Roland McIvrey had always avoided her room while Marion was visiting.

Harry Willoughby had judged his wife correctly. He knew she would never ride competitively again, but he also knew that a life without horses would not be much of a life at all for his Duchess. Empty stables would be a constant reminder of what had been.

And Fern liked fine things. It was Fern who had gone right through the collections of china and lacquer work at the Hall, cataloguing. She had the sort of eye which could instantly tell the good quality from the poor. She also had the sort of tongue which would occasionally point it out, but he forgave her that as he forgave her everything else.

And of course, she liked to role-play. After all, hadn't he, in the tradition of the English aristocracy, married an actress? An elegant carriage she could learn to drive would certainly appeal to her. And Seamus could learn, too, so that she could be driven about, rather like something out of a Jane Austen novel.

The barouche had been mouldering in the stable block for decades, probably for generations. Its panelling was dull, its half-hood ripped, the suspension seemingly hopeless. But Marion, as kind-hearted as she was noisy, said she 'knew a little man', a saddle-maker by trade, who could restore it. The job had taken months. Harry had wanted it for his wife's homecoming yesterday, but today was just as good.

And driving was an equestrian sport, increasing in popularity since the Duke of Edinburgh had taken it up. Willoughby thought Fern might rather enjoy the chariot-race drama of it all, the costume and the whip-cracking. If she did, he'd fix her up with a team of horses and a newly-built coach. He felt there was nothing he wouldn't do for her.

Yes, she loved the idea, hugging the Duke of Mercia where he stood on his own ancestral gravel and kissing her thank yous.

'When Charlesbury is built,' she said, 'I shall drive you round for a triumphal tour!'

The Duke looked as pleased and embarrassed by her display of affection as if he had been a sixth-form boy kissed by a pretty cousin. Fern ran her fingers over the shiny doors, the smooth wheels of her barouche and kissed him again.

'You're feeling fond of me?' Harry asked in half-belief.

'Oh, I've *always* been fond of you, darling.' Was there was something which sounded like 'but only fond' in her words? The Duke couldn't tell.

Nor could Fern, who wandered off after breakfast for a stroll about the deer park she hadn't seen for months. She needed to be alone.

'Week after week of staring at that blasted hospital ceiling and I want to be alone?'

It seemed ridiculous, yet there was something nagging at Fern that the hospital solitude and even the moment of crisis in the tackroom last night hadn't sorted out. All those men . . .

All those men she had craved and had over the years. Oh, she'd never pretended love for them, never claimed it was anything but a physical need which had to be slaked for her comfort – slaked in a variety of ways which would have added a few inches to the index of most sex manuals.

It had been fun – exciting, risky, an exercise in power and fantasy which men had scarcely believed possible in the minutes before. Or after for that matter. But still it had to be said that not one of those men, not the film directors or the London party set, not the fellow horsemen or even that silly, open-mouthed young curate, had shown the slightest interest while she had been in hospital with a broken back.

God knew, there'd been enough publicity. She'd made both the gossip and the sports columns of the national press. Her absence had left a hole in the county scene. But no-one had given a damn except Harry, wondering what he could do to make life more bearable for his broken wife when she came back. Harry, mooching sadly about the estate out-buildings and coming across a decayed thing of beauty and thinking he would make it lovely again for his Duchess.

'Dear Harry!'

Fern leant against a chestnut tree and looked back at Willoughby Hall. So many windows, so many rooms, wings knocked down, added, burnt down and altered through the generations. If only she'd been able to produce an heir to the Mercia title and for Willoughby Hall, instead of amusing herself by having sex with strangers in as many of its rooms as she could. All those rooms. All those little blue crosses. She leant against the trunk, deep in thought, until an ache in her back told her it was time to return to the house.

In a display of untypical tact, Marion had gone away after delivering the barouche. There was no sign of Harry and the house felt strangely empty. Fern was unused to being at a loose end. She needed action, and that was rather limited at the moment. She drifted aimlessly around the house, from the library to the foot of the staircase and around the upper rooms. She didn't want to admit, even to herself, where she was going.

There was a room at the far end of the second floor which was all light and sunshine in good weather because it had windows on two sides. Fern had fallen in love with it when she first became mistress of Willoughby Hall. In those days she had sat on the wide sill thinking what a charming room it would make for a teenage son or daughter – large, light and conveniently removed from the rest of the house.

A foolish thought! As the childless years went by, it became a guest bedroom like the others, kept ready for visitors by the staff. And Fern had very rarely found her way in there. Now she was drawn to it again, without really knowing why she had come. She stood in the doorway, watching the figure sitting on the sill, gazing out on the grounds towards the deer and the chestnut.

'Harry.'

She caught him unawares. He had been watching her as she leant against the tree, watching his wife lost in thoughts which he yearned to read. And when she had come back into the house, he had remained there, pondering, thinking a little wistfully of what his life might have been. If only *what*? He couldn't change the way he was.

He stood up as she came into the room, just as he would have stood for any woman. He studied those green eyes and searched them for a sign of emotion, for something like affection. He didn't exactly know why he still hoped after all this time, but he'd sensed a sea-change in their relationship since Fern's horrible accident. What did it mean? Was it simply his own pity for her that he felt, or had she been affected, too?

Harry Willoughby was a restrained Englishman. Something deep inside stopped him from asking what he hungered to know. One look at his drawn face told you that here was a man who didn't know whether he was loved, but who desperately needed to.

'Fern.'

It was all he could manage to say.

She nodded, as much to herself as in acknowledgement of her name. Quite suddenly, she knew what she was going to do. It was the right thing and she wanted to do it very badly. Once more she was her old assured self. For the first time in months, life felt laughably simple.

So laughably simple, in fact, that she had a little smile on her face as she approached him. That habitual languid expression of hers had entirely gone. Willoughby saw a slight flush about her long white neck, saw her breasts rise and fall under the magenta dress. Its simple cut showed the slight roundness of her belly.

It was years since he had felt licensed to look and frankly admire. He reached for her hand and, feeling her move still closer, pulled her gently to him. He still half expected a laughing rejection or a sisterly peck on the cheek, but the whole length of her body was suddenly against his, squirming. He felt their thighs pressed hard together.

There was no resistance. He felt the upward surge of his swelling member and knew she must feel its hungry thrust against her stomach. The mere thought of that gentle curve between her hips made it harden to steel. Still she held him, breathing as he breathed, shallowly, pantingly. He saw her nostrils flare.

God, the warm pulsation of her! Willoughby closed his eyes with the joy of being wanted. This was a Fern from dim memory, from the days of his heady initiation into the glories of rampant, earthy sex. She wasn't simply tolerating his physical needs, she wasn't wielding the power to say yes or no – opening or closing her legs depending on whether it was friendship or boredom she felt for her Duke that night.

He inhaled her fondness, knowing he could take his time to enjoy her, that she wasn't going to run away. It gave him a confidence he'd never known before. He was the master, not the awkward learner. He stroked her hair, lifted it gently to finger the soft nape of her neck. He ran his hand along the undercurve of her arm, moving down to the pronounced waist and sliding his palms over firm buttocks until his fingers probed the soft and yielding flesh between her legs.

'All yours,' she murmured.

She moved against him, the slightest wriggle. He cupped her face in his hands and planted little kisses along her mouth. Pulling away a few inches, Fern slipped her hands under his jacket, squeezing.

'Where are you . . ?'

Now her hands were suddenly everywhere, deftly loosening, unfastening, unbuttoning. He joined in, tearing off his clothes in savage haste to stand before her stark and rearing.

'But me,' she said in a voice strangled with lust, 'I'm not wearing much at all.'

She turned her back towards him, inviting him to undo her dress. He ran his hands firmly up her sides, feeling every curve, so that she raised her arms high in the air, swaying and sighing. Then he tugged on the zip, and the dress gaped open. He unhooked her bra, found her full breasts and pulled her towards him. The dress fell to the floor. She shifted against him as he kissed her shoulders. His nose was full of the musk smell of her. He began to explore her warm flesh, all over. He felt the change from smooth flesh to thick hair under her silk French knickers. She was dripping wet.

'Hungry,' she muttered, wriggling out of the knickers and turning to face him. 'Fern's hungry.'

He stood rapt, unable to move. She put her head forward, pouting, letting him kiss her mouth to mouth, full and deep. Then she knelt in front of him, running her tongue down his chest to the navel, where the line of black hair began.

'Don't stop,' he said.

She crushed his upright member between her breasts, squeezing his buttocks. He closed his eyes, feeling her nails scratching lightly through his pubic hair towards the root of his cock. He groaned. Holding his balls with one hand, she took him all into her mouth and, not using her lips at all, simply ran her upper teeth lightly over the dark blue vein which stood out proud.

Then he felt himself held in the warm wet lips and felt her tongue find the slit. It darted in and out. There was a joyous confusion of probing and sucking as a finger slipped deep between his buttocks made him gasp with pleasure. He could feel the blood beating and the seed almost bursting as Fern took her mouth away and began to press herself against him, moaning.

He bent down and, gently raising her by the elbows, brought her to the bed. The skin of her nipples was dark and erect. As she lay down, her eyes swam with longing. Inside she was taut and throbbing, beyond doing anything but cry out for what she needed.

Now he parted the full lips of her sex and stroked. Fern, her eyes closed, took his hand and guided it to her clitoris, engorged and red. She shuddered, rearing towards his fingers as they worked her to pleasure.

'Please. Oh, please!' Her voice was husky with lust: 'I want you inside me.'

Through the mists of his desire, Willoughby remembered her damaged back. He wanted nothing more than to bury himself in the hot moistness his fingers could feel tightening to receive him, but not for worlds could he bring himself to hurt her.

'This way.'

She turned from him, lying on her side. As he nestled in behind her she raised a leg and he was able to push inside her, feeling her grip on him. She made a catching noise in her throat, like a little choking, as he drilled deep and filled her. Her buttocks were warm on his stomach. He was on the verge of coming, a thrust would do it. He held back.

He had one hand under her breasts and now he felt for her clitoris with the other one. Taking its wrinkled moistness between finger and thumb, he rubbed it, pushing slowly, rhythmically in and out, feeling her tightness push the skin backwards and forwards over the tip of his restless cock.

They came in a rush of wetness, seed and tears, finally panting to a calmness which neither wished ever to break.

28

'If we could have a little order, gentlemen,' Brent Lorimer pleaded. He'd entered architecture thinking it a civilised way of earning a living, but it seemed to him that it had changed a great deal very quickly, and entirely for the worse. If you couldn't ever have a quiet, sensible board meeting at Broughton, Hughes, Lorimer of all practices, what hopes were there for the less-established firms? 'Comments through the chair, if you don't mind.'

'Through the chair, with your permission,' hissed Langton Meredith, 'I should like to say that Jake Broughton is smug, self-satisfied and, from any sound business standpoint, suicidal.'

'That's preposterous!' exploded Broughton. 'Through the chair.'

'Moreover,' Meredith continued, 'through the chair, I wonder if it isn't time he resigned and made way for someone more suited to architecture at the beginning of a new millennium.'

Lorimer began to sweat. If anyone was on the point of resignation it was the senior partner and supposed chairman of this meeting. Any authority he had was being mocked by these two colleagues who seemed determined to split the practice in two.

'Do we need to make this personal?' he asked lamely.

'Something I wish as fervently as you,' Meredith said. 'Unfortunately it seems our friend Jake is determined to question every move I make.'

'If merely asking questions is disallowed,' Broughton countered, 'we're running our affairs like a fourth-rate, banana-republic dictatorship.'

'And if every enterprising deal is ruled out of court,' snapped Meredith, 'a fourth-rate power is exactly what we shall become. Or don't you know it's a ruthless world out there?'

Brent Lorimer brought his fist down on the table with a crash. It worked, probably because nobody realised his gesture came not from strength but weakness: the frustration had built up inside him to such a pitch that he thought he would crack. When his fist hit the veneered surface everyone stopped talking or even fiddling with their pens and pads. The silence held for several seconds.

'You've said nothing, Stew,' Lorimer turned to McClear, hoping the young Scot would get him out of a hole. 'How do you see this thing?'

McClear frowned and pushed his glasses against the bridge of his nose: 'This is big money,' he said. 'I suppose there are two questions that come to my mind. One, do we know enough about this Brazilian to trust that he'll pay up on time, keep to the rules and so on? Two, how do we keep an eye on the work at such a distance?'

'Thank you, Stew,' Broughton broke in before Lorimer could reply. 'They're the very questions I was trying to ask myself.'

'Except,' snarled Meredith, 'that you weren't able to ask them without resorting to personal invective and snide comments.'

'That'll do, Langton,' Lorimer said, surprising himself. 'Let's not start that up again.'

Meredith smiled: 'Listen, Brent, I'd like to make one comment. Through the chair. Then I'll do nothing but answer your questions. All right?'

'All right,' Lorimer conceded.

'I'd like to remind you that when I first suggested entering the Charlesbury competition I met with some hostility in this room. It was claimed that we were overstretching ourselves. I was later accused of behaving improperly in the Bunny Simkins affair, even though there wasn't the slightest evidence to sustain that allegation.

'What happened when this practice reached the short-list for the competition? I met with nothing but luke-warm praise for my efforts, and I was again regaled with warnings about interfering in the affairs of our rivals. I had to point out to you then that we were not a bunch of boy scouts or some form of holy order, but a business operating in a cut-throat industry.

'Now that I have negotiated a highly lucrative contract with one of the wealthiest men in South America we hear again the cries of alarm about risk and the supposed over-stretching of our resources. It's a Little England approach, a timid stepping back from the reality of the world as it now is.

'Why the hell can't someone say that what I've done is for the long-term benefit of this practice?'

For once Jake Broughton made no effort to intervene. There was simply a sneer on his lips. It implied that Meredith's complaint wasn't worth arguing with.

'I'm sure that we all appreciate what you've done, Langton,' Lorimer said in soothing tones. 'But it is, of course, quite proper to ask questions about something which is entirely unknown to most of us. Tell us, for instance, about this Diego Morais. Who is he?'

Meredith picked a pile of papers from the table and pulled out several sheets, tossing them in front of his colleagues so that each could take one.

'This is his CV,' he said. 'As much as I could get on one side of A4. He owns huge areas of land in the Americas and these, of course, include the sites we're involved with on the outskirts of Brasilia. The man is more than credit-worthy – he simply doesn't need to raise the cash.'

'What's the deal on payments?' McClear asked.

'The best. He'll pay an advance, and there'll be regular fees twice a year, with penalty clauses if there should be any hold-ups. I expected some very tough bargaining, but he agreed to nearly every demand.'

'And this doesn't sound too good to be true?' queried Broughton.

'If you mean to suggest,' Meredith said icily, 'that I've been taken for a ride, I can assure you that I haven't. Naturally Morais has made demands of his own, but every one of them is within our normal terms of contract. If you're asking what Morais gets from the agreement, I'll tell you. He gets the very best English design.'

'You've met the man personally?' McClear asked.

'Naturally,' Meredith said, taking up his papers again. He found a batch of large, shiny black-and-white prints and tossed them on the table top. They showed Meredith shaking hands with a stout and swarthy man; Meredith and the swarthy man sitting side by side with pens in their hands; a line of men in dark suits, with Meredith and the swarthy man at the centre.

'Pictures courtesy of one of the newspapers in Brasilia,' he explained. 'You'll notice the caption on the back. The translation reads: "distinguished British architect signs development agreement". It's an outline agreement, of course – but I hope you're going to sanction the final document, once you've studied the details.'

'And if we don't?' Broughton asked.

'Oh, you will,' Meredith replied scornfully. 'If you know where your bread's buttered.'

• • •

Bunny Simkins had discovered that he wasn't the type to commit suicide. If he had been, he consoled himself, he would have done the deed by now. He'd been through nearly every bad emotion these past few months, from anger, through shame and self-loathing to fear. He'd had the one prize he still coveted, the Charlesbury project, denied him by a dirty trick which made him feel dirty himself – yet here he was, sipping tea on a bright May afternoon by the Thames, and he wasn't finished yet.

'Sorry I'm late, Mr Simkins,' Martin Kingsley said, joining him.

They'd arranged to meet in the cafe of the National Theatre. You can sit on the balcony there, with a view along the river, and it's easy to feel that the rest of the world no longer exists. Bunny Simkins had often wished that it didn't just lately.

'I thought of throwing myself in,' he told the journalist, 'but it turned out to be only an idea. I did stand on Blackfriars Bridge on one occasion and I tried to imagine leaping over, but all I got was a sense of vertigo. I don't think I'm cut out for that kind of thing.'

'Pleased to hear it,' Kingsley said, stirring his tea. He'd felt bad about the Simkins affair from the first, and he knew he'd have found it hard to live with himself if the thing had ended in any kind of tragedy. It was his feelings of guilt which had led him to investigate the affair on Simkins' behalf. He didn't think there'd be any journalistic mileage in it for himself.

'Well?' the architect broached the subject at last. He watched a string of barges moving slowly past against the tide. It was highly embarrassing. 'Did you manage to find anything?'

'Nothing absolutely conclusive,' Kingsley said, 'but I think it's pretty clear what happened. Quite frankly, Mr Simkins, I don't think you've got a lot to worry about.'

'Oh.' The words should have been reassuring, but somehow they weren't. 'Even though I get visits from the police, threatening me?'

'Standard police practice, Mr Simkins. Have they been back again?'

'Just once. They were very unpleasant. They said they thought I needed another warning.'

'They've got nothing on you that can stick, Mr Simkins. Just tell yourself that some policemen are bastards and you happen to have picked a couple.'

'And I'll be on an official file somewhere. One day fifty years from now someone will open that file and say Bunny Simkins was a pervert. There's no way I can stop that, is there?'

'No, there's not. You could make a fuss, of course, and try to have the information removed. Write to your MP, for instance. But I don't suppose you want to do that, do you?'

'Certainly not.'

Once a rumour started, he'd come to realise, it was almost impossible to stop it in its tracks. If you protested, people who'd never heard the rumour before suddenly knew all about it. And everyone said there was no smoke without fire. Perhaps it was true. The frame-up wouldn't have been devised in the first place if he didn't have certain tendencies, if only in his head.

That was another thing that sickened him – that people looked at him and knew what was in his head. He felt exposed. He felt that fingers were pointing at him wherever he went.

'You've guessed why all this happened in the first place, Mr Simkins?'

'I'm afraid not. I can't think why anyone should want to do it.'

'Look, I don't want to accuse you of being naive. But you've realised that it probably had something to do with the Charlesbury project?'

'I don't like to think so,' Simkins said. He stood up abruptly: 'Would you like another cup? I'll get it. And a tea cake?'

Now that the moment of truth had come, he didn't really want to know. If those photographs had been taken to stop him winning the Charlesbury competition, it followed that a fellow professional had been behind it. Bunny Simkins had been brought up in a world where such things didn't happen. It was horrible to think that anyone who knew him would think so little of him that they could callously ruin his reputation. He queued for the tea and cakes, and he carried the tray outside to the balcony very slowly.

'I've done quite a lot of digging,' Kingsley said.

'That's very kind of you.'

Kingsley waved the thanks away: 'I wanted to do it, for myself as much as you. No one likes being set up like that. All of us were used in one way or another.'

'I got the other journos working on it, too. We'd all received personal tip-offs, anonymous of course, to turn up at the Old Rooster that evening. I got them to go through their contacts books so we could discover whether anything pieced together – whether there was any common factor. One person we all knew, for instance, who might have any interest in pulling this thing off.'

'And it worked?'

'Like a dream, Mr Simkins. Mind you, I already had half a suspicion, knowing things that I knew.'

They sat in silence for a while, sipping their tea and nibbling their cakes. Kingsley wanted to be asked. Like any journalist, he relished a good yarn. He especially liked telling one. He liked to be the first to break the news.

'It's someone I know?'

'Naturally, Mr Simkins. Another architect. I can't prove it, of course. It wouldn't stand up in a court of law. But you can trust it, all right.'

'Tell me,' Simkins breathed, and almost stuffed his fingers in his ears.

'If I told you it was Langton Meredith, would you be surprised?'

'Meredith!' Simkins exclaimed. 'You mean Meredith of Broughton, Hughes, Lorimer? I don't believe it!'

God, Kingsley thought, he *is* naive.

'He'd ruin his grandmother for half a crown,' he added.

Simkins put his head in his hands and stared at the table. He hadn't realised how dreadful he would feel to know who had betrayed him so cruelly.

'Why?' he asked, tears in his eyes. His voice trembled. 'What had I done to him?'

'Charlesbury.'

'But can it have mattered so much? To have done a thing like that?'

Kingsley stood up, feeling strangely deflated. A rotten job badly handled, he thought. This was one piece of news it hadn't been a bit enjoyable to break. He touched Simkins lightly on the shoulder and hurried to the door. When he looked back, the architect's head had sunk onto the table.

• • •

The Barracuda was another journalist who relished the breaking of a first-rate story. And why not? She recognised it as an occupational disease, and she was glad to suffer from it. There was nothing like that excited atmosphere when someone bowled into the newsroom or the pub crying: 'You heard what's happened to X?' or 'You'll never guess what old Y's done now!' Everyone would gather round, egging the story-teller on, hanging on every word so they could spread the tale themselves in another newsroom or another pub.

And the best thing of all was to be that story-teller yourself.

'Meredith,' came the languid voice at the other end of the telephone.

'Oh, we're acting sober citizen of the world this morning, are we?' fired Ella Lepard, blowing smoke from her cheroot across the mouthpiece.

'Ella, darling!' cooed Langton Meredith. 'Well, I do have a certain role to play.'

'Several, I'm sure, my sweet. That one doesn't really convince. Does *anyone* take you at face value?'

'Now that's not kind. I do have a sound reputation in certain quarters. As for my bedside manner . . . '

'Spare us, ducks!' guffawed the Barracuda and instantly became caught up in a bout of coughing. 'And damn these cancer sticks.'

'I sometimes wonder,' Meredith said, 'whether I'm the only person I know without a vice of any kind.'

'Save pride,' she noted tartly. 'And whatever bribery counts as in the catalogue of sins. Don't forget that you shamelessly fed me tempting prosciutto and mozzarella at Orso's purely to soften me up as an informant. *Im*purely, I mean.'

'One reason among many, Ella, and you know it. I find your particular charms irresistible.'

She gave a bark of a laugh, and then all he heard was the blowing of smoke, a sucking sound as she inhaled and another expiration of air.

'Ah, I see,' he said. 'Slow of me. You mean you've actually got something to tell.'

'I thought you'd never ask,' she chided him. 'But probably not, really. I don't know how relevant it is.'

'Let me be the judge of that.'

She paused. A good story-teller needs the right atmosphere before the tale begins. There wasn't quite the necessary air of expectancy yet.

'You were asking questions about Calla Marchant, yes? We spoke about the Jason Andover connection, and all his little . . . problems?'

'Of course I remember. Don't tease, Ella!'

'I'm not teasing, Langton. I simply don't know whether this story will interest you. It concerns Jason Andover's litte pet, Peta Abercrombie. Perhaps she's a little too remote from Calla Marchant to interest you.'

'By no means, darling. Do tell me.'

'Well . . . ' she drawled. 'Hang on, Langton. Let me close the door.'

Meredith waited. He was a patient man. He knew that the sort of information he was after filtered through piece by piece. He'd been hard at work on both Calla Marchant and Grant Locke these past few months, and he was confident he'd have something damning on one or even both of them before competition time had arrived. The secret was never to say no to a story.

The Barracuda began to wind herself up to reveal all: 'What do you know about Peta?' she asked.

'She's a model. Blonde and blue-eyed. She also shares her boyfriend's drug habit. Right? And that's all I know.'

'Yesterday,' Ella Lepard began, 'we had a *Chic* fashion shoot. Out in the country. Do you know Lord Thurley's place in Buckinghamshire?'

'Never been there.'

'I don't know how we came to choose it – my fashion editor deals with that sort of thing. A gorgeous spread. Usual thing. Tudor manor house, walled garden, lawns, a spinney or two, paddocks. Every Englishman's idyll. Too bloody draughty by half as far as I'm concerned. Give me London every time. The only greenery I enjoy comes served up on a plate.'

'Go on, Ella.'

'Two models, okay? A classy brunette who's going places – and I mean really going. It's not often you meet one of these girls and immediately see *everything*. Not only the looks, I mean, but brains and sass and drive. Not gooey ambition, Langton, but drive. Claudia Marlin. Make a note of that name, and tell me I told you so five years from now.'

'And Peta Abercrombie.'

'And the bimbo, yes. Listen, I said to my fashion editor, do you know this girl's track record? Well, she says, she's been used by the best. How long ago? I ask. This one's unstable. But very pretty, she says – and how can I argue? The deed's been done.'

'She ruined the shoot?' Meredith asked, anxious to have the tale told.

'Don't jump in, Langton. Who's telling this story?' The Barracuda took another pull on her cheroot. 'It's a long shoot, right? Lots of changes of costume. Cars on the drive. Moose heads on the wall. Loads of interior and exterior shots. That's hard work, believe me.

'So I take a close look at our Peta, and I don't like what I see. She's acting jumpy, and it's still early in the day. Well, it's mid-morning, but that's early for me and it's a bit damn soon for a model to feel tired and edgy. She's a real pro, so she looks great for the camera if you like that artificial sort of thing, but as soon as one sequence of shots is finished she disappears for a while. Doesn't say where she's going, just disappears.'

'Did you follow her?'

'Slightly *infra dig*, wouldn't you say, Langton? I am the editor of this illustrious magazine, after all, not a paid help or baby-minder. I was out there principally to have a good time on the pretext of keeping an eye. Lord Thurley has his own deer park and the venison's unsurpassable.'

'You have excellent taste, Ella.'

'Over luncheon I had a few words with the girl, and she had a frightened, distant look in her eyes. I felt quite motherly towards her, if you can imagine such a thing. She told me she was all right. Hadn't slept very well, that kind of thing. Then she disappeared again, and when she came back she seemed revitalised for a time. What does that tell you?'

'Drugs, I assume.'

'Must have been. This shoot was running way over time, but everyone was happy to carry on and the gracious lord offered his floodlighting for some evening shots. Ball gowns with a background of creepered walls. It's hard to believe, but my fashion editor does come up with some bright new ideas from time to time. This just wasn't one of them.

'The girls were doing fine, but Peta wasn't talking. I mean, not even twittering, which is what you normally get from these pretty deadheads. She was just perfect for the pictures – do take a peek at the next issue, Langton – but as soon as the cameraman had finished she wilted.

'It went on like this all day and into the evening. She looked about to fade away, and then she'd disappear and come back temporarily radiant. Then it was a downhill slide all over again.'

'Half piste,' Meredith murmured, enjoying his own little wordplay.

'No, that was me, darling,' the Barracuda said. 'Let's not confuse our substances. By the time darkness fell I'm afraid I was swimming in the stuff. Lord Thurley has a wonderful cellar.'

'Perhaps you might introduce us....'

'So I'm rather losing touch with the shoot,' she continued, ignoring the hint. 'I've left that to the others to deal with. I do hear quite a lot of calling out, and a bit later on there's this terrible commotion. Not at all civilised. Lord T. and I have to struggle to our feet and open the french windows onto the verandah.'

She paused, and took a few short pulls on her cheroot. Meredith dutifully waited, recognising a climax when it was offered to him.

'What's happened is,' she said in an almost off-handed manner, 'that the beautiful Peta's gone missing when there's still one more picture to pose for. Most unprofessional. To be fair to her, I suppose you have to say it's not at all characteristic. They've looked all over the house for her and called out through the grounds. All to no avail.'

'And?'

'They keep looking, darling and – I'm afraid this is all very Agatha Christie Country House Drama – they find her at last in the summer house, huddled in a corner and stone cold dead.'

• • •

'Don't do it, Bunny,' Calla pleaded. 'I'm sure you've got everything out of proportion.'

'No.' His voice down the telephone sounded firm, determined. 'I've been thinking about it for some time. I've made the decision.'

'If you'd already made it, you wouldn't be talking it over with me,' she insisted. 'It sounds more like one of those famous cries for help.'

He laughed: 'Would you blame me?'

'Of course I wouldn't. You've been abominably hounded and persecuted. I tell you, Bunny, if I ever discover who the bastard was who did that–'

'Careful, Callalily,' he broke in. 'I think I know who did it, and I don't want to be responsible for murder.'

'You *know*, for God's sake!'

'Probably, yes. But don't ask me now. Not over the telephone.'

'When?'

'In a few days. I'm going away to think over the other business.'

'Didn't I say you hadn't made up your mind?' she exclaimed triumphantly.

'Oh, I've made my mind up. It's a question of how I go about it. Of who'll buy.'

'Bunny, there'll be a queue of people wanting to take over your partnership. That's not a problem. It's just that if you go now, people will say you ran away. They'll believe all those stories.'

'I don't care,' he replied. 'Not any more. There comes a point when you get too weary to fight it. I'd have retired soon in any case.'

'Stick with it!' she urged him.

'We'll talk, Calla-lily,' he said, and put the phone down.

• • •

Jason sat in the back row of the chapel, his face pale against the black of his suit and tie. The organ was coming to the end of 'What a friend we have in Jesus'. After years in which he had never attended a funeral, he was now at his second within weeks.

'My friends,' the chaplain said. 'We are gathered together to remember Peta, and to give thanks for her life among us . . . '

His mother's had been a full fig affair, of course. The church had been packed with mourners, many of them people who very much wanted to be seen attending. The sheer volume of wreaths had been an obscenity. The rector had spoken of the deceased in terms which would have flattered a saint.

That had been a grand burial in the family vault. This was a humble cremation with the ashes soon to be taken away in a small casket. That had been a celebrity event. This was pathetically anonymous. Jason supposed that the half a dozen people clustered at the front were family, but he had never seen any of them during the time he had known Peta. She'd never referred to relations even once.

'Peta gave pleasure to thousands who never knew her, through her work . . . '

And look how much the thousands cared! he reflected. It was all skin deep. At his mother's funeral he had felt desolate, but he had been untroubled by difficult thoughts. The sadness had been everything. Today he couldn't pretend to be heart-broken, for he and Peta had never loved one another, but he found himself racked by guilt and anger.

It was easy enough to feel guilty. He knew how much he and Peta had encouraged each other in their blind folly. He knew that, like all drug users, they'd both been looking for excuses, both wanting to hear that their habit was natural and justified and harmless. Yes, she doubtless had as much responsibility as he did for that, but she was dead, poor thing. Her responsibility was erased by her death. His swelled up like a malignant growth.

Why hadn't he once told her what an idiot she was? Why hadn't he told her that her life was blighted? Obviously because he couldn't have done that without condemning himself. But it still hurt him to ask the question.

'Let us pray . . . '

His anger was directed at the people who might have helped Peta but who didn't. Her family, for instance. Presumably that was her mother in the centre of the front row, her face veiled by black lace. She was the only older person there. What had she been doing on her daughter's behalf these past few years?

He wanted to shout at them all above the stupid, sing-song voice of the chaplain: 'Bugger your sham sorrow! If you really cared for Peta you wouldn't be here now.'

When the service was over they trooped out to look at the wreaths – just a few useless bundles of spring flowers. There were tears on the faces of a couple of the girl mourners. Who the hell *were* they? he wondered. What gave them the right to cry? Everyone read the messages on the wreaths with great care, as if they contained some hidden truth. As if they meant anything at all.

No, Jason thought, he hadn't ever loved Peta, but they had, for a brief time, drawn close together in their despair. They had shaken with the same terror. They had stood on the edge of the same pit and seen the same snakes writhing in its depths. That was a rare kind of bond. They had known things about one another that nobody else understood.

'You've got a damn nerve!'

It took him some while to realise that the remark had been made to him. A tall young man of about twenty, his fine-boned face surrounded by neatly cropped blond hair, separated himself from the other mourners and stood a few yards away, his fists clenched.

'I beg your pardon,' Jason said.

'Coming here like this. You're Andover, aren't you? You're the man who brought her to this.'

'I'm Jason Andover, yes.'

It would have been embarrassing, except that everyone was full to the brim with emotion of some kind – the girls' sentimental sorrow, the young man's anger, Jason's intermingling of anger with guilt. It might have been frightening, but he was feeling strangely detached. He couldn't see that these people were part of the story, his and Peta's story.

'Got your kicks, did you?'

Jason began to move away. He couldn't possibly explain all that he'd come to understand about his addiction and what he knew about Peta's. Not in these circumstances, anyway.

'Come back here, you bastard!'

Jason turned: 'Who are you, sonny?' he asked.

The condescension worked a treat. The young man looked as if he was going to throw a punch.

'I'm only Peta's brother,' he said. 'Did she ever tell you she had a brother? Did you ever ask?'

'The answer to both questions is "no".'

'No, you were too busy feeding her that shit. They ought to put people like you inside and throw away the key. So you can't corrupt lovely young girls like my sister.'

He didn't throw a punch after all. Instead, his face puckered up, tears ran down his face and he began to whine like a baby.

'I'm sorry,' Jason said.

'Sorry? You bastard!'

'I'm sorry,' he went on, 'for every lousy minute you might have been comforting your sister but weren't. I'm sorry for every second Peta suffered and I didn't know what to do for her. And I'm sorry for all the thousands of poor souls who cry out for help but don't know themselves what it is they want.'

He began to walk across the grass towards his car, his body shaking. What had caused that violent outburst? Why had he made that dramatic little speech in front of people he could only despise?

Jason knew what it meant. He knew it was because he himself had plunged into that seething pit of snakes and had managed to climb out the other side. That was why he could stand back and feel sorry. He understood. He *did* know what it was he wanted.

The only question was whether he had a snowball's chance in hell of getting it.

29

'I've got you in at Green's, one thirty,' said Adam. 'In your name, natch.'

'Good. This is my treat.' Calla had no intention of finding herself under an obligation to Philippe Beauvoir, not even to the extent of a lunch. The relationship was strictly business now.

'Expensive treat, you know. Unless you have the fishcakes ' speciality of the house and at least half the price of the rest of the menu.'

'One of your haunts, is it, Adam?'

'Not on my salary. But I've been treated, too, in my time, you know.'

'I'm sure you have,' teased Calla. 'But have you ever been to Green's?'

Adam decided to ignore his boss's cruel jest: 'Are you meeting Phil at the airport? Is he bringing his well-groomed *femme* with him?'

'God, I hope not. This is a working trip. A flying visit at that. God knows, he's delayed long enough. The Charlesbury deadline's getting uncomfortably close for having half the partnership on the opposite side of the Channel. He'll have a good hour or so to look at some of these plans before we go for our working lunch.'

'You're lucky he didn't pull out, don't you think?'

Adam was rather proud of his first foray into the art of blackmail. He longed to tell her exactly how he had persuaded Philippe to stay in the Charlesbury project, but he didn't fancy contending with a furious Calla. The revelation would have to wait for a special occasion. For the day he left?

'He's the lucky one. This is *the* project of the twenty- first century he's in on. To answer your other question, we arranged to meet here.'

Calla didn't think she could stand another airport welcome scene with Philippe.

'Oh, how nice,' Adam cooed. 'I wonder what he'll wear.' He disliked Philippe – and envied his wardrobe intensely.

The sarcasm wasn't lost on Calla, but she had a ready supply of her own: 'You won't believe this, Adam, but Calla Marchant Practice is not run specifically for your pleasure.'

'A fact which had somehow escaped me,' he replied with a little smile.

He turned his attention to the coffee machine, knowing when he was beaten. It was one of his most endearing qualities, in his own opinion, that he knew how to accept defeat graciously. Working for Calla, you needed to. The woman could be a vixen. A real foxy lady.

And she was looking especially bright-eyed and bushy-tailed, he thought. Hard work and a challenge, not to mention a fair amount of risk, suited Calla Marchant's constitution. Those violet eyes were absolutely bewitching today. It made Adam quite glad to be gay. He'd have been powerless under their gaze otherwise.

But seduction wasn't on her lunchtime menu, he could tell. The look was rather more rustic than ravishing. Oh, she looked terrific, but it definitely wasn't Calla out for the kill. A softly gathered Edina Ronay skirt came down to her booted calves. A wide belt showed off an enviably slim waist and a vintage Caroline Charles tweed hacking jacket with a velvet collar followed her contours.

Adam, with his eye for sartorial style, understood the message. It was womanliness all wrapped up, alluring but not meant to start a fire in a man's loins. Not, at any rate, in the space of a lunch-hour at a place as formal as Green's. The St James's fish restaurant, frequented by royalty and Fleet Street editors, each pretending to be unaware of the other, wasn't a place for wooing. It was business, entertaining and superb food. Calla had chosen well.

But she had a little time before Philippe was expected and these days time couldn't be wasted.

'Get me the Rilcon estimates department on the phone, will you, Adam? I need to know clearing and dumping costs, and urgently. They've had our bloody submission for over a week now. It's time we made them jump a little.'

There you go, thought Adam with a sigh. She looks like a *Vogue* cover, swears like a fishwife and talks about clearing and dumping. No wonder sensitive boys like me have identity crises.

All the while he dialled the number Calla was tapping the table with her pencil. She did want to sort Rilcon out, it was true. Most of all, though, she wanted to take her mind off Philippe until the moment he got here.

It was a difficult balancing act, trying to keep a man like him at arm's length but no further. She didn't want to bed him anymore, but she needed him around for Charlesbury. She needed that very badly indeed.

'Estimates department,' Adam sang. 'Unless everyone's at lunch, of course.'

She knew she would have to steel herself to resist that fatal sexual attraction there was between the two of them. And she'd have to be quite tough with him if she found that the influence of Yvette the maman-to-be had hindered his work. No, bloody tough.

Adam handed her the telephone with his hand over the mouthpiece: 'There's a woman here making life very difficult,' he said.

'This is Calla Marchant,' she said vigorously. 'I want to speak to the head of estimates.'

She paused. A cab drew up outside, but she didn't look. She disliked being given the run-around by an over-protective secretary, and that battle for the moment took every ounce of her concentration.

'If he's still in that meeting five minutes from now he can kiss goodbye to ten thousand pounds. You understand that?'

Adam went to open the door.

'You need to ask *me* how to do it?' he heard Calla roar. 'Don't they pay you anything for initiative at that place?' She slammed the receiver down. 'Bloody men and their precious little office wives!'

She swung round in her chair to face the door – and received a very nasty surprise indeed.

'Yvette!'

Adam, looking on, thought there couldn't have been a greater contrast between the two women. Calla was flushed and vibrant, like some exotic creature startled by a strange noise. Yvette was subdued by comparison, but she was undeniably in control of the situation. After all, the element of surprise was all hers.

'But of course.'

He realised in that second that she knew. This was a wife who'd found out about her husband's infidelity and had decided to cope. Fearsome, thought Adam. Like a deathcap mushroom: pale but deadly. He very much doubted that Philippe would show his face.

'I am not welcome, perhaps?'

So much for his blackmail, he thought. Thank God he'd said nothing. But what was Yvette's game? And how would Calla cope? He switched his gaze from one to the other like a spectator at a tennis tournament. Only there were no written rules for this kind of confrontation.

'Of course you are,' Calla lied impeccably. 'How nice to see you! Adam, a chair for Madame Beauvoir, please. And a coffee?'

'Thank you.'

She watched with a mounting irritation as Yvette, now clearly pregnant, sat down very carefully, then arranged herself in an annoyingly unhurried way. As if her pregnancy made her someone uniquely special. As if nobody in the history of the world had ever had a baby before, for God's sake. What the hell was this about?

'Good flight?'

Yvette smiled that calm smile and shrugged: 'Thank you, it was fine. Tiring in my condition, but fine.'

She wasn't the sort of woman to hop on and off planes during a pregnancy. Something must have driven her to it. More infuriating still, she wasn't in a hurry to mention her husband. But, Calla decided, if the idea was to put her in the embarrassing position of having to ask, it damn well wasn't going to work. Hell would freeze over first.

'Shall I change the lunch booking to three?' Adam asked, right on cue. If that wasn't worth a pay rise, he didn't know what was.

It was Yvette who replied: 'That won't be necessary. My husband hasn't come, you see.'

Calla found her voice, despite herself. It was deep and rather dangerous. 'Hasn't come?'

Yvette was still smiling, hands still resting calmly in her lap, looking like the perfect model for maternity wear – all calmness and contentment.

'I'm afraid he has other things to do.'

'Other things to do!' Calla's tone was grim. 'Too busy is he?'

Maddeningly, Yvette took a few seconds to consider Calla's words: 'Too busy? No, he is not too busy.'

She's enjoying this, Adam thought. She's enjoying her sweet revenge. So how would Calla react? He'd put money on her in most situations, but this wasn't most situations. This was a damage-limitation job if ever he saw one. And he certainly wasn't leaving the entertainment to make coffee.

Calla, though still boiling inside, was determined to be polite. After all, she thought desperately, Philippe might be ill. Shit, no: in that case, his office would have rung. There must be something in this for Madame Beauvoir.

'Yvette,' she said. 'May we come to the point? Why hasn't Philippe come?'

Yvette looked her straight in the eye. Oh, she was a lovely looking woman, this Calla Marchant. It wasn't surprising Philippe had fallen for her. Yvette wrinkled her fastidious nose. No doubt Calla had all the animal appetites which she, *grace a dieu*, wasn't troubled by. She didn't care to imagine the scenes of their passion, didn't dare to. The truth was that Yvette's imagination wouldn't stretch that far anyway.

'Because I wouldn't let him.'

Yvette saw Calla's black eyebrows arch. But that was exactly how it had been. Philippe, for all his charm, wasn't difficult to handle, not for a Frenchwoman with an instinct for these things.

Oh, she'd had no positive proof, just her observations when he'd returned from his first trip, plus that almost tangible sexual tension between the two which she'd sensed a couple of months ago.

'Really?'

'That is so, yes.'

She'd faced him with it as soon as he started making plans for his visit to England on Charlesbury business. Her instincts had been sound. It was almost comical at first. Philippe, for some reason assuming that Calla's girl-boy of a secretary had informed on him, instantly gave himself away. How sick he'd looked to learn that he'd been betrayed simply by the instincts of his wife.

But he didn't want to alienate her. Yvette had money of her own, the sort of money which could be used to shore up his architecture practice while he was competing for big schemes. There were always plenty of those in the French capital, which welcomed architecture that was bold and not afraid to shock.

The cost of his unfaithfulness was Charlesbury. He was to have no more to do with it, no more to do with Calla Marchant. Yvette's conditions were tough ' her or Charlesbury. And, after all, he did love his wife, in a fond, unimpassioned way. Wasn't it by far the simplest thing to obey?

And there was the baby, of course – Yvette's trump card. Philippe, like most Frenchmen, was nuts about children. He wanted lots of them. He actually wanted more than Yvette was willing to supply, but he didn't know that yet. The baby had won the day, and he had crumbled.

And now Yvette, having taken her husband's seat on the aeroplane, was enjoying her victory. And how! Adam could sense her quiet delight, but he was also aware of signs which meant nothing to Yvette. A Marchant eruption was on its way.

'*You* wouldn't let him?' The contempt in the word *you* was withering. Calla, her chair turned round from her desk to face Yvette, looked at the pale creature as if she were a stone which had suddenly found a tongue. 'And what the hell has it to do with you?'

Yvette seemed surprised by Calla's raw energy, but she was game: 'I'm his wife, I think,' she remarked coolly.

'Quite!' Adam winced at Calla's dismissive scorn.

'My husband is having nothing more to do with the Charlesbury project, Miss Marchant. He has decided to withdraw from it.'

'*He* has decided? Oh, come on, Yvette! Don't play games with me. You're the one who makes decisions in the Beauvoir menage.'

Yvette looked around her edgily. She disliked an audience to any kind of disruption. The girl-boy was quite clearly relishing the whole thing, not to mention any other members of the architectural staff who might be around the building. The noise level had already risen considerably.

'Please, I don't like scenes.'

'You don't?' Calla rose, her colour high and her eyes blazing. She thrust her jacket back and stood with her hands on her hips, looking down at Yvette. 'Well, I do! I love them! And I want to know what this is all about!'

She did know of course. It was just that she hadn't wanted to know. And she also knew that at any minute Yvette would be driven to announcing the details to anyone within earshot. A scandal? Quite honestly, she couldn't care less. All she wanted right now was to see Yvette looking thoroughly uncomfortable. She'd ruined Charlesbury for her, so let her pay too.

'You must know, I think.' Yvette's voice shook, but she spoke determinedly. 'It's about your affair with my husband.'

'Hooray! The little woman pronounces!'

'I don't mind saying so. I'm not the one who acted like a whore.'

Calla laughed loudly, tossing back her mane of hair: 'Oh, Yvette! I'm shocked! What weapons did you use to subdue him? Refuse to press his trousers unless he stayed put in Paris? Isn't that the sort of thing that wives do?'

'I have someone to do my ironing.'

One to Yvette, thought Adam.

'Really? So what's next? Someone to do your screwing?'

Adam briefly closed his eyes in distaste. It must be the influence of the long-lost sister, he thought. He'd met Nerissa for the first time a few days earlier and truly felt he would never forget the experience. Some of that colourful vulgarity seemed to have found its way into Calla's vocabulary.

His boss was in full flood now. Yvette had won the war, there was no doubt about that, but Calla was determined to make this a bloody last battle.

'Not that you'll need to spend time on it, Yvette. Philippe will find someone soon enough.'

'Please, no,' Yvette protested.

'You're missing a treat, you know. He's very good at it. Expert, in fact. Knows more positions than a chess grandmaster. Shall I tell you some of them? No?'

My mistake, Adam thought. He should have made the coffee after all. He'd never thought of himself as squeamish before.

Yvette's creamy face for once showed a little colour. She was rattled, but she simply didn't have it in her to give back as good as she got. Dignified withdrawal was more in her line. She stood up, shaking slightly, and left the room, pausing only to stare at Calla's beautiful and angry face for the last time.

'What a peasant you are,' she said as she left.

'Send Philippe my regards!' yelled Calla after her. 'Tell him the quickie in the lift was the best!'

The door slammed. Calla grabbed the nearest thing – a pair of dividers – and hurled it against a wall.

'Damn! Damn! Damn!'

'You didn't, surely!' said Adam, bending to pick them up. 'Not in a lift!'

'Of course I didn't, acid-head! But I bet Yvette thinks about that all the way back to Paris. What a conniving bitch!'

Adam reflected that now was perhaps not the best time to ask where stealing another woman's husband featured in the top ten bitchy acts. Calla still looked in the mood for throwing something and he didn't want to end up on the street.

'Get me that treacherous little worm on the phone!'

Calla was pacing, or rather prowling, up and down the room, fury etched on her face.

'The Phil worm?'

'Mais bloody oui!'

Adam dialled the number. 'But I think he *will* want to take this call,' she heard him say. 'I'm ringing on behalf of Madame Beauvoir.'

Calla grabbed the receiver, holding it like a javelin. She heard Philippe's voice, edgy and concerned.

'Allo! Yvette? Ca va?'

'It's not Yvette, Philippe. And it's not ça va, not at all ça va.'

She heard Philippe breathe in sharply. Let him squirm! Her voice was calm, but heavy with irony.

'We've just had a social call from your Madame Beauvoir. Is it true you're letting me down?'

'Calla, I'm sorry. Yvette insisted on telling you herself. I've so much work . . . '

'Spare me the apologia, Philippe. I can't take another performance. Yvette's just given a very convincing rendition of wounded and virtuous wife. If you do the overworked and misunderstood husband, I shall throw up.'

There was a pause.

'She gave me an ultimatum, Calla. I'm saving my marriage. Charlesbury is out as far as I'm concerned. What more can I say?'

'Nothing. There's nothing you can say that won't confirm my opinion of you as an out-and-out, lily-livered shit of the first water. But just listen. I still can't quite believe you're doing this to me after our plans, after all your talk about the philosophy of Charlesbury. Do you realise how close the dealine is, for Chrissakes? What am I supposed to do now? Couldn't you have been man enough to make up your own mind and stick to it?'

'I'm sorry, Calla. It's made up now.'

'Oh, there's strength!'

'Don't mock me.'

Calla gave Adam a massive wink: 'Yvette's on her way back to you, by the way. Don't try denying what happened in the lift.'

'The lift?'

'And I hope she makes you suffer!'

'Calla, Calla . . . I wish you well with Charlesbury . . . '

There was a click. The phone had been put down in London.

'Could you use that coffee?' Adam asked, so gently that she hardly heard him.

Wishing was cheap, she thought. All around her, on the drawing boards and pinned to the walls, were the Charlesbury plans. Neither a wish nor a prayer would be enough to finish that project. She ran her hands through her tangled black hair. She felt like pulling it out.

'Did you say coffee, Adam?'

'Extra strong, I suggest.'

'Coffee, hell! I'm all dressed up with nowhere to go and you're *always* dressed up.'

'So?' he purred.

'So let's use that blasted table at Green's, dumbo. I need someone to chuck oysters at!'

• • •

Calla threw her pencil down and rubbed her eyes. It was late Sunday and she was at work in her studio at the top of the house. Since Philippe had dropped out earlier in the week, she'd been working almost every waking hour.

'I'm tired, tired, tired. Christ, why am I doing this?' She pushed her chair back and walked across to the high window which looked out over the street below.

'You're doing it for the biggest architecture prize of your generation, that's why you're doing it,' she told herself.

A keen eye would have noticed that even in a few days she had lost weight. The truth was, she'd hardly stopped to eat. When she did finally put her plans aside, it was to sleep.

She leaned over the stairwell and shouted into the depths of the building: 'You there, Neri?'

A stupid question. Her older sister wasn't the sort of person whose presence you could ignore. Days after their first meeting she had moved in with Calla, the two of them delighting in one another's company, but Nerissa was spending most of her time away, taking pictures of buildings the length and breadth of Britain. She just wasn't a home-bird, that one.

'Damn!' she said out loud. Did architects in their garrets ever go mad? she wondered. She needed someone to talk to. Tonight, thank God, she'd arranged to see her old mentor, Bunny Simkins, but she still had time to kill before setting off for his elegant home in SW3.

She threw herself on the settee to leaf through the arty magazines which she and Nerissa had collected between them over the weeks. There was often an idea in the glossy pages – the line of a painting, the angle of a photograph – which inspired her own architectural designs.

A name jumped out of the *Tatler* as she browsed: *Jason Andover*. It was a review of an art exhibition in Fulham. Amazed, she checked the date of the magazine. This week. He was back.

> *Ariana Muller's 'Menstrual Moments' makes me rejoice in two things: that I do not live with Ms Muller and that she does not have my address. A woman who can do this much violence to red paint would have no mercy with a critic's blood. My one comfort is that if she did find me and take aim, she would almost certainly miss.*

'That's Jason, all right.' Calla sat as if dazed, the magazine on her lap. She had tried not to think about Jason over the last few months. Charlesbury had helped, but there had still been moments when the memory of him had filled her with a yearning which surprised her. And, yes, which irritated her no end.

For didn't she pride herself on being an independent woman?

She'd felt it that time at the Grosvenor House Hotel when she knew she'd reached the final of the Charlesbury competition. And she'd felt it most of all when she heard that violin music filling her opera house during her Glasgow visit with Philippe.

But her anger against him had been there all the time as well. She wasn't one of nature's forgivers and forgetters. On balance, she did rather wish she had cracked open a vase of flowers on Peta's pretty head that night she found them in the flat, instead of smashing the Stradivarius. But she certainly felt no regret over walking out on him.

That, at least, was what she told herself – though she had problems convincing herself sometimes. Jason would wander into her dreams unbidden, smiling that winning smile and being so warm and witty she would sleepily reach out in bed to find him.

'And now he's back.' She closed her mouth firmly on the words 'And he hasn't been in touch with me.' After all, what were they supposed to be to each other? Ex-lovers, that was all. And exes were two a penny.

She wondered how he was, whether he was coping. And she realised that she very much wanted him to cope, to be all right and not to slip back. Was he free of the drugs or simply learning to live with them? He'd obviously renewed professional contacts in the magazine world, she reasoned. He must have begun the long fight to prove that he was trustworthy once again, that he could meet deadlines. But it was a world riddled with the sort of temptations he didn't need. Was he strong enough to turn them down?

Perhaps he needed a hand.

She got up to pour a glass of sparkling mineral water. 'And why should I even think for a mini-second that the hand might be mine?' she asked herself. 'Just don't be a stupid, sentimental bitch.'

But on the way back to the settee, she picked up the phone. She looked long and hard at his byline on the page – a classy upper-lower case italic. Then she took a sip of water. 'Dammit, why not?' Impulsively, she dialled the number which for so long had been hers. She felt her grip tighten as the phone began to ring.

A damn answerphone! Jason's voice: *Sorry I'm out earning a crust. Leave your number and I'll ring you.*

She felt herself flush warm at the sound of his voice. And immediately she knew what a fool she was. Really, why in hell should she ring? If he needed her, he could get her. And she certainly didn't need him.

'Forget it,' she told herself – and put the phone down.

● ● ●

'It's my refuge, Calla-lily. More than ever, in fact.'

He looked a little worn, thought Calla, but he could still smile. Bunny was one of life's optimists.

The white-painted regency house stood in a fine crescent of four-floored houses opposite the park. Inside it was a marriage of old-fashioned English good taste and pre-Napoleonic France. Bunny was comfortably off and, though he was generous in his donations to various charities, had enough left to indulge a taste for the elaborate and antique.

There was more than a touch of Louis Quinze about the place. A beautiful roll-top desk, with gold inlay, was the pride of his sitting room. Pretty French clocks, with all manner of gilded statues atop them, adorned most of the rooms. On the first landing stood an enormous bow-fronted gilt chest. He paused in front of it as they walked upstairs and Calla felt a short lecture coming over him.

'Its pair is at Versailles. I have the guidebook showing it. This one came out with the aristos who fled to England when Madame Guillotine got to work. I was lucky to get it, very lucky.'

He wasn't a vain man, but he took enormous pride in what he called 'my pieces'. Kind visitors let him chatter about them for a while, but Calla had too many things on her mind to allow him the indulgence.

'So tell me,' she said. 'Who was it?'

He poured her a vodka and tonic: 'Who was *what*, Calla?'

351

'Do you really have such a short memory?' she asked with an incredulous laugh, sinking into one of his plump armchairs. 'The last time we spoke you put the phone down on me – very politely, of course – because I was asking too many direct questions.'

'Ah,' he said. 'And one of them concerned the perpetrator of my unfortunate little episode, yes?'

'The bastard, if you'll excuse my French, who stitched you up. Who was it?'

'And what will you do if I tell you?'

'I don't know, Bunny. I really don't know. But I promise it'll stop short of murder. I haven't got the courage to serve a jail sentence.'

'It was Langton Meredith.'

His abruptness took her aback. She didn't know which name she had expected to hear, but it certainly wasn't Meredith's.

'You've crossed swords?'

'Never, to my knowledge. I've only met the man a couple of times. No, as far as I can tell it was simply a question of narrowing the field for the Charlesbury. But probably I wouldn't have made the short list anyway.'

'Probably you would, and you know it.'

'As for the other matter we spoke about, I've definitely decided to sell. I'm getting out,' (he wagged a finger at her) 'and there's nothing you can do to persuade me. The business is already in hand.'

'It makes me so cross that you should let those filthy-minded creeps drive you out!'

'Oh, I might be grateful to them one day. An early retirement with lots of time to scour the auction rooms and the antique shops rather appeals to me. I shall become the profession's amiably cranky elder statesman within a few years.

'You know the sort of thing – asked to judge competitions and write articles for magazines. In fact, I shall probably be offered the chair of architecture at one of those trendy polytechnics which look as if they've been built out of self-assembly blanket boxes. I shall be in charge of a curriculum which includes Darl Pannick. It may even include a special option on Calla-lily. I shall allow only students of exceptional refinement on that one.'

Calla dipped her tongue in the vodka, deep in thought. It seemed such a short while ago that life was simple. She was an up-and-coming architect with a few good commissions under her belt, and Bunny was her mentor, at the peak of his profession. Now nothing was the same.

'I don't know how the hell you're taking this so calmly,' she said.

He smiled: 'Because I've been through it and come out the other side,' he explained. 'There's nothing that can hurt me now. The worst has happened – and I've survived it.'

'And still smiling,' she observed, wonderingly.

'Why not? I've come face to face with myself through all this, Calla, and now I'm able to look myself in the mirror as I couldn't before. I've thought everything through. I've been to hell and back – and believe me, this place is far better.'

She said nothing, and he caught a look in her eyes as she sat cradling her glass.

'Whereas you, young lady, have everything going for you, yet you look tired and what I can only describe as haunted. Or am I imagining it?'

'Dear Bunny,' she began – and then, dammit, felt tears coming. She jumped out of her chair and began to pace the room. The exercise helped to stimulate her anger, which always felt a better emotion.

'I think I've blown it,' she said. 'I got so blasted caught up by the excitement of this project that I didn't see the danger signs.'

'Such as, Calla-lily?'

'Such as, first of all, the horrendous cost of the whole thing. You warned me about that. You told me that people ruined themselves entering these competitions. I didn't listen. So what's happened? I've spent so much time on the Charlesbury work, I've neglected so much of my other work, that I've had to borrow from the bank, and the bank's getting difficult. If I don't win this competition I'm in a bad way. I mean rocky. That's really stupid, eh?'

'The judging is only a few months away, Calla. Can't you hold on until then?'

'Wait till I tell you the next bit. Do you remember how Jason put all that money into the practice? It came with strings attached, thanks to that worm of a brother of his, Patrick. What I've discovered is that Patrick's bought out Jason's investment in CMP, and now he's leaning on me. Heavily.'

'In what way?'

'He wants me to fix business for his contracting company or he'll withdraw his stake. I don't think I can raise that much in a short time.'

'How much?'

'I don't know, Bunny. But it won't be peanuts. As for when – in about eight weeks' time. Before the judging. That damn competition!'

She sat down again, her cheeks flushed, her eyes blazing with anger and despair.

'But if you win it . . . ' he began.

'So now we come to foul-up number three,' she almost howled. 'What do you think happened this week? Shall I give you a few guesses?'

'I think I'd rather not.'

'This week, Bunny, Philippe Beauvoir pulled the plug on me. He's not playing. He quits. He's staying in Paris with his wretched, pregnant little wife. I don't even know whether I'll be disqualified because of it, let alone whether I've the strength to finish the damn blueprints.'

Bunny poured her another drink and, muttering something about a little concoction in the oven, disappeared into the kitchen. She knew her old friend. He was mulling everything over in his mind. Now that she'd unloaded everything in a great flood of emotion she could wait a while for his verdict.

'Courage!' he counselled at last, as they sat down over lasagne and green salad.

'Where can you buy it?' she asked ruefully.

'Mercifully it's one thing you're not short of, Calla-lily. Your spirit has put the fear of God into me more than once in the past. But let's deal with your problems in reverse order. Beauvoir. There's no way he'll change his mind?'

'Not after a few things I've said.'

'Will he let his name be attached to your project?'

She shrugged: 'Probably. But I think I'd rather be without it in the circumstances.'

'A short-sighted view, in my opinion. Carry on as you were, I'd say, and face the problem when it arises. The Duke may not care. Now the money. Is Patrick Andover open to negotiation?'

'God knows. In what way?'

'Might he sell his interest in CMP?'

'Who to, for Chrissakes?' Calla demanded. 'Who'd want to buy into a lame duck outfit like mine?'

'I might,' Bunny said simply.

She might have thrown her arms around him had she thought there was the slightest chance she would accept the offer. As it was, she allowed the tears to well into her eyes.

'Stupid,' she said.

'You think about it, Calla-lily. I shall get much more from selling my own business than I would need to invest in yours. I'd be a partner, but largely a sleeping one. An adviser.'

He took a pad from the table, hunted through his pockets for a pen and scribbled what seemed to be a row of figures.

'Don't look at it now,' he said. 'That's how much I can afford. If Andover will sell, I'm interested.'

30

'The way I see it,' Barney said sagely, 'we share the same problem.'

'And just what *is* this problem, Blarney?' squeaked Malibu ecstatically, rocking back and forth on the floor, hugging her knees. She'd been delighted by him the moment she met him, but he was still capable of new surprises. For instance, the way he'd just marched to the hall cupboard and taken out the ironing board.

'Partial parental deprivation is how I'd put it.' He ran the steam-iron into the corners of a handkerchief, put it down, folded the cloth with great precision and pressed with the iron once again so that it hissed.

'You mean because Nerissa's gone missing again?' Malibu asked. 'On safari in the English outback, taking pot-shots at wild buildings?'

Barney shook his head: 'You're kind of weird, Malibu, you know that? You have this strange way of saying things. I guess I don't entirely understand you.'

Malibu grinned and watched him at his labours. Where on earth had he picked up these quaint domestic habits? She knew that if she once tried to use an iron she'd burn the house down. Perhaps all American kids were like this. In that case, what in God's name happened to them when they grew up? What was left?

'So how are we deprived, Blarney?'

'It's Barney,' he instructed her doggedly. 'It seems you have a problem remembering that. Is this maybe a dyslexial dysfunction?'

'Just another problem, Barnum,' she giggled. 'I've stopped giving them names.'

How hugely entertaining he was! It made Malibu sad to think that he was already half way through his holiday in England. He said things your stuffy parents were supposed to say but never really did, being too damn liberal. He took everything so seriously that it made you glad you were flippant. You could tease him as much as you liked and he never quite got the point.

'What I had in mind was our common single-kin, uni-parental situation,' he went on.

'Oh, *that*! Whatever it is . . . '

'Research has shown that thirty-five per cent of children raised by a single parent, and I checked it out only this morning, suffer interpersonal relationship difficulties.'

'As few as that, Barnum?' Malibu responded, wanting to plant a big juicy kiss on his forehead. That would flummox him!

'Barney.'

'And Bailum. It's a circus, isn't it? Anyway, Bailum, don't you and I get on fabulantly?'

He finished the handkerchieves and started on a pile of socks: 'And the figure rises to seventy-four point six per cent for only children of single parents. That has to be an alarming statistic, is my view.'

Could this pint-sized sociologist, psychologist and philosopher truly be her own brother? she demanded of the universe. Okay, half-brother. But where were the similarities between them? And how had he come about? With what shiver-making, gross, abnormal creature had Nerissa mated to produce such a prodigy?

'Do you iron your shoelaces, Bailum?' she enquired.

'Barney. Of course.' He gazed at her as if she were a primitive from some newly-discovered forest tribe. There was no doubting, as far as he was concerned, whose daughter Malibu was. 'And the incidence of teenage crime is also at disturbing levels among this group.'

'Scarifarious!' she cried, jumping to her feet and padding lightly to the kitchen in search of sustenance. She'd never felt as hungry in her life as he had these past few weeks. Maybe that was purely a stage in her physical development, but Malibu herself put it down to sheer bowled-over happiness. Hadn't she been longing to know something about her mother? Her prayer couldn't have been answered more positively.

More than that, though – she couldn't have asked for a mother better fitted for the job. Nerissa was an unreal as she was. Malibu never once asked herself what kind of a woman abandons a mewling, puking baby. That was irrelevant. In any case, it was seventeen years ago. What mattered was that here was an outlandish, vibrant, exciting woman, and she was Malibu's own mother.

'Can I get you anything, Bailum?' she called, sawing herself two great chunks of wholemeal bread. She reached for a huge tub of peanut butter. 'A working man needs heavy-duty fuel, after all.'

'No thanks. What my aunt's larder tells me is I don't get to eat properly again until I'm back home.' He finished the socks and glumly began to tackle a dish-cloth. 'Did you ever find a pretzel in this place? Or root beer?'

And the extra wonder of it was finding an aunt like Calla. The three of them had hit it off stupendously. True, Nerissa was away more than she was here, and Calla was up to her eyes in her architectural competition, but whenever they spent time together it was like fireworks night, with the sky full of brilliant tracers and colourful meteor showers. The trio only had to walk down the road to catch every eye, and if they went on a shopping expedition they practically brought trade to a halt. They weren't trying to: they simply couldn't help it.

'Personally,' Barney said as she returned to the room, 'I'm coping with this thing. I work at it, and I gauge that I have it under control. How about you? You holding up okay?'

'Haven't robbed a bank in days,' Malibu chirped, finding her place on the carpet again and eagerly devouring her snack. 'How do you resist the dreadful temptation, Bailum?'

'Barney.' He placed the iron on its stand and fixed her with a grave expression. 'I once had a fantasy,' he said.

'*You* did, Baloney?' she asked in amazement. 'And it wasn't terminal?'

'I had this dream I could work it so my mother and my father got together again. It's a common fantasy. It's reported by eighty-nine point two of young people in our situation. I even wrote my father a letter. But it was no good.'

'The letter wasn't any good?'

'The fantasy. I never sent the letter. I came to see my desire for wholeness was a pathetic infantile aberration.'

'Jezebel!'

'Our problem is out of our direct control, Malibu. We have to cope with that fact, I guess. Day by day. It's kinda hard.'

She sat chewing her second slice of bread. Just for a second, to try it out, she attempted to feel sad and deprived. For some reason it wasn't working. On the contrary, she felt bubbly with happiness. But naturally she did!

'Excuse me, Baloney . . . '

'Barney.'

' . . . but something's gone wrong with your sums. I *have* got two parents.'

'Sure,' he conceded. 'We all do. You didn't know that?'

'I mean here and now. In London. Within easy reach. So where's my problem?'

He sighed, a look of weary patience on his face: 'Your problem is, our mother flies back to New York in a few weeks.' He bent down and carefully picked up three crumbs which had fallen from her plate. He put them in his pocket. 'So that's identical to my problem, is how I see it.'

Malibu frowned, hugged her knees afresh and began rocking with renewed energy. She could think better that way. She wasn't the sort to look to the future – butterflies enjoy the sunshine while it warms their wings, they don't worry about autumn frosts – but now the thought of Nerissa's departure hit her with a sickening jolt.

Of course her mother would be leaving. She'd known that all along, but had pushed the idea out of her head.

On the other hand, did she really have to go?

'Let me help you with the housework, Baloney,' she offered, a strangely determined note in her voice. She leapt to her feet, grabbed a pair of tights and, before he could warn her, covered the iron with a sticky mess of overcooked black nylon.

• • •

Darl Pannick answered the door in a mood of scarcely repressed anger. It was a hard-hitting speech he was in the middle of writing, and putting his ideas into words had brought out all the strength of his feelings.

'Please come in, Sir Isaac,' he said.

His visitor smiled ingratiatingly and followed him into the sitting room. Sir Isaac Gower was one of those lesser-known pillars of the establishment who keep English public life on an even keel. He was on the board of several public companies and any number of charities; he'd served on some important Government-created commissions; he was on the committee of the MCC; and he dabbled in the adminstration of the arts in various forms. He was an expert in nothing, but he knew everybody. And he was regarded as 'sound'.

'I do apologise for the short notice,' he said, taking the chair he was offered and accepting a whisky and soda. 'I shan't take up too much of your time, I hope.'

Pannick wasn't in the slightest overawed by the visit of so patrician a figure. Although he'd been brought up in England, and understood its institutions well enough, he always thought of himself as an outsider. There was, he thought, something comical about the English way of doing things – the perpetual nudge and wink which encouraged charges of hypocrisy. Nothing was ever out in the open. Darl Pannick liked to be more direct.

'I assume it's to do with the Pring Memorial Lecture,' he said flatly.

Sir Isaac laughed: 'It must be taking most of your time at present,' he suggested.

That's it, Pannick thought. Don't answer my bloody question. Try to play me like a trout fisherman with his fly. Only, I won't be played.

'Probably too much,' he replied. 'But it's almost done. How can I help you?'

The Pring lecture was a prestigious event in the architectural year, and to be chosen to give it was a considerable honour. But he didn't *feel* honoured. In fact, Pannick thought he'd been overlooked for too long. His reputation and his seniority demanded that he be asked to give the lecture, and this time his turn had come.

'I'm not sure that "help" is the word,' Sir Isaac murmured. 'As you're well aware, I'm no architect myself, though I do have a great interest in the subject.'

And I'm supposed to say, Pannick thought, what a profound knowledge you really have, how much you've done for architecture and all that bullshit. But I won't.

'You've come here to nobble me,' Pannick accused him, not even bothering to smile.

'Ah no, no, no, no, no!' sang Sir Isaac. 'Please don't place such an interpretation on what I have to say.' He took refuge in his scotch for a moment. 'I'm merely someone who has gauged the opinion of certain people in the profession and who has come to make the knowledge of that opinion available to you.'

'That's generous of you,' Pannick said, not caring if the sarcasm showed. He fully guessed what was coming. He wasn't sure he could remain civil if the conversation lasted for very much longer.

'Not at all. I regard myself as one of life's middlemen. If I can help to oil the wheels, so much the better.'

Yes, you're oily, all right, Pannick thought. He poured himself a cognac. Clearly he wasn't going to get rid of this man for a little while yet, so he might as well listen in comfort.

'I've always understood,' he said, 'that the Pring lecture is supposed to be a personal view. That is its strength. We don't have to toe some party political line, or even the RIBA line.'

'Quite so, Mr Pannick.'

'And I don't see, therefore, how it can be of any help whatsoever for anyone to make any representations to me. I know what I want to say.'

God, he knew! He felt it even more strongly now than when the doorbell had rung. He couldn't wait to get back to his desk and write the damn lecture.

'Please, Mr Pannick! It's not a question of what you want to say. Far be it from me to make a single suggestion on that score. It's more a question of, ah . . . ' (he raised his glass to his lips and fixed the architect with a stare across its rim) . . . more, I suppose, of the *tone* of the thing.'

Vicious, Pannick thought, if I can manage it. Murderous. He'd decided to let rip on the subject of the Duke of Mercia and his influence on modern British architecture. The Duke had had *his* say, on television, in the newspapers, even through a coffee-table book on the subject. Now it was time for the architects to hit back.

And it was pretty obvious that word had got around.

'It might perhaps not be a good idea,' Sir Isaac said softly, 'to rock the boat. If you follow me.'

'Whose boat, precisely?'

'Let's put it this way,' said the supreme society fixer. 'Many architects share your views, Mr Pannick. They're entirely reasonable views, of course. But the great British public, perhaps unfortunately, may not be in a state of readiness to accept them.'

'The great British public are pig-ignorant, you mean.'

'What I mean,' Sir Isaac continued, a little more forcefully, 'is that strong criticism of the Duke of Mercia and his plans might be counter-productive. It might be better not to stir things up too much at present. Do you follow?'

'I follow,' Pannick said. He made great play of tightening the top of the whisky bottle and replacing it in the cabinet. He downed his own drink and placed the glass upside down on the tray. He stood with his hands behind his back, in a gesture which couldn't be mistaken.

'Well, thank you so much, Mr Pannick,' Sir Isaac said, rising, 'for allowing me to state the profession's case.'

Darl Pannick followed the worthy knight to the door, congratulating himself on keeping his temper. He even managed a courteous farewell. Then he hurried back to the desk, took up his pen and began to write at a furious pace.

● ● ●

'Jeez, this is a new Calla Marchant!' Neri exclaimed as she took the three darts which had been thrust at her. 'Where was this strange playfulness hiding all these weeks?'

Calla laughed: 'Behind a whole host of problems, I suppose. But now, as Rhett Butler said, frankly I don't give a damn.'

'Right on, little sis! Think wild. How many points for braining the guy?'

'Twenty. Ten for the body, five for extremities.'

'And the other creeps in the picture?'

'Zilch, as I think you'd say.'

They were in Calla's studio on the top floor, and Neri was taking aim at a full-page newspaper cutting. The photograph at its centre showed Langton Meredith standing with a row of stuffed shirts. The first dart missed completely and ended up in a Charlesbury blueprint pinned to the wall.

'Lack of practice,' Neri said. 'I haven't thrown a dart in anger since I gave up marrying people.' Her second shot stuck in the text of the article. 'So why the change of heart?'

Calla shrugged

'Bloody-mindedness, mainly,' she explained. 'I suddenly asked myself what I was doing worrying when I could be out there doing.'

'That's my girl,' Neri said, clipping Meredith's arm. 'Five points!'

What Calla didn't say was that Bunny had put the bounce back into her stride. For one thing, if her old friend could put all his troubles behind him, why the hell couldn't she? She'd never been a quitter. But the meeting had also given her notorious anger a vital boost. She *would* win Charlesbury, if only to deny that bastard Meredith the prize.

If at the same time she was giving two-fingers to Philippe Beauvoir and his little wife, so much the better for that!

'Your architecture is always like this?' Neri asked, surprised by the raw atmosphere of competition and back-biting she'd come across in England. 'You guys are always hurling arrows at one another?'

Calla, her dander up, hurled her first dart perilously close to a window.

'This man,' she told her sister, 'is 22-carat shit. If I don't attack his picture I'll end up using his person.' The second dart crashed against an angle-poise lamp, so that the sound echoed through the room for several seconds. 'Which may be a better idea.'

Neri laughed like a drain: 'Have I seen any of his great works?' she asked. 'It feels like I've taken shots of just about every last building in Britain these months, ancient and modern.'

'You'll have to go abroad,' Calla told her. 'That's where he does most of his business.' She took careful aim with her third dart and speared one of the other men in the photograph. 'My apologies,' she grinned, peering at the cutting, 'to Senhor Diego Morais himself.'

Neri swung round: 'Say that again!'

'I said apologies –'

'No, the name, dumbo.'

'Diego Morais. You've heard of him? Meredith's involved with him. An extremely wealthy Brazilian. Owner of half of Brasilia as far as I can make out. A developer.'

'Sure,' said Neri, 'and a drugs dealer.'

'A *what*?'

'Names I don't forget. I've had too many myself – why do we always take *their* names, for Sweet Jesus? This guy is bad blood, Calla, believe me.' She cocked her head. 'You want that I should get proof of this, little sis? You could use the info, maybe?'

Calla's eyes were alive and her blood raced: 'You're damn right I could!' she answered.

Nerissa's next dart went clean through Meredith's head.

• • •

361

'No, Malibu,' Grant Locke spoke very firmly into the telephone. 'There's no way I'm picking you up this evening . . . I daresay that does seem unreasonable to you, but the taxi service isn't functioning at present . . . Because the proprietor has had some kind of a brainstorm and joined an architectural practice, that's why.'

He held the receiver at arm's length and grinned, rather sheepishly, at Dulcie. She was in the act of putting a mug of very hot coffee on the desk in front of him.

'If I'm allowed to make an observation, Malibu . . . That's very generous of you. All I'd like to say is . . . Malibu?...What I'd like to ask is why they don't give you a bed over there, you're such a regular customer . . . No, of course that wasn't sarcasm . . . Yes, I do like you living here with me . . . Very much . . . Extravagantly . . . From the very core of my being, for God's sake . . . Ciao, sweetheart!'

Locke seized his coffee, sniffed in its heady aroma and wished the steam would become a cloud which would surround him and shut him off from the world. To one side of him was his drawing-board, and the wastepaper bin next to it was full of crumpled sheets of paper.

'Sweet enough?' enquired Dulcie, who was busy backing up files on her computer.

Shut him off from the female world in particular. That was how Locke felt right now. He was besieged. How simple life had once seemed! All right, he'd had the Malibu problem for some time, but he'd been able to shelve it. He'd been aware of Dulcie's growing craving for intimacy, but he'd thought he could push that into the background, too.

'Fine. It's just fine. Perfect in fact. Best mug of coffee I've had in a long time.'

What the hell was the matter with him? he wondered, noticing Dulcie's sharp, querying expression. It was a run-of-the-mill, one-tea-spoon-of-instant, small-splash-of-milk, two-sugar mug of coffee. Why the song and dance about it? Why couldn't he say what he felt any more?

'Would you like a biscuit?'

Please no! he thought with an inward groan. Not another decision. How could he be sure of saying the right thing? He didn't even know if he wanted a biscuit or not. That was the state he'd been driven to.

'If you're having one.'

Perhaps Charlesbury was getting to him, Locke thought. He certainly hadn't been conscious of worrying about it. He was the front-runner, after all. Everyone knew he designed the sort of schemes the Duke liked. It was one hell of a job preparing for a competition like that, but it was normally no sweat for him. Was being the favourite beginning to put a strain on him?

'I won't, thank you, but the packet's open if you'd like one.'

No, it was nothing to do with the competition. The difficulties he was having with these blasted blueprints were only the symptom of what he thought of as The Woman Problem. His emotions were in turmoil.

'I think I won't, Dulcie, if you don't mind.'

A short time ago he'd had only one goal on the sexual front, and that was the conquest of Calla Marchant. His lust for Calla hadn't been without its complications. He'd known she was the sister of his former lover, and he'd known that she was entirely ignorant of the fact. That had always given a spice to their relationship, from his point of view.

But did that mean he still hankered after Nerissa? Was it the echo of the violet of her eyes in Calla's that had turned him on? When he had stumbled upon her that night he'd picked Malibu up from Calla's house, he had felt sick to the stomach, but he hadn't known why. He didn't know what he wanted, and that was part of The Woman Problem. Oh, Lord!

'Why should *I* mind, Grant?'

And just when he thought he could breathe easily about Malibu, now that she had a job which satisfied her, the girl's feelings had been put in turmoil by the sudden discovery of her mother. She was crazier than ever, dammit. She didn't seem to know whether she lived with him or with her mother at Calla's. And because she was so mixed up, she seemed to be always trying to entice him over there for little impromptu parties.

'Perhaps I will have one, Dulcie, after all.',

He heard the impatient intake of her breath. Wrong move, he thought. Especially as he really didn't want a biscuit, for heaven's sake. *He did not want a biscuit!* He could feel the tension mounting. Oh yes, Dulcie was still very much part of The Woman Problem.

She had come back to him because she had sensed he needed her. Dulcie desperately wanted to be needed. She craved the closeness it brought on. But she particularly wanted to be needed by Grant Locke. It was unfair, he protested to whichever cosmic forces it was which controlled the human heart. He'd done nothing to encourage her. He only wanted a good secretary – which she was until the trembles came over her.

He'd been relieved when she left, much as her absence had wreaked havoc with his office systems. And he'd tried very hard to resist her offer of coming back. He was too soft, that was the trouble. And she had sensed his weakness, knowing that he was going through a bad time in every way. She knew him better than anyone, she told herself. Yes, she doubtless knew him better than he knew himself. She would return in triumph, Dulcie to the rescue. She would nurse him, coddle him, make his coffee, provide his biscuits . . .

'Mint chocs,' she whispered in his ear, her arm rubbing against his as she slid a plate onto the desk next to his coffee. 'New recipe.'

His voice was heavy Yorkshire: 'Ay, but I'm nobbut an old-fashioned lad, Dulcie.'

He wished he was, sometimes. His father had never had The Woman Problem. He'd married one, stayed with her and stopped where he was all his life. That way, surely, lay peace and contentment.

'I think at heart you are,' Dulcie said in a matter-of-fact tone. 'And you need protecting from the wicked world around you.'

He smiled helplessly: 'I'm really not worth the effort, Dulcie. As you well know. I'm difficult, bloody-minded, cantankerous . . . '

'And it may surprise you to know,' she told him, 'that there are people who enjoy the challenge of taking someone like you in hand, whatever the inconvenience – and the pain.'

He grunted: 'There's an expression where I come from . . . '

'I know it,' she said, imitating his northern accent. 'There's nowt so queer as folk.'

• • •

London at its worst can be the greyest, most oppressive of cities, but when the June sunshine is filtering through the fresh green leaves in its extensive parks it becomes magically transformed. Then you forget the millions of people slaving at screens in those thousands of cramped offices. Out in the fresh and balmy air you're persuaded that there's nothing quite like city life, where practically everything has been created by human hand precisely for rich human enjoyment.

Nerissa, bowling along in a taxi towards Darl Pannick's office with the window right down, felt suitably elated. Life was darn good. She watched the people in the street and thought they looked a happy breed. The breeze cooled her forehead and rustled this morning's copy of the *Independent* which she was flicking through in a lazy, desultory way in between her people-watching.

Some day soon, she supposed, she'd have to go home. She always began to experience this nagging feeling when she was a few months on the road. You couldn't stay away for ever. This time she'd had the wit to bring Barney over for a time, which appeased her conscience no end, but she had a pile of queries piling up from dear Betsy, and her agent kept leaving messages about lucrative deals he could fix if only she'd let him know her intended movements. As if she knew!

She'd never for a minute felt homesick when she left England all those years ago. Calla was the only person she had missed at all, and that pain had soon dimmed in the busy press of her life. But now she was back in the country of her birth she did feel as if she belonged. Sure, some things were different. The English seemed a lot more polite than the people she was used to, but they'd sure as hell forgotten what service was, and they didn't seem to know whether they were 24/7 go-getters or gentle, caring souls who followed some earlier philosophy. They seemed a bit lost, in fact.

But this London she was spinning through (they'd got as far as Oxford Street) seemed a welcoming place to Nerissa. She'd been away too long to realise how much it had changed, how much dirtier and more cut-throat it had become. She compared it with New York and it made her feel comfortable.

Her eyes were drawn to a front-page headline: *PRING LECTURE ASSAULT ON CHARLESBURY.* She'd got to know this newspaper because it gave the best coverage bar none to the world of architecture. It also, as it happened, had the best photography of any of the Fleet Street papers, too.

She was on the second paragraph before she realised just what the story was about – and who was involved.

'Jesus,' she muttered. 'The little creep.'

> *In his hour-long lecture, Darl Pannick not only accused the Duke of 'wilfully turning the clock back two hundred years', but made a detailed attack on each of the three schemes chosen to contest the final of the Charlesbury competition.*

'Excuse me,' she barked to the driver, 'but how long before we get there?'

'About five minutes – if this twerp in front of me ever gets out of first gear.'

'Okay, just take it slowly, will you?'

'Slowly, you said?'

'Sure. I want to read this article properly before I arrive.'

Judging from the quotes the paper had picked up from around the profession, Pannick's speech of the night before had stirred up a hornet's nest. He'd gone for the jugular. In fact, Nerissa had never heard of such vivid language in a public lecture. That was great, of course. There was nothing she liked better than pricking pomposity, giving the establishment a kick in the fanny.

But she didn't always appreciate his aim.

The joint Marchant-Beauvoir scheme, Pannick suggested, had
'more sophistication than substance'. There was no evidence in
the entered blueprints, he claimed, that the finished project would
be anything other than 'a charming but irrelevant appendage'
to the existing town, rather than a creation 'genuinely born of
the millennium.'

'Up yours, Darl Pannick!' Nerissa growled, climbing from the cab and paying off the driver.

She was secretly pleased to have something to lambast him for. Otherwise, she'd have felt at a distinct disadvantage. Here was a man who had pulled strings to land her a wonderful assignment in England, and all she'd done was given him the slip. Even someone as thick-skinned as Nerissa knew that this was a tiny bit naughty.

The fact was she had so many other things on her mind, she didn't want the complication. Who needed it? Next to old husbands, old flames were the worst sort of hindrance to a carefree, happy life. With ex-husbands you spent your time thinking how godawful the relationship used to be. With ex-lovers you thought how much better it was then than now.

Really, the wisest course was to give men a miss altogether.

'Neri!'

He had come down the steps to meet her. For a moment she did actually forget to remember her maxim. Perhaps it *could* be as good now as before. That worn, experienced face of his – it was fascinating to read between the leathery lines. There was a history in it. And that slightly gravelly voice. She remembered it in her ear at that hotel in Rio.

'Darl baby.' She linked her arm with his as they climbed the steps to his offices, a two-storeyed Queen Anne house with a pretty shell-shaped canopy over the door. 'You don't practise what you preach, I see.'

He ignored the remark and led her through a spacious, elegant entrance lobby into a room with chairs, a sofa and low tables which matched the period of the house immaculately. There was a chimney-piece heavily framed in marble, with curly mouldings, and several glass cabinets with finely moulded legs. The walls were sprinkled with water-colours, tastefully hung. There were sash windows, open to let the warm summer air blow in.

'Helluva strain,' she suggested, 'not having the waste pipes crawling all over the walls outside. How do you cope with that?'

He motioned her into a chair: 'Please, Neri,' he said. 'I don't want to talk about architecture today even for a second. You've read the papers?'

She tossed the *Independent* at his feet with a dismissive gesture: 'Sure.'

'Then that's enough. The subject is taboo.'

'But I want to talk about it, Darl baby,' she cried. 'You've just slandered my little sister.'

'I beg your pardon.'

'You stood up in a public hall last night and knocked six shades of piss out of my kith and kin. You took a megaphone to the task of belittling the woman who'll be building the wonders of the world when you're a forgotten graffito on the cracked wall of post-modernist architecture. How do you plead, Lego-brick Man?'

'Calla Marchant is your sister?'

'I read that as a guilty plea.'

Pannick stared at her in silence for some time.

'Yes, there is a resemblance,' he acknowledged. 'Why didn't I notice it before?'

'Quit stalling, crumbum – the judge might just interpret it as contempt of court. That girl never harmed a hair of your head, yet you've dragged her reputation through the mud.'

'Don't be ridiculous, Neri. It's not personal. Someone has to make a stand against this duke and his wretched competition, and nobody else seems to have the nerve to do it.'

'So it's bold Darl Pannick to the rescue, eh?'

'You like to mock me,' he said. 'I don't doubt your sister's qualities, but she's been seduced by the promise of glory, just like all the others. She's helping to betray her own profession.'

'Balls!' exploded Nerissa merrily.

She didn't have a strong view about modern architecture, much of which she quite enjoyed. And she knew full well that Pannick's motives were of the very highest. But that was trivial detail. The point was that he'd presented himself as a sitting target. She could never resist one of those, especially when there were high stakes to play for.

He shrugged: 'This is fruitless, Neri. Let's talk about something else. About all this work which is occupying all your time, for instance.'

'Exhausting,' she gasped, hoping that her sudden limp pose was movingly convincing.

'I had hoped,' he said, 'that we might see a little more of each other.'

'There's something we missed?' she queried with exaggerated innocence.

He grinned wickedly: 'That was a good time in Rio, yes? I've often thought about it. What energy!'

'Hey, don't make a girl blush, bad boy. I'm a reformed character these days.'

'No, I don't believe it.'

Didn't want to believe it, she thought. How come men had the ability to play the old tunes over and over again? On the other hand, maybe it wouldn't be so bad. She remembered the tenderness as much as the obstacle race. He was one hell of an attractive man. You could spend too much of your time working.

'I was thinking,' he said, 'of an evening meal, perhaps? A night on the town? You'd like that?'

'Maybe,' she replied off-handedly.

'Tomorrow night, say?' he suggested, whipping out a pocket diary. 'I'll call for you at seven.'

She stood up and strolled to the window, apparently lost in thought. A couple of minutes passed. He heard her humming softly to herself. Then she turned and perched on the arm of a chair: 'I'll come,' she said, 'on one condition.'

'Which is?'

'No, foxy man, you have to give me your word. That's the deal. You promise?'

He laughed, defeated: 'Okay, I promise. What's the condition?'

'That you tell me,' Neri said slowly, 'every last damn thing about Diego Morais.'

31

When bad times came to Patrick Andover he always looked for revenge. Because this was the worst time ever, he was after the ultimate revenge – which was why he'd invited Calla Marchant to meet him for lunch at the Stafford.

What infuriated him most of all was his own misjudgement. He'd counted on getting his hands on the bulk of his mother's fortune, either in his own right or indirectly through his children. He hadn't doubted it for a second. It was pre-ordained. It was what was due to happen to the Andover money. It was what his father would have wanted, and his father's wish was the family law. Because he'd been so certain of that, he hadn't made any effort to make sure nothing went wrong. That was so uncharacteristic of him, it so contradicted every rule he'd ever lived by, that just for a moment – and for the very first time in his life – he had doubted his own ability.

That night after he had knocked Jason to the ground at the manor house, and roared off into the darkness in a paroxysm of fury, he had begun a desperate attempt to save the money from falling into his brother's hands. He spent hours on the telephone, arguing, cajoling and bribing. He called in old favours. He leant on the susceptible.

It was all to no avail. His mother grew more stubborn the more her advisers tried to reason with her. She knew. She was ready for them. She expected to have her good sense, even her sanity, called into question and she upstaged Patrick at every turn. The rector, an incorruptible man, paid her regular visits and made it clear to all and sundry that he found Sarah Andover to be in her right mind and that, if required, he would testify as much to any court of law. She had her last will and testament signed in the presence of the kind of witnesses whose integrity nobody could impugn. Not only that, but she seemed to gain strength from the experience. There was a bit more colour in her cheeks for a day or two. She talked a lot. She regained her appetite. She even sent her maid Carrie out for a bottle of port, saying she suddenly had a fancy for it, and she worked her way through it in no time at all.

Patrick continued to pull every string that remained to him, but he felt each one slip inexorably from his grasp. His mother refused to talk to anyone about her money. The will had been written and signed, and that was that. When he made his last, despairing effort to make her change her mind, sitting by her bed with a well-rehearsed plea for her to remember her great responsibilities, she resorted to the unanswerable ploy of fading away beneath his gaze.

'Mother!' he called urgently.

Was that a smile on those thin lips? The eyes seemed to burn through him for a second, their glance bitterly triumphant, and then they closed for the last time. Her head flopped onto the pillow and her hands released their grip on the sheet. He was beaten.

There was a black void inside him. The money itself wasn't the worst thing. Patrick Andover would never be anything but rich: every day he earned a few thousand pounds more to add to his children's legacy. No, what gnawed away at his entrails was a kind of shame. He'd been caught out in a stupidity. The man who had lived by his proud, masculine manipulation of everything and everyone had been made a fool of by his own mother. His own weak, foolish, artistic, unrealistic mother.

As he recovered from the shock of her betrayal, as he felt his old ebullience gradually returning, so his contempt for what he saw as feminine values intensified. Sarah was for ever damned in his memory. His brother Jason, who had inherited their mother's useless sensitivity, was a worm to be crushed underfoot. Patrick Andover made a vow to himself never to be outmanouevred again, not by anyone. Ever.

Those who knew him well had never seen him so purposeful. He strode around with a menacing determination. He asked more questions and gave more orders in an hour than most businessmen managed in a week. People kept out of his way. In his intense moods he was never a man to be crossed, and this was the deepest, darkest mood they'd ever witnessed. He gave off an energy that had his colleagues sliding away out of sight and which made his rivals quake.

During those weeks after the death of his mother, Patrick shook up Andover International as if it was a mere corner sweetshop with marketing problems. It wasn't as if he had ever let the company run to seed, but now he tackled its every last problem with a ruthlessness which was excessive even by his own standards. Managers were sacked, less profitable products were killed off, bold new initiatives were taken in areas entirely new to the firm. Nothing could stand in his way.

It was as if he had to prove to himself that his instinct was still sound. Many of the changes he was bringing about would take months, even years, to reach fruition, but he'd weighed up all the possibilities and he knew that he was doing the right thing. The force was with him. He was like a snooker player on song, judging all the angles to perfection.

'Thank you, mother,' he muttered to himself on one occasion as he put the phone down on an especially adroit deal. It had been hovering at the back of his mind for months, but only now had he been inspired to carry it through. He blessed his mother for giving him a new sense of purpose. It was the challenge he'd needed, he told himself. Sarah

Andover had made her little protest, and he was replying as his father and his grandfather would have done. The male principle had reasserted itself.

And the Calla Marchant business? That was just one more of his affairs which had to be dealt with. It had, however, a special component – the Marchant woman herself. Andover's brain was doing its arithmetic, all right, but in its current hyped-up state it was capable of calculations of quite another sort at one and the same time. He knew exactly what he was doing, and he'd never felt in better form.

He was waiting for her in the characterful terrace bar of the Stafford, one of that rash of small, historic hotels which has thrived in London during the past few years. He liked its atmosphere of a private club. He liked its setting in a cobbled mews, and he liked its SW1 postcode. He was also best friends with the head porter, a man who could work wonders.

'Bloody Mary?' he asked as she arrived, his knowledge of her preference immediately establishing an intimacy which took her by surprise.

In the hot July sunshine she was dressed only as much as she needed to be for the occasion. She wore a flimsy strawcoloured dress which clung to the thrusts of her curves and which emphasised the honey-brown of her slender arms and her firm, bare legs. She had a pair of simple leather sandals on her feet.

'Orange juice, please,' she said, holding out against him already. 'In this weather.'

He kept his eyes off her. One glance had been enough to remind him of her brimming sexuality, and his game plan was to start in a strictly businesslike, even an off-hand, manner. He knew what he was doing.

Calla had come to the meeting with a determination of her own. If he would agree to sell his share in CMP back to her she would pay to the limit of Bunny's offer. She certainly wouldn't spend a penny more. She wasn't going to put her practice into even greater jeopardy by mortgaging its future. He had the whip hand, true. He could decide here and now to carry out his threat, to call in his interest in the business and force her to raise the cash from the bank – if she could.

But she wasn't going to crawl!

He surprised her again by making no mention of CMP whatsoever over the drinks. Instead, he began to talk about his own business deals, high-level meetings, hirings and firings, the money markets. He spoke about these things in such an impassioned manner that she felt almost inspired by them herself. It wasn't dry accountants' talk, but vigorous and colourful reportage from the front line. Yes, that's what it was like. Andover had been over the top where the bullets were spitting and the bombs exploding, and here he was, alive to tell the gripping tale.

And he was very much alive. She remembered the first time she had met him – how she'd been at once repelled by his hardness and, at the same time, drawn towards it like a magnet. She experienced that again now, his raw dynamism somehow rubbing against something similar in herself. And once again she fought against it.

His gutsy cut-and-thrust business talk continued in the restaurant until, despite herself, she began to feel herself caught up in a world of high drama and consequence. Inevitably, too, he himself appeared a strong, outsized character as the main actor in the play he was describing so vividly. She found herself enjoying his stories, coming to recognise his little mannerisms as he brought each one to a close. And she responded on cue. If he gave a short laugh, at the climax of part of a story, she would laugh, too, and in a similar vein.

Andover noticed all this, of course. Because he despised women, he was able to observe them analytically. It was one of the secrets of his success with them. He knew how to make them respond, and he enjoyed manipulating those responses. He wasn't talking business because he wanted to, but because it was part of this particular plan of campaign. He was the performing fox mesmerising a rabbit.

When, at last, he turned to Calla Marchant Practice, it was with an air almost of condescension. What was her small firm compared with the corporations he controlled? But he flattered her that he wanted to know. He asked how the Charlesbury project was going and, almost before she knew it, she was talking of it with the same rampant enthusiasm as he himself had shown only minutes before. As if they were two of a kind.

'You've thought about what we spoke of last time?'

His question brought her up short. She had to check herself, to remind herself that, far from being some kind of feisty soulmate, Patrick Andover was a ruthless businessman who was a danger to her very survival.

'Naturally.' She suddenly knew that she couldn't hide. This man was one of life's natural dealers. He read people, and he acted on what he read. Hot weather or not, she felt a shiver of apprehension run along her spine.

'And?'

'I don't believe,' she said, 'that I could have much influence on the Duke, whatever the outcome of the competition. I can't see that you and I would work usefully together.'

Her words hung in the air. Andover broke off a piece of bread roll and chewed it very slowly, his eyes elsewhere. She observed how comfortable he seemed in his surroundings, how much at ease he was. It increased the sense of power he gave off. It made her feel extremely vulnerable.

'You've considered the consequences of that?'

For the first time he looked her full in the eyes. His were blue, hard and searching. Hers held the gaze. She had to draw on all her reserves of grit to hold them there, not to flinch and look away.

'I'd like to make you an offer,' she said.

He laughed: 'You're in a position to do that?'

'I'd like to buy back your share in CMP.' She watched his face and had to admire the lack of any give-away expression. 'How much would you want?'

Andover studied her face and then, as if involuntarily, allowed his eyes to wander briefly down her neck to the top of her dress.

'Hey, not so fast,' he said lightly. 'Why should I even consider doing that?'

'Because I may not be such a sound investment,' she said. 'I've won nothing yet. What use would your money be if it was tied up in a busted flush.'

He nodded: 'A reasonable argument. But suppose that I enjoy being involved with this particular enterprise?'

As he said it he screwed up his eyes and puckered his lips in an expression she knew very well. Calla Marchant had never been short of admirers, or of men who made their admiration glaringly plain. Sexual advances in business meetings had always seemed insufferable to her, yet this one didn't, she conceded, strike her – as it really should have done – as a vulgar come-on. Why was that? What had he done to make both the remark and the gesture nothing more than chivalrous?

Andover knew the answer to that. He knew the sexual potency of power. He knew how to lead a woman into the kind of situation and the kind of conversation that maximised the whiff of power in himself. And when a woman of Calla Marchant's vibrant temperament and ambitious drive was involved, the vibes of suppressed energy seemed to magnify of their own accord.

'But assuming you don't,' she smiled, 'how much?'

'More than you could raise.'

'You don't know that.'

'I've a very good idea, Calla.'

He had never used her first name before and it seemed to sting her very flesh, so that she blushed. She cursed herself for blushing. The thought rolled dimly across her brain: *What in the hell's happening to you?* She reached for her wine glass and emptied it.

'I'd like to make you an offer,' she insisted.

'No, I don't think so.'

'You don't know how much it is, dammit!'

Andover shrugged: 'Well, perhaps we'll see,' he said vaguely, in what seemed to her an unusually kindly tone.

Over the coffee they spoke little. The atmosphere seemed mellow. Calla remembered the vow she'd made to herself – that she wouldn't crawl. Well, she wouldn't. She'd said her last word on the subject. If he did want to sell his stake, he'd have to say so. She knew how much she was prepared to pay. If he chose to keep his stake, she'd deal with the consequences of that when they arose.

'Let's finish this elsewhere,' he said comfortably, after he'd signed a chit for the meal. 'I've got a room upstairs. Why don't we have a drink up there?'

She nodded and followed him from the table. What he had in mind she didn't doubt. She understood Patrick Andover well enough.

'Everything's in order, sir,' the head porter said with the hint of a bow as they passed.

'Thank you, George,' Andover replied briskly, pressing the button for the lift. 'Damn good man,' he confided quietly to Calla as the doors opened.

They rose slowly to the top floor, Andover managing to control the feeling of triumph which flooded through every atom of his being. This, he told himself, was the final settling of the scores. After this he need never think about his mother's legacy again.

Because what he knew, and what Calla couldn't possibly know, was that he no longer owned the all-important stake in her practice. He had sold it this very morning, to Jason. He had the cheque in his pocket now. Her reaction when she eventually discovered this would be wonderful to behold.

'Champagne!' exclaimed Calla as they entered the bedroom, its curtains drawn across the window but fluttering in the breeze. Damn obvious, she thought – but just right all the same.

'Only the best,' he said, expertly uncorking it and filling the two glasses which stood on the table alongside the ice bucket.

The investment in CMP had been a mere bagatelle for Andover. In the reassessment of his finances caused by Sarah's wilful stupidity, it had made sound sense to dispose of it. The practice might, indeed, be a busted flush. Even if it wasn't, his money could earn him certain dividends elsewhere, whereas with CMP it was tied up in something purely speculative. It had to go.

But there was a symbolic aspect to the CMP stake, too. By simply unloading it, he could be seen to be acting out of weakness. He might appear a victim of his mother's will. More than that, he might seem to have been bested by his own despised brother. Patrick Andover wasn't prepared ever to be a victim, and Jason was the last person he would allow to best him, so the deal had to be obviously to his advantage. He sold his stake for twice what he'd paid for it.

Right and proper, he told himself. The cash would only go to waste in a puff of narcotics otherwise. Jason had paid up like a lamb, easily persuaded that the stake was worth much more now that CMP was a Charlesbury finalist.

Honour was, therefore, almost satisfied. But Patrick had one final move to make – a move which would give him the sweetest revenge on his brother.

As Calla raised her face to drink the champagne, he lowered his lips to her neck. He held them there, savouring the warmth and the smell of her, then stood back before he might be overcome. He was an expert in self-control. He was an expert in mastery.

'I always want the best,' he said.

'And usually get it, I assume.'

'Always.'

He took her glass and dropped it on the carpet, enfolding her in his arms in the same movement. He held her lightly, but she felt the strength of him against her, one knee pushing against the inside of her thigh. His hands ran down her back to her waist and pulled her still closer.

'Yes,' she whispered.

'Wait.'

He disappeared into the bathroom. Calla kicked off her sandals. She reached behind to unzip her dress, using both hands to release the clip of her bra. She shook it down the inside of the dress, then tugged her pants off and hurriedly tossed them away from her. The cloth clung to her breasts and her stomach, which felt moist in the heat. She sat on the edge of the bed, waiting.

Patrick Andover had a perfect body. He stood in the doorway, flaunting it. His shoulders were broad and square, and a full chest, with a neat triangular mat of blond hair, tapered to a waist kept taut and slender by hard exercise. His thighs were long and well-muscled, and rearing up between them from its deep-hanging sac, was a gigantic throbbing cock which seemed to have a hungry, rapacious life all its own.

Calla slipped the dress from her shoulders and, standing, let it fall around her ankles. She was breathing deeply.

'Christ,' he said, 'I'm going to enjoy you.'

Bending, he picked her up in an effortless swinging movement. He raised her breasts towards his face, rubbing his lips against them, then lowered her to the bed. She lay outstretched, awaiting his touch.

He knew how to play the game. *His* game. Patrick Andover had honed the humiliation of women to a fine art. He recognised all the signs of arousal, and he knew how to work his victims either slowly or at speed. If he brought them quickly to excitement, it was only so that he could immediately thwart their desire by holding back, delaying, transferring his attention to some other erogenous zone. Then slowly, agonisingly slowly, he would bring them to screaming pitch.

Now he turned Calla over and ran a finger firmly along the cleft of her arse. She pressed her knees into the bed and opened her thighs, inviting a deeper probe, but he pulled away, kneeling beside her with his manhood hard and tight. He tried not to look at her. If she was his greatest prize, she was also his greatest temptation, and he knew to keep his passion in suspense while he carried out his task, expertly, relentlessly.

'Pussy,' he murmured, his finger brushing high inside her thigh then, as she squirmed to meet it, lifting away from her again. He lowered his head and gently nibbled at the flesh inside her knee. She shuddered and tautened, and he heard her gasp with a little intake of breath. Her hands were stretched above her in a gesture of utter submission.

Sliding from the bed, he took her feet in his hands and licked the soles, pressing hard with his tongue. She writhed and murmured. He put his head between her calves, nosing gently upwards towards her sex. Then he knelt above her and his hands found her buttocks, massaging them, his thumbs close to the cleft again, so that she heaved almost into his face.

He turned her over and, eyes closed, she reached out with her arms to take him. But he refused, wary of being overcome by the feel and taste of her. He pushed her arms down, forcing them under her, and lipped the swell of her heaving breast and its rigid nipple until she muttered something he couldn't make out.

'You want, eh?' he asked through clenched teeth. 'You want?'

But it was too soon to finish it. She was simmering, she was close enough to boiling over, but he was going to make her run the whole gamut of frustrations. The palm of his hand made a slow, stroking motion beneath her breasts, moving down to her stomach, where the muscles hardened. She wriggled upwards, bringing her throbbing mound of venus closer and closer to his hand, but he retreated, pinching the flesh of her loins, first gently, then more severely.

She sat up, her eyes glazed, and pushed him back into a sitting position. Her hands seized his cock, her splayed fingers stroking the sides of it. As her hair tumbled over it, he pulled away, taking her hands in his and kissing each fingertip in turn. He kept his eyes averted from her, feeling the juices stirring within him.

His lips pressed against her lips, firmly, forcing her head to the pillow. But she had come alive now, and she slid free, putting her forearms around his waist and snuggling her head under his armpit. He felt the tongue working, and then a little bite. His cock sprang upwards in response.

'Bitch!'

His nails ran down her back, not cruelly yet but roughly enough to leave their mark, two red tracers on the firm flesh. He brought his hands round to the front and took both her breasts, manipulating the nipples. He was working faster now – anything to avoid his own capitulation. He tried to make his mind a blank. He told himself he was a machine, a cold arousal machine, doing its job with great efficiency. He only wanted to hear her moan and plead.

She wrestled with him, fighting to excite his flesh as much as he was stimulating hers, her fingers running towards every crevice, every tender spot, her tongue finding the secret chamber of his ear for a moment until he tore himself away and pinioned her with the weight of his body.

So he was the master again, with her body under his. And now he tried to slow the motion of her desire with soothing sweeps of his closed fists down the length of her thighs. Then he opened his hands and used the fingers, down the thighs and off, down the thighs and off . . . until he realised, with a sudden catch of fear, that he was using greater energy than he meant to, bringing his hands down again too rapidly, impelled – *oh shit! oh fucking shit!* – by what he realised too late was his own gathering lust.

'No!'

He knew it had all gone wrong a split-second before Calla rolled away from him and sprang deftly to the floor. He knew, with a devastating incomprehension, that this beautiful, ripe, pulsating woman wasn't *(for God's sake, why not?)* at the screaming-for-it stage. And he knew for sure that if he didn't bury himself inside her this very second and lose himself in the primal explosion of a massive ejaculation he would burst into a thousand million pieces.

Calla stood by the door, her eyes gleaming with a triumph which seemed to make her whole body quiver and glow. He watched her slip the dress over her head and shake it down that damnable, desirable flesh. She picked up her bra and pants and stuffed them into the toes of her sandals. She was smiling. No: it was soundless, but she was laughing.

He rose from the bed, a hoarse rattling sound in his throat. His face was dark with the fury of his pent-up emotions. His great unsatisfied cock seemed to lunge forward, out of control.

'No!' he shouted again from sheer, hopeless despair.

377

Calla pulled the door open. That had been one hell of a close thing, she thought. She'd gone into the room knowing exactly what she intended to happen, but you couldn't tumble in bed with a man without having the occasional feeling here and there. Not every gasp and wriggle had been fake, she had to admit. In fact, quite a few of them had led her somewhat further along the road than she'd wanted to go.

But she'd upstaged the bastard, she knew. She'd given him something he'd deserved for years. And she reckoned, in a funny way, that she'd avenged Jason, too.

She smiled sweetly: 'Shall I ring for service?'

The vision she carried with her as she padded barefoot along the hotel corridor (a vision she was to relish for the rest of her life) was of Patrick Andover, his eyes wild with anger, waddling awkwardly towards her – almost overbalanced by the weight of his rearing, purple, gushing member.

32

A good story always put Martin Kingsley in a happy frame of mind, and an exclusive made him ecstatic. Right now he was over-the-moon jubilant.

He had first given the thing an airing in *Private Eye*, that magazine which thrives on leaks from journalists who have information which their own proprietors can't or daren't use. It was an excellent way of getting your story out into the open where it couldn't be ignored – even by your own proprietor.

> *Would-be ducal architects Broughton, Hughes, Lorimer aren't averse to mixingwith less than polite company in the furtherance of large ackers.*
> *Dirty deal of the month is a mega-cruzeiro contract with South American drugs king Diego Morais.*

The essential trick when you played this game was to have the facts fully-researched and the quotes in the bag by the time the *Eye* hit the street. All you had to do was drop the hint to your editor that you had a lead or two, making you the obvious guy to tackle the story, and you'd be in print while your rivals were still fishing around in the archives.

It had worked a treat. That was why Kingsley had been promised the front page the following morning, with a splash that would make the rest of Fleet Street sick with envy.

He hammered away at the computer keyboard. Some of his colleagues had been under the doctor with Repetitive Strain Injury when they first moved over to the new technology, but Kingsley's vicious two-fingered assault hadn't changed its style one bit since the old typewriter days. The machine would need treatment long before he did.

> *BHL partner Langton Meredith stitched up the deal on a three-week, all-expenses-paid trip to the Brazilian interior.*

Kingsley hadn't yet persuaded his editor that it was necessary for him to take the next flight to Brasilia, but he was working on it. In the meantime his original tip-off had led him into some very murky waters indeed.

> *My investigations have revealed that the design contract is only the tip of the iceberg as far as the involvement of British firms with the Morais empire is concerned.*

But don't run away with it, he warned himself. This story's good for several episodes yet. At this stage, just hint at what's to come. Whet the appetite. The Meredith angle is strong enough to major on for now.

> *Meredith is known to have pushed ahead with the Brasilia deal despite reservations expressed by his colleagues. One of them told me: 'He's probably the most ambitious architect in this country, and he's prepared to take big risks if the rewards are good.'*

If the story itself gave Kingsley pleasure, the exposure of Langton Meredith was icing on the cake. Very tasty icing. After being involved with that tacky Simkins affair, it made him feel clean again. He was settling a score.

> *Now the authorities are investigating the handling of the contract, hoping it will shed new light on the way the profits from drug trafficking are laundered through foreign bank accounts.*

Okay Meredith, he thought, pounding away on the keys like some manic vulture pecking at a carcass. Just try to get out of this one!

● ● ●

'This thing cannot work, Malibu,' Barney said, holding the tray very tightly. 'Do I actually need to tell you? This is a dream you have. I think it's called a chimera.'

'Course it can work, Brainy,' she grinned, loading the tray with bowls of guzpacho. They were in the kitchen. They were in charge of the meal. 'It's going to be the best *au revoir* and *hasta luego* party you've ever had.'

'Are we on the same planet? I find myself asking. That is not what I mean, Malibu. It may be a swell party, who knows, but this plan of yours is doomed. Your father and my mother . . . '

'*Our* mother, Brainy.'

'Barney. They just are not compatible. I see a multi-faceted conflict situation here.'

She opened the door and Barney carried his burden slowly to the table. Grant Locke sat at one end, with Calla and Nerissa at either side of him. This was Barney's farewell supper. He left for New York in the morning.

'Malibu,' Locke chided with mock seriousness, 'you've let the soup go cold.'

Neri snorted: 'Do I remember this guy ever cooking soup in all the years I knew him?'

'Was it years?' Malibu asked cheerfully, in a desperate attempt to keep the conversation lightsome.

'All too few,' responded Locke chivalrously.

'Felt like the complete Seven Ages of Man,' Neri said, starting on her soup.

Calla, Malibu noticed, seemed far away. It wasn't as if she seemed unhappy – indeed, she'd come bounding down the stairs at lunchtime saying she'd cracked all her Charlesbury problems and couldn't wait for the judging – but she wasn't really listening to the conversation.

'You've forgotten,' Locke said, rather ruefully Malibu thought.

'Forgotten? You bet I've forgotten! Look, Grant baby, I married four impossible guys after you and I've forgotten everything about *them* except the severance cheques and the portable property.'

Barney paused with the spoon to his mouth: 'Which is my classification, I guess,' he said philosophically.

Calla was in a state of mental limbo for two reasons. One was her work. She'd been on a high for days, shaping up her blueprints with the feverish certainty that at last they were everything she wanted them to be. In this mood she found it almost impossible to break off for food or sleep. Last night she had reached the critical point in her design and so she'd carried on, the curtains pulled, the lights blazing, until she finished – at what she was amazed to find was eight o'clock in the morning. Then she fell on her bed and took a few hours' very deep sleep which had left her glowing with health and confidence.

The other reason was what she found when she came downstairs. It was a large white envelope with three things in it: two sheets of paper and a card. The first sheet was the original of Patrick Andover's letter stating that he wished to withdraw his cash from CMP. It had been torn in half. The second was a photocopied document revealing that Andover's stake in the practice had reverted to his brother Jason.

Calla gazed at this document for several minutes. Its message was clear, but she found it difficult to take the information in. Thoughts and feelings came crowding in upon her, and she felt herself trembling.

She at last looked at the card. It was an elegantly printed invitation.

You're invited to a glass of bubbly and a few nibbles
– but espcially to view London's finest exhibition at

THE ANDOVER GALLERY
St Anne's Court, Soho

Friday August 24th 7.30pm

There was an *RSVP* which had been crossed out. Of course. If she was ever to meet Jason again it certainly wouldn't be across a plate of canapes at an art gallery. Not even his *own* art gallery.

But Jesus, she thought, what could it mean? Running a gallery was a tough business, however fancy it might seem to those who didn't know. Was he capable of that? Did he really have the patience, the discipline, the steel? She began to ponder what might perhaps have happened these past months while she was wrapped up in her Charlesbury competition. What was this envelope and its contents trying to tell her?

'My little sis remembers my own past better than I do,' Neri laughed, mopping up the remains of her soup with a bread roll. 'The day I left home, Calla – that's a blur to me.'

Calla came to with a start: 'You left home?'

'In disgrace, as I vaguely recall. Howling parents. You remember that?'

'Oh yes,' Calla said. 'Who could forget the drama? Thrown out on the streets!' She smiled towards Locke. 'And all because of a no-good man.'

'I believe I was flattered,' Locke said. 'I thought I must be a bit of a rogue. There's no smoke without fire.'

Neri guffawed: 'Fire, he says. More like the fizzle of a damp matchstick!'

'Not always, Neri,' Locke protested. You remember that evening at Battersea Funfair?'

'Did I ever visit Battersea once in my life?' she demanded. 'Other than the time I first collected you from the famous dogs' home?'

Malibu followed Barney into the kitchen with the tray of soup plates.

'Don't say it, Brawny,' she threatened, opening the oven to check the turkey. She picked up the carving knife. 'Please.'

His perplexed expression revealed that a battle was going on between prudence and his burning need to clarify the situation. He edged closer to the door.

'No way can this thing work,' he declared – and fled.

● ● ●

Fern Willoughby was beginning to become just the teensiest bit bored by the Captain's Table. She caught her husband's eye and knew he felt the same. It was funny how often that happened these days.

The *Ocean Dauphin* was no doubt a beautiful cruise liner. The sights of the Mediterranean and the Adriatic were no doubt beautiful sights. And the loud American couple who were also the captain's guests were no doubt beautiful people.

It was just that right now she couldn't quite appreciate any of this.

For the Duchess had something on her mind. It certainly wasn't the legends surrounding their various ports of call during the cruise. Amazingly, it wasn't even the Captain's likely between-the-sheets proficiency: Fern found her Duke learning so fast in this field that she'd more or less stopped thinking about other men.

The cruise had been his idea – a combination of second honeymoon and convalescence. And it had been tremendous fun for a few days. But now Fern thought she really wanted to go back to Willoughby Hall. If she were shown one more temple ashore or one more seafood feast aboard, she'd make the first officer walk the plank.

He looked across fondly at his wife. She was a damned fine looking girl, no doubt about it. She looked a bit preoccupied just now, but that was probably the effort of being polite to their rather wearing fellow guests.

And Harry Willoughby? He looked better than he had done in years. And he felt good, too. Many happy returns to that little used and sunny room at the far end of the house had worked wonders on him. There was a confidence and happiness about him which were entirely new.

A flunky approached and whispered to the captain, who turned to his guests: 'We are about to pass Stromboli.'

'Stromboli?' barked the American woman at Fern. 'What's that? Sounds like a dessert.'

'All our guests will be going on deck to see it,' the captain said, suppressing a smile. 'I suggest that we beat the rush and go up to the bridge now. I hope you'll return for coffee and liqueurs.'

On the bridge, Fern leant against a rail to watch the volcano, which erupts every fifteen minutes or so. It poured out white sparks against a black sky. No question, it was beautiful, but Fern still had no clue why tears came to her eyes.

She hid them in the darkness, her wrist tucked through the warm crook of Harry's arm. Soon they'd be back in Venice on a plane for home. She couldn't say why, but this seemed to matter enormously. Was something the matter with her? she wondered.

'Harry,' she said urgently.

He squeezed her arm by way of response. The Duke was enormously pleased with his wife these days. The shadows of the last few years which had sometimes made their marriage look rather a sham to him had completely rolled away. She was all his again.

The cruise had done so much to restore her strength, he thought. Plenty of seafood, sunshine and swimming in the on-deck pool had done them both good. It had given them a chance to be together away from Willoughby Hall while the blessed Hon Marion oversaw the sale of Fern's competition horses and the reorganising of the stables.

Yes, he felt as though they were on their honeymoon again, but his contentment this time round was greater still. Fern's attitude to him had changed, though he wasn't quite sure how. What she had regarded as a weak-kneed toleration of her infidelities she now saw as patience and forgiveness. And now that she was wholehearted about the marriage, she found in her husband a passionate lover she had never dared to imagine.

'Harry! We *are* okay aren't we, you and I?'

'Okay, darling? Of course we are. What do you mean?'

'Us, the marriage, our life. Everything, dammit.' Her voice was low, but intense. 'We're for keeps, aren't we?'

'Fern, are you about to confess to some heinous sin or another? Of course we're for keeps. Now concentrate on the volcano like a polite guest – or the captain will serve you stromboli for supper!'

She concentrated for another explosion of white sparkles, then squeezed his arm again.

'I need cheese, Harry,' she said, aware that she sounded half-hinged. 'That runny ripe stuff we were just about to get when Stromboli happened by. I need it badly.'

'Badly? You can have it when we go back for coffee, can't you?'

'No, I must have it *now*.'

He watched in amazement as Fern, slender and elegant in her simple off the shoulder gown, clambered down from the bridge and headed for the restaurant Was she perhaps suffering some sort of delayed reaction to her injuries and going quite off her head?

He was to be worried again the next day when the *Ocean Dauphin* visited the discreetly expensive Italian harbour town of Portofino. The harbour, brilliant in the August sunshine, was too small to take a ship the size of the *Ocean Dauphin*. Tenders ferried passengers from cruise liner to shore.

'Beautiful!' murmured the Duke, helping his wife into the boat. 'You once filmed here, darling?'

'An absolutely dreadful Romeo and Juliet storyline. Thank God I've forgotten most of it! Can we *not* eat at the Hotel Splendido? Too grand, too vulgar. A good place spoilt by the likes of Elizabeth Taylor.'

The Duke laughed. Fern was in good form these days.

'We'll find somewhere very shabby, Fern. Somewhere quiet and unpopular. Or would you prefer a packed lunch on a seafront bench?'

'Actually, Harry – yes!'

Sailing into Portofino gives you one of the loveliest sights on the Riviera. Buildings of faded yellow and pale pink stand amid rich green trees on a horseshoe-shaped cliff around the port. Private yachts the size of houses swing lazily at their moorings, the richest owners kitting their crews out in uniform like Royal Navy summer gear. At the water's edge there's a crescent of exclusive shops and restaurants. No trinket sellers gather round the wealthy cruise passengers as they step off the tender. Wealth is commonplace here.

The Willoughbys strolled along the front and into the shops. Fern loitered meaningfully outside Hermes until Harry took the hint and whisked her inside to choose a present. Hermes had always been her favourite accessory designer. She liked all those horsey motifs on silk, and now she picked up a scarf to run it sensuously through her fingers.

It was as she lifted her head to smile at her husband – a smile which said that this was the little gift she would like to take away from Portofino – that her head began to swim and she fainted away.

Harry caught her. The assistant rushed round the counter with a chair and produced a glass of water.

'Are you all right, my darling?' The Duke's voice was full of concern.

'I'm fine.' Fern sat up. She was white but quite alert. 'I don't know what came over me, Harry. Maybe it's the sun . . . '

'We're going straight back to the ship so the doctor can look at you.'

What on earth, she wondered again, taking his arm, is the matter with me? She wasn't the fainting type. She'd always looked down on the wilting violets of this world.

On the tender back to the ship, the Duke kept a tight arm around his wife. He was genuinely worried. He'd heard plenty of unnerving things about the sort of medical men who became ships' doctors. He'd go with Fern to the surgery – and if he had the slightest doubt about the fellow's competence he and Fern would fly back to London directly.

'Really, I'm all right,' she protested in vain. 'I don't need a doctor.'

The surgery was on one of the lower decks. Cruise ships can make big money out of portholes with a view, and essential facilities like the doctor's room tend to be tucked away down below. In a GP's waiting room you'll often watch fish swimming around in a tank: here they're just outside the window.

'Sorry to bother you,' Fern said, feeling guilty.

The doctor was a tall thin woman with white hair. On her desk were a box of Earl Grey teabags and a tin of chocolate covered Bath Oliver biscuits. She looked the sort who even made a serious business of her pleasures, and she certainly wasn't the disreputable drunken barber-surgeon Harry Willoughby had imagined.

Elizabeth Drew had got out of the National Health Service when the cockroaches, the cuts and the first outbreaks of MRSA had combined to make hospital surgery thoroughly unsatisfying. Years of study, long hours and damn hard work had left her precious little time for travel or for men. At 52, still an elegant woman, she had given up all hope of men, but that had seemed no reason to despair of travel. Practising her skills at sea seemed the answer, at least for a few years.

You saw all sorts on a cruise ship. There were the rich old men, the young girls they brought with them, as absurdly skinny as their sugar daddies were fat. There were those who had old money, often the most discreet with it. There were the two sets of widows – the merry ones who travelled to find husbands, and the sad ones who travelled to talk to each other about their lost husbands and to escape homes full of so many happy, painful memories.

Her work was mainly hangover and seasickness cures. There were occasional lively episodes when she had to 'cut out and keep' as she often thought of it – hack out an offending bit and keep the patient alive. But most of it was routine and, with a surgery below the waves, less than exciting.

But what was this coming in? She recognised the Duke and Duchess of Mercia from the captain's dinner table. Fern Willoughby had been looking rather peaky, she thought. Probably not a good sailor. Why had she brought her husband with her? Elizabeth Drew didn't like doing joint consultations. Theatre work was one thing, an audience quite another.

'Which of you is the patient?' she smiled.

'I am. It's probably nothing. I rather stupidly fainted. It's never happened to me before. I feel rather queasy, too.'

'My wife had a very serious fall from a horse a few months ago. She broke her back . . . '

Elizabeth Drew nodded: 'Let's examine you,' she said, leading Fern into a tiny examination room and closing the door as politely as she could on the worried husband.

The examination was thorough. Fern, having spent months being treated like an important piece of plasticine in hospital, thought nothing of it. But to Harry, on the other side of the door, it seemed a dreadfully long time. What in God's name might be doctor be discovering?

'Okay, sit up,' Elizabeth Drew said briskly. 'I think you're pregnant.'

Fern looked at her and laughed: 'Now, that's one thing I can't be.'

'Really?'

'I can't have children, doctor. I'm infertile. I don't ovulate.'

'You mean, you *didn't* ovulate. I can't be a hundred per cent sure just by feeling at this early stage. I'll give you a definite answer if you bring me a sample in the morning.'

'Believe me, there's no point. I can't have children. If I could, I'd have had them by now.'

'You mean you don't use birth control?'

'No need. I have it inbuilt.'

'But you have periods?'

'Oh yes, I have all the fun bits. I bleed, but there's no egg.'

'Had any periods lately? Say, for the last two months?'

Fern paused. She hadn't bled since she left the hospital. Even while she was in Stoke Mandeville, it had been erratic because of the shock following the fall. She'd put the later absence of periods down to the trauma of moving back to Willoughby Hall and her new life.

'Now you mention it, I haven't.' She spoke slowly. She already felt the spark of hope deep within her womanhood. It was a spark she feared to nourish. 'But things have been very unsettled and I thought . . . ' Her voice tailed off.

'Your husband mentioned a fall.'

'Yes. I fell off a horse while I was taking a jump.'

'I think that fall may have kicked your ovaries into action. They've started producing eggs.'

Fern stared and said nothing. Elizabeth Drew sensed that she was on emotionally fraught ground. This was a woman who had wanted children and, judging by her expression now, had gone to enormous lengths to repress her disappointment – and her longing.

She put a hand on Fern's shoulder: 'I'd guess that you're eight to ten weeks pregnant. Come and see me first thing.'

Fern's head was in a whirl. She couldn't think. She couldn't believe it. But she also couldn't bear the thought that this promise, held out to her once, might be dashed away in the morning. How would she get through the night? Harry, waiting by the porthole, saw that his wife's bright green eyes were wide and wondering as she approached him.

'Well?'

'The doctor thinks I'm pregnant.'

He looked from one woman to the other: 'But you know that's impossible!'

Christ, could it be true? Was there the slightest chance? He put an arm round his precious wife. No, he wouldn't believe it. Pointless to hope, he quickly told himself. It would be too cruel if the doctor had made a mistake.

'Not after a fall such as your wife has had. She'll tell you what I think. Go and talk about it.'

Proper sleep that night was impossible for Fern. She lay on her back, one hand resting lightly on her stomach, the other in Harry's. Could she really be expecting a baby? She dare not think of it, but she couldn't think of anything else.

As for talking about it, neither of them had the courage.

The morning came after what seemed an age. The ship was on the move again, and the sun blazed down on a passing coastline of craggy cliffs covered with shrub. They were oblivious of it, hurrying to the doctor with the sample as soon as breakfast was over.

When Elizabeth Drew emerged with the result, she couldn't prevent a smile lighting up her face: 'It's positive,' she said, putting a hand on Fern's arm. 'No doubt about it.'

They heard a thump behind them, as if something heavy had hit the deck. It had. Harry Willoughby had fainted.

• • •

'Very sexy,' Malibu said, taking the colour print to the studio window. It was a still life of an apple sprinkled with water droplets on a dripping black slate. 'But I suspect skulduggery.'

Rudi Kazinsky opened a fresh bottle of single malt whisky: 'Don't change the subject,' he boomed. 'Here you are breaking my heart, and all you can do is talk about the tricks of the trade.'

'You haven't got a heart, Rudi.'

'Don't be so damn sure,' he grinned. 'The answer to your question is that first I brushed the slate with cooking oil and then I sprayed it with a solution of water and glycerine. As for the apple, I worked wax polish into it so the water droplets would cling. I give you that information for nothing, though God knows why in the circumstances.'

Malibu frowned: 'It's not as though I'll be gone for ever. For just six months, in fact.'

'And the rest,' Kazinsky said, sniffing his scotch and then rolling it round his mouth. 'These plans depend on your mother, right? Well, I know your mother. I've worked with her. I've *survived* working with her.'

'She speaks rather better of you.'

'Listen, I love your mother, Malibu. At a safe distance, anyway. She's a great character and an even greater photographer. But she has no idea of time. Sure, she plans to have you with her in New York for six months. I'd put money on it being closer to six years.'

Malibu shook her head: 'You forget I've got a Daddykins this side of the Atlantic.'

She looked from the window over the London skyline. Her father was the only thing she'd miss, really. She hadn't lived in the city long enough to take it to her heart, and New York did sound very exciting. Suppose, she thought with a pang, that after six months with her mother she found she never wanted to come back? But that was easy – she'd find work for her father in America. He was famous, wasn't he? If only he hadn't got that stuffy Charlesbury project to work on he'd probably jump at the chance. Then he could fly out to join her. To join *them*.

Malibu was an incurable romantic.

'Come on then, genius,' Kazinsky said, recharging his glass. 'What else can you tell me about our apple caught out in the rain?'

'Easy. Camera, Bronica SQ-A. Am I right?'

'Good God! How did you know?'

'Mainly,' she giggled, 'because you've left it out on the table.' She ducked to avoid a lens cap he hurled in her direction. 'Anything else, maestro?'

'Lighting.'

'You've used a single source.'

'Correct.'

'The Hensel mini-lite, I assume. Through a softbox.'

'Good. So?'

'So I think you'll have needed reflectors to balance it up. That's what I'd have done.'

'Because,' Kazinsky said warmly, 'you're already bloody clever, Malibu. You've got one hell of a future. That's why you'll break my heart if you don't come back.'

'It's not personal?'

He laughed: 'Sorry, kid. That kind of heart I *haven't* got.'

• • •

Now that the meeting had come round, Brent Lorimer was anxious to get on with it. He'd been worrying about it for days, feeling quite certain that it would run completely out of his control and fearing that it would have some catastrophic, blood-letting conclusion which would bring disaster on them all.

Those were the kind of grim thoughts which came to him in the early hours of the morning, when he'd wake in a sweat with the dim shadows of a nightmare hovering in his brain. He wasn't a detailed dreamer, but he always knew that Langton Meredith was in there somewhere. The hissing voice still echoed in his head as he sat upright in the bed, clutching the blankets.

He looked at his watch. Ten past three. They were ten minutes late starting, and Meredith hadn't yet arrived.

Lorimer was comforted by one thing. He'd acted in the best interests of the practice. Whatever flak he received during the next hour, he was confident that the decisions he'd made and the actions he'd taken were absolutely sound. He just hoped to God enough of his colleagues would back him up.

'Shouldn't we start?' Jake Broughton asked, turning to look at the clock on the wall. 'I can't stay late.'

True to form, Lorimer thought. None of them could resist trying to run the damn meetings. Perhaps you couldn't expect anything else from a highly motivated team of individualists, but he'd had enough of it. Two hundred and six, he thought.

'Let's give it five minutes,' he said.

He was counting off the days in his diary. Two hundred and six days until he retired. It sounded better somehow than six months and a bit. He wasn't ancient, but architecture today was a young man's game. Or, he reflected, a young woman's.

'Because the star turn isn't here?' queried Stew McClear.

'Exactly, Stew.'

He really couldn't be bothered to argue the toss. This wasn't a meeting to discuss the coffee machine or supplies of paperclips, and they knew it. There was only one topic on the agenda. An outsider would have known what it was simply from a quick browse through the photocopied press cuttings which had been set out at every place at the boardroom table.

The first article, in *Private Eye*, had been the worst shock. All the rest had followed from it with an agonising inevitability. As soon as he'd read the *Eye* article Lorimer knew that he was partly to blame. He cursed himself for his own weakness. Why hadn't he led from the front? All the right questions had been asked, but he hadn't pushed them hard enough.

He followed Martin Kingsley's daily expose with a feeling of dread, and then watched the rest of the Fleet Street pack climb on the band-wagon. As the Diego Morais scandal broadened, so mentions of the architectural contract abated a little – but it was always quoted as the deal which had broken the silence. Lorimer pored over the papers with a morbid curiosity. At a single glance he could pick the name *Broughton, Hughes, Lorimer* from a dense four-column broadsheet report. It was like the urge to keep finding a jagged piece of tooth with your tongue. It eventually rubbed the tongue raw, but you couldn't stop doing it.

'I vote for starting,' McClear said, polishing his glasses. 'We could wait all day.'

Lorimer pulled himself together. Hell, they were nearly twenty minutes late now. He'd been deep in his own thoughts. Yes, it was high time to call the meeting to order.

'Well, gentlemen,' he began briskly, shaking his papers into a neat pile – and at that very moment the door swung open and Langton Meredith strolled in.

'My apologies,' he murmured. 'I've been serving someone with a writ.'

The immediate silence seemed to gratify him. He picked up a carafe of water and, his lips forming a little smile, poured himself a glass. When he sat down it was at the end of the table opposite from Lorimer. That outsider would have been unable to tell which was the chairman.

'I thought,' Broughton said, 'that only solicitors and officers of the Crown could do that.' Bastard, he thought. Sleek, self-satisfied bastard. 'Or have you switched professions?'

'Not yet, Jake, I'm sorry to disappoint you. If I must be tiresomely exact, I accompanied my solicitor in the act of serving a writ on a journalist.' He looked slowly around the room. 'It won't be the last.'

Upstaged again, Lorimer thought. How do I start this thing off? Meredith isn't going to make it easy.

'All those stories have been lies?' McClear asked sharply. 'Is that what you're telling us.'

Meredith sighed: 'Do you believe everything you read in the newspapers, Stew? I'm afraid I lost my innocent trust in journalists many years ago.'

'Especially those you were able to manipulate,' Broughton accused, rising from his seat.

'Gentlemen . . . ' attempted Lorimer weakly.

Meredith lowered his voice and fixed Broughton with a malevolent stare: 'I should be very careful what you say, Jake,' he hissed. 'Writs aren't only served on journalists, you know.'

Mercifully, from Lorimer's point of view, the secretary chose that moment to come in with the tea. Everyone stopped talking while she was in the room. The spoons rang against the cups like bells. Bloody funeral bells, Lorimer thought.

'Shall we attempt a rational discussion, gentlemen?' he suggested even before the door had closed behind the girl with her tray. 'We've nothing to gain from a slanging match.'

'Quite agree,' Meredith threw in quickly.

'It does appear,' Lorimer went on, 'that we've acted unwisely, however much in ignorance that may have been. Would you like to give us your view, Langton?'

Meredith leaned forward, his fists clenched: 'What do you mean *unwisely*? Because a scrum of ignorant Fleet Street hacks choose to dig up dirt and try to make it stick on us? That's what you don't like. I don't like it either, but it's a triviality. I know it doesn't matter. Are you telling me that we should lose sleep over it?'

'I've certainly lost some,' Lorimer replied.

'But that's because you're a frightened rabbit! You don't care about the best deal this practice has ever won. I mean *ever*, Brent.'

'The newspapers,' McClear's Scottish accent broke in, 'are saying we've used improper accounting. They're accusing us, for Christ's sake, of actually helping Morais to launder his fucking drugs money.'

Meredith's face turned white: 'Am I being tried in a court of law?' he demanded angrily. 'If so, I'd better ask for the case to be adjourned while I call my solicitor. I certainly don't believe I'll get a fair hearing in this room.'

'Just answer the question,' Broughton said. 'We're all partners in this practice, and that means we're all responsible. That means if you end up in prison we've a fair chance of joining you.'

'Ha!' Meredith laughed harshly. 'More frightened rabbits, eh? Well, I'm almost sorry to tell you that you've got nothing to worry about on that score. Whatever deals Morais has done with other companies, our contract was drawn up by the book.'

'To the letter?' Lorimer queried.

'Absolutely, Brent. You have my word on that.' He looked at his colleagues with an expression of disgust. 'I had hoped to enlist your support today in a campaign to silence the newspapers who've printed lies about us. But I can tell that your heart wouldn't be in it. You haven't got the guts.'

Broughton pushed his cup and saucer away from him with a force which sent them spinning to the centre of the table: 'Hasn't it occurred to you, Meredith,' he asked bitterly, 'that there's something dirty about dealing with a man like Morais, however squeaky clean you may have been over the accounting? Haven't you been reading those papers? Don't you know how many thousands of young people have had their lives ruined by the drugs he peddles?'

Meredith shrugged: 'We're architects. Or so I believed. Perhaps we're supposed to be missionaries after all.'

'If you're the role model of an architect,' Broughton spat out, 'I sure as hell don't want to be one.'

'Then presumably you won't be sharing in the profits we make from the Brasilia development? Anyone else feel that way? How about you, Brent?'

Lorimer shook his head: 'There won't be any profits from Brasilia, Langton.'

'No profits?'

'We are, of course, pulling out of the deal. Did you really imagine we could go ahead with it?'

'You, Brent, are a miserable little shit!'

'I've consulted the other partners. I believe I have their support in this?'

'Absolutely,' said McClear, among the grunts of assent. 'Count me out.'

For the first time there was a silence. All eyes were on Meredith's face. The flesh was tight on the bones. He was fighting to keep his self-control.

'I see little point in continuing as a member of this practice,' he said calmly. 'We have been poised to secure two contracts which would have swamped BHL with cash. You tell me that we're dropping one of them, and I have no faith whatsoever in your support for the second, should we win it. I refer, naturally, to Charlesbury.'

Brent Lorimer cleared his throat.

'No, Langton,' he said quietly, 'we shan't be winning the Charlesbury contract.' He held Meredith's gaze, despite its venom. 'I rang the Duke of Mercia this morning to withdraw our entry from the competition.'

'You *what?*'

'He was extremely grateful to us. Charlesbury has already been mentioned far too often in these Morais stories, and we're entirely to blame for that.'

'You bastard!' Lorimer hissed, leaping to his feet so that his chair clattered to the ground. 'Do you know how hard I've worked on that scheme? Do you know what effort I've put in behind the scenes?'

'We can guess,' Broughton said.

'Our reputation is what matters to me,' Lorimer explained. 'I want us out of the headlines. I want us to be known for good, clean architecture. That's what matters.'

Meredith opened the door: 'When I joined this practice,' he said coldly, 'I looked at it very carefully. I knew it was dead from the top downwards. That was a challenge to me – to shake this dreary firm to life. And I did it, didn't I? My mistake was to think that the corpses would thank me for raising them from the dead.

'You'll have my letter of resignation in the morning.'

As he closed the door behind him, Jake Broughton thrust two fingers in the air. It might have been a victory salute, but it wasn't.

33

'Is this a tease?' Calla looked up as Adam came into the office, carrying a large bag. 'Or did you actually manage to get it?'

'I've got it,' he said, pouting. 'Some personal assistants would take it rather badly, you know, being asked to trot round to South Molton Street in the middle of the rush-hour.'

'But they close at six, Adam. What can a girl do?'

'Suppose I shut up shop at six, eh? Suppose I, leaving the shop on the hour, had gone home for the day?'

'I'd have gone to the Minister's reception stark-bollock naked, natch. Only I don't have bollocks. Oh, come on, Adam, admit you're dying to see it on.'

'Daresay I can live without it. I got caught in the rain you know. One little cloud in the whole sky and it got me.'

'Don't worry, your mascara hasn't run. Draw the blinds, will you?'

'Am I safe?'

'We're both safe.'

The other staff had gone, but there was no chance of going home herself for a quick shower before the House of Commons cocktail party. Life didn't seem to have those little gaps in it any more. She'd have to change here. Calla wriggled out of her clothes, revealing loose silk underwear and long legs. First she checked her stockings for snags, then she unpinned her lustrous black hair and brushed it out.

'Lovely,' Adam nodded in approval. 'Looks newly washed.'

He unfastened the bag and carefully shook out a Chanel button-through dress in mustard and navy, something Calla had seen in the new collections in *Vogue*.

'Hope it fits.'

'It'll fit,' she said, stepping carefully into it. She buttoned it over her spectacular body while Adam looked on in a matter-of-fact way. 'What do you think of the tulip hem? Curse this place for not having a full-length mirror. Remind me to tick off the proprietor.'

The hem was cut in such a way that it came up at the front to meet the last button, giving the impression of two upturned tulip petals parting. It was made for legs like Calla's.

'Terrific. Coco would have signed you!'

She gave him a flamboyant kiss on the lips: 'Take tomorrow off!' she offered generously.

'Thanks, it's Saturday.'

'Oh, too bad!' she grinned, grabbing her handbag.

A maddening employer, Adam thought, but he couldn't imagine working for anyone else. A personal assistant's lot wasn't really deeply fulfilling, but Calla's combination of style and vivacity gave the job a special zest.

'I suppose Monday wouldn't do?' he suggested hopefully.

It was too late. She was gone, in a cloud of familiar scent and a taxi. He sniffed the air. 'Chanel no 5. Of course.' He sighed and locked up.

The Houses of Parliament were floodlit by the time Calla arrived at Westminster. She'd passed that way time without number, but to see it in the evening always filled her with pleasure. They'd cleaned the London soot off the building a few years back and it gleamed like something out of a fairy tale.

A junior civil servant took her through the small but lofty central lobby, past statues of famous parliamentarians to the reception room.

'Good heavens,' muttered Frank Benton as she came into the pannelled room. Calla Marchant wasn't quite what the secretary of state for the environment had expected of this gathering of RIBA members. Calla paused slightly and her colour heightened a degree or two. She sensed that crackle of excitement which her entry always created in a room filled mainly with men.

Benton was one of the prime minister's good grammar school lads, who had made Oxford and the upper echelons of the civil service through scholarships and hard work, not through privilege and the right gentlemen's clubs. Although most of the edges had been smoothed off, he lacked the aplomb of those members of the the government who took the view that they'd been born to rule. So the PM had given him the environment post.

He was an able minister, who tackled easily the complex demands of lengthy public inquiries into unwanted development. Able but unnoticed. In the early days he'd rarely been in the limelight. Environment secretaries made far fewer appearances on television than chancellors of the exchequer or home secretaries. Those jobs were best filled by people with a greater degree of charisma.

But then the Green explosion had happened. Global warming and climate change had become household words and Benton had become, through the small screen, almost a household face.

As if that weren't enough, the Duke of Mercia, instead of living a quiet life in his west country mansion, had dragged architecture to the front of the public arena. By daring to speak his mind he'd enraged any number of architects and given the common man a voice about the buildings in which he lived and worked. Now architecture was a regular television subject and newspapers devoted regular features to it. There was even to be a whole new town of Charlesbury, very different from the new towns of the post-war era.

Benton decided, in his slow way, that he'd better get to know something about architecture. The Prime Minister, in anything but a slow way, had suggested he set about it in fairly rapid order.

'We'd better have a party,' Benton had instructed his under secretary.

The faithful under secretary had duly consulted minions further down the line, producing a list of architects who the RIBA though the secretary of state might like to meet. And now the same under secretary was bringing Calla across to him.

'Ripe,' was the word that came to mind. This wasn't what the word architect normally conveyed to him. He'd imagined a breed of crusty, dusty, slightly mad dreamers, pursuing their odd visions at dusty drawing boards. He'd never imagined violet eyes, sensuality and long legs.

'Good heavens,' he repeated, shaking Calla's hand as if he were trying to detach it.

'Miss Marchant is one of the Charlesbury finalists, sir,' the under secretary said quickly, desperately attempting to disguise his boss's lack of poise.

'Ah yes, Charlesbury. Of course. And what have you done before?'

Calla could see it written all over his face. He had her down as the token woman in the competition, a sop to the feminists and the young. It was the sort of assumption which made her very cross indeed. No, it made her bloody furious. She felt like seizing him by the tie, giving him a severe shaking and pointing out that she was one of just two finalists, dammit. She would have added that there was no way she wasn't going to win the competition, either. But the House of Commons was hardly the place for a scene. She ran through the list of her projects, answering the predictable questions. The most predictable of the lot was his last one.

'And who do you work for?'

Calla smiled: 'For myself,' she said. 'You should try it one day.'

That would give the slime-ball something to chew on, she thought, sliding away to mingle with the other guests. God, she *did* feel a scene coming on. When you were very young you put up with people out of some false sense of politeness. Those days were long gone. She didn't intend to waste time with an ill-mannered politico who'd probably be eased out at the next re-shuffle in favour of a sleeker, higher profile model.

Slime-ball? Her big sister's rumbustious visit had even affected her use of the language, she thought. Life seemed one hell of a lot quieter now that Neri had flown back to New York. Was that why she felt so keyed-up this evening, so restless? For days now she'd had the uneasy feeling of looking for something – she wasn't sure what.

It certainly wasn't anything to do with Charlesbury. She was right on song there, working as sweetly as she could have wished, detailed plans gushing from her computer. The deadline was a week away, and she was definitely going to meet it.

No, it was as though there was something missing. That was how it felt. And every time she'd seen the invitation to the opening of the Andover Gallery on her fireplace – an opening that was taking place this very evening – she'd had the uncomfortable feeling that she really did know what it was, in her heart of hearts.

'Ladies and gentlemen, architects all . . . '

She saw, to her horror that Benton was beginning to make a speech. That was when she knew she couldn't bear to be in this place for a minute longer. She felt trapped, stifled. Did she have some sort of duty to be here, for Crissakes?

'It's a great pleasure to meet you here this evening . . . '

There was a soft click as Calla Marchant closed the door behind her. Her heels echoed through Central Lobby. She hadn't a clue where she was going or what she was doing, but she trusted her own instinct.

Outside, in New Palace Yard, she took deep breaths of fresh night air. It was a balmy evening. Big Ben struck nine, and when it had finished everything seemed very quiet and calm. The sky above was clear, and she could easily distinguish the arrangement of stars the English know as the Plough. Neri, she remembered, had called it the Big Dipper.

'Shall I get you a cab, Miss?' It was the policeman on the gate.

'Thank you.' But then she changed her mind. 'No, I'll walk.'

For suddenly she knew where she wanted to go. It was stupid of her. It was pointless, horribly sentimental. *But what the hell!* she thought.

She took the steps down to the Victoria Embankment and walked alongside the Thames in the direction of St Paul's. The silky black waters twinkled in the city lights. Traffic whizzed by en route for Pimlico, Battersea and Belgravia.

On the other side of the river stood County Hall, a white pillared curve on the bank. She passed the ugly railway line across the water from Charing Cross, then drew level with the Royal Festival Hall, the finest public building of its era. In the distance she could see the stubborn concrete form of the National Theatre. She was nearly there now.

A drunk staggered across her path, but Calla wasn't frightened. She recognised his helplessness. She remembered a time when she, too, had been lost and lonely at this spot. And she remembered that a drunk that night had made her shake with fear.

At Cleopatra's Needle, she stopped. *Okay, clown*, she ridiculed herself. *Now what?* But now nothing. This was where she'd first met Jason that crazy and beautiful night everything had begun. That was all.

Now nothing.

• • •

'I think it's super!' Ella Lepard called across to Jason, waving her cheroot in perilous fashion.

Jason nodded, smiled and hoped the room was too crowded for Ella to buttonhole him. The Barracuda was the sort of person you had to have at a gallery opening – *Chic* was read by the wives of money, after all. But he'd been putting off a personal encounter for as long as possible. So he waved a champagne glass at her and tried to mingle madly at the far end of the room.

'Seems to be going well,' remarked a tall and balding man, wearing a dinner jacket like the rest. He was Graham Sinclair, a Sotheby's valuer.

'Some people will go anywhere for a caviar canape,' Jason smiled.

'You've got a name, Andover, that's what it is. A name in your own right as well as in your mother's.'

'My mother's?'

'Oh I can see a few faces here tonight who are more than interested to see some of the Sarah Andover collection. Small English is back, you know.'

'I'd have to be pretty hard-up to sell those off. I love them too much, Graham.'

'So what's the speciality going to be?'

'Things I like. Why have your own gallery if you fill it with stuff you can't bear to look at all day?'

'Oh, quite! You've got a decent smattering of the fourth estate here, eh? I can see old Ella Lepard over there. What does she know about art?'

'Enough to cover the bottom of a whisky glass, probably, but she commands an awful lot of glossy pages.'

'For her sake, I hope she keeps moving. There's so much paint on her face, someone might frame her.'

'She's on the look-out, you know. I recognise that hungry expression.'

'On the look-out for what? Picassos? Corots?'

'Men, Graham, men. Younger, prettier and poorer than herself. Terms include an allowance, a Renault 5 to run about in and generous severance gifts. Interested?'

'I'd rather have the severance first, painful though it might be. Whoops! She's coming this way! Must go and talk to old Joshua. You know Joshua? Picture restorer at the Tate. Come and see us when she's spat you out.'

La Lepard wore white trousers and a white beaded sweater. The tan was darker than ever, the hair blonder and even more distrait. The scent was Giorgio and overwhelming.

Jason braced himself. Yes, he could stand it. He could stand anything, even the Barracuda, now that his gallery was open – now that his dream was realised. He had almost everything he'd ever wanted.

Except, maybe, the most important thing.

He hadn't really expected Calla to come tonight. The invitation had been another sort of message altogether. He'd trusted Calla to read two things into it. The first was that he was back in the land of the living and fulfilling his ambition. The second was that he wanted her back.

It was a plea, but would she answer? He hadn't expected her here, but he couldn't help looking whenever the door opened. She must have received his package. She must have read everything it contained. How had she reacted? he wondered. Had she ripped it up? Had she left it carelessly lying around? Or had she, just possiby, felt a pang of the old love?

Not knowing frankly hurt. He didn't even know, dammit, if there was anyone else in her life now. She'd been so lovely when he first met her, and she was absolutely gorgeous now in her prime. He'd walked into too many parties with Calla not to know the kind of an effect she had on men.

Sure, she wasn't the sort to let herself be picked up by just anyone. Calla was quite capable of the unforgettable put-down of an obtrusive male ego. She was well practised at it, too, come to think of it. But equally, she had strong passions which were unlikely to lie dormant for long. She was a vibrant, healthy woman with lusty appetites. Had she been satisfying them?

He realised at that moment, and very clearly, that no matter how many men there might have been during the last few months, if his Calla would just walk in now, by herself, his happiness would be more than complete. To hell with pride, he would do everything to win her back. He needed her.

But instead, he had Ella Lepard.

'Love it! Reeks of taste and quiet money, my darling! Where did you get the dosh?'

'I robbed a glossy magazine editor, leaving her for dead on her white carpet and making off with her Fabergé egg collection which I traded for cash off the Portobello Road.'

'Sorcerer! How did you know about my white carpet?'

'You once offered to do unspeakable things to me on it, that's how.'

'Really?' Thoroughly enjoying the repartee, she drew deeply on her cheroot. 'Must have been before I bought the black satin sheets.'

'A great attraction, I'm sure. But where's the current *jeune fils*? My instructions were to admit La Lepard plus accompanying teenage boy. Or boys.'

'Given them up, darling. These days I look better unruffled, that's the truth. If I settle down, it'll be with someone who at least remembers where he was when Kennedy was shot. You look a sight too vigorous for me.'

She blew smoke over his head: 'No, you're not the Jason of old. What's come over you? Dare I ask if it's a lady? It certainly can't be anything in powder form. I perceive a genuine healthy glow about you.'

'I'm cured, Ella,' he said. 'I don't need drugs any more.'

'There's a triumph!' The Barracuda's voice was hard-edged. 'Join the ranks of the self-sufficient. Cyanide tablets available from this PO box.'

Jason smiled. He had no intention of sharing his secrets with Ella: 'So tell me what you think of the gallery.'

'Great. I think the lighting is perfection. The decor is subtle. The exposed beams are authentic. The stripped floorboards concentrate the mind wonderfully on the canvases. I think it's just the right size. I think your opening party would have been well-graced by Calla Marchant.'

Did she see him wince? She was in full flow: 'Sadly, the last I heard she was with a devastatingly good-looking Frenchman. And his eyes, to mention nothing else, were roving all over her. But cheer up, Jason, these cross-Channel romances never last long. He'll soon find another bit of brioche.'

'Your glass is empty, Ella.' He waved the waiter across and, as the liquid creamed into the Barracuda's glass, he asked innocently: 'You hear nothing from Julio these days?'

She frowned in an effort to recall her last toy-boy, he of the olive-skin and slicked back hair.

'You do know,' Jason went on, 'that he's dining out on the story of your plastic surgery?'

'My what?' Ella hissed. 'You mean the little tyke's claiming I've had my face lifted?'

'Who said anything about your face?' Jason murmured triumphantly. She had rather walked into that one. 'Ah! There's old Joshua from the Tate. I need his advice on a damaged canvas. Do excuse me, Ella.'

Too bad, he thought, if she decided to exact a little revenge through the pages of her magazine. He didn't rule out good publicity from *Chic* but he could live without it. He was relieved when he saw her leave, stubbing out a cheroot in a potted bay tree as she was helped into her fox jacket. He wanted his gallery to be respected in the art world, a place where good modern work would hang side by side with older pieces. The last thing he was striving for a was a trendy repuation which depended on the latest acquisition of Britart canvases.

The party was beginning to break up, save for one or two last animated conversations. The evening had gone very well. In a field known for its bitchery, he'd managed to contrive an atmosphere in which the art spoke more eloquently than the guests. No doubt it was sentimental of him, but he couldn't help thinking that Calla would have been proud of his performance, not to speak ofd his witty victory over the Barracuda.

She'd have liked the place, too, he thought. It was such a surprise, behind that unassuming little Soho doorway. When he'd first stepped inside, it had seemed an unlikely proposition. He wasn't after a smart area, but perhaps this was rather *too* bohemian.

And then he'd climbed the narrow wooden staircase to the first floor. Christ, he'd been almost literally knocked out by the light! It flooded in from ceiling fanlights, from windows high in the walls and from a gigantic double door which led out to a lower roof, no doubt once used for hoisting during the building's time as a shoe factory.

It smelt of leather and wood. It was bigger than he had dared to hope, large enough for an office as well – and even for a small restoring room at the back if he ever managed to employ an Isaac of his own. Quite simply, he'd fallen in love with the place.

Having a project definitely suited Jason. He looked well. He felt happy. He found the extra time to work on the gallery and write the music and art reviews for which he was in demand again. He was even playing his violin, the beloved Stradivarius which he'd had restored after Calla's slight mishap.

Calla! If only she'd been by his side this evening, he thought as he tidied up. God, had he blown it entirely? He'd certainly heard nothing from her. And who was this bloody Frenchman the Barracuda had been going on about? Did he exist? And was he still around?

It was nearly ten o'clock as he dropped into the seat of his navy blue Morgan and steered his way through Soho. *Where the hell am I going?* he asked himself, taking a route he'd never used before. There were, after all, far quicker ways home to Fulham than along the Embankment. In fact, it was pretty much in the wrong direction.

You stupid, sentimental bastard! he accused himself.

He was driving, he knew, towards Cleopatra's Needle, the place where he'd first met *his* Cleopatra. His head was suddenly full of that distant, magical night when he and his friends had formed their own imaginary orchestra – when he had found Calla, a confused, embarrassed young girl who'd told him very seriously that she played the flute but was out of practice.

His head was full, too, of all the years since then, so many of them wasted. He scarcely noticed how clear the sky was, what a beautiful evening it was. Driving along by the river, he slowed to gaze across at the obelisk. He saw, through the confusion of the passing traffic, that a woman was sitting on the plinth, just as Calla had sat on it all those years ago.

Shit, what he'd give to be the young man he was then!

• • •

It was, she thought, the most beautifully played Elgar she had ever heard. It was almost agonisingly sweet, aching with a longing which only music could express – which perhaps only a violin could express.

'He can play like *that?*' she asked the night air, strangely moved.

Why had he never played for her like that?

The rooms facing the street were in darkness, the curtains drawn. That sound was coming from somewhere deep inside the house. She couldn't bear to stop it. It would be a profanity to ring the bell. If necessary she would stand outside all night, listening, the tears welling up in her eyes.

Only it wasn't necessary. She still had the key. She'd often come across it in her handbag and thought of throwing it away, but something – some fugitive tinge of sentimentality – had always prevented her.

Now she turned it in the lock and quietly entered the shadowed hallway.

Music had such vivid colour. She stood still for a while in the darkness and experienced a powerful sensation of rich blues and greens and tangerines mingling inside her brain. Did music have smell, too, or was that simply the familiar odour of home? Because it *was* familiar, wonderfully familiar. The prints on the wall were mere squares in the gloom of the hallway, but she knew each one. And her feet, as she began to follow the music up the stairs, remembered every single step and every turn of the landing.

There was only the sitting room door between them. She turned the handle and gently pushed it open. The light inside was dim, cast by a shaded table lamp.

Jason half stood, half leant against a high stool, his eyes closed as he played. He was facing her, but oblivious of her presence. With his hair flopping over his forehead, his sensuous lips, his slim figure, he was every bit the Jason she had loved when she was a very young woman and life had been so simple.

But his face: she had never seen him look like this. Not with this expression of impassioned striving, of hard-won joy. She knew so well the Jason who was gentle, rather sadly amused by the passing scene, the Jason who let the world go by instead of leaping onto it himself. She had loved that Jason with a devotion which had in the end threatened her own wellbeing. But this was new, this was a Jason utterly absorbed and committed to what he was doing – and so obviously expressing something which would otherwise have remained hidden, perhaps even from himself.

A glance around the room revealed the old turmoil of magazines, mugs and books. A bottle of red wine stood half consumed on the table. On one wall there was a portrait of herself which Jason had painted in oils. She remembered how he'd told her that water colours would never do her justice.

He had no sheet music. How could he be playing such a wonderful, detailed piece from memory? It held her spellbound and she dared not move.

Then he opened his eyes and saw her. He continued to play. The music wrapped itself around them. They were two ghosts, hovering in the gloom. He gave no sign of recognition, but put his bow to the strings for an aching adagio. Calla felt herself float into the room. Blindly she sat on the balding arm of the aged sofa on which the two had so often embraced. Only when a tear fell upon her hand did she realise that she was crying.

He finished, put the violin aside and, like a sleepwalker, came towards her. He lifted her by the elbows.

'Why did you never tell me?' she whispered.

'It doesn't matter,' Jason said as he drew her closer to him. 'Nothing else matters just now.'

They kissed, gently and slowly. Then he pressed his lips to each of her closed eyes: 'You're back?'

She said nothing, but led him round to the sofa and they sat down, knee against knee and hand in hand.

'I never knew you could play like that.' Her voice was low and soft. Jason thought he had never seen the outer ring of her irises such a deep and lustrous violet. 'Why didn't I know?'

He stroked her cheek, upwards to those finely arched dark eyebrows: 'You're in the mood for a story?'

She nodded.

'I'm not sure that I can tell it properly, even now. You know that I've been shutting myself away in a clinic? That's where I learned to tell the story to myself, all the way through. The first part's easy, and the end – well, I'm not quite sure how the end works out. It's the middle chapters which have always been the problem.'

'And I was I involved in your middle section?'

He stroked her hair and put his lips to her forehead.

'Yes, dear Calla. I wrote you into my disturbed chapters. I haven't been able to forgive myself for that. You suffered because of my own confusion, my incurable disease of the spirit. At least, it seemed incurable.'

'Tell me,' she said simply.

He smiled: 'Once upon a time there was a young violinist,' he began. 'One of the most promising in the country, they said. He did everything that was expected of him – leader of the National Youth Orchestra, university music scholarship, the lot. He loved his playing, but there were plenty of other things in his life, too. It was a charmed life he led. Everything came easy.

'The young man was tipped to become one of the youngest orchestra leaders ever. "This boy's playing," some critic actually wrote, "is proof that the soul is lodged in the finger-tips." Scarcely my critical style, but still . . . '

He paused and poured out some red wine. They both sipped from the same glass. The silence lengthened.

'Are we reaching the middle chapters?'

'Yes, we're there. We're at a powerboat race off the Isle of Wight. Calla, I'm not sure I can carry on with this.'

'Please try,' she whispered.

My father's boat was the *Andover Ace*, capable of more than a hundred miles an hour. Patrick and I were his crew. We were all damn good at it.'

Calla nodded. She knew that Jason's father had been killed in an accident while racing, but she had never even guessed that Jason and his brother had been there at the time. She began to realise how little she really knew of the man she had loved so long.

'Near the end of the race we were in with a chance, but the water was incredibly choppy. The boat in front blew up. Patrick was on the throttle, driving us forward like fury . . . '

Jason's voice was coming in short breaths. He sweated. He was no longer seeing the room, Calla could tell. In front of his eyes were only the foam-flecked waves and his brother's relentless expression.

'My father signalled to him to slow down, but he didn't. All right – he *wouldn't*, blast him. We smashed into the catamaran in front of us. That was it.'

He paused for breath and another sip of wine. Calla said nothing. She could see what the tale was taking out of him. She could also see how important it was that he tell her the whole thing.

'My father was dead, floating on the water.' Jason's lips were dry. 'Patrick was trapped in the upturned boat. I dived for him and managed to free him from the straps.'

'You saved his life.'

Jason shrugged his shoulders: 'If you like. It wasn't at all heroic, believe me. What matters for those middle chapters is that, as he came free, I felt something give in my left wrist. I'd injured myself.'

'Badly?'

'Trivially for anyone else. Crucially for me. It was more a lack of flexibility than a matter of excruciating pain, though it hurt enough at the time. But the damage was permanent. In short, I could never be the violinist everyone said I was going to be.

'That was when the rot set in.'

'The drugs?'

'Not immediately, but I suppose they were inevitable – especially with the kind of money I could lay my hands on. I understand it pretty well now. You can't spend months with the shrink I had and not know everything about yourself, right down to why you put your left sock on first.'

Calla squeezed his hands and raised the fingertips to her lips: 'It was because you couldn't play to the standard you wanted?'

'Not as simple as that, I'm afraid. Nothing ever is. No, it was partly the shock of my father's death and partly the death of my musical career, but there was something else much deeper down. Something to do with my brother.'

'With Patrick?'

'Ah yes, you've met him, I think. Patrick's everything I'm not. I used to despise his ridiculous masculine drive when I was young. It seemed so stupid, so boorish.'

'And I think you were right,' Calla said.

'But after the accident I somehow felt that I couldn't fight it any more. Can you understand that? I'd always put him down with a little wit and sarcasm. I thought my art, my finer sensibility, was more than a match for all his rapacious business nonsense. He was a financial wizard when he was still at school, dammit!

'And then I was unable to perform any more. Even my wit wouldn't perform properly. I know you always thought me bright company, but already I was beginning to despair. Already I knew that, however humorous and intelligent I seemed, I wasn't amusing myself. I looked on myself as something useless.Writing clever things for magazines is entertaining enough I suppose, but it's no substitute for the agony and triumph of making something yourself.

'I saw myself, if you like, through Patrick's eyes. He'd caused that stupid, tragic accident, and now I was letting him ruin my life. I couldn't do what I wanted to do, Calla. I was frustrated, bored.

'And you came into it, as well. You had your passion. Buildings are to you exactly what music was to me. Everything you touched seemed to turn to gold – except for me. I felt tarnished by your side. You needed me at first, you know, and then all that came to an end. I couldn't really see what I supposed to do with my life.'

'I didn't help,' she said. 'That was happening to you, and I didn't even notice.'

'How could you? It would have been impossible. There was too much going on inside my head for anyone to cope with. I turned to the drugs, because the drugs put me to sleep. I needed something to numb the pain that started that day in the water and had never gone away. It never went away because I wouldn't face it. That's what I learnt to do in the clinic.'

'And now?'

'Now I know that I *was* right about Patrick all along. About what he stands for, I mean. He's a man who always has to win. Nobody ever gets the better of Patrick Andover.'

'They don't?' she smiled, remembering a certain hotel room.

'And I'm able to believe,' Jason continued, 'in the old values again. That's why I've opened my gallery. I don't want to be a flea on the rump of the art world. Oh, I'll still do reviews for the magazines, but at last I can make a mark of my own. It's what I should have been doing years ago.'

He paused: 'I've learnt one or two other things as well. Very important things.'

Calla leaned forward and kissed him. He didn't need to say what it was he had learned, but he was going to tell her anyway.

'Like that I still loved you.'

When they disentangled themselves again, he stroked her stockinged thigh and asked quietly: 'Is there anyone else?'

She shook her head. 'There's been no-one who mattered. I'll tell you some day, if the conversation ever flags. I heard about Peta.'

'Poor Peta. It was over, whatever it was, while I was still in the Bowerman. What about Charlesbury?'

'Tenterhooks time,' she smiled. 'Can I meet the deadline?'

'My money's on you – in more ways than one.'

She laughed: 'You don't know what a relief that is,' she said.

Patrick took up the violin again and, still sitting, cradled it under his chin. Closing his eyes, he played the most beautiful, soaring music she had ever heard, and she knew it was a celebration that was pouring out of him. When he stopped they both had tears in their eyes.

'You had the Stradivarius repaired,' she said simply.

'Yes, some unspeakable hoyden smashed it in a rare display of temper.'

That familiar lop-sided grin stirred all the old feeling in Calla.

'Still need a flautist?' she enquired impishly.

'Desperately!' He held her face in his hands. 'When can you start?'

'Now, but . . . '

'But you're awfully out of practice?'

She nodded, and they both laughed.

'Home tuition on offer,' Jason said. 'Easy terms. But *no vandalism* is a condition of contract.'

They were still smiling as they closed the bedroom door behind them.

Epilogue

Gazing down from the first floor window as her husband and Calla Marchant strolled across the frosty lawn, Fern was surprised to feel herself shaken by a little spasm of jealousy. It was foolish, and it passed in a second, but she knew it was something that would never have happened a year ago. She hadn't cared enough about him then.

'I wonder if they've reached the all-important topic yet,' she murmured.

The light was already beginning to fade, and a large sun hung red above the horizon. Jason, who was standing next to her at the window, shook his head: 'I'd see it in her movements,' he said. He feasted his eyes on his beloved Calla, dressed for this bright but glitter-cold November afternoon in a tweed trouser suit with flared, belted jacket. 'She's waiting.'

Calla *was* waiting, but she was feeling very relaxed about it. Harry Willoughby had been more affable than she could ever have imagined over lunch, full of jokes and pleasantries and engagingly proud of his wife and her swollen belly. The difficulty he now had in getting to the point didn't embarrass her one bit. They leant in silence against a fence, overlooking the river and, beyond it, the land where the new Charlesbury would blossom.

Life was damn good, she thought. Her 'personal relationships' paragraph in the horoscope must be sensational right now. Jason was more loving and attentive than any woman had the right to expect, and there seemed to be a spin-off from that throughout the rest of her life. Not only hadn't she shouted at anyone in weeks, but – even more amazing – she hadn't once felt deprived of her verbal brawls and noisy spats. Shouldn't she be experiencing withdrawal symptoms?

On top of all that, she had her new family. In her pocket was a letter delivered just before they left London this morning. She wouldn't have expected more than the odd transAtlantic phone call from Neri, but her quirky niece was proving to be a regular, if not exactly reliable, informer:

> *Dearest Auntette,*
>
> *Superfetatious hiyas and howdees from yr newly-orphanised nieceling, who grievously laments loss of mother due to Snappers' Disease. Said parent last seen boarding flight for Delhi, swathed in camera bags.*
>
> *Joysome to report yrs truly faked identity of famous disappeared one, earning greatsome praise and dollars for prestigious Big Apple*

magazine assignment. Yeah!
Barney says this is unethical.
Deserted nymphet still hopeful of dis-orphaning. Treacherous
mother's return predicted this year. (Don't count on it, Barney says)
And – oh, wondrousness! – dearest Daddykins promises visitation
if dreadful competition ends dreadfully . . .

'I suppose we should begin as soon as possible?' Harry Willoughby broke the silence at last.

'Begin?'

'Once I've made the announcement to the media, I mean. Can we get down to work before Christmas, do you think?'

Calla smiled: 'I think there's something you haven't told me,' she said.

'Really?' He looked into the distance, as if he could see the new settlement taking shape before his eyes. 'Forgive me,' he said awkwardly, 'but I thought I'd more or less made it plain. I'd like you to be the architect for my new Charlesbury.'

Before she could check herself, Calla had bounded towards the Duke. *Steady on, girl!* she mentally warned herself – but it was too late. She was already planting a firm and juicy kiss on his cheek.

'I take it,' Willoughby blushed, 'that you're pleased to accept.'

Jason and Fern missed this piece of most unprofessional conduct. They were on their way down the stairs to meet their partners.

'If you don't mind my asking,' Jason said, pausing by the door, 'what are all these little crosses doing on the plan of Willoughby Hall? I noticed them on the way in.'

'I don't think you'll ever guess,' Fern replied.

'Something to do with maintenance?'

She laughed: 'How very perceptive of you! Yes, the blue crosses refer to the little men I've had in over the years.'

'And the red ones? There seem to be rather more of those.'

'Ah, the red ones. Well, it may surprise you to learn, Jason, that Harry has become very skilled in that field himself. They all refer to my husband's recent . . . handiwork.'

They began to stroll along the path. Calla and the Duke were a few hundred yards off, walking towards them.

'To be honest with you,' Willoughby was saying, 'for a long time I thought Grant Locke was the man I'd choose. The architect I'd choose, I mean. He has an excellent track record. A very sound chap.'

'A good, safe choice.'

'Exactly so. But I decided in the end that safety wasn't enough. I know the popular press paints me as an old fuddy-duddy living in the past, but I've had a bit of a sea-change just lately, you know. It's made me a bit more adventurous.'

'The baby?' Calla suggested.

'Perhaps,' he said, reflectively. 'Something like that, anyway. All I know is that when I sat down with the plans to make my final decision I realised that yours had a flair which appealed to me very much. You'll create a townscape which respects tradition, I'm confident of that – but there'll be a new spirit at work that's going to make Charlesbury a by-word for imaginative architecture.'

The four of them made their farewells by Jason's car. The glint in Calla's eyes was enough to tell him that Harry Willoughby had at last got round to breaking the news which Fern had passed on to him a full hour ago.

As they roared along the drive towards the impressive gateway (Portland stone pillars, decorative ironwork with the aristocratic crest inlaid) their front wheels struck a sleeping policeman and the navy blue Morgan took flight. They landed on the tarmac with a crunch.

'Bloody hell!' Jason exclaimed, jumping out to inspect the damage.

But Calla only laughed: 'God bless the Duke of Mercia!' she said.

THE END